DUKES OF PERIL

ROYALS OF FORSYTH U

ANGEL LAWSON

SAMANTHA RUE

NORTH SIDE

COUNTS
KNT

KING: LIONEL LUCIA
CHILDREN: LAVINIA (SOLD), LETICIA (DEAD)
COUNTS: BRUNO PEREZ, LARS
COUNTESS: SUTTON
PLEDGES: CASH "MONEY" MALLIS (DEALER)
LOCATIONS: THE LUCIA MANSION

WEST END

DUKES
ΔΚΣ

KING: SAUL CARTWRIGHT
DUKES: NICK BRUIN, SY PERILINI, REMY MADDOX
DUCHESS: LAVINIA LUCIA
DKS MEMBERS: BRUCE OAKFIELD, KAZ, PORTERFIELD, GRANT
PLEDGES: BALLSACK, WEASEL
MANAGER: MAMA B
CUTSLUTS: VERITY, HALEY, LAURA KATHLEEN, GRETA
ARCHDUKE: KITTEN OF CUTE
FAMILY:
SARAH (MOM/FORMER DUCHESS)
DAVIS BRUIN (DAD/FORMER DUKE)
MANNY PERILINI (DAD/FORMER DUKE)
TIMOTHY MADDOX (DAD)
TATE (FRIEND/DEAD)
LOCATIONS: THE CLOCK TOWER (HOME)
THE GYM (TRAINING/FIGHTS)
THE BUNGALOW (PARENTS' HOUSE)
THE CLIFFS (WIDOW'S ROCK)
THE DINER

BARONS
BPN

KING: TIMOTHY MADDOX
BARONS: LIAM, WILL, BILLY
BARONESS: REGINA THORNE
LOCATIONS: THE CRYPT, THE CEMETERY

SOUTH SIDE

LORDS
ΛΔΖ

KING: KILLIAN PAYNE
LORDS: TRISTIAN MERCER, DIMITRI RATHBONE
QUEEN/LADY: STORY AUSTIN
FAMILY: DANIEL PAYNE (DAD/FORMER KING/DEAD AF)
POSEY PAYNE (IMPRISONED)
WORKERS: MRS. CRANE (BAMF), AUGUSTINE (MANAGER)
LOCATIONS: THE VELVET HIDEAWAY (BROTHEL)
THE PAYNE MCMANSION
THE CRANE MOTEL (CHEAP BROTHEL)
THE AVENUE (MAIN STREET IN SS)
THE LDZ BRWONSTONE

EAST END

PRINCES
ΨΝΖ

KING: ASHBY
FAMILY: FELIX ASHBY (MURDERED BY NICK)
SONS:
WHITTAKER "WICKER" ASHBY, PACE ASHBY, LEX ASHBY
LOCATIONS:
THE PURPLE PALACE

AUTHOR'S NOTE

Royal Readers,

We've made it! Dukes of Peril is here and... whew. These bears were giving us the fight of a lifetime.

Let's start with **Warning #1:** We're going to remind you that this is a series and Dukes of Peril is the 6th book. Have you read Dukes of Ruin and Madness, as well as the Lords? Each of these books is interconnected as we go deeper into the series the universe of Forsyth will grow inextricably linked.

But! If you're just here for the dark, delicious, sexy-times? Please continue, we think we've got what you're (ahem) coming for.

That leads us to **Warning #2:** As always, **friends and family–turn around now.** We love your support. We do not love having to make eye contact after reading the darkness and smut in our books and frankly, our hearts. Thanks for everything tho.

If you're still here, **Warning #3:** Don't read this book if you don't enjoy dark bully romance. Don't. Because you're going to have a problem and that's okay. It's okay not to like dark romance. It's NOT okay to read stuff you don't like and then bash it all over the internet like it's your J.O.B.

Anyway...

Now that it's just us, lovers of the dark and depraved…

Warning #4: T/W: this book has and is not limited to: dubcon, mental health crisis, self-harm, sleep disorders, drug abuse/addiction, mentions of past off-screen abuse, violence, murder, gore, past OW, gaslighting, and emotional manipulation.

For the full list of warnings (as well as other Forsyth U extras) please visit our <u>website</u>.

Angel & Sam

~

To keep up with Angel & Sam please join our reader group at Angel's Antics on Facebook.

ANGEL'S ANTICS
READER GROUP

1

L avinia

The fall doesn't even last the space between two heartbeats.

If I'd had any expectations about it, I think it would be slower, like moving through molasses, two bodies fluttering away from the edge of the universe like some birds shed feathers. My life should be flashing before my eyes, a slideshow of hurts and mends and bitter wishes for revenge. But that doesn't happen. It's just... so fast. *So fucking fast.*

Remy and I, we're not feathers, and that's the only profound thought I have time to acknowledge. That we're solid and real and painfully heavy and the universe doesn't care about us. Not as specks, nor air to be exhaled from its lungs. We're two pieces of lead hurtling through a gravity that's pushing us down.

I barely register the wind in my hair, the crushing pressure of Remy's arms as he squeezes me close, the surface of the water rushing up to meet us. But it's not the jump that scares me. The real fear is from the realization that the man holding me as we fall, the man with a fragile psyche, has a tighter grip on reality than the rest of us.

That's what consumes me as we smash into the black, icy water. It's only when we hit, sternums slamming against one another, that I realize Remy's turned us during the fall so that his back hits first. I think I might hear the air punching from his lungs, but it's instantly covered by the muted garble of the water swallowing us whole.

And then, it's a lot like the fall.

One minute we're conjoined, and the next, our bodies are cleaved apart by the rush of the water. Feeling the power of the surge, I understand with an aching clarity that this is how we'll die. It's not the fall. It's not even the landing. It's the blind fury of the water, tossing us about like grains of ineffectual sand.

Fifty-fifty shot—luck.

I'm instantly turned around, body thrashing against the current, the water dark and endless, and there's no space for any other thought but this: survival. I can't tell what's up or down. I kick, but I don't know if I'm rising or just burying myself deeper into a grave. My body feels pulled in five different directions, and I can hear it– the rush of water, the call of the void.

I rage against it, pushing and flailing, spreading my hands, seeking air, ground, rocks, anything. It's not long before my lungs begin burning, muscles seizing against the cold and the power of my punches through the water. For a split second, I pause, and I realize my sister was here once. She was in this water. She felt this coldness. She knew the burn of two lungs, suffocating. She died here, just like this, determined but powerless.

It's only then that I see it.

A faint glimmer of something in the distance, through the water. A gap in the emptiness. A pale light guiding me.

The moon.

My kicking leg slams against the craggy darkness, and I can finally orient myself. I'm deep in the water and being battered against a wall of rock.

I kick off of the stone, propelling myself frantically toward the light, arms extended, palms grasping, lungs aching like needle-fire. Where the fall toward the surface seemed to have lasted a mere blink, the ascent to it takes centuries, and with every sweep of my arm, every kick of my legs, I'm filled with more and more confidence that I won't make it. That my lungs are going to win this battle to inhale, filling me with the ice I'm fighting against. That someone is going to find me later, bloated and still. That I wasn't able to keep my promises. Not to Nick or Sy, or even Remy.

I'm almost not even expecting it when I finally arrive, breaking through the surface with a gasp so loud that it's mingled with a cry. I go back down instantly, but try frantically to kick myself back to the surface.

And then someone grabs me.

Hands pull me toward the light, hauling me back to the surface. My lungs expand gratefully before expelling a series of wet, hacking coughs that seize my body, a phantom fist around my diaphragm. There's no instinct to relax. The adrenaline—fight or flight—still courses through me.

"Get off of me!" I cry, but most of it is lost in a gulp of water. I'd fight harder, except my body doesn't know who to fight against; the water or the hands.

"Come on," I hear over the sloshing water in my ears. I kick out, using my foot to drive him away. "Fucking hell, Vinny!"

Vinny.

I heave, gagging, but manage to suck in air. "Remy? Remy is that you?" I spin, struggling against the darkness to make out a face.

"Jesus, you got me right in the balls," he wheezes. Relief floods through me as he drags me along, his inked forearm wrapping around my body like an anchor. It's solid but lacking strength. I kick my feet, helping propel us toward the rocky outcropping that I can hear the waves crashing against.

"Almost," he grunts, "there." His voice sounds as ragged as I feel, winded and wan, but there's a power to it that drives me harder.

We made it.

We cheated death and its disciples.

Only a little further to go.

My knees graze the bottom suddenly–hard, sandy rock–and I feel the skin tearing absent of pain. I plant my feet just as Remy releases me, and I press my hands to the stone, so thankful for solid ground that I could kiss it. The cold air stings my skin, but I want to get out of the water—away from here.

It's loud on the shore. The water is frothing a lot more angrily than it looked from above, slamming against the rocks and pelting us with its mist. I think at first the earth is trembling beneath my feet. But no. That's just me. My body is wracked with shivers, and as my eyes adjust to the darkness, I finally get a good look at Remy.

He looks pale and grim, eyes glazed as he stares out over the river's water, watching.

It occurs to me this isn't his first time standing here like this.

"Remy?" I croak, climbing unsteadily to my feet. "Are you–"

His eyes snap to mine, losing some of that dazed sheen. "We made it." He reaches for my hand, levering me up with a pinched, pained expression. "We made it. Right? Didn't we make it?" Green eyes scan my body, as if he's searching for proof that I'm really here. Only then, he pauses. "Oh. You're hurt." Ducking his head to look at my knee, he lets go of my hand only to wipe the blood away.

"It's just the rocks," I say, still struggling to catch my breath. In the dim moonlight, I check him out, too, looking past the tattoos and defined muscles. His shoulder sags. I touch the rounded junc-ture, alarmed. "You're hurt, too."

"I think it's dislocated," he says, still touching me, mapping out my body. His fingers land on my hip, tracing the star, and I'm surprised to realize the action grounds us both. "It's not the first time. Happened in the third grade, seeing how far I could swing off the monkey bars."

"Remy," I say, drawing his gaze to mine. "I didn't believe you before. About your dad. I'm sorry, I thought–"

"Don't," he says, his tone harsh. I think the anger is meant for his father, or maybe even me, but he continues, "Don't apologize. I'm the one who didn't believe you. I'm the one who fucked up, Vinny." His face falls, and he looks away, swatting wet hair from his eyes. "I fucked us up so bad."

Haley. The memory of her on her knees before him burns sour at the back of my throat, but I bite it back. Everything we talked about on the edge of the cliff comes with caveats.

"I love you, Vinny."

He said those words. I heard them, felt them, let them soothe something wounded and sore inside of me. But now that we've survived the fall, I can't help but wonder if it was the truth or just a last-minute, panic-driven confession. Pretty words to send a dying girl off the edge of the world with.

I won't hold Remy to it, even if the thought of him loving me warms me like a blanket.

Maybe that's the hypothermia setting in.

There's no time to ponder the hurt that brought us here or the truth about the man who sent us over the edge. "Hey," I say, pulling myself away from this train of thought. "We can talk about that later, when we're safe and warm. But right now, I need you to think. Do you know how to get to a road?" I ask, wrapping my arms around my upper body, trying to control the shivering. "How did you get out of here before? Do you remember?"

He winds his arm around me, the good one, engulfing me with his skin as I'm clutched to his chest. It's just like it was before, when we were falling, and it's odd, I think. That something so fast can be burned so precisely into my memory. "We need to wait."

"It's freezing," I say through chattering teeth, but that's the least of my worries. The Baron King won't give up on his son that easily. "We can't just sit out here until sunrise."

"They'll come for us," he says, looking up at the sky.

I stare at the patch of skin below his chin and shiver. "That's what I'm afraid of. Your dad isn't going to let us get away twice."

Remy looks down at me, blinking away a drop of water. "You're right, he won't. But my father isn't going to chase us. He'll wait for our bodies to surface down-river. Just like..." He doesn't say her name, but I know he's thinking it. *Just like Leticia.* His fingers curl against my bicep. "But my dad won't find us. Not before they do."

They.

The Dukes.

Nick and Sy.

I glance out at the river, dark and empty. "How do you know?" I have no doubt they're looking for us, but we're at the base of a cliff, carried down by the current. How the fuck are they going to find us?

"They'll come for us, Vinny." His fingers, trembling from cold, graze the side of my face, lingering behind my ear. The tracker. "They'll come for *you.*"

Eventually, we collapse against the rocks, legs bent at the knees, my cheek crushed into his good shoulder. I'm not sure how Remy can stand it. With his arm hanging unnaturally like that, he must be in more pain than he can bear, but aside from a grimace every now and then, I wouldn't know it to look at him.

There's a stretch of silence where the trees on the opposite bank rustle in the wind, leaves chattering just as hard as my teeth. My eyelids are feeling heavy when Remy's gruff voice suddenly shatters the quiet. "I hit my head against the rocks," he says, voice thrumming beneath my ear. "There was blood everywhere, but it wasn't red. It looked black, like ink." My gaze snaps up to him in alarm, but I don't see any blood–red, black, or otherwise. His eyes are full of exhaustion, fixed sightlessly to the sky. "It wasn't like it is now. It wasn't cold that night. I kept bleeding and bleeding, and it wouldn't fucking stop. The river had a smell to it. Goldenrod and dead things. It made me want to puke my fucking guts up. I remember falling now, Vinny." His gaze dips down to mine, something flat and angry swimming within it. "I remember landing."

And then he looks away.

He doesn't talk after that. I almost wish he would go on one of his epic babbling sessions, with the colors and vague explanations, but he doesn't say a word. He clutches me close, but remains eerily still, as if he's shutting down, or perhaps lost in the memory of the first time this happened to him. *Goldenrod and dead things.* I know it'd be the right thing to do, to talk to him, to keep him stimulated, to keep him alert, to ask him everything he remembers.

The problem is, I sack out first.

THE SUMMER AFTER THIRD GRADE, I had this phase where I followed Leticia everywhere. It was partly just to drive her crazy, piss her off, make her lash out so I could lash back even harder. It was our cycle. Lucias being Lucias. But it was also partly because there was no place or purpose for me. Leticia had dancing lessons and friends and duties—a *life*—and all I had was her and my father. So I'd follow her to her friends' houses, to the dance studio, to the river, waiting for the moment where she snapped, erupting like a volcano. The phase didn't last past that summer, but the effect of it did. Even well into our teens, before she'd leave for the night, she'd throw me this venomous look, full of mascara and threat, before saying, "Don't follow me."

Now, she's on the other side of the river.

I can see her across the water, so small over the distance that she's barely more than a blonde wisp. She's too far away to make out any details. It could be anyone, but somehow, I still know it's my sister, the moon reflecting off her shiny hair like the edge of a knife. She doesn't call out for me. She doesn't wave her arms. She just stands there, watching, just like that dream I once had of her on the swingset. A snapshot in time. An echo of a memory. A reminder that she was here once, too.

Don't follow me.

I jolt into awareness with the memory of those venomous words throbbing through my head, a low hum occupying the space where they should be.

Only, it's not the memory humming.

I lurch up and whirl toward Remy, a spike of panic lancing

through me at the pale, slack look on his face. "Remy!" I hiss, grabbing his face. "Wake up!"

Luckily, his eyes flutter right open, dark swirls of green and pupil. Strangely, the second he registers me in front of him, the corner of his mouth lifts into a lazy smirk, and for a split second, it's almost as if we're just waking up in his bed after a good, slow fuck.

"Someone's coming."

The smile plummets.

His eyes harden as they scan the water, but he's already rising, tugging me up off the ground with him. He moves stiffly, shoulder still sagging, but he doesn't falter in lifting me, gentle but strong. My legs wobble and I can no longer feel my fingertips, but I'm just as desperate as his words sound when he whispers, "Get ready."

"Ready?" The hum grows louder, filling my ears like a buzzing bee. I try to tug Remy back into the shadows. "What if it's your dad?"

He just stands there with his chin raised, looking for all the world like a man ready to meet anything. "To the victor, Vinny."

"For the record," my jaw clenches in frustration, "I'm getting really sick of the spoils being our own fucking lives."

But try as I might to tug him back, Remy doesn't budge, and why should he? He's right. *To the victor.* Remy is a Duke, and Dukes don't hide in the shadows like snakes, coiling under rocks and waiting in damp holes. They fight under the sharp heat of a spotlight.

Fog hovers over the dark water, but as the sound increases, ripples of water wash against the shore. A light emerges, and then the front of a small boat. Fear grips me. Maddox isn't our only enemy here. What if it's *my* father? He's the one that put out the hit —the contract Maddox was simply willing to take. Nick making me their Duchess wasn't just an act of defiance. It was the start of a war, like we're the fucking Hatfields and McCoys.

Remy hooks his arm around my waist, holding me to him, but it doesn't stop my knees from buckling when the fog finally parts, cutting two broad-shouldered silhouettes that I'd know anywhere.

I burst forward, almost collapsing in a frantic attempt to wave my arms. "Nick! Sy! Over here!"

Nick jumps into the water before I even finish saying his name—before the boat even reaches the shore.

Remy catches me, saying, "I told you they'd come." There's no smugness in the tone, only relief and weariness. The shiver that wracks though my body is intense and Remy shudders next to me. I'm not sure how much longer the two of us would've lasted out here, wet and exhausted, but I should have known. These two wouldn't leave either of us behind. Fleetingly, I wonder how anyone can function in this town without having what the Dukes do. A brotherhood. A surety that when you're too tired to go on, there'll be someone there to carry you the rest of the way.

Suddenly, the Royal houses make a little more sense.

Nick splashes across the distance with a wide stride, running through the water to us, and every yard he gains brings the hard edges of his face into sharper relief. What I see in his eyes makes me shiver just as hard as the temperature.

Death.

Mine and Remy's. Our fathers'. Maybe even his own. There's death in Nick Bruin's eyes, and when he finally reaches the shore, his stride doesn't even falter. He marches right to me, waterlogged and full of that Bruin fury that still makes me shrink back.

He grabs me before I can, two wide palms clutching my face, and then his mouth is devouring mine, hot and hard, painfully demanding. "I saw you," he says, panting with the exertion of the run. "I saw your tracker in the river, and I–" Any other words are poured into the crest of a bruising kiss, and then I understand.

He didn't know what he was coming for.

Me, or my body.

I try at first to kiss him back, but it doesn't last. It's not that kind of kiss. It's brutal and claiming and too intense, and I cling to it like a tether. Being loved by a psycho like Nick Bruin might mean hurting sometimes, but there are some advantages to knowing he'll never let me go.

"Are you okay?" He releases me just to grip me even harder, fists tangling into the wet fabric of my shirt. "Tell me you're okay. Tell me who to fucking *kill*." Up close like this, I can see the bright ring of panic in his eyes, the worn crease in his brow, the stiff set of his jaw. I bet he's been like this for hours.

"I'm fine," I say, curling like an animal toward his heat. I nuzzle my mouth next to the tattoo of my kiss-print on his neck, hoping it soothes him. "Just cold. Really, really cold."

I feel his head turn more than I see it. "Remy?"

There's a grunt, and then Remy's wry, "No caveman kiss for me, huh? I see how it is."

Nick bends, hooking an arm behind my knees, and suddenly I'm hoisted right up into his arms. "Can you walk?"

Remy and I both answer, "Yes," but only my response is laced with indignation.

Nick just gives me a jostle, cradling me tightly against his chest. "Maybe you can, Little Bird, but you won't."

I know better than to argue, and even if I wasn't exhausted, his warm, strong body feels so good to rest against. He carries me through the knee-deep water, and I can feel the power of his muscles and tendons against me, shifting beneath his skin. Just the scent of his neck is enough to make the memory of the last time I saw him—naked and sated and happy—slam to the forefront of my mind.

I physically have to force myself to let go when we reach the side of the boat, the water up to Nick's stomach as he hands me over to his brother's waiting hands. Sy clutches for me, hauling me easily against his own chest, and I get my first glimpse of him since the morning before.

He's practically buzzing with energy.

"I told you I'd come back," he says. The wounds between us are still raw. There hadn't been time for healing, just an uneasy truce. But it's the second time he's held me like this, scared and on the run from a deranged Forsyth King. Sy is there when I need him. I can admit that.

I hold his gaze. "And I told you I'd bring him back to you."

Something complicated passes over Sy's face, but before I can parse it, he's pressing a kiss to my forehead, lips so warm against my cold skin that it feels like a brand.

So low that I can barely hear the words, he says, "Thank you."

After lowering me into a bench seat, he quickly wraps a blanket around my shoulders, pulling it so tight that it nearly chokes. I get this macabre moment of clarity that they didn't know which purpose this blanket would serve when they brought it. The thought of it being used to wrap up my lifeless body makes me shudder, and Sy crouches down to rub some quick warmth into my arms.

"You okay?" His eyes darken, rising over my head. He's not asking me.

"Fuck." The boat tips from Remy's weight and he stumbles into one of the cushioned seats, collapsing like a sack of rocks. "I've been better." After a beat, he quietly adds, "I've been worse."

Sy's jaw tightens. "Head check?"

I twist just as Remy throws his head back, releasing a jarring, maniacal laugh. "Brother, we're so far past being able to use a number system for this shit. But yeah, I'll give you a number. Negative six." He dips his head, mouth quirking. "*Thousand.*" Sy rises, as if he could even do anything about Remy's current mental state, but Remy waves him off. "Trust me. Nothing that a hot shower, a beer, and a nice hit of Scratch can't fix."

I don't miss the look Nick shoots Sy when that word comes out of Remy's chattering mouth. Scratch. *Viper* scratch. It's North Side's most insidious creation, a potent drug that has spread throughout Forsyth's frat scene. My father has always been in the drug trade, but something about Viper Scratch is next level. He's not just trying to make money, he's working on eliminating his enemies. Two birds, one addictive stone.

It's impossible to know if Remy's joking, but Sy tosses him a second blanket while Nick climbs back in the boat, which sags a lot less with Remy and Sy on the other side. He manages to bring in half the river in his soggy jeans, soaking the floor in the process. His eyes are wild, ticking over me again and again as he readies the boat for departure.

"You got the coordinates?" Sy asks, drawing his attention away.

"Yeah," Nick says, approaching the wheel. There's a small box on the console, a pistol sitting beside it. I hear the beeps as he enters numbers into the GPS. He cranks the engine, and it rumbles under the surface, churning up water.

"Everybody ready?" he asks, making sure we're secure.

"Y-y-yes," I reply, teeth chattering. Nick gives me one last, long look, before he aligns the boat and heads across water.

Remy pulls the edge of my blanket over his shoulder and drags me close. "My dad—" he yells over the roar of the boat's motor.

"He's the Baron King," Nick shouts back, sparing him a quick glance. "I believe you. I always believed you."

"I'm sorry I wasn't there," Sy says, squeezing next to me. He throws an arm over my shoulder, but extends it far enough to reach Remy, sharing his warmth. "I should have been there." One glance at his stony face reveals that Sy's probably been beating himself up about this all day, all night. "It was fucking stupid."

Remy shakes his head, huddling closer until we're both snug against Sy. "You know, you're actually allowed to have your own breakdown on occasion."

"Not like this," he says, cutting his blue eyes at me. It's only a split second, but I get a glimpse of all the emotions swirling within them. Guilt, anger, humiliation.

"Are you still my girl?"

He'd asked me that yesterday before leaving to find Nick, and I'd never answered. I didn't know how to, and I still find a painful clench in my chest where the answer should be. This thing I'm doing with Nick–letting him in, allowing myself to accept whatever twisted love he might have for me and trusting that he won't use it to hurt me again–it's an experiment in forgiveness that's still up in the air. The thought of having to do it again for Sy–fuck, for *Remy*– makes my stomach turn anxiously.

"We're the Dukes," Sy goes on. "Our job is to fight, and what I did that night—" He tenses, eyes staring out into the dark river. "I should have stayed. I should have fought." Suddenly, he whips his gaze to me, adding, "I should have fought to keep you." The moment is too acute, too intimate. Even Remy squirms beside me, Nick carefully not looking back, as if they both realize this demands privacy. But then, like a string being cut, Sy averts his eyes, adding, "I mean, all of you."

I squint against the wind, not knowing what to say. The apology up in the belfry was a start, but these guys... it's like they had a glimmer of something good coming, and they sabotaged the hell out of it. "J-j-just get us somewhere warm and dry, and then we can do all the fighting we want."

Nick glances back, hair ruffling in the wind, and steers the boat across the dark water. I look back, watching the rocky face of the cliff we just jumped from growing smaller in the distance, and feel my face paling.

Remy and I share a long look.

We really jumped off that?

"Does he know where he's going?" I ask Sy.

"My little brother has more connections than an airport," is all he says, but Nick shifts the boat into gear, making it impossible to hear or speak.

It's a long while later, in the gray dawn, that houses rise on the banks. Nick steers the boat toward a dock that he seems to recognize more than the others, but Sy jumps up instantly. Together, they ease the boat into the slip, securing it to the hooks with rope, and watching them move like this, smooth and powerful and efficient, is almost enough to distract me from the heaviness of the moment.

I look past the boathouse, toward the steep steps that climb up the mountainside. Behind the trees looms a gray house with big windows that reflect the muted light of the sunrise.

"Where are we?" I ask, clutching the blanket to my chest.

"A place to hide out." Nick tucks his gun away before offering me a hand. "Sorry it's not the Crane Motel."

I snort and climb over the edge of the boat. "If I never see that shit hole again, it'll be too soon."

He grunts in agreement while Sy keeps the boat steady for Remy's exit, and then the four of us start the hike up the hill.

"So how did you find this place?" I ask, my calves burning.

"I did a security job here for Daniel last summer," Nick says, clutching my elbow to help me up each step. "It's owned by some jack-off that lives in the Caribbean nine months out of the year. They leave after Labor Day. The whole thing was wild—I've never been around that much money. Diamonds on every finger, Viper Scratch piled in candy bowls," we reach the back door and he opens a security box, "and, of course, Daniel's hustlers providing the best pussy in the city." Remy and Sy wait impatiently, eyes on alert through the trees as Nick stabs in a code. "Which is why I have the security details. Daniel didn't play when it came to his pussy." He glances at me, mouth in a tight line. "We had contingency plans in case something went to shit."

The light on the box blinks from red to green, the bolt sliding open.

He explains, "I figure we can hide out here until we come up with a plan."

"If that plan doesn't involve taking out my father—" I start.

"Or mine," Remy adds.

I nod. "Then add them to the list. None of us are safe while they're around."

Sy touches my lower back, ushering me deeper into the house. "We'll get your hit list together, but first, we need to patch you two up."

I'm not in the mood to argue.

We all follow Nick deeper into the house, which is a little North Side-esque for my liking. Although he's loose here–relaxed in a way that broadcasts how secure he feels in this strange place–the rest of us are on alert, tense, our footsteps quiet. Nick, however, starts turning on lights, even stopping at a thermostat to crank up the heat.

From behind me, Sy clears his throat. "Come on, Remy. Let's check out that shoulder. I hurt just looking at you."

Nick and I watch as Sy helps Remy out of his shirt, and I'm not thinking much of it just then; what happened while we were falling. But then Remy twists, hissing as his damp shirt flops to the floor, and I catch sight of his back.

It's mottled with black and blue, blooming out toward his shoulder, his lungs, his spine.

So when Sy inspects his arm pensively, muttering, "Shouldn't be too hard to pop it back in," I lurch forward to stop him.

"I'm the Duchess. I'll do it."

Sy swings those blue eyes on me, blinking. "Lavinia, you look like you can barely stand. I've got it. I saw someone do this at the gym once, so it's not–"

"No," I demand, stepping between them. Remy watches me, head tilted, like he's confused why I would possibly be so eager to pop his shoulder back into the joint. But then, his face clears.

Remy turned.

While we were in the air, falling to what easily could have been our deaths, he turned so that he took the brunt of it. Right there, at the end of the world, he was protecting me.

"This one's on me," I explain. "Plus, I–I've done it before."

Remy dips his chin in a nod. "Go ahead. I trust you."

Nick and Sy help him onto the kitchen table and I gather my hair up, knotting it into a sloppy bun. "Sorry I only know the street-triage version of this. I'm sure a real Duchess knows the tendons and nerves and–"

"Vinny," Remy cuts me off, green eyes holding mine. "You are a real Duchess."

Nick holds his other shoulder, saying, "Just make it quick."

Sy snatches a dish towel from a hook and twists it up, ordering Remy to, "Open wide."

Remy bites down on it, wriggling his hips, taking a deep breath, and then he nods. His arm is warm, and for a second, I trace a vein on his bicep, praying to a god I don't believe in that I don't mess something up. Remy isn't just a fighter. He's an artist. The gravity of his trust slams into me and I'm momentarily paralyzed. This isn't one of the North Side henchmen my father used to throw my way for a quick mending job. This is the man who put stars into my sky. The man who first showed me what it felt like to be touched with reverence. The man who looks at me as if I could save him, even though I can't.

Do I have it in me to cause him pain?

Sy is gathering ice from the freezer, but Nick notices my hesitation.

"He can take it," Nick insists. When I just stand there, Remy's elbow cradled in my palm, Nick offers me a word of encouragement. Or at least, that's what I think he's going to do. Instead, in a voice blasé as ever, he says, "I bet Haley didn't miss a beat when he whipped his dick out for her. I wonder if he kissed her first. Did you, Rem? Of course, you did. No way you get a girl on her knees without tasting her–"

I yank the arm upward violently.

Pop!

Remy's scream is muffled into the towel, but his throat still swells with it, eyes clenched tight as his heel comes down hard on the table–once–twice.

Sy appears instantly with the bag of ice, pushing it into Remy's shoulder. I flee the room more than anything, too exhausted–physically, emotionally, mentally–to untangle the look Remy gives me on the way out, full of anguish and hurt.

"Sorry," Nick says, catching up to me in the hallway. "I just knew you needed–"

"I know," I snap, immediately deflating. Quieter, I repeat, "I know."

I pause, listening for Remy, but other than some basic swears hurled at Sy, he seems okay. Nick leads me deeper into the house, to a large bedroom on the main floor. A wall of windows overlooks the water, anemic morning light filtering in. The room is decorated in dark blues, but accented with warm golds. Like Nick said, these people are rich-rich. The bed is the most inviting thing I've ever seen, but tonight, I'm so tired, I'd happily take my nest up in the loft.

I turn to him before we walk in. "There's something you need to know. My dad—the hit–it wasn't on Remy."

"It was on me." Nick's dark eyes take me in, and then he shrugs. "Your dad wanting to kill me isn't anything new. Look at me, baby." He holds up his arms, drawing my eyes to his broad chest. "Any girl I ended up bagging was going to have a pissed off father who wanted to kill me." He reaches out, tucking his fingers into the waist of my pants, drawing me closer. "The way I see it, things are right on track. At this rate, we'll be married by May." The words are spoken with that sly, cocksure smirk that always makes my stomach flip, but I just shake my head.

"This isn't a joke, Nick."

He raises an eyebrow, reaching for my hand. "Who's joking?"

I look down as he touches the ring around my thumb. My heart skips at the reminder I'm still wearing his Bruin ring. So fucking careless. This thing has probably been passed down since his great-great-grand-whatever. It could have gotten lost in the water, forever abandoned in the river bed.

Hastily, I tug it off, pressing it into his palm. "You should be wearing this, Nick."

When I glance back up, his face is sharp and severe. "I gave it to you."

"And you shouldn't have," I stress, just as sharply. "You're a Bruin. You're a *Duke*. And you're the next in line to lead them." I shove the tip of my forefinger into his chest. "You're West End's only hope of fixing this fucked-up ecosystem, Nick. You don't give something like this away. You harness it. You fucking own it."

He scoffs. "Big words coming from North Side's only surviving heir."

"North Side doesn't want me, and I sure as hell don't want

them," I point out, holding his gaze. "But West End? I've seen you, Nick. You're one of them. You have the name, but you also have the spirit. You have the chance to maybe build something here. Something worth half a shit. Something that lasts." Just in case that's not enough to drive it home, I add, "Something for us. All of us."

Nick watches me, looking all at once confused and annoyed. "What are you saying? You want me to be King?"

"I want you to be alive," I say. "As a Duke, as a King–I don't care about titles. I just know this is bigger than me." I close my fingers over his, curling his fist around the ring.

"You're wrong," he replies, searching my eyes. "But if that's what you want..."

There's something in his eyes when he puts the ring back on. Disappointment, perhaps. Maybe even some of that hurt I'd seen in Remy's eyes back in the kitchen. It's a strange feeling. I finally have the power to hurt these three, and I'm gaining zero enjoyment from it.

He nudges me against the doorjamb, and his fingers reach out, tracing along my neck. "All I care about is that you're safe."

"I'm fine," I tell him, although it's followed by a massive shudder. It's not as much about the cold as the sudden release of tension. All the tears I've been holding onto fill the corners of my eyes. "I swear I tried to get him out of there safely," I whisper, needing Nick to know this. Remy hurt me, but it'd never once crossed my mind to leave him there. "I'd almost done it. I talked him off the edge, and then his fucking dad showed up." Shaking my head, I swat at the falling tear. "He threatened to send him away to some long-term hospital, and then–"

His body tenses. "That's not going to happen."

I cut my eyes at him. "You can't promise that. These men are too powerful and fucking deranged."

"Hey," he says, fingers curling around my neck. His ring digs against my skin. "If deranged is a criteria, then I've got us covered. Plus, Sy is the most powerful man I know. And Remy? He's stronger than you think." He presses his forehead against mine. "Especially with you in his life."

I don't know how Remy is going to handle all of this once the dust settles. I don't know how *I'm* going to handle it, but just having Nick here, having Sy and Remy in the other room, makes me feel like it's possible.

"Thank you," I say, trying to keep my eyes open, "for coming for me."

"I made the mistake of letting you go once," he says, guilt etched into his features. "*Once*, Little Bird. It'll never happen again."

2

N^{ick}

I DON'T HELP her shower.

I sit on the bench in front of the bed and spin the ring on my finger, round and round, listening to the sounds of water hitting her naked body. If things were different–if I were actually fucking normal–I'd be thinking about this ring, and how, for the first time, I feel the weight of its responsibility. I'd be thinking about this hit out on my ass. I'd be wondering what to do about it and when to make a move.

Instead, I'm thinking of her skin.

Consuming it. Biting it. Claiming it. Making her bleed just so I can swallow it down, giving her a home inside of me. It takes a level of willpower I don't have to stop myself from bursting into that bathroom, slamming her up against the tiles, and fucking her until she's black and blue.

It's not because I'm horny–although I absolutely fucking am, twenty-four-seven, three-sixty-five. It's because my mind keeps going over seeing that dot in the river. A vision of her had settled in my mind, dead and cold and still. Maybe someone like Sy or Remy could react to that with romance and tenderness, but my fucked-to-shit lizard brain wants nothing more than to poke her, just to see if she twitches. It wants blood and tears and *life*. It wants to shoot my cum inside of her and know, deep down, that it's meant to be there.

I ball my fist, the ring digging into my palm, and resist the urge.

She walks out twenty minutes later, and the first thing I do when I see her standing there, swimming in some rich fucker's oversized sweater, is whip off my shirt.

"Take it off." My voice is sharper than I mean it to be, but she doesn't flinch. Not because of me. Not anymore.

She gives me this little exasperated sigh and lifts the sweater over her head. "It's cold, Nick."

But she doesn't fight when I lower my shirt over her head, wet hair dripping little dots into the dark fabric. I pull it down over the swell of her chest, but my hands go right beneath it, palming her tits idly, letting myself be comforted by their warmth.

"Get some rest." I say this as if my lips aren't suddenly on her neck, thumbs caressing her nipples into peaks. It really isn't fair. She's barely been mine for a day. I haven't even had time to explore what that means, how far she'll let me take it.

She isn't pushing me away.

Clenching my jaw, I force myself to let her go. To guide her into the bed. To lift the blankets around her shoulders and watch the heaviness of her eyelids as she settles on her side, a palm between her cheek and the pillow.

The feeling that tugs at my chest at the sight of her so small and weary is different than it used to be. I saw her like this plenty back in our old Crane Motel days. Restless, yet somehow still tired. Weighed down and deflated. I used to imagine taking her away from that place, but there wasn't anything noble about it. I'd just wanted to own her. Didn't much care what condition she came in.

Now, I just want to make the darkness haunting her eyes go away.

When I go to move away, she grabs for me, wide eyes flashing to mine. "You're leaving?"

"Responsibilities." Unthinkingly, I lace our fingers together, letting her feel the metal of the ring between our knuckles. "Remember?"

If she hears the apprehension in my voice, then she doesn't mention it. She just says, "Oh."

"I'll be in… after," I promise.

After I find a way to fix something. After I pick up the pieces–at least some of them. I don't know how to tell her that I can't be what she wants. I can't save West End. I can barely fucking save her. But I guess I don't need to. This is a secret that only the two of us can really know: Bruin–much like Lucia–is just a name. It's not imbued with divine grace. It doesn't make me special or qualified or *good*. It's just a series of letters on the end of a driver's license.

But if she wants me to try, then I will.

That's the only reason I pull away.

"Hey, Nick? Could you…" She hesitates, teeth digging into her plush bottom lip.

I press, "What?"

"Could you bring Sy with you?" she asks, pulling the blanket higher. "Later, when you come to bed?" After a short silence, she adds, "It's just… I sleep better when he's–I mean, he knows how to–"

I nod. "Yeah, I'll bring Sy in with me."

There's a flash of surprise in her eyes, as if she's expecting my mood to turn at the request. The truth is, I'm not gatekeeping Lavinia anymore. The thought of her belonging to Sy and Remy isn't so bad when I already know she's mine. If anything, it makes her feel *more* like she's mine, as if nothing in this world ever truly could unless I was sharing it with my brothers.

That is, if they can keep her.

I find Remy in the den, tipping back a bottle of scotch.

Crossing my arms over my bare chest, I prop myself against the jamb and watch him swallow it down, pulling a face when he looks at the label.

"Fuck, I hate scotch," he croaks, pinching the bottle between his knees to hold it steady as he screws the cap back on one-handed. I look him up and down, and beneath the exhaustion there's something else. The tremble in his limbs from the Scratch working out of his system, the red eyes from being up for days, the random bruises mottling his skin. He's coming off a fucking bender.

His hand is shaking.

"You good?" I ask.

He looks up at my tone, carefully absent of any inflection. "Oh, I'm fucking stellar, Nicky. I just leaped off a cliff. My dad wants to lock me up and then kill my best friend. I've got one good arm and half a Duchess." He leans forward to place the bottle on the coffee table, but he doesn't straighten, the line of his shoulders cutting a dejected figure. "Man, I'm not having the best day ever."

I nod, thinking over his words. "And whose fault is that?"

Slowly, he raises his gaze, eyebrows dropping to a scowl. "You can't put all this on me."

"Not all of it," I agree. "I should have seen it–your dad being the Baron King. I was around him enough. Plus, I'm the one Lionel's got beef with. That's got nothing to do with you." This is the problem with Remy and Sy. No tough love whatsoever. If someone's got to tell Remy how it is, then it has to be me. "And maybe if you'd been taking care of yourself, you wouldn't have been up on a cliff, losing your goddamn mind and taking our Duchess with you."

"Oh, that's rich." He gives a low, humorless laugh, eyes flashing bitterly. "Last I heard, you were the one taking her to see my father for a fun little round of Russian Roulette. Are you really going to pretend you haven't been our albatross for three years running?"

"Yeah, I've fucked up," I admit. "But I'm fighting like hell to be better. What are you doing?"

Remy inhales deep, nostrils flaring. "I can't do this right now."

"Then when, Remy?" I hold his gaze. "When you get your

hands on some more Viper Scratch? The next time you go off your meds? Maybe during your next paranoid delusion about everyone being out to get you? I guess I can catch you at the next funeral. Mine, Sy's, *Vinny's...*"

"Stop," he snaps, digging his fingers into his temple, eyes clenched shut.

I look at him, this guy who used to be the life of West End, and all I see is the living embodiment of misery. "What happened to you?"

Remy gives me a long, incredulous look. "You want a fucking list?" He throws his hand in the air, ranting, "I didn't ask to be like this. You think I like being paranoid? You think it's fun being completely fucking unable to rely on your own executive function? You think I liked seeing the look on Vinny's face when she—" The words clip off, and I don't even know which way they were going. When she saw him with Haley? When she jumped off that fucking cliff with him? He doesn't finish, though. He just hangs his head, fingers clawing roughly through his hair as he grits out, "You don't know how hard it is."

"You're right. I don't." A silence swells between us, because I might have impulse issues of my own, but I can't actually imagine what it's like to be in Remy's head. Probably chaos. "But right now, we need a fighter, and the one thing I do know is that you're not fucking fighting."

His head snaps up. "What are you talking about? I fight all the damn time!"

"You fight for DKS. For me and Sy. You'll fight for Lavinia. Hell, you'll fight just because you don't like the color of someone's shirt." I jerk my chin toward the bottle of scotch. "But you don't fight for yourself, Remy. You let everyone else do that for you." He just stares at me, unblinking as I turn away. "That's our albatross."

∽

I FIND Sy in the kitchen, a gleaming white and stainless-steel monstrosity that looks like Martha Stewart should be behind the stove, not my brother. He's searching the cabinets, opening and closing doors. He'd slam them if they could, but there's nothing but the soft hiss of the cabinets easing back into place.

When my brother is at a loss for what to do, he falls back on three things: fighting, working, and cooking. There's no one here to fight and all his books and journals are back home, so all that's left is feeding us.

There are cans and boxes all over the counter. Random stuff. Pasta, canned olives, waffle mix. I push aside a can of chickpeas and sit at the barstool to watch him. The frantic energy of it all is weirdly soothing, like we're back in high school, him tearing through Mom's kitchen at six in the morning for a ridiculous pre-SAT meal.

He bends over, digging around a cabinet, grumbling, "How the fuck do you have a million-dollar home and not have a quality non-stick pan?"

"Remy's sacked out on the couch, and Lavinia's in the bedroom," I say, ignoring his pan tirade. "I think they'll be asleep for a while." This whole thing where I play damage control to the people closest to me is a role that fits as awkwardly as the ring on my finger.

"Good," he grunts, nodding to a package from the freezer. "Maybe there'll be time to defrost some of this steak. Remy needs protein, and she needs iron." He wrangles a frying pan out of the cabinet, but three other pots come flying out, clattering to the floor. "Goddamnfuckinghell!"

"Sy," I say, aware that my brother is teetering on the edge of a tightrope. "Chill."

His eyes snap to mine. "Don't you fucking dare tell me to chill. Not after the last twenty-four hours."

"They're fine. We're fine. Everyone made it out alive."

Sy and I were at my storage locker the last time we spoke to Lavinia. She'd texted and said she was on her way. She never showed up. I know Lavinia hates the tracker, but I've never been more thankful—especially since one minute she was up on the cliffs, and then next she was lost in the abyss, a dot bobbing in the nether.

Across from me, Sy shoves the pots back into the cabinet. One slides out, clattering against the tile. I watch silently as he picks it up and beats it against the granite countertop. "Stay inside you motherfucking son of a whore! Just stay fucking inside!" He shoves it in one more time, slamming the door shut before it, or anything else, can fall out.

"They're cold and banged up," I say, reaffirming. "Nothing that can't be fixed."

He looks up at me, eyes rimmed in red. "The pots?"

I glare at him. Jesus. "Lavinia and Remy, you fucking basket-case."

"But what if it couldn't?" His words settle in the room. When he speaks again, it's low and strained. "What if Maddox killed them? What if they jumped and didn't make it? What if we couldn't find them?" He pales, the set of his chin uncomfortably vulnerable. "What if it was like last time, when we lost him for months? When Tate *died*." His eyes flick to mine. "When you left."

"None of that happened, big brother." I jerk my head toward the bedroom. "They're both alive. They're safe. And trust me, I'm not going anywhere."

That's how I know everything is different. Back in South Side, I'd wanted to take Lavinia away. Now, I want to stand my ground to keep what I've got. Sy doesn't know that, though. He stands there, frying pan in his hand, looking lost and worried and completely overwhelmed. If he looked like this after Tate died, then I didn't see it, because he's right. I left. Sure, I had a purpose–a mission–but that's not what he saw. For the first time, I feel the bloom of regret in my chest for it. If I'd told him why I was going to work for Daniel Payne...

Well, he would have followed me into the filth of South Side.

He would have fought with me about it. He would have said it was a stupid plan–and he wouldn't have been wrong–but in the end, he would have come with me, because that's just who Sy is. For better or for worse, even when I'm a complete shit who doesn't deserve it, he's looked out for me. Cleaned up my messes. Let me back in.

Remy wasn't wrong before. For three years, and possibly even longer than that, I've been the unbearable weight around my brother's neck.

I step around the counter and wrench the frying pan from him. "What the—"

I haul him into an aggressive, crushing embrace. A real hug. A bear hug. A *Bruin* hug.

He stiffens.

"I'm sorry I left last time," I say into his shoulder. "It was selfish, but I wasn't doing it to be a dick. I had to do something, Sy, or I would have gone fucking crazy."

He slowly returns the hug, giving my shoulder a firm pat. "Yeah." He sighs, heaving his other arm around my shoulders, palm tight on the back of my neck. "I know, Nicky."

Hearing him say my name like that–*Nicky*, without the spite or sarcasm, just like the old days–feels like something slotting into place. It's a synchrony I thought we'd regained when I became a Duke, but I was wrong. I see that now. It's always been off, slightly off-kilter, soured. A tension in my back, older than my flame for Lavinia, suddenly unwinds, falling away at the sound of it.

Gruffly, I confess, "I really fucking missed you when I was away, you know."

"Jesus, Nicky." Sy's voice sounds thick, like there's a lump in his throat, and he gives the side of my head a hard slap. "I didn't miss you at all, you gigantic pain in my ass."

Snorting, I jab my fist into his side and he feints left, only to dart forward and put me into an abrupt headlock. "Hey, you fucker!" I kick at his feet, plant my elbow into his ribs, and he digs his knuckles into the top of my head. The scuffle is quick and painful, just like they should be, but we're both visibly fighting back laughter, struggling to keep our scowls in place as we land playful slaps and sloppy punches.

When I finally shove him off, breathless and amused, I glance at the counter filled with cans and boxes; the scattered efforts of a man trying to stay sane. "We're Dukes," I tell him, catching his gaze. "We're brothers. And fucking hell, we're fighters. But we don't fight each other anymore. We *can't* keep fighting each other."

Inhaling deep, he crosses his arms, giving me a firm nod. "No, we can't."

I grip his shoulders, willing him to see how serious I am about this. "From now on, we work together, and we stop this bullshit— all of it. We keep our girl safe."

In the space between the hug and his nod, something shifts in his expression, jaw firming, eyes clearing. "We keep *all of us* safe," he says. "And if you mean it–if you'll really work with us on this– then you'll listen to my plan."

My brows rise. "You already have one?"

Sy shrugs. "It's not the best, but it's worth a try."

Maybe that's why this ring–why being a Bruin–fits so uncomfortably on me. The thought of sitting above everyone else, no one at my side, makes me squirm with the wrongness of it. I wasn't built to walk alone. I didn't understand it then, but I do now.

This time, I'll take them with me.

I LET HER SLEEP.

I do.

I don't even bother her once.

Sure, I check on her a couple of times, making sure she doesn't have a concussion or a fever. I can wait, even knowing she's half-naked under that blanket, because it's not about wanting her, or knowing how warm and tight her pussy is, or the fact I want so goddamn badly to fuck her again, just because I can—because she's *mine.*

It's not about those things.

It's knowing I could've lost her.

I spend the next two hours inside that house making a pretty good show of having my shit together. When Sy disappears through the side door, phone pressed to his ear, I don't hover and wonder what he and Dad are talking about. I trust him. My time working alone in South Side was never about that.

When he comes back, he doesn't say anything. He just walks into the hallway where I'm waiting by the door to the bedroom, and gives me a jerk of his chin.

"Tonight." He keeps his voice low, pocketing his phone. I don't miss that his eyes are ringed with just as much exhaustion as I feel. "It's all set."

"We should get some rest, then. Just in case..." My words trail off, unable to form around the thought of shit going south. Yeah, my problem was never that I didn't trust Sy. It's everyone else I don't trust.

Sy cuts his eyes to the door and instantly averts them, ducking his head. Reaching up, he palms the back of his neck. "There's another bedroom down the hall. Guess I'll take that one."

I reach for him when he goes to walk away, grabbing his forearm. "Like hell you will. I promised her I'd take you to bed with me."

He blinks at me. "Why?"

"Because she asked me to." I nod toward the door, knowing that when I open it, I'll find the shape of her beneath the blanket, cold and alone. "She said she sleeps better with you. I don't know, man."

There's a tightness to his mouth that wasn't there three seconds ago. "I can't."

"You can't?" I shift, preparing for a fight. "Why the fuck not?"

He gives me a long look. "Come on, Nicky. You know how it is when we're close to her. We get..." Sy makes a wild, vague gesture. "... all fucking crazy."

Tiredly, I wonder, "Sy, is this about your dick?"

"It's not my dick," he hisses, jaw tense. "It's what I want to do with it. It's what I *can't* do with it."

"So because you can't fuck her, you're just going to blow her off?" I glare at him, anger welling up as I shove his shoulder. "Fuck that. Your Duchess asked for you. Do you know how many times she's asked me to come to bed with her? Once. Four hours ago. *Barely.* But you know what she was crystal fucking clear about? That she wants me to bring you with me. So suck it the fuck up, wrangle your cock into submission, and get into that goddamn bed."

Christ.

This shit is the blind leading the blind.

Knowing instinctively he'll follow me, I push the door open. It's just past noon, but the shades are drawn. They weren't like that when I tucked her in. She must have gotten up at some point to close them. The sun filters through in a muted, eerie glow, just enough to make undressing quick and painless.

Beside me, Sy follows suit, taking off his shirt, stepping out of his shoes, peeling off his socks. He hesitates with his thumb over the button of his pants, but eventually decides to shuck them off, just like I'm doing.

We climb in slowly, wordlessly, Sy taking the left side, me the right.

Lifting the covers, I'm hit by a wave of her scent. The punch of white-hot need that slams into me isn't unexpected, but I still have to take a second to shove it back down, teeth clenched on a shudder. It's worse than it used to be, which is saying a lot. Sy wasn't lying before. Something about Lavinia just makes us fucking crazy.

She's on her back, hand curled delicately on the pillow beside her head. Her hair has dried, the blue-dyed ends matted into an impossible nest. She's in nothing but my dirty shirt and a pair of panties, tits pushing at the fabric. Sy and I both pause halfway into the bed, staring. She looks like the personification of sex. My mouth practically waters at the sight of her like this, so soft and ripe and finally *mine.* How many times did I see her like this on

Daniel's security monitor? How many times did I walk into that motel room and fucking *ache* with the impulse to throw her into that bed and fuck the threat of myself into her? How many times back in the tower did I imagine coming home to her like this–in my bed for once, instead of Sy or Remy's?

I'm so busy obsessing about it that it takes me too long to realize her eyes are open.

Shaking out of the trance, I whisper, "Hey," and reach out to brush a lock of hair from her cheek. Her eyelids look heavy, slack, but she's staring sightlessly into the darkness, lips slightly parted.

She doesn't move.

I touch her cheek. "Little Bird?" Her eyes twitch, but she doesn't respond, and that punch of need from before is joined by a sledge-hammer of panic. I shake her shoulder. "Lavinia!"

Sy's voice penetrates the staccato of my racing heart. "Hey, hey, chill." It's only when he pries my hand from her neck that I realize he's beneath the blankets beside her, propped up on an elbow. "She's okay, Nick. She gets like this sometimes. It's just sleep paraly-sis." He leans over her, searching her eyes, and his lips form a tense, unhappy line. "Shit. No telling how long she's been like this. She can go in and out."

I stare at her slack face, muscles still coiled tight against the urgency to wake her. "Sleep paralysis?" Little things are more noticeable now. The small, thin divot between her eyebrows. The tightness in her arms. The little jerking movement of her chest. I whip my gaze to Sy, suddenly horrified. "She can't fucking move?"

"It's a really common thing," he assures, but the way the words are rushed out tells me he knows why I'm staring at him like this. Lavinia is claustrophobic. Being completely unable to move has to be fucking agony for her. Sy exhales heavily. "Yeah. It's probably related to... well, you know."

Her dad locking her in that chest.

Daniel locking her in that motel room.

Me, locking her in that goddamn elevator.

Sy pushes his fingers through his hair. "I guess with the river and everything, she was bound to–"

"How do we wake her up?" I ask, voice hard and demanding. "Hey!" I snap my fingers in front of her face. "Wake up, Lavinia!"

"That doesn't work," Sy says, voice clipped. "I need to–" I glance over at my brother when his words cut off. He's sitting up now, avoiding my gaze. "*You* need to... stimulate her. When it's bad like this, that's the only thing that's guaranteed to break her out of it."

"Stimulate her?"

"You know, like..." He makes a slow, rolling gesture. "Physical arousal." When I just stare back at him expectantly, he palms his face, groaning. "*Jesus.* Rub her pussy, Nick."

My eyebrows shoot up. "All this time, you've been rubbing her pussy to wake her up?"

"Only when it's really bad." He shrugs, flicking his eyes toward me. Whatever he sees in my face makes his eyes harden. "It's not like that. I just rub her a little and she wakes up, and then we go back to sleep." A little more defensively, "Genital stimulation is a valid vasovagal maneuver, okay? It's... fucking clinical."

I'm remembering now the other reason why I couldn't let Sy come to South Side with me.

My brother can't lie for shit.

It's not all a lie–that much I can see–but the tips of his ears turn a bright magenta, which tells me there's some shame underneath all that righteousness. Something happened. Something he's not proud of. Something that meant taking advantage of the vulnerable, frightened, incapacitated girl sleeping in his bed.

It's not like I have any room to judge.

I add that to the bucket of reasons he's telling *me* how to do it instead of doing it himself. Whatever that shame is about, it's joined by the fact he doesn't trust himself, as well as the certainty that Lavinia might not, either. Not after what he did that night at the party, forcing his cock into her.

I don't stand for it. "What's more important here? Your fuck-up or helping her?"

He curses at me under his breath, but rests his hand on her wrist, touching her more softly than I knew the brute could muster.

"Just draw her out of it," he says, watching her face closely. "It's like she gets stuck in that same shitty moment and can't force her way back out."

Tucking myself in close to her warm, soft body, I don't hesitate. I don't have the patience my brother does. A day. That's how long it's been since shit hit the fan. Since Remy fucked up. Since Lavinia was beneath me and I was inside of her. Since we found out about the hit, about Maddox, the jump. It swirls in my head over and over, so many chances for everything to go wrong.

My heart pounds in my chest, hard and drum-like—beating in warning. I stroke her neck with my thumb. Her skin is so soft. So fragile. I skate my palm down her body, grazing the peak of her nipple as it descends, pressing into her ribcage, her belly. When I reach my destination, I can feel the heat of her through her panties, but that's just background noise to the static that fills my chest when I look at her.

Sy says, "Do it, Nick."

She's lifeless, sightless, and silent, just like she'd looked in my head when I saw that blinking dot, floating over the void of the water.

I flinch against the memory, but it's *right fucking here*. It's in the blankness of her eyes, the scant part of her lips, the way the lines of her face look as though they'd frozen in a moment of unspeakable fear.

I kiss it away.

Her lips are soft against mine, and when I lick out to taste her, I can feel her breath, hot and quick. "It's me," I tell her, wondering how cognizant she is under there. Is she trapped in a dream, or is she just trapped in her body, listening to me and Sy talk about this? I'm not sure which is worse. Pressing the tips of my fingers right into her clit, I whisper, "Come back to me, Little Bird."

If I didn't have my lips on hers, I wouldn't have heard the sound she makes. It's small and quiet, delivered on the crest of her exhale, and there's fear within it. Confusion.

A plea.

My eyes dart to my brother's and he nods encouragingly. His fingers are still on her skin, rubbing small circles on her wrist with his thumb, as if he's afraid to do more.

I'm not afraid. I'm emboldened and that impulse I've had all day–to poke her just to see her twitch–surges through me like a lightning bolt. It drives me forward, crushing my mouth to hers as my hand plunges into her panties.

I use my knee to wrench her thigh open, parting her legs for me, and *fuck*, I can feel her already getting wet. I slick my fingers with it, sliding one into her tightness as my thumb works her clit. Her mouth is slack against my tongue. I force it through her lips anyway, feeding her a rough, gritty, demanding sound, not even thinking of how this must look to Sy.

Then again, no one knows me better than him. "Easy, Nicky." He says the words like he's talking to a wild animal, because Sy sees this for what it is. This sudden, aggressive urgency isn't because I'm horny. It's because a Lavinia who doesn't kick, scratch, or strike back is just... so goddamn *wrong*. "It takes a while. Be patient."

But I see in my periphery that it's working, the fingers of the hand Sy is touching, still resting on the pillow beside her cheek, give a strong twitch. And when I look at her, she's looking back, her eyes staring right into mine.

They're fucking *screaming*.

Not even Sy can stop me now. Maybe for him, fumbling in the dark to keep his touch quick and clinical, it took a while. But nothing about the way I shove her panties down her thighs is clinical. I ruck up the shirt to get a rough handful of her tits, already rolling between her legs.

"Nick," Sy hisses as I wedge my hand between our bodies, pulling my cock, excruciatingly hard, from my boxers.

I grab her thigh, hiking it up around my hip, and then line myself up. A shudder rolls through her, muscles flexing weakly.

Holding her gaze, I push inside, slow and slick. The last time we were together, she asked me to make love to her, but this is beyond that. So fucking beyond.

Her mouth falls open, chest expanding on a gasp as I sink the length of my dick into her. Tipping my forehead to hers, I watch her watch me back, understanding now. She's in there. She's so warm, so tight, so goddamn perfect–everything I think and dream about. I linger there, letting my cock expand inside of her, stretching her muscles. I want her body to remember me. To know that I can be the one pulling her free from the darkness. To know that I'm never again going to be the one to put her there.

She gives a long, slow blink back.

"That's it, Little Bird. Follow me back."

Suddenly, her fingers move.

It's jerky and slow, but her fingers seek Sy's, threading between them, grounding the two of their bodies together. Well, three, since I'm buried inside of her. It doesn't even matter that her forehead screws up, like she's in pain, because I know exactly how to ease it.

My cock punches into her, desperate and needy. She gasps at the invasion, but her hips roll, rising back to meet me. I pull out slowly, deliberate, before pushing in again. Her eyes are on mine, tired but bright, worn but alive, and her other hand finally finds some strength.

She uses it to pull me down.

This time, her lips move against mine. The sound she makes is so guttural, so wanting, that it's all too easy to let go. To punch my hips into hers. To trail my lips hungrily down her neck, capturing the peak of a nipple. The sheets beneath her pillow get mangled in my fist as I clutch the fabric, slamming into her with a force that makes her whimper.

I don't mean to use my body as a weapon–not here, not when we're like this–but I still find my body surging into hers. Powerfully, relentlessly, like a threat. As if I can break whatever chains are holding her with nothing more than the snap of my hips. It's wild and mindless, and when I catch sight of Sy beside us, still half-reclined in the bed, I see the shocking rawness of it reflected back at me in his stare.

His mouth is slack, pupils so blown that they're pools of black.

Beneath me, Lavinia comes to life. First her hand on me, nails digging divots into my nape. Then she lifts her knee, spreading herself wider for me, and I gladly take it, grinding in deeper, until there's nothing between us but the building slickness of sweat. On the bouncing jostle of my thrust, her neck moves, head digging back into the pillow as her eyes screw shut. A tear squeezes free from the corner of her eye and runs down her temple. I catch it before it can fall, retracing its wake with the point of my tongue.

"Nick," she gasps, never letting go of Sy's hand.

"Look at me," I demand, fucking into her hard and frantic. Her lashes, wet and dark, flutter as her eyes open. "Talk to me, tell me you're back."

Her lips tremble, but she raises her knees, winding her legs around my hips. "I was drowning," she croaks.

I chase her gaze, not letting her hide. "There's nowhere you could be that I couldn't get to you. You understand me?" If my voice weren't so sharp and punctuated with a smash of my hips, that might not sound like a threat. "Nothing can keep you from us, Little Bird. *Nothing.*"

I crush my lips into hers and thrust my tongue inside. If I could burrow into her I would, but then her nails dig into my bicep, teeth bearing down on my lower lip, and finally, everything is right.

Loving Lavinia should never be painless.

"Ah!" she cries, arching her back. I run my hand between us, down her stomach to the liquid heat between her legs. I find her clit, throbbing and slick, and fall into rhythm.

"Come for us, baby," I tell her, wanting to feel more of that clench building around me. "Let me feel you. Let us hear you."

Her head falls back, and she turns, swinging glazed, heavy eyes on my brother.

"Give it to him." Sy's voice is pure gravel, but the way he touches her, pushing her hair off her damp forehead, is slow and gentle.

She finally comes, the orgasm shuddering through her. I feel her tighten around my cock, her muscles tensing and drawing me toward my own release. I fuck her harder, unleashing the emotions of the day; fear, want, anger, loss, until I'm on a pinpoint, the sheer face of a cliff–one that doesn't lead to death.

Maybe it leads us to destiny.

It's on that last punch, the last thread of control, that I grab her chin and force her to look at me. "You're mine."

"Yes." Her fingertips ghost over the tattoo of her lips on my neck, eyes sparkling up at me. "I'm yours, Nick."

The sound I make when it finally happens–when my cock begins filling her up–is raw and frayed. I bury it into her neck, and there's no way she comes out of this without bruises, because I'm clutching her like a punishment I'm not even intending to give.

We stay like this for a long moment, her pussy milking my cock for every last drop. As much as I hate it, I pull out, afraid that if I stay one second longer, I won't be able to stop myself from telling her that I love her again. She didn't believe me before. I don't know if she'll believe me now.

I kiss her and ease out, rolling her toward Sy. Their fingers are still linked, but not in the same death grip as before.

Beneath the hard lines of his face and the tension of a body desperate for relief is a worried frown. He whispers, "You okay?"

Nodding, she tugs at the sheet, fixing her gaze on Sy's bare chest. "I could hear you, talking him through it. Thanks."

I feel his shrug on the mattress, but I also see the pleased flush behind his ears. We got through it. We'll get through everything else tossed our way, too. I have no doubt.

That confidence is what propels me to say, "We could have lost you." She starts to argue but I shoot her a look. "And don't tell me it couldn't happen. It already has. To Tate. To Leticia." Lazily, I skate my fingertips over her chest, the death's head moth dark against her skin. "The cliff does terrible things to powerful women." My hand wanders under the sheet, pushing back to the heat between her legs, feeling my warm cum between her thighs.

Beside her, Sy's eyes zero in on the motion, like he's wishing for x-ray vision.

She sighs against my touch, voice lax and sated. "You're right. It was scary as fuck. We were scared, but at the same time... we weren't. We had each other, and somehow I just knew we'd make it." She tilts her head, flashing me a weak smirk. "Fifty-fifty shot."

I snort, remembering saying that in the Baron's crypt. We can't keep putting our lives in his hands.

Sy's eyebrow arches and he says, "Those are shit odds."

"Agreed," I say. "That's why, starting with your meeting tonight, we flip them back in our favor."

My brother's eyes meet mine over Lavinia and he nods in understanding. No more jealousy, no more pettiness, no more rash decisions. From now on, we fight as we were always meant to. We fight as one.

We fight as a family.

3

S ^y

I ONLY SLEEP for a few hours, dipping in and out of awareness every time Lavinia shifts, rolling back and forth between me and Nick. In sleep, she seems conflicted about who to press up against. I lift my arm to welcome her when she turns my way, clearly seeking out my heat, and for a good while, I'm halfway to contentment, pressing my nose into her hair as I doze off again to the feel of her skin against mine.

But she always rolls back to Nick.

That's where she is when I wake up, struggling to orient myself within the strange surroundings. The light struggles through the blinds, signaling late afternoon, early evening. I spend a long time there on my side, watching the shape of them as they sleep. Lavinia and Nick. He's on his back, and much like I've been doing, he's extended his arm to tuck her in close to his side, palm resting on the delicate expanse of her back. Her cheek is resting right in the nook between his shoulder and neck, arm thrown over his waist. Below the blankets, halfway to being kicked off, I can tell her leg is threaded through his.

They look perfect, like a Greek painting of mythic lovers, the woman wound around her man. It's impossible not to remember the way they'd looked hours ago, passionate and powerful as they fucked their way to whatever little bliss is available in this messed-up world.

It's not jealousy–not anymore.

But there is envy.

Nick can do that. He can wake her up by thrusting into her. He can let the man inside himself free and know that she won't come out of it bleeding and crying. Nick doesn't need to ask or plead or plan. All he has to do is roll between her legs and give it to her. Nick and Remy are allowed the heat of a moment.

I leave them there in bed, my neck feeling too heavy as I force myself to turn away from the sight. To not edit the image in my head, putting myself in Nick's place. To not get caught up in the hardness of my cock, balls aching from a lack of release.

I check in on Remy instead, ducking out of the hallway to seek the long line of his figure reclined on the couch. His face is illuminated by the glow of the absurd flat screen on the wall, and I realize he's already awake.

"Hey," I say, glancing down to make sure my cock isn't still bulging with need before I step out of the hallway. "How's the arm?"

He gives me a look before raising his hand, pressing a tip of each finger to the tip of his thumb. "My dexterity is still solid," he says, voice low and flat. "I don't think there's any damage."

He certainly looks like there's damage. His face is drawn and ashen, and as I observe him, his body erupts with a shiver. "Want a blanket? Another ice pack? Something to eat?"

He shivers again. "No."

Falling into the armchair, I shrug. "Alright."

He cranes his neck, giving me a suspicious look. That's fair. In any other circumstance, I'd be forcing food down his gullet and hounding him into a hot shower. Berating him to take his meds. Demanding a head check. Jotting any observations down in my journal–were I to have it with me, which I don't.

"I really want you to be okay, Remy." My voice is quiet and worn, just like everything else in this house. "I want that more than almost anything. I think I might want it too much because I've been ignoring what's been right in front of my face all this time." I slide my tired gaze to him, watching as he pushes himself to a sitting position. "You can rely on me–you can *always* rely on me–but you can't be dependent on me because I'm not perfect. Sometimes, I fail." I walked away that night, left him on his own for a week, and he crumbled. Nick told me all about it. The drugs, the lack of meds, the insidious delusions. Maybe all this time, I haven't been helping him. I've just been giving him crutches. "I can't control you." God knows I've tried. "And I can't make you care about *you* as much as I do."

"So it's finally happening." Pushing his hair out of his eyes, his mouth curls into a bitter, joyless grin. "You've realized you can't win. You can't fix me."

"I can't win because it's not a game. Look at me," I demand when he scoffs, eyes rolling. "Man, I love you. But I can't always be there to play warden for your worst fucking impulses. I would if I could. Believe that. But the only way it'd be effective is if I locked you up and threw away the key. And then how would I be any different from your father?" Leaning forward, I prop my elbows on my knees, willing him to hear me. "This is something you need to do yourself. And the thing is? You can, Remy. You're stronger than me. Hell, when it comes to knowing yourself and fighting your demons, no one is stronger than you."

"I don't feel strong." He stares at the floor, his eyes welling with anguish. "I feel like I'd rather rot in the green than destroy one more thing I give a shit about."

It takes everything in me to not go to him and make him impossible promises, like that I'll make him better. That we'll go back to the schedules and the graphs. That I'll stick by him every day and make sure he stays level. If he asked me to do any of those things, I would.

He never actually has, though.

The hardest thing I've ever had to do, possibly in my whole life, is say this:

"Then that choice is yours to make. I can't stop you." I struggle not to break when he looks up at me, eyes rimmed in red. The only reason I say it at all is because I'm confident in this one thing. "But deep down, we both know that's not who you are."

"Oh yeah?" He gives a mangled laugh. "Then who am I, Sy?"

"You're an artist. A Maddox. A Duke." I level him with a look. "But most of all, you're my brother, and no brother of mine could be anything but the most stubborn asshole on the goddamn planet."

His eyes flick toward the hall, where I know Lavinia is still curled around my other brother. "So you're telling me I'm on my own," he mutters.

I straighten, shooting him a glare. "Fuck that. You're never on your own, Remy. *Never.* I'm telling you that it's time to walk beside us instead of being dragged on a leash. Either that's something you want, or it isn't. You need to figure that out."

His head bows, fingers raking through his hair. "It's too late. Everything's fallen apart."

"Then we'll put it back together," I insist, voice brooking no argument. "It's never too late."

Something in his posture uncoils at my words. *We,* not *him.* Not alone. He swings his green eyes on me. "You think?"

"If that's something you want to put the effort into doing?" I dip my chin, my tone serious. "Always, Remy."

He falls back against the couch, looking deflated. "I guess she hates me now."

"Open your eyes, dude. She doesn't hate you. If she hated you, do you think she'd be half as hurt as she is right now?" I kick out, catching his ankle with my foot. "She cares about you, dumbass.

She was head-over-heels for you before she even knew what hit her." This is the part that worries me, though. He's strong–I meant it when I said that–but he's also so fucking fragile. "Remy, not everyone is as forgiving of your antics as I am. Maybe you can fix what's broken there between you and Lavinia. But maybe..."

Tonelessly, Remy says, "Maybe I can't."

He fucked around with Haley. Nick told me everything. Lavinia's never asked or expected us to be exclusive with her, but Remy knows as well as I do that he's not the only fragile one here. That shit probably cut her deep. That's probably why he did it, too, and it's probably just going to make it that much harder, knowing he did it out of malice, contempt.

I wince. "I need to know you have what it takes to accept that."

"Yeah," he sighs, looking nothing like the snotty, rebellious rich kid everyone's known him as. It makes my heart sink to see him like this, diminished and defeated. But then he meets my gaze, lifting his chin. "I won't accept that."

Hope swells in my chest and I feel a slow smirk curving my lips. "No?"

He crosses his arms and I finally see what I've been searching for all day. The fight. He's still got some in there, buried beneath the shivers and sickly pallor. "Either I can add auditory hallucinations to my rapidly expanding list of problems, or I heard her and Nick fucking earlier."

"Yeah. They do that now." I see what he means. Nick fucked her up pretty bad. He betrayed her. And yet? "They're... together now."

"You know what this means, don't you?" Remy leans forward, holding my gaze. "We're going to have to ask *Nick* for *relationship advice.*"

I drag a palm down my face, hiding my laugh. "God, help us."

〜

THERE'S ONLY one thing that would bring my dad back into Forsyth politics, and that's a threat to one of his sons. That's why I asked him to set up this meeting. I was backed in a corner, swinging, but missing every shot. Pride falls when it comes to the Bruin-Perilini family. For him. For me. For all of us.

I get to the club, Underworld, just before midnight, rolling my eyes at the name. Of course Maddox, the crypt keeper, wants to meet at a bar named after the pits of hell. He's a goddamn demon. Even more than we ever thought.

"You guys know what to do," I say to the two pledges in the backseat. "Ballsack, you're with me."

"Got it," he says, and we both climb out of the SUV. I see the black gun tucked into the back of his pants as he adjusts his jacket. "Anything I should know before we go in there?"

Nothing I can tell him. The whole point of this meeting is to make it clear the Dukes can keep their mouths shut—as long as the hit is taken off my brother.

"Sit at the bar. Order a drink. Just stay frosty. I can deal with Maddox." I should be able to, I've known him since I was a kid. But the idea that Maddox is King of the Barons… it's made me question my intuition. "I just don't want to get ambushed."

"Right." He claps me on the shoulder. "I've got your back."

The bouncer waves us in, barely glancing at our IDs. I see why when we get inside. Some of the clientele is young—catering to the nearby women's college and the boarding school, Preston Prep. The interior lives up to its name, dark and gloomy. We're a long way from the country club.

Ballsack peels off, slipping into the crowd, and I scan the room, checking out the bar and tables around the cavernous space. There's a staircase that leads upstairs, roped off. I instinctively walk toward it, knowing Remy's father would never deign to lower himself to mingle among the masses. A tall guy stands at the bottom, eyes pinned on me. His hair is blond and tousled, and he oozes an annoyed, rebellious rich kid vibe, just like Remy once did. Something about him is familiar, and I think at first it must be that.

And then he speaks.

"Simon Perilini, right?" He thrusts his hand out. "I'm Heston

Wilcox. This is my establishment. I told Mr. Maddox I'd escort you up, personally."

I raise an eyebrow but shake his hand. Something niggles at my brain. Wilcox. "Any relation to Sebastian?"

"Only by blood." He gives me a sharp, sarcastic grin, unlatching the rope. "I saw you fight at the Shell a few years back, actually. Fucking grisly."

The 'Shell' is a half-built amphitheater the city of Northside began constructing before running out of money. There's a platform and a half-covering the shell—which is mostly used for underground fights and skateboarding. Before I landed a spot in DKS, I threw myself into a few fights down there to hone my skills. Sebastian Wilcox was a legend in his own regard, even back then, barely in high school. Scrappy. Strong. Fast as hell. "I heard Sebastian quit fighting."

I don't say it, but there had been talk about recruiting him to Forsyth and DKS. Last I heard, he'd moved up north.

"A few too many concussions." He shrugs. "It didn't hurt that the girl he's banging told him it was the fights or her pussy. He chose the pussy."

I grunt in response. Three months ago, if someone had told me I'd change my life over a woman, I would have told them they were fucking crazy. That, of course, was before Lavinia crashed into our lives.

We reach the top of the stairs, and I finally see him. Timothy William Maddox. He's lounged back on a red velvet couch, and it takes me a second to process the scene. There's a girl perched sideways on his knee. Her arm is wound casually around his neck, and her eyes, tinged with shame, are turned away, as if she's avoiding his gaze. His hand caresses the small of her back, which is bared by the sluttily-low scoop of her dress.

She has a pentagram tattooed there.

The gold ring on his finger catches my eye. The King's ring. His fingertips trace the tattoo slowly, sensually, but his green eyes are bored, staring out over the dance floor. I'm not sure if it's this new knowledge of him being another Royal that makes him seem weirdly human all of a sudden, or the rumpled appearance. I've known Remy's dad for years, and never once have I seen him look anything but eerily immaculate. Tonight, he's shucked his tailored suit jacket, the top three buttons of his shirt undone. His eyes are heavy with the drink he's holding, a glass of amber liquid resting on his other knee. His head is tipped back so that he stares down his nose at the people below, but there's a visible exhaustion–or maybe disappointment–in the set of his mouth.

He's never resembled his son more.

It's only when the girl turns, catching sight of me in her periphery, that I announce myself. "Am I interrupting?"

The girl springs to her feet, looking relieved. "I'll be downstairs!"

Maddox's hand falls away from her skin, eyes narrowing as she saunters away.

"Thank you, Wilcox," he says, leaning forward to place his drink on the table. "Make sure no one bothers us. Simon and I have some private matters to discuss."

Irritation flickers across Heston's face, his jaw tensing at the command. I get the feeling he's not used to taking orders. It's an indicator of Maddox's power, one he's used to flaunting. Like Wilcox, I'm not interested in measuring dicks. Not tonight. I need solutions.

The minute we're alone, he turns his cold eyes on me. "How's my son?"

"Alive," I reply, not willing to give him more than that.

"Obviously." He flashes me a condescending grin. "I could tell from the call. Otherwise, I wouldn't be celebrating."

A bottle of brandy sits on the table, along with two glasses.

"Do you always celebrate by railing your Baronesses?" I sneer because it's downright illicit. Kings do, take, and keep whatever they damn well please, but there are some lines that just don't get crossed, and fucking the current leaders' house girl is one of them.

Unbidden, the thought springs to mind–Saul on top of Lavinia–and I ball my fist.

"Ah, you really do have that Duke charm, don't you?" He reclines back, nodding at the space beside him. I take the chair directly to his left instead, disgusted by this new view of him. "Regina simply needs to be brought to heel. That's the problem with recruiting brides from the wicked path. Fickle, psychotic little bitches. She's driving my poor boys up the wall. But I suppose you know a thing or two about that." He holds my stare, which is how I realize he's halfway drunk already. *Good.* "Not that it's any of your business, but the only Baroness I've ever 'railed' was my own, twenty-three years ago, and I've been carnally faithful ever since." Maddox raises an eyebrow at my snort. "Does that surprise you? I suppose it would. This new guard doesn't value loyalty at all."

"It's more that my brother has pretty expansive knowledge of the Hideaway's clientele." I give him a long, meaningful look.

Flippantly, Maddox waves a hand. "A man has needs and a myriad of ways they can be met."

"Oral doesn't count, huh?" I scan the floor below, looking for anyone wearing just a little too much black. "See, that kind of pedantic horseshit is exactly the kind of 'loyalty' I'd expect from the old guard."

Maddox leans forward and refills his glass, spilling a little down the side, and then pours the brown liquid into the empty one. He pushes the fresh one toward me. "Tell me, did the Lucia girl survive?" At my dark, warning look, he hums. "Well, of course she did. Else, it would have been my son coming up those steps, ready to kill me." Sipping his drink, he adds, "Or ready to try, in any case. Still, I'm a bit offended they sent you instead of Nicholas."

I roll easily with the topic change. "Well, seeing as how you want to kill him, I'm not sure who else you'd expect."

"Want is a strong word." He tips his chin and leans closer, as if he's about to tell me a secret. "Irritating as he may be, Nicholas is merely a job. He understands being in that position more than any of you, so I know for a fact he has the guts to look me in the eye.

Most importantly, he has a name fitting of someone who'd hazard to negotiate with a senior member of the highest Royalty." Maddox tsks. "What gives you the authority to make this kind of arrangement? You aren't the Bruin Heir."

It's meant to be an insult, but my patience has run thin. "No, I'm not. But it's not safe for my brother to be traipsing around town right now, is it? Don't look a gift horse in the mouth, Maddox. If you want to start a war, you call Nick. If you want a negotiation? You talk to me. " He eyes me long and hard, realizing the truth of that statement.

"Still, Perilini doesn't strike fear into the hearts of men."

"Maybe it should." I point out, "I've taken down a lot of men–all bigger and better than you."

"Yes, the fighter. Catch and release." He raises his glass to his lips, which are curled in obvious distaste. "I do wish it'd been Nicholas. He's insufferable as a person, but as a murderer? He shows potential."

I give him a grin as cold as his own. "Next time, I'll be sure to bring you his autograph. In the meantime, you want to cut to the fucking chase?"

Maddox regards the sweep of my hand with a dark, severe expression, and I try to reel it in. This is why Nick couldn't come. Not because he's afraid. Not even because I was afraid for him. It's because Nick is an escalator. Unfortunately, sitting like this with my best friend's father, it's easy to forget he's a King–one out of the five most powerful people in Forsyth.

So I tack on a belated, "...sir," and try not to pull a face.

"I'll admit," he says, holding up his glass, "things didn't go as planned last night. My intention had been to get Remy somewhere safe." He takes another sip, savoring it. "But, as usual, the interference from the Dukes and your Duchess ruined my best laid plans."

I stare at the glass, unable to look this man in the eye. Not now that I've been reminded how close he'd come to taking the most important people in my life away from me. "I happen to know a little about not being the man your father wants you to be. Like you, my fathers never wanted their sons to be Dukes. They thought this life was too violent. Too deceptive. They opted out—for me. For Nick. For their Duchess." I pick up the glass, giving it a covert sniff.

"It's the fatherly Forsyth curse. Look at Daniel Payne." His voice turns casually conversational, just a touch of a booze-slur, as if we're just two friends meeting for a drink. "We raise defiant men because we want them to survive. If we ask them not to pledge Royalty, they'll do it just to spite us. If we ask them to lead our houses, they'll ultimately come to overthrow us. There's no winning, Simon." He tips his glass toward me. "No victor. No spoils."

Hearing the solemness of his tone, I try to reason with him. "Remy isn't made for the darkness of a Baron's life. It would consume him, and you know it."

He laughs. "Oh, it's much too late to think he'd ever take the Baron's path. Especially now that he knows I'd like him to." The bright lights reflecting off his green eyes make him look sinister. "Naturally, I'd hoped to have my heir serving my house, but I gave up on that the moment he pledged to the fists."

"And the alternative is what?" I ask, fighting back the welling anger. "Locking him in an eight-by-ten room for the rest of his life, painting watercolor landscapes? It'd drive him to suicide."

"It'd mean that he's safe," he says, a bit too sharply. "He'd be medicated and well cared-for. He'd be with his mother." There's a flash of angry, bitter grief in his eyes. It surprises me to see something so familiar. A feeling I know like the back of my hand.

It's the anger of someone who loves Remington Maddox, but is completely fucking unable to save him.

I feel it every single day.

More reserved, he looks out over the pit below. "In any case, you're wrong about why your fathers didn't want you and Nicholas to become Royals. They didn't care about the violence of this life. Your mother, maybe. But for those two, it's the secret. It's the *shame*."

I balk. "What's that supposed to mean?"

"You see," slowly, he turns to look at me, "in Forsyth, a Royal man can only lead a house that's willing to follow him. Imagine how terrible of a leader your father–a Bruin, born and bred–must have been to have lost the loyalty of his entire territory to Saul Cartwright."

"You're not going to rile me up," I insist, pretending to be bored by this tidbit of information.

Maddox leans back and throws an arm over the back of the couch. "If you're not going to encourage Remy to come home, then why did you ask me here, Simon?"

"You know why I'm here." I hold the glass to my lips and tip it back, swallowing the drink in one gulp. It burns, giving me the courage I need to make my demand. "I need you to get the hit on Nick removed."

Once again, he looks bored. "Lionel made that hit, not us."

"But you're carrying it out."

Maddox releases a low, insidious laugh. "If you think I can control Lionel Lucia, you misunderstand the application of my power."

Shrugging, I keep my voice matter-of-fact. "Then you're going to have to figure that out, because if you don't?" I pause to make sure he hears the gravity of my words. "Every citizen in Forsyth is going to know who and what you are."

He watches me back for a long beat, not even breaking my gaze to set his glass down. "You're threatening me. A King."

"To them," I gesture to the dance floor, "you're a King. To me, you're just Remy's sperm donor."

"Hm." He rubs his fingers together, swaying a bit from the liquor. "In truth, that makes this all much easier."

I barely see him move, a shadow zipping over the distance. Before I can do more than tense, flinching to bolt, he's behind me, fisting a handful of my hair.

Something cold and sharp digs into my throat.

A knife.

He speaks into my ear. "It's been so long since I felt blood on my hands." Maddox's voice is suddenly crisp and fierce, the slur now completely absent. "That's why I took the hit, you know. An artist has to keep the gears oiled."

I rest my hand on the arm of the chair, sighing in annoyance. "Come on, dude. You're not going to kill me."

The knife digs in deeper, his voice a low growl. "And why is that?"

"For one, because this place is public as hell." Rolling my eyes, I add, "But also because Remy would never forgive you."

My scalp stings as he pulls it, extending my neck for the blade. "I think that ship sailed when I took the hit on Nicholas."

"Maybe," I concede, because he's right. Remy wouldn't have forgiven him for that, either. "But there's another reason you're not going to kill me, and it's a lot more convincing than the others."

I can practically hear the mocking smirk when he asks, "And what's that?"

With one jerk of my legs, the chair jolts backward, knocking into his chest. I snatch his wrist before he can react, spinning, leaping from the chair and shoving him back.

I have him pinned against the wall, knife pressing into *his* throat, before he even knows what's hit him. "Because," I smirk, "I'll win."

He fights back, which I expect. Years of training, scuffling with Nick and Remy and the guys at the gym, have taught me just about every maneuver. Maddox lifts his knee, but I lift mine first. He tries to wrench my wrist back, but even though he's not soft like the other Kings–there's definitely a lot of muscle and strength hiding under all that darkness–I'm younger, hungrier, and definitely stronger.

When he finally huffs, furious eyes glaring into mine, I give the signal, a quick sharp whistle.

The footsteps ascending to us are quick and loud, just like Baroness' panicked breaths. "Daddy," she says, voice frantic and gasping. "Help!"

Maddox's gaze flicks over my shoulder, but I don't need to look behind me to know what he's seeing. Regina Thorne, the Baroness, with her wrists bound and the barrel of a pistol to her head.

Nick's idea.

Behind me, Ballsack cocks the hammer. "Ready for your signal, boss."

Maddox's eyes move back to mine, nostrils flaring wide. "You said you'd come alone!"

"Yeah." I shrug. "But I lied." *Lavinia's idea.*

"No true Baroness fears her death," he barks, speaking just as much to Regina as he is to me. His eyes flick back and forth between us, and it's clear as day, really. He'd let this woman die.

"I bet her Barons do." I lean in close, trying hard not to see the similarities between him and his son. I bet Maddox ran wild back in his day. I bet he could do it now, just like Remy, catching the eye of women half his age. "Imagine the ways you might lose the loyalty of *your* territory. For instance, killing their woman over some bullshit contract that you only took because you value your heir more than them." *Remy's idea.*

He presses against the blade, slowly, deliberately, smiling as blood trickles down. "They worship me. She's just a warm hole."

"You really don't know the new guard, do you?" I wave the knife between us. "We all get a little psycho over our girls. Probably something to do with how we were raised by people like you."

He looks at Regina again, jaw tight, and I know I've hit a nerve. He's as good as lost Remy–his one true son. Does he risk losing the three stand-ins? "Make your fucking terms."

Bingo.

I back off, glowering down at the knife. "You get Lionel to call off the hit. We'll keep your secret, and I'll even offer something you want more than that."

Maddox straightens his shirt aggressively, not even bothering with the cut on his throat. "And what do you think you have that I want?" he asks, sneering.

Spinning the knife, I offer the hilt to him. "I'll keep your son safe."

He doesn't take it. He *laughs*, the sound jagged and grating. "Oh, you've done a real bang-up job of that so far, haven't you?"

Sighing, I make a gesture to Ballsack, watching him pocket the gun. "No, I haven't. But now I understand where I went wrong." To Maddox, I cock my head. "Have you?"

Maddox twists the ring on his finger, the lines of the pentagram catching the light. My heart hammers in my chest. What I'm doing, it's unheard of. A no-name Royal making a deal with a King. I should've gone through Saul, but I don't know who I can trust right now, only who I *can't*.

"Fine," he says, finally swiping out to snatch the knife from my hand. He bares his teeth in a sadistic grin, reaching up to smear the blood on his neck. "But I only make deals in blood, Perilini."

I stare at his out-stretched, blood-stained hand. "Fucking gross." Nevertheless, I play his stupid, unhygenic game, flicking at the blood on my own throat before taking his hand, matching his strong grip with my own.

He leans in and says in my ear, "If any harm befalls my son–if my secret gets out to anyone–it won't be like it was tonight, boy. You won't see me coming for you."

He steps back and gestures over my shoulder, Regina rigidly sprinting the distance to him.

Maddox may not be the devil, but I still have the feeling I made a deal I may regret.

I DROP Ballsack and the other guys back at the gym, then take a long, convoluted way back to the house on the river. All the while, I keep vigilant, making sure I'm not being followed. I still feel grimy from the meeting at Underworld, and I'm glad that this isn't my destiny; making deals in shitty bars, with narcissistic assholes fighting a decades-old turf war. Nick gets the pleasure of dealing with Kings in the future, not me. My dreams are bigger than being a Duke. I'll get my degree, go to med school, become a psychiatrist and rise above it all.

I pull up to the house, parking next to the garage. Slumping back, I scrub a palm over my face and get a look at myself in the rearview mirror. *Jesus*, I look like shit. I've barely slept since I left my parents' house. I'm lucky it didn't give Maddox the upper hand.

Or maybe he just let me win out of pity. The Dukes, in the current form, are a fucking shit show.

I get out of the car and walk to the house, the crunch of gravel under my feet. I need a shower and about sixteen hours of sleep—preferably in my own bed.

No. Preferably in my own bed with Lavinia curled up next to me.

But no, I fucked that up, too.

I punch in the code for the security system and walk in the foyer. The house is quiet. Remy is hopefully still asleep. I feel like we'll have a few hours before we get the signal from Maddox. *If* we get it. Fuck knows what we do if he can't get Lionel to cooperate. There's no way he'd negotiate with one of us.

I slide the keys into my pocket and walk into the kitchen, heading to the cabinet for a glass. A rustle across the room draws my attention. I peer around the corner and catch a covert peek at Lavinia and my brother on the couch. She has her elbow propped on the arm, eyes fixed on an open book, while he lounges beside her, shirtless and in his boxers, scrolling on his phone.

I can't help but notice his hand on her thigh.

The hem of Nick's oversized T-shirt is stretched out over her knee. From where I stand, I can see the white of her panties underneath. Seeing them like this, calm and casual with one another, is a shock to the system. Lavinia and Nick, who just weeks ago couldn't even be in the same room.

Nick's hand glides up and down her leg, pushing at the hem with every pass. Lavinia ignores him, focused on her book. I'm frozen, watching the two of them, trying to figure out how they went from wanting to murder one another to this? How do you get to this?

Do I need to decapitate someone? Hound her relentlessly?

Fuck, maybe Remy was right.

Maybe Nick has the answers.

Nick's hand vanishes under her shirt, and she shifts, thigh dropping. My instinct is to leave, put myself out of my misery, but I stay, watching the two of them, trying to untangle this mystery.

She didn't say no, back when I asked if she was still my girl, but she also didn't say yes.

Nick leans in, kissing her neck, fingers vanishing between her legs. Lavinia continues to ignore him, but I see the flush on her cheeks, the way she doesn't fight back, the subtle rise and fall of her chest. I know her well enough now to understand that reading is an escape for her, something she uses to fade away into another world, life, thought. But right now, it's not working.

Her eyes aren't even tracking across the page.

She's not even trying.

And Nick is in full pursuit, sucking the lobe of her ear, dragging his teeth down her jaw. He pulls his hand out from beneath her shirt, fingers slick, and slowly slides them between his lips, sucking the taste of her off. The action works, and she looks up for the first time. I wait for her to recoil, to be grossed out, but she tilts her head to the side, hair falling over her shoulder, and kisses him.

My cock, already pressing at the seam of my jeans, threatens to rip through.

This... this is what I don't understand. What women want, what turns them on? Why didn't that piss her off? Why does it work for him now, but not before? I've watched Remy eat her out. Hell, *I've* eaten her out. I've watched this woman manipulate the three of us into a hand job competition. And I've taken it too far, used her trust and broken it.

But I just don't get her.

With her tongue in his mouth, Nick reaches out and deftly closes the book. He tosses it aside with one hand while dragging her into his lap with the other. He looks up at her, eyes clear, mouth red, and he's excited in every sense of the word, tongue poking into the corner of his self-satisfied smirk. She lifts her shirt over her head, giving me a full view of her slim back, the skin pale from so many years in captivity, but she's more sturdy now from our weeks of training.

His hands cup her tits, kneading them together. The arch of her back gives my brother all the access he needs to drop his face between her tits. He mouths them like a man deprived, hungry and desperate.

I wince, the pain in my pants is so intense that I know I need to be careful. I'm better at controlling myself now—she helped me with that—but I've still got a hair-trigger, and apparently watching my brother fuck my girl–*twice now*–is what will set it off.

Nick's hands splay across her back, and she lifts up on her knees, bracing herself with a hand on his shoulder. The two of them fumble with their clothes, panting loud enough that even across the expanse of the room, I can hear the little hitches of her inhales, the gruffness of his exhales. But even as he pulls out his cock, my brother's movements are sure, confident. I mean, I see the urgency in his eyes, the tension in his neck. He's holding back, letting her set the pace. I guess he knows his Little Bird and how fucking easy it'll be to scare her off.

But she's not scared. Not when he yanks the crotch of her panties aside, or when he threads his fingers in her hair, dragging her mouth to his so that he's kissing her right when she takes him in. There's not a trace of visible worry or tension while she rides him. Nick is domineering, he always is, but this is different.

Why is it so different?

There's the size obviously. But there's other stuff. Patience. Communication. She falls open for him like a flower, not wound up so tightly that she could shatter.

And he talks to her.

I can't hear all the words. Most are mumbled right into her mouth or muffled against her skin. But I do catch some. The low inflection of a drawn out, "Fuck," the hissed rise of, "... tight," the rumbled, "Ride me so good," and eventually a string of expletives that indicate he's about to come.

I look away before that happens, a crushing wave of jealousy rolling over me, and if it was just that one emotion, I could handle it. But add it to the ache in my balls and the guilt I have for hurting her, and it's just...

It's too goddamn much.

I don't see them, but I hear it when they come, her first, my brother second, the room filled with nothing but their strained fricatives and panting breaths. I stand there for too long, hands clenched into fists, emotion welling in my chest. I hear them clean up, speaking softly, and a few minutes later my brother leaves the room.

I muster up every ounce of courage I have left, more than it took to walk into that club tonight and face Maddox, to stride into the room.

Lavinia is only just pulling the shirt over her head.

"Oh," she says, stretching it over her thighs. Her cheeks are a bright, vivid pink. "I didn't know you were back. H-how did it go?"

I'd called as I was leaving Underworld to give them an update–let them know I was alive and unmangled-so she already knows the gist. Still, I say, "Just waiting on the signal."

"Oh, good," she rushes out, looking painfully uncomfortable. "I worried maybe–oh, god!" In a flash, she's against me, fingers pushing up my chin. "Sy, you're bleeding!"

I shudder at the feel of her fingers on my skin, reaching up to gently pry her wrist away. "It's fine, it's just–"

"Your throat is cut," she gasps, wide-eyed and... yeah. Definitely pissed off. "That son of a bitch! He said no violence, and–he totally lied!"

Snorting, I remind her, "So did I." Before that flame in her eyes can evolve to something impulsive and destructive, I explain, "It's just a scratch. In no universe is Maddox single-handedly overpowering me."

Huffing, she grabs a handful of my shirt and orders, "Come on." I let her drag me toward the bathroom. I'd let her drag me anywhere when she's like this, all rumpled and sex-sated, irritated and bossy. She swipes a washcloth from a bundle above the sink and goes about wetting it. "Did you at least hit him a little?" she mutters.

"No." My eyes dip to the backs of her thighs. Briefly, I wonder if my brother's cum is trickling downward. "I cut him back, though."

In the reflection of the mirror, she flashes me an impish smirk. "Good." When she turns to me, I stand still, eyelids slouching lower as she blots gingerly at the cut. "I don't think it'll need stitches," she sighs, her fingers soft on my skin. "Maybe there's some bandaids in–"

"Can I ask you something?"

Her expression turns wary, but she nods. "Sure."

The words tumble around my brain, so easy but so hard. Nick or Remy wouldn't even have to ask, they'd just assume. "Fuck," I mutter, running my hand through my hair, feeling like an idiot.

"Sy?"

My eyes snap to hers. "Shit. Right." I swallow, my skin bursting into flames. "Dinner. Tomorrow night."

Her head tilts. "Dinner?"

"I mean, we should go, right?"

She nods. "Yeah, I definitely need some real food."

"Good," I say, taking a step back. "Good."

I leave before I can ruin it. Say something–do something–to make her change her mind. Before I fuck it up.

4

———

L avinia

Sy GETS the call at three in the morning.

The hit on Nick has been removed.

What Maddox used to convince my father is unknown, but that's not a surprise. The Baron King is the master of secrets. The Kings go way back, decades now. The dirt and literal dead bodies they must have on one another is enough for a landfill.

The ride back to the tower is spent in a complicated silence. Sy is pushing at the edges of exhaustion. I keep darting glances to his reflection in the rearview, checking how alert his eyes are. Beside him, in the passenger seat, Nick looks relaxed, knees spread, head tipped back against the seat as his thumbs fly over his phone screen. I guess three rounds of sex–once in bed, once on the couch after we woke up, and once in the shower before our departure– plus the knowledge that he's no longer kill-on-sight, tends to put a guy into a lax state. Nevertheless, I can tell he's being watchful of a tail, eyes flicking to each mirror, head occasionally twisting to check the side streets.

Remy, however, is slumped in the backseat beside me. His arms are wrapped tight around his body, which radiates discomfort and tension. Every now and then he'll turn his head, watching me, but every time I glance over to meet his gaze, he just gives me this stiff little bullshit smile.

He looks like he's going to hurl.

I inch to the left.

"Do not," Sy says for the third time, "puke in my car."

Remy swallows thickly, giving a clumsy thumbs-up. "S'all good. Car rides are a fucking blast."

"They're all there," Nick says, the light of his phone going dark. He lifts his hips to tuck it into his pocket, giving me a glimpse of skin above his waistband. "Hope you're all ready to face down forty sober, half-asleep DKS."

"I hope you are," Sy says. There's a push pull going on between them. I buy into the fact they want to get on the same page, but saying it and doing it are two different things. Sy throws out a dozen questions, including; What do we tell the members? How much can they know? How do we keep this from escalating? I'm not sure they've totally figured it out by the time Sy parks the car under the shadow of the clock tower—hands frustratingly in place.

I never thought I'd call a dark, damp, beer-soaked room 'home', but walking through the tower doors, that's exactly what it feels like. Even when the entirety of DKS stands, watching the four of us filter through, I'm still filled with a strange sense of relief. It's as if finally, for the first time in two days, I can actually relax. Let my muscles uncoil. Stop listening for sounds outside the doorway.

I'm safe here.

Sure, this is the room where Remy coaxed me into blowing him in front of the group and Sy possibly irreparably mangled my pussy, but it's also where I got to hold the tattoo gun on a pledge, and where Nick revealed my kiss print on his neck.

It's a room of definable moments, some good, others shitty, but I understand it for what it is now. DKS is a pack, this is their den, and my role as Duchess makes me one of them.

This *is* home.

The energy that meets us is full of anxious agitation. Pledges bright-eyed and hard-jawed. Members who are already halfway to loading guns, dressed for a scuffle, a couple in the back even wearing brass knuckles. These are fighters who are ready to fight. They need direction and a leader willing to point the way, which is why they gravitate toward Sy the instant he crosses the threshold, peppering him with questions and demanding answers.

"Who should we hit first?" one of them asks. Another speaks over him, demanding, "We shouldn't wait for tonight, we should strike now." A third guy busts through to say, "We should call Mama B."

Sy absorbs it casually, like it doesn't even bother him, but it makes my gut clench in nervousness. It's an intensity I don't quite expect, along with the wary glances a lot of them are casting Remy's way. He drags through the door, sunglasses firmly attached even though it's a windowless room. Nick, being Nick, simply avoids the entire scene, sweeping out an arm and catching me smoothly around the waist, stride never breaking.

Wordlessly, he leads me to the back of the room, among the bar lights and sofas, and drops his duffel bag, kicking it beneath a pool table.

"I guess we might be here a while," I say, glancing over my shoulder at the mass of bodies.

Two strong hands grip my waist, effortlessly lifting me up to perch on the edge of the pool table. Nick wedges his way between my legs, shoving my knees apart to make space for him. "Who knows with Sy, you know he likes to yammer." He tilts his head. "Why? Thinking about how long it'll be before I take you upstairs and get balls deep in you again?"

My cheeks burn. He's giving me that *look*, blue eyes caressing down my body as his palm skates up my thigh, and it's like I'm the only person in the room. Like he wants to devour me.

And sweet Jesus, I want to let him.

Maybe it's the craziness of the past two days. Maybe it's that Nick's desire for me is so easy to get lost in, just like a really good, long book. Maybe it's that the longer I'm immersed in his rough touches and starved kisses, the longer I can avoid looking at the men closest to him and wondering where we stand. Hell, maybe it's just because it feels so fucking good. To be wanted so intensely. To be touched so powerfully. To look at Nick's hard, tattooed body and know that it's mine to take pleasure from, because he'd let me.

But most of all, it's the way he looks at me–before, during, and after. Nick might stop fucking me, but his eyes never do.

Yes, I want to have sex with Nick.

All day.

All night.

Suddenly, it's all I want to do, as if my libido is punishing me for years spent rejecting his advances. I'm paying some serious back-taxes on my lust for Pretty Nick Bruin.

But I can't get lost, and for once in my life, I don't want to escape. So I say, "Nick, I'm hungry." He leers, pressing his growing hardness into my center, and I roll my eyes. "For *food*. We skipped breakfast."

Remy tumbles into a leather chair nearby, groaning loudly and palming his shoulder. It's still tender and I'm pretty sure he needs to get it looked at, but I avoid bringing it up until something can actually be done. Sy says this is the worst he's ever been. Remy's had ups and downs before, but the severity of this bender, plus the Scratch, kicked it up a notch. He spent most of last night and this morning caught in a cycle of puking his guts out and sleeping heavily. The combination palls him with a gaunt eeriness, but with his lanky frame and harsh, modelesque features, it doesn't detract from his looks, it just makes him appear more dangerous.

"He shouldn't have come," Nick says, reaching between my legs and touching me there, firm and insistent. "He looks like shit."

"He wanted to," I reply, trying futilely to close my legs. "Which... is good. It means he's still invested. Cutting him out would be the worst thing to do." Yeah, reading those psychology books is the gift that keeps on giving.

"We need to look strong," Nick mutters, fingers tracing down the crease of my leggings, hovering right against my hole.

I squirm just as much with discomfort as pleasure. No one except Remy is really paying attention to us at the moment, but they could. "Nick, not now." When I go to wrest his hand away, he's as immovable as iron, leaning in to plant a long, sucking kiss into the skin below my jaw. "*Nick.*"

He makes a low rumbling sound. "Fuck, I miss being inside you."

Behind him, one of the DKS members is watching, eyebrow curving curiously. My stomach rolls with the memory of what it felt like to be in this same room, Sy forcing his cock into me as everyone watched. Remy pushing me to my knees so Haley could watch.

And now Nick is shoving his hands down the front of my pants.

I guess I'm about to find out if giving into my feelings for Nick was a mistake. If the heat in his eyes can warm, but will still burn. If the power in his touch is there to hold me close or just hold me down.

"Nick." Curling my palm around his warm neck, I put my lips to his ear, whispering, "Please, stop." He goes rigid, but just in case the nice way doesn't work, I add, "If you humiliate me in front of this frat again, you can say goodbye to your balls."

He pulls his hand back, the muscle in the hinge of his jaw tensed into a tight knot. "Shit." When he finally looks at me, pupils blown into wide pools of black, it's all I can do to not tell him to just take me upstairs and have his way. The lopsided, rueful smirk he sends me doesn't exactly help matters. "Sorry, Little Bird. Wasn't thinking straight."

I glance around the room to make sure we haven't made a scene, realizing I'm still the only girl in the room. "Hey, where are the cutsluts?"

Nick bows his head, palms braced against the table on each side of my hips, and then takes a series of long, calming breaths. "No chicks invited for frat business."

I card my fingers through his hair, hoping I'm helping more than hindering whatever situation is happening in his pants. "What about me? Am I not a chick?"

He looks up, scoffing. "You're the Duchess. You pull rank on the cutsluts, you know that." He nods at the guys making their way to the folding chairs set up across the room. "These pricks know it, too. They answer to you."

That's not exactly how it works with the Counts, but I've seen the way the Lords and LDZ fuss about Story when I've seen her on campus. They'd probably carry her around on their backs if she told them to. I've sensed a little of that power with the pledges, but that's to be expected. They're still fighting for a spot in the frat.

Sensing my skepticism, Nick straightens. "Watch," he says, lifting his chin. "Hey, Porterfield!"

A beefy guy I've seen at the gym jumps out of his chair and runs over. "Yes, sir?"

"The Duchess is hungry," he pushes my hair off my neck, eyes going glazed at what he sees there. Probably the hickey he just left. "What do you want, babe? Tacos? Candy?"

I lock up, realizing Porterfield is standing at the ready. "Uhhh…"

"Vecino has good tacos, but they don't open until ten," Porterfield says, forehead etched in thought. "But if you want candy, I can hit the corner store." His dark eyes jump between us. "Or both. I can find somewhere that's open, maybe in Northridge."

"That's not necessary." I give Porterfield an apologetic smile. "It's fine, but thank you."

"You just said you were hungry." Nick looks genuinely disappointed that I won't boss this poor kid around.

But then Porterfield levels me with a pleading look. "Duchess, if you don't give me a job, I'm going to go out of my goddamn mind. Really, you'd be doing me a favor." Adamantly, he insists, "It's not a problem. Promise."

Looking around, I still feel that energy, like the static in the air before a lightning strike. These guys are all twitchy and coiled, and Porterfield has a point. They need something to do.

Deflating, I cave. "Is anything closer than Northridge open?"

Nick pipes in, "There's a breakfast sub place just before you hit East End. You know it?" When Porterfield nods, reaching for his wallet, I jump down, ignoring the way Nick clutches for me.

"Just a second." I pat his chest reassuringly before approaching the front of the room, weaving around high-strung bruisers and over-excited pledges. No one really looks when I climb up on the bar, calling out a weak, "Excuse me?" At the lack of response, all of them still chattering over one another, I try waving my arm. "Hey, guys?"

I catch Sy's gaze, his large form standing in the middle of the crowd. He looks baffled, gesturing to the frat as if to say *'Really?'*

Okay, point taken.

So I stomp my foot, barking, "Hey! Listen the fuck up!" Instantly, the noise falls away, forty men turning obediently toward my voice. Blinking, I try not to shrink under their scrutiny. "Uh, thanks. Okay, so... by show of hands, how many of you rushed over here without eating breakfast first?" As I feared, a sea of hands goes up. "Porterfield is going to come around and take your orders. He's going to need two volunteers to help bring back the–oh, yeah," I say, pointing to a pair of fighters in the back who look like they might actually die if I don't notice their hands are raised. "You two can go with him."

Once that's all in motion, Sy gives me a grateful look and steps forward. He extends his hand to help me down, arm wound around my waist to steady me. "Good thinking, Duchess."

"Yeah, well..." I glance up at him, caught beneath the force of his gaze and the softness within it. I'd seen it earlier when I cleaned up his cut and it's no less jarring six hours later. My face heats as Nick approaches us, breaking me out of it. "Forty hungry athletes, shut up in a room, already itching for a fight doesn't sound very conducive to peace."

Sy nods at Nick. "I guess this is as good a time as any to get this started." Clapping his hands to get their attention, Sy climbs up on the bar. "Everyone shut the fuck up. I know you have a lot of questions, but first you need to sit down and chill out."

This seems to have the opposite effect, which I guess isn't a shock when you consider the temperament of the average DKS. One kid jumps up and says, "Is it true you got in a shootout with the Counts?"

From the back, "I heard Remy ODed at the Hideaway from some tainted Viper Scratch!"

Quiet, almost whispered, "Did the Duchess really hit him with a car?"

My jaw drops. "I don't even have a car!"

"That's enough!" Sy cuts an authoritative figure, hand whipping out to snap fingers at a group off to the side. "You bitches gossip worse than a knitting circle. We know you've been hearing a lot of bullshit, so we're here to set the record straight before you start a fight we're not equipped to win." There's no doubt he can get this group under control, but just as he opens his mouth to get started, something flickers across his expression. His eyes dart back to his brother. Flexing his fists, Sy says, "Uh, Nick, can you come up here?"

Nick tenses and I rest my hand on his shoulder, giving him a little nudge. Sy crouches down to meet him, beckoning him close. "You've got to be the one that does this. You're the leader."

Nick stares blankly. "Sy, I don't do public speaking. I break faces professionally."

"Tough shit." Sy gestures to the ring around Nick's finger. "I've got your back, we all do, but you've got to step up. They need to see you up here taking charge. It confuses the hierarchy if I do it."

It's a strange dichotomy. Sy is the older brother, but Nick is the heir. They were raised together, fought together, but Sy has done the work in the frat, while Nick was working outside–for their rivals. No matter the history, I know better than anyone that in the Royal system, legacy and blood matter—and Sy doesn't have it.

"He's right," I say, nodding at Nick. "It has to be you. Plus, look at these guys. They don't need a politician, Nick. They'll actually listen to a professional face-breaker."

There's a wild glimmer in Nick's blue eyes, like he'd rather set a bomb off and take down the whole tower before stepping up on that bar. But something transpires between the brothers, a flicker of understanding, and then Nick sighs. Cracking his neck, he grabs Sy's hand, letting his brother haul him onto the bartop.

Nick looks even bigger from this vantage. Stronger. More intimidating. Royal.

Idly, he palms his fist–the one with the hand bearing the ring–and cracks his knuckles, staring out at the crowd.

"The rumors aren't all untrue," he begins, a wave of disgruntled whispers working through the room. "Some serious shit's gone down in the last couple days, but you've got the details wrong. All three of your Dukes are standing here—" his eyes flick to Remy, still curled up on the couch, "or... laying here," Without moving anything else, Remy's fist rises, forefinger and pinky extended, "with our Duchess, and all of us are fine. That's the only fucking thing that matters. We're solid." This time he looks at Sy, a grimace rising on his mouth. "*Ish*. We're solid-ish."

The room flutters with reluctant chuckles, and that seems to give him a boost.

"So here's the thing. I know you probably want names–houses, Kings–and I don't blame you. Truth is, if it were up to me, I'd be filling at least two corners of Forsyth with bodies."

The room erupts in a sudden, booming cheer, and Sy swings furious eyes on his brother.

Nick pushes his fist into his palm, eyes narrowing. "But that's how houses fall, boys. I've worked in the other Kingdoms. You all know it. It's why you'd probably rather Sy be up here." A tense hush falls over the crowd and Nick pauses. "Shit, I'd rather him be up here, too. But that's not how this works, which is unfortunate, because he'd give you the kind of speech that would turn you from boys to men. I don't know how to do that. I'm a soldier, like all of you. A fighter."

"A kick-ass fighter!" Ballsack shouts from the middle of the room. "3-0, undefeated!" he adds, noting Nick's score from the ring.

Nick shrugs. "So if my history in South Side bothers any of you, then no offense, but I don't give a fuck. It's how I learned we can't be messy. Not anymore. Rule one." He sweeps his gaze over the men. "No more Viper Scratch. I've seen that shit eat through more brains than are in this room. If we see anyone holding, doing, or selling it, you're done as DKS, and the door *will* fucking hit you on the way out." The threat is delivered like a boulder, Nick's eyes narrowed. "We're not here to fund the Counts. Got it?"

A murmur of agreement surges throughout the room, although some of the guys glance back at Remy's form on the couch.

Nick pretends not to notice. "We need to worry about *our* product, our coffers, and our legacy. We'll do that by running a tight ship. We need to be more like the Lords and less like the Counts."

This doesn't go over half as well.

"The Lords are trash!" a tall guy up front insists. I remember him from family dinners, always trying to get up the cutsluts' dresses.

Nick takes a long, restraining breath. "You know what running these streets makes perfectly fucking obvious? That Forsyth isn't a boxing ring. Out there," he thrusts a finger to the east, "the hardest punch doesn't win. You know who wins?" Nick moves the point of his finger toward the ceiling. "The motherfuckers in the box."

"The Kings," someone in the back yells.

Nick raises his chin, seeking him out. "You're right, Hernandez. Or at least, they did. Which is why I'm going to confirm another rumor." Nick's eyes flick to his brother–not for reassurance, but in warning. "I helped Killer Payne take down his father."

The room swells with shifted movement, the DKS members all turning to look at one another. Some of them look worried. Some look mad. Some look completely unsurprised, and a few even look disappointed.

"The Lords are our rivals," Nick explains, "but they aren't our enemy. And if working with them will help West End strengthen our territory, then you can bet your asses I'll do it."

"What about the Princes?" Someone shouts.

Nick scoffs. "Fuck those pussy-ass bitches. If we need a pregnancy test, we can call them." He flicks a sharp, roguish smirk my way. "Maybe one day."

My face explodes with heat, and I turn to shield it from the prying eyes. More from embarrassment than anything. As I want to recoil at the thought of being pregnant, it's not as horrifying as it should be. Not if Nick's the one putting the baby in me.

"I know the last few weeks have been hard. You were told a Bruin was coming back to the belfry, and you probably had a lot of expectations I haven't met. So if you can't trust me as the leader of this frat, I understand. But here's something you can always trust, no matter what I've done or what I'll end up doing." There's a beat of silence where Nick's eyes turn stony. "In one way or another, everything I care about–everyone I love–is a part of this club. And I'll defend it with my life."

The room is so still that his words are like a physical presence, and I can't possibly miss the eyes flicking over me.

"For now, we circle up, look out for one another, keep a brother close. Protect the cutsluts. Protect the *Duchess* at all costs."

Nor can anyone miss the muttered, "... but she's a Lucia."

Nick's eyes dart around the faces, shoulders tensing. "Who said that?" Everyone glances around, looking, but when no one fesses up, Nick gives a chilling grin. "Boys, I'm tired and hungry, and I've got the promise of a tight pussy coming to me later on, so if you've got something to say, grow a pair of balls, look me in the eye like a man, and say it. I'm not here to break faces this morning."

After a moment, someone steps forward.

Bruce.

The guy who attacked me in the gym, my first real day as Duchess. The man who Sy was ready to trade me to for a wristwatch. The guy who held me down, eyes full of thrill as he tore at my clothes. He doesn't come around often for the victory parties, but I've seen him at the gym, at the fights, and up until now, he's carefully avoided paying any attention to me at all. My blood buzzes with futile, bitter anger.

When I look away, my eyes stutter over Sy and the curve of his neck. Though his head is bowed, his posture is stiff, fists flexing.

Bruce's mouth tilts unhappily, but to his credit he does look Nick in the eye. "I get what you're saying, Duke. You're a Bruin. You've got West End running through your veins, and whatever we might think about you working with the Lords, we can put our faith in that." I feel more than see Bruce's eyes on me, his voice turning cold. "But if that's true, then we have to also trust that our Duchess–a *Lucia*, for fuck's sake–has North Side running through hers." Bruce looks at the men around him. "Doesn't anyone else think it's weird that Viper Scratch is suddenly all over West End? Before she came, it wasn't a problem. Are we just supposed to think that's a coincidence?"

Nick's face hardens. "It's not a coincidence. Lionel Lucia has lost any hope of an heir. He's on the ropes and spreading his product to all four corners. It's not just West End."

Bruce's face twists, like he's smelled something unpleasant. "You didn't even fucking brand her."

For a heartbeat the room goes still, until every eye snaps to Remy, who moves with a speed and agility I didn't know he could access in his current state. His eyes flare with possessiveness as he grabs me by the waist, spinning me around while yanking the shoulder of my shirt down, revealing the bruin tattoo he gave me at the Hideaway. "The Duchess is marked. By my hand. Assisted by your Dukes."

His eyes meet mine and we both know, we *all* know, they marked me with more than ink that night.

Fuck *anyone* that says I'm not branded.

Bruce holds up a hand, undeterred by proof. "Yeah, okay, but look. It was one thing when she was just a fun toy for Sy to show off in the locker room, but now you're acting like... You're acting like she's one of *you*."

Something in Nick snaps to attention, but just as quickly settles. "When we'd show her off in the locker room?" I'd know that look in his eyes anywhere. It's the same efficient, terrifyingly *aloof* menace I'd seen in him the night he killed Felix. Nick nods, like he's coming to a decision with himself. "You're the one who tried to buy her with the watch."

I'm not sure who jumps first–me or Sy–but we both dive for Nick at the same time, me clambering up onto the bar and Sy lunging for the hand Nick's reaching for his gun with.

"Let it go," Sy growls into his ear. A stiff, tightly contained tussle is taking place at the small of Nick's back, where his pistol is located, but I don't bother with that.

I grab his face, hissing, "If you kill this fucker right now, they'll never follow you, and they'll sure as hell never respect me." But his murderous glare is fixed like a laser on Bruce, and I shudder at what I see in it. The soldier. The cold-blooded killer. The machine. "He doesn't matter. He's *nothing*. Nick, look at me." Unthinkingly, I strain up on my toes to press a kiss to his lips. "Please don't," I whisper, gentling him with another caress of my lips. "For me?"

Nick blinks, and when his eyelids lift, those blue eyes finally connect with mine. Sy jerks, the gun being suddenly released, and Nick grabs my neck. But instead of the hard, consuming kiss I'm expecting, he spins me around, forearm loose around my shoulders.

"This Duchess you think so little of, Bruce?" Nick's lips brush across my temple. "She just saved your life."

Bruce's face is ashen but twisted in anger. Enough to know that this isn't over.

"That wasn't on Bruce," Sy says, sliding the magazine from the pistol. "It was on me." His eyes flick to mine, expression rigidly blank. To Bruce, he says, "Yeah, she was just a toy back then. Now she's ours. If you've got a problem with that," Sy jerks his chin, "there's the door."

Bruce holds up his hands. "Man, I'm just saying. One second, you're offering her up on a platter, and the next you're asking us to give our lives for her. Make it make sense."

"It doesn't need to make sense to you," Sy barks. "Know that it makes sense to us."

Nick's arm tugs me firmly into his chest, voice full-throated against my back. "You all hate Lionel Lucia a lot. I hate him more than you ever will. But no one in this room," he insists, voice growing louder, "no one in this whole fucking *city*, hates Lionel Lucia as much as this woman right here."

My heart pounds at all the eyes on me, scrutinizing, looking for a crack, a reason to rebel. I'd say something in my defense, but I can see it'd be pointless. From Nick, they need words. From me, they need to see actions. A Lucia's word isn't worth anything. So I respond by reaching up, fingers curling possessively around Nick's forearm.

Nick goes on, "You're all nervous she's feeding intel about us back to the Counts, but you need to stop and think that maybe the Counts should be the ones worrying about the kind of intel she's offering us."

I can practically hear his arched eyebrow, but more than that, I hear the slight shift in the room–forty men considering my use as an asset. Little do they know, if I thought it could truly help the Dukes, I'd tell them anything and everything.

Nick is right, no one in this town hates Lionel Lucia as much as I do, and with DKS supporting me, I'm going to be the one that kills him.

~

SY SAID SEVEN O'CLOCK.

This is why I'm sitting on the bottom step of the staircase leading to the loft, stuffing my feet into boots, wondering why the hell Nick is still in the shower.

"Why is Nick still in the shower?" I ask Archie, who is deter-mined to chase the laces on my shoes. "Ow!" I snatch my hand back from his claws, glaring playfully. "You're a menace, just like the rest of them."

His big eyes look up at me. "Mew."

I tighten the knot and pick Archie up, pressing my nose to his head. "I know. You're not a menace, you're the sweetest baby I've ever met." I kind of regret having to leave him again so soon. We only just got home this morning, and most of that was spent wrangling the DKS boys, trying to feed the DKS boys, and then cleaning up after the DKS boys. Point being, much of today has been about the DKS boys, and after a lengthy late-afternoon nap, I'm ready for much needed downtime and the illusion of normalcy, however flimsy it may be.

The Archduke squirms out of my arms and darts off, disappearing into Nick's bedroom.

"Hey," I say, leaning into Remy's dark, hushed room. The door is open, but he's just lying on the bed, shirtless, exposing the dark lines of art inked across his shoulders, curled up in a ball. "Sy says we're leaving at seven. Do you want to–" He's asleep, I realize, a pillow clutched to his chest.

I'm prepared to wake him up, though. He finally stopped vomiting, and I'm pretty sure he needs food. From across the living room, Sy's door opens. Still trying to decide if I should wake Remy up, I explain, "Well, Remy's asleep, Nick's in the shower, and I'm fucking starving, but I guess we can wait—"

I turn and the sensation in my gut is somewhere between a sucker punch and a burst of butterflies fighting to escape.

Sy is in a suit.

And not just a suit, but a *nice* suit. It's dark blue, with a crisp white shirt that highlights his warm brown skin, and a skinny black tie. His curly hair has been wrangled into control, the top half tied at the back.

"Jesus," I mutter, resting my hand on the doorjamb for support. Either all the sex I've been having with Nick is fucking with my hormones, or Simon Perilini is seriously revving my motor. I live in a house with three incredibly attractive men, and at least two of them are athletes who treat their bodies like temples. I'm accustomed to their muscles and sexy bodies, but they're usually clad in workout clothes or, at best, ratty jeans.

This?

This is too much.

"You look..." I gape at him, trying to think of a word that doesn't drip with subtext. "*Nice*. Really nice." He adjusts his tie, blue eyes fixed to mine, and I struggle to find my bearings. I look down at my basic sweater and basic jeans and basic scuffed boots. "I didn't know we were having a formal dinner. I just thought–I mean, I can change if you think..." My words cut off when I look downward.

He's holding flowers.

The bouquet is being clutched at his side, half hidden behind him, as if he were about to tuck it away like a gun. The flowers are light blue, but in different types. Hydrangea, bluebells, periwinkle. The soft femininity of the colors contrasts with the striking masculinity of the dark blue he's wearing, and for a moment it stuns me speechless.

"You don't need to change," he says, awkwardly shifting his weight. "You look fine. Good. Great." Clearing his throat, he explains, "I guess I didn't tell you we were going to Stock and Barrel. That's, uh, on me."

Stock and Barrel is an upscale place on the water. My father took me and Leticia there once, for Leticia's sixteenth birthday. It's not a place to go hang, it's a place to go on a—

"This was going to be a date," I realize, the color draining from my face.

Now, it's Sy's turn to be speechless. He's frozen with his hand still halfway into his tie, blue eyes caught on mine. "Was that not obvious?"

"No," I blurt, and then, "I mean, maybe. I just assumed when you asked, that you meant, well, all of us. As a group."

Sy looks around the room shiftily, brows crouched low. "It doesn't... have to be," he mutters, moving to stiffly place the flowers on the end table.

Last night, when he'd asked me, things had just been so fuzzy. Nick's cum was hot inside of me, and I was still in a weird fog from the whole... running for my life... *thing*. It never would have occurred to me that Sy might want to take me on a date.

Frozen, I begin to panic, because I have no idea if that's something I'd want to do. Being the Duchess–being their Duchess–has only meant a few things. Weird, spontaneous, and overly intense orgasms, life-threatening situations, and hurt.

A lot of hurt.

More than a little of it at the hands, and cock, of the man in front of me.

But the more I think about the hurt, the more I remember why it cut so deeply. Sy was my safe harbor for so long. Comfort when I needed to heal, instigation when I needed to fight. He rescued me once, pulled me from the darkness and into his warmth. I've seen the sort of man Sy can be, the good and the bad, and weighing them up against one another, I have my answer.

"Let me change into something a little less comfortable."

He stops me before I climb the steps to the loft, heaving a big sigh. "Look, you don't have to. I'll cancel the reservation."

"No." I touch his arm, gazing up into his blue eyes. "If I'd known what you were asking, I still would have said yes."

He searches my eyes, a crease between his brows. "Really?"

I glance over at Remy's room. "Lucky for you, my sugar daddy bought me a bunch of outfits perfect for this type of thing."

A small, reluctant smile breaks through his panicked expression, and I give him one in return.

5

R^{emy}

I WAIT until I hear the door shut to pry my eyelids open.

Vinny and Sy.

Going on a date, if I heard that conversation right.

I'm pretty sure the closest thing Sy's ever had to a date was busting a nut in his pants at a Fourth of July party a few years back. First and last time he ever made out with a girl at a function. Well... until Vinny.

I wallow in the ensuing self pity for a bit, not bothering to get out of bed. I've done nothing but sleep all day, so I'm caught in the web between being wide awake and too exhausted to move. My muscles feel like they've been beaten with a meat tenderizer made of needles and regret. My throat feels like fire, stomach burning, but the urge to retch up the acid has thankfully passed. My shoulder is stiff and still swollen, and a big part of that 'not moving' thing is a deep desire to not feel the heavy, aching twinge of it.

All of that could be tolerated, though.

The problem is that there are no colors.

Red or green would guide me. Black or white would offer some relief. Blue would make me feel better. Purple might make my muscles move, drive me into action. Orange would make me fucking miserable, but at least there'd be something. Instead, it's all just...

Gray.

I put my palm over my eyes as if I could call them back with a prayer. *Our colors who art in heaven, sallowed be thy name.* But I already know it won't work. I can feel it inside, the empty pit where they used to be. I'd probably cry if I had any yellow to spare.

I've hit a lot of rock bottoms, but this time I must have rolled my sorry ass into a trench.

"Get up."

I let my hand fall away, squinting to see Nick's figure in my doorway. Get... *up?* "Worst idea you ever had," I say, voice rough as gravel. "And that's saying a lot."

Nicky doesn't look any more mad at me than he already was, entering the room and walking to my dresser. "Clean yourself up and put on something loose and comfortable. We leave in an hour."

Every inch of my gut recoils at the thought of walking. "Leave for where?"

"The gym." Nick throws me a pair of boxers and a t-shirt, not meeting my eyes. "Pauly's going to take a look at that shoulder. Make sure everything's kosher."

My gaze falls to my hand, and I curl my fingers. "It's fine."

The dresser drawer slams, making me flinch painfully. "Goddamn it, Remy." Nick braces his hands on the dresser, not even turning to look at me. The line of his shoulders is as tense as his words. "I'm not going to stand here and order you around like a fucking toddler. Either you get out of bed and handle your shit, or you lay there and rot. I'm not going to be your new Sy." Straightening, he strides to the door, flicking a hand dismissively. "Meet me downstairs at eight if you find your balls."

Taking a stealing breath, I go through the motions of sitting up, my head throbbing like a wound for a good second. Usually when Nick's pissed at me like this, he either avoids me like the ice prince he's so good at being, or he just straight up punches me in the face. Since no punch of his could hurt more than what's already going down inside my head, all that's left is avoidance, and that's not an option, either.

Groaning, I push myself to my feet, fist pressed into my gut. I give it a few seconds to make sure nothing is about to come up before gingerly making my way out of the room. Flipping the bathroom light on is roughly the equivalent of stabbing hot pokers into my eyeballs, so it takes me some time to adjust.

When I do, I wince.

The man staring back at me in the mirror is just as gray as my mind.

My hair is gnarled and dull, cheeks gaunt, eyes rimmed with red. Unbidden, Sy's voice rises in my head. *You're dehydrated.* I turn on the faucet, duck my head, and take large, greedy gulps of water from the stream, trying not to hear the way it sounds, rushing and wet. Just like the river.

I jolt out of the memory, slamming off the tap, which is when I see them. The orange bottles are lined up in a nice little row. One, two, three.

See no evil, hear no evil, speak no evil.

It's been a week since I took my meds—for '*see no evil*', maybe more. I look at them, their presence as unavoidable as a heartbeat, and then look back up at my reflection. The first real memory I recall having at Saint Mary's was being convinced that I'd died. I didn't know why at the time. Back then, the memory of jumping into the river was still a red riddle inside my memories. But I knew something happened. Something enormous. Something unsurvivable.

Something horrifically yellow.

The feeling never really went away. That much I do remember. It's always been there in the back of my mind, this possibility that everything happening around me isn't... *life*. Just synapses firing off inside my brain on the moment of impact. An infinite loop of days meant to provide me with the physical chemicals that made dying a bearable thing.

It's not something I tell Sy about, because it isn't all the time. Sometimes, like right now, everything feels *too* real. The smoothness of the pedestal sink. The buzz of the overhead light. The drip of the showerhead. The scent of Nick's body wash. The dampness of the mat beneath my bare feet.

I haven't had that feeling in days.

Not since I jumped with Vinny.

Reaching out, I begin opening the bottles, ignoring the orangeness of them, and dump one of each pill into my palm. They go down harshly, scraping at the back of my raw throat, but something inside me strengthens with resolve afterward.

I keep my shower quick, washing my hair one-handed. After, I consider shaving the five days of growth from my face, but doing that one-handed just seems fucking stupid, so I brush my teeth instead. Can't be having all those pills on an empty, upset stomach, so after getting dressed, I stop by the kitchen for a bagel and one of Sy's protein shakes.

By the time I step into my boots, the thought of my bed is feeling pretty tempting. My shoulder hurts like a bitch, but there's nothing anyone can do about it anyway. What's the point? Sleep is healing. I could do that for two more hours. Or, like, thirty.

You're just cycling, comes Sy's voice. *Crashing from the mania.*

Oh.

Right.

Even knowing that's probably true, it still tears something within me to pass my bedroom. To reach for my coat, wallet, and keys. To make all the motions of stepping through the door. To leave the hope of crawling into a hole behind.

Nick is waiting in the party room.

I pause at the bottom step, only halfway into my jacket because

I refuse to consider how much it'd suck to thread my arm through its sleeve.

He looks me up and down with blank, assessing eyes, and then nods. "Good."

If I had the energy, I'd be glaring back. "Stellar."

The walk down the stairs is excruciating. Every step makes the protein shake slosh around in my belly, and even if it didn't, my legs consider mutiny halfway through. Nick stays quiet ahead of me, but keeps my slow pace, glancing over his shoulder at me, each flight.

"I'm going as fast as I can!" I finally snap, but even that takes too much energy, so I end up slumping on one of the steps.

Nick turns, lifting an eyebrow. "You could have taken the elevator."

"Fuck you."

"Fuck me yourself," he says, watching as I sprawl out. His eyes are annoyingly alert, scanning the stairwell before he lowers himself to one of the steps below me. "We can rest for a second."

Bitterly, I mutter, "Go ahead." He twists, giving me a questioning look, and I huff. "Tell me how this is all my fault, and I'm a pussy-ass bitch who should have pledged to the Princes, yadda fucking yadda."

Nick rolls his eyes, turning his gaze forward, forearms resting on his knees. "Well, it's no fun if you do it yourself." I cradle my shoulder, hissing at the tug, wishing for a bottle of whisky and the sweet, sweet release of oblivion. Nick's quiet, pensive voice breaks the silence. "When I looked at the tracker and saw her in the river, I knew you were with her, and I–" I can't see his face, but I can hear the distress in his tone. "I can't lose you, Remy. If I'm a dick to you, it's only because I love you. And because I know you can be better." Turning just enough to show me the cut of his jaw, he adds, "And also because I can't punch you in the face when you already look so pathetic."

Snorting, I just shake my head. "Take your shot, Nicky. Fair is fair."

He twists to meet my gaze, and I know he's remembering that

day in the Pit at the Hideaway. I wanted so badly to beat his ass for handing Vinny over to the snakes. And he let me–would have let me do a hell of a lot worse.

Nick gives me a wry, knowing smirk. "Like I said, it's no fun if you do it yourself."

I kind of wish he'd beat my ass, too. One of the best things about Nick is how willing he is to call me on my shit. "I want to ask you something," I start, throat already tightening. "And I need you to be up-fucking-front with me, okay? No bullshit."

Hearing the seriousness in my tone, Nick turns, giving me his full attention. "Shoot."

"Do you think..." I can barely say it. Admit it. "Do you think I could have killed Tate?"

Nick's eyebrows crash together. "What?"

"I was there with her and Leticia. I don't know what frame of mind I was in, or what I saw, or whether or not I was cycling, or..." I look at Nick, searching his expression for some kind of confirmation. "She was running around with a Lucia behind our backs. What if I thought she sold us out?"

"Remy–" Nick tries.

"It was one of your guns. I had access, Nicky, and don't fucking tell me I'd never–" My words choke off. "Because look what I did to Vinny. If I'm capable of that–"

"You did not," Nick's gaze is rock solid, voice sharp with vehemence, "fucking kill Tate."

My heart pounds, and this time when my stomach rolls, it's not from the withdrawals. "Are you sure?"

Without hesitation he says, "Yes."

"How can you be sure?" Even though it's a question, it emerges with all the desperation of a plea.

"Because if you did, your father would have known," Nick says, holding my stare. "And he would have used that shit to lock you up for the rest of your life."

I blink. He's right. The conversation with my father up on that cliff made one thing certain. He'd take any chance he could to lock me away forever. To keep me under his thumb and away from the DKS. Nothing could have turned Nick, Sy, and West End away from me faster and more effectively than the knowledge I'd killed Tate.

The nausea dissipates, relief whipping through me at the new certainty. The resolve from before returns in full force, and I promise him, "I'm going to make it better. With you. With Sy and Vinny. With DKS. I don't know how yet, but I do know one thing."

"I know."

"How?" I ask.

"A man who's cheated death twice doesn't just give up."

"He *fights*," I add, feeling it in my chest. God, it's the first real feeling I've had in days not engulfed in regret and cravings.

Nick stands, brushes himself off, and then offers me his hand. "Then let me help."

❧

PAULY MEETS us at the gym, sizing up my shoulder in the training room off the main room.

"An x-ray would make me feel better," he says, raising my elbow and ignoring my grimace, "but I think it looks pretty good. Range of motion is all there. You should start some light exercises tomorrow. Nothing too strenuous, but you need to loosen up this joint, son."

Nick's expression is skeptical, but I'm confident in Pauly's skills. He joined DKS before he failed out of med school. 'Something came up' is what he always says whenever someone asks why he didn't graduate. Verity told me once that he was kicked out during his residency for stealing drugs from the pharmacy at his hospital. That tracks, to be honest. I see it in the shake of his hands and the mottled scars on his upper forearms. But he's the closest thing the gym has to a medic, although he's actually just a trainer, and even then, only part-time when his real job allows it.

His real job.

As a line cook.

It's no wonder the Duchess is always meant to be pre-med.

"No shit." I hiss when he drops my arm, rounding the chair to get another look at my back.

"These bruises worry me more," he says, giving the large black and blue patch a poke. "The fuck did you do, jump off a building?"

I glance at Nick, whose eyes darken. "Something like that."

Pauly makes a thoughtful noise. "Well, you're going to need something for the pain if you plan to rehab that shoulder. We've still got some codeine in the back."

Fuck.

That sounds like heaven wrapped in pussy.

I deflate. "No, wait." Knowing I'm going to end up regretting this, I meet his gaze. "Don't bother, man. I'm coming off a bender. Trying to clean myself up. You know how it is."

Pauly, who's probably done and quit more drugs than I'll ever see, spits a low curse. "You're going through withdrawal, too? Don't tell me. Viper Scratch?"

Nick's standing off to the side, arms crossed. He's the one to say, "I think the worst has passed. He stopped ralphing around noon."

"So you've got a shoulder that needs rehabbed as you detox from some of the worst dope around." Pauly shakes his head. "Keep on burning that candle at both ends, Maddox, and all you're going to find is ash."

I struggle back into my shirt. "You don't know the fucking half of it."

He leaves us with a couple of exercises but mostly wants me to rest it and allow it to heal for the next few days. "Pushing it will only cause more pain and more pain will drag you back to the scratch, baby."

"Come on," Nick says, "you can spot me on the weights."

I know what he's doing. He's keeping me busy. *Babysitting* me until I'm ready to go to class or pick up a paintbrush again. My hands have been shaking so bad I won't dare get near the tattoo gun. Jesus. I value my art—my *reputation*—too much to risk it.

Nick racks the weights then lays back on the bench, beneath the bar.

"You know if this falls on you there's not much I can do with this fucked shoulder, right?" I tell him, eyeing the amount of weight he added to each end.

"This?" He nods to the weight. "Total cakewalk," then grips the bar. His muscles tense, but he pops it off the rack and brings it down to this chest. I roll my eyes, knowing Nicky can't stop pushing himself. Sy has that too. That determination and grit.

The Maddox genes didn't pass that down.

A door slams across the room and I glance up. "Shit," I mutter.

"Wha–" Nick starts, but it ends in a grunt. Sweat blooms in the center of his gray T-shirt.

"It's Haley," I say, feeling the tickle of anxiety on my spine. I'm not a big fan of confrontation. Or accepting responsibility. Or cleaning up my messes.

More Maddox genes.

My signature move here is to just dip. Get the fuck out. Avoid whatever hellfire is going to come my way from engaging with Haley any further.

I'm about to notify Nick of my super mature plan, that I'll meet him in the car, when he says, "Rem. A little help?"

His arms wobble the massive amount of weight threatening to crash down on his chest. "Jesus. I told you!"

I grab the bar with the hand on my good arm and the two of us struggle to get it back on the rack. "See?" Nick says, wiping his face. "Cakewalk."

I shake my head but then I see her crossing the gym. "Dammit. Now she's coming over here."

"Dude, you dug this hole. Fix it. Own up to your bullshit." He tosses his towel over his shoulder. "I'll be over there on the treadmill."

"Whatever," I say, "Haley loves me. I'm sure she's fine." I run my hand over my face and when I look at her again, I see she's got her shoulders back, pushing her chin and tits out. A coy grin toys with her lips. I try to pull out her colors, get a feel of her vibe, but they're lost to me right now, like so many other things.

"Hey, babe," she says, eyes skating over me. "You okay? I tried to find you after the fight and you were just gone."

Gone is the right word. Out of my goddamn mind, climbing cliffs, confronting demons and jumping for my life. Declaring my love. She has no fucking idea what I've been through since the locker room.

"Look, Haley..." I start, aware of the steady sound of Nick's feet pounding on the treadmill.

"No," she says, voice hard.

"No, uh, what?"

Her hip juts out and her hand lands on the curve. "You are not about to 'look' me."

"'Look' you?"

"No good conversation starts with 'look,' I know that. I've been on the receiving end enough times in my life." Her tone is sharp. Bitter. "So let me jump to it. *Look,* Remy, you and I are good together. We rock some serious orgasms. You're hot. I'm hot. You obviously want me because you keep coming back." Her eyes narrow when I open my mouth to cut her off. "And don't give me that Duchess shit. You got busted. Who cares? You're a Duke. You can fuck or get blown by anyone you want, and it's obvious you want me."

Across the workout area, the thud of Nick's foot missing a step, bounces over to us. I shoot him a hard stare and the cocksucker has the nerve to laugh. He's loving the fact this is not going my way.

"L–"

She glares at me.

I swallow. "Haley, what happened the other night wasn't just a mistake, it was a capital F fuck up. I was high on scratch, high on the win, and completely convinced that everyone in my life was out to get me." I soften my expression. "I shouldn't have used you like that. It was shitty. Especially since I know how you feel about me."

"How I feel about you?" she snaps. "You have no fucking idea how I feel."

I mean, I think I do, but my radar could be a little off.

"Okay, well," I rub the back of my neck, "I apologize. You can take it or leave it. I didn't mean to lead you on or whatever." God, I hate this. My stomach hurts. My shoulder hurts. I search over her head. Maybe Pauly still has that codeine in the back.

"Hey," she says, drawing my attention back down. "I know what this is about."

"You do?" Worry adds to the mix. Does she know my father is the Baron King? What the hell did I say while she was sucking my cock? Anything is possible.

She steps closer, planting her hand on my chest. "This is about that interloper, Lavinia, isn't it?"

I frown. "Well, yeah."

"You've changed since she showed up. We used to have so much fun. You'd strip me down and draw on me. We'd fuck and get high. Stay up all night, riding across town on your bike." She jabs her finger into my chest. "But you couldn't resist that fresh piece of pussy. Royal pussy. Count pussy. God, in the end you're just another fucking typical man, you know that?" She pushes up on her toes. "Wanting what you can't have. You're such a dumbass, Remy, letting her get under your skin–probably letting her sleep in your bed. *Tattooing* her. She's using you." Her eyes flick to Nick who has slowed down and is listening carefully. "She's using all of you, and I'm here, as one of your loyal cutsluts to give it to you straight." Her eyes glimmer with hate. "She's going to ruin you, *all* of you, before this is over."

Her nail digs into my sternum, and I snatch it off at the wrist. "Step back, Haley, before you say something you regret."

She snorts. "Or what? You'll push me to my knees and make me suck you off? Don't forget, baby, I do that for free. Does she?"

Her other hand reaches for my waist, but I knock that away too. Before I can react, Nick is by my side, jerking his chin at her. "You're embarrassing yourself, H."

"See?" she says, "That's where you don't get it. I'm not embarrassing myself. I'm loyal. To all of you, but you're the ones willing to toss it away." Her shoulders square and she finally steps back. "But I know how it is; you'll be back. Crawling to me after some win or some loss or whatever it is that spins you out, and unlike your little Duchess, I'll be here."

She turns, hair flouncing behind her.

I open my mouth and start to follow, to tell her to get the fuck out of here but Nick says, "Let her go."

"Seriously? After what she said about Vinny?"

He shakes his head. "She's hurt, but she'll get over it. Verity and the others will calm her down. She's not worth it."

He says that, but Haley's right. I know her pretty well, and something tells me she's not going to let this go–let *me* go–so easily.

WE STOP at the diner on Sixteenth on the way home, grabbing hamburgers and fries. The sugar and grease help get the food down, even if the harsh fluorescent lights make my eyes hurt.

"What do you think they're doing on their date?" I ask, sucking on a chocolate milkshake.

Nick pops a fry in his mouth, checking the window beside us every now and then. We're in West End, but only just, and I can see it makes him twitchy being this close to North Side. He hums, talking with his mouth full. "I know what they're *not* doing."

Having sex. He's right. That's going to take a minute.

There's a long moment where I pick at the remnants of my burger, wishing I could look up and see something other than gray. Knowing it sounds sulky and stupid, I mutter, "I could take her on a date." *A better date than Sy.*

Nick narrows his eyes at me, stabbing his shake with his straw. "Yeah, you could."

I push the rest of my food to the side and confess, "I told her I loved her."

"Yeah?" Nick looks at me over his glass as he sips, eyes intrigued. "What did she say?"

"Mostly, uhh... incomprehensible shrieking?" I shrug but Nick's expression forces me to add, "Well, we jumped right after I said it."

Putting his glass down, he gives me a blank, mystified look. "You told Lavinia you loved her right before you threw yourselves off a fucking cliff?" He shakes his head, shoulders bouncing with a laugh. "It really is always life or death with you, isn't it?"

My back straightens. "It's not like I planned it!"

He sighs, tossing the fry he's about to eat into the trash pile. "I told her I loved her, too. A few times, actually."

I fight a wayward shiver, watching as he dusts the salt from his hands. "What did she say to you?"

"The first time?" Nick slings his arm over the back of the booth, sucking his teeth. "She laughed in my face, called me crazy, and then tried to kick me in the balls."

I wince in solidarity. "Yeah, you win."

Nick grabs his milkshake and holds it in the air. "To the fucking victor, brother."

My eyes follow his gaze through the window, to the corner across the street. It's lit up with a single flickering light, a couple guys in dark hoodies tucked close, talking. I already know who they are. I knew Cash Mallis was standing there the second we rolled up. Maybe the resentment should burn that Nick brought me here of all places to grab a quick bite, as if neither of us know the boundary between west and north, but instead I just feel hollow.

"You can beat it, you know." When I look up, Nick is watching me carefully. Closely. "Viper Scratch made its rounds in South Side before it came here. I once saw Daniel Payne's best girl, Augustine, so strung out that Mrs. Crane had to tie her up just to stop her from clawing out her own eyes. She looked fucking possessed."

I shift my eyes back to the corner. Mallis is leaning into a car window, a little hatchback having stopped to make a purchase. "It's where it gets its name. Scratch." I can still feel the phantom tug of needing to dig my nails into my arm. "Whatever it's cut with, it makes you itchy as hell."

I see Nick nodding in my periphery. "You just did it a couple times, though. Enough to get the bug, but not enough to really get its fangs into you." Leaning forward, he lowers his voice. "It's the next time that'll get you, though. You'll start lying to yourself. You'll think," he shrugs, quick and casual, "whatever, you kicked it once. No big deal. It wasn't so bad. You can just do it once or twice. Three times, since it's available. Four, because you had a bad day. Five, just on account of wanting to." There's a pause where we both watch Cash salute the driver of the hatchback, slinking back to his post. "And you won't come back, Remy." When I swing my eyes to his, Nick's mouth is pressed into a tight, grim line. "Not if you do it again. One more time is all it'll take."

I drop my eyes, wishing he was wrong but knowing he's not. I'm no Augustine. No one's going to tie my ass down and get me clean, because if that fraction of the pull I felt a few days ago grew big enough, no one could stop me.

Lifting my hips, I take out my wallet, pulling out a wrinkled twenty. "Let's go home," I decide, dropping it beside my plate.

6

____

S ^y

EVEN WHEN WE walk into the restaurant, the thought is still knocking around in my brain like one of those medieval, spiked maces. As if the entire concept of going on a date with Lavinia wasn't fraught enough, the fact she didn't even realize it was a date just makes it...

Fuck fuck fuck.

Unbearable.

"Let's not make a big deal about this," she says for the third time.

The dress is shiny and tight, her breasts peeking out the top, and she keeps plucking at the straps, inching them just a little higher on her shoulders. My eyes snap to the jiggle of her tits every time she does, cock threatening to swell with the idea of slipping the straps off, watching as the fabric catches on her nipples before finally falling away, revealing her soft, supple, flushed–

My eyes dart up, and I can't even imagine how harried I must look, desperate to plant my eyes anywhere else. It's been an inner battle all night, but I no longer try to shove it away, willing the waves of my inner ocean to calm. I accept it, acknowledge it, let it pass.

I want to fuck her so badly, it hurts.

Despite the fidgeting, she wears the dress like a second skin, her shoulder blades elegant beneath the spaghetti straps as she stands tall.

Except for the fact she can't stop trying to smooth things over.

"We were all tired and everything was crazy. Obviously, you asked me out–like, *obviously*." She gives me a tense grin. This might be the most I've ever heard her talk about something that wasn't related to her kitten or her hatred of jogging. "I just got my wires mixed up."

"Lavinia." The hostess is walking toward us. I keep my voice low.

"Yes?"

"No offense, but please shut up."

Her eyebrows rise, shocked. "Rude." But then her lips twitch, some of the tension shattering with her ruby-red smirk.

"Sorry," I mutter. "That was harsh."

We both let out a nervous laugh.

I pretend like I'm not remembering what she looked like riding my brother's dick.

"No. You're right. I'm finished." She toys with the beaded fringe on the bottom of her skirt. It hangs like a curtain, shouting, 'pull me up and come to the show.'

The hostess arrives, giving me a nod. "Your table is ready, Mr. Perilini."

"Thank God," I mumble, gesturing for Lavinia to go ahead of me. It's a mistake. Every step sends that fringe swaying back and forth and my cock reacts predictably. Like a feral animal trying to escape a cage. I place my palm on the small of her back, not leading so much as allowing myself one small indulgence of her heat.

Accept. Acknowledge. Let it pass.

When I step in front of her to pull out her chair, she pauses, an odd look coming over her face. It's gone just as quickly as it came. "So how'd you score a last-minute reservation at Stock and Barrel?" she asks, lowering herself into the seat.

"I have my ways." Carefully, I push the chair back to the table. So far, despite the utter humiliation and the fact I want to rut her like a goddamn dog, I've managed to tick off every box in the gentleman playbook. Flowers. Holding the door for her. Taking her hand to help her out of the SUV. Walking closer to the street.

"I hear the waiting list is months long." She freezes, eyes snapping to mine. "Wait. Unless it wasn't last minute. Have you been planning this for a long time?"

I take a second to interpret the confusion in her eyes. I could lie. If I'd planned this during my week away, then it would have been a statement. A gesture. An apology. She might appreciate knowing I'd had the forethought, because yeah, of-fucking-course that's what a guy does when he's messed up.

I tell the truth instead.

"My mom is the owner's therapist," I explain, draping my coat over the back of the chair and taking the seat across from her. The table is next to the wide windows that overlook the water. It's small, suffocatingly intimate, and with my large frame, not at all unlike sitting at a child's play table. I tuck my limbs in close to avoid knocking anything over. One wrong move and my shirt cuff could catch fire on the centerpiece candle. "He told her that whenever she wanted a table, it was waiting."

She reaches for the menu. It's narrow, on thick cardstock, and offers a limited selection. According to my mother, that's how fancy places work. "It's cool that your mom has her own career," Lavinia says, eyes sparkling in the candlelight. "It's very non-Royal. For a woman, I mean."

I pick my menu up more for something to do with my hands than anything. My pops already told me what to order. "It's one of the reasons my fathers decided to get out. Mom wanted to be a psychologist, not a Queen. They didn't want to hold her back from her dream."

Not that the comment from Remy's father hasn't taken root inside my mind.

"...for those two, it's the secret. It's the shame."

My parents almost never talk about their time in West End, but I've never gotten the impression that there's shame in their past. That my Pops lost the loyalty of his men. That my dad and him left not because they wanted to, but because they didn't have a choice.

Then again, it wasn't a week ago that Remy thought his father was just a lame, boring old real estate developer.

She stares at the menu, but sensing that she's not really reading, I wonder, "Are you thinking about your own mom?"

She blinks up at me, the fog clearing from her eyes as she shrugs. "Or what our lives might have been like if my father had sacrificed his ambition the way yours did."

Reasonably, I offer, "Abdicating has its own issues. My parents have had to look over their shoulders their entire lives. Career opportunities–the good ones–are hard to come by in Forsyth for an ex-Royal." I take a sip of water. "And it's one reason the Dukes are viewed as the lowest tier frat. Saul hasn't been a failure as King, but he doesn't have the bloodline. He has no heir, and it gives us weaker positioning. Like Nick said. It's all about lever- age." My eyes meet hers. "We don't have the luxury of losing. Ever."

She tilts her head, something soft and pensive in her eyes. "It's a shame, isn't it? That people from good, strong, loving families are never the ones who take the crowns. It's always the snakes and the rats."

"Snakes eat rats," I point out.

Lavinia's red lips curl into a slow, knowing grin. "Bears eat both."

My dick is instantly, unavoidably, fucking *agonizingly* hard. "Can I kiss you?" The request tumbles out with all the grace of a boulder, my voice dropping two octaves. I don't actually mean to. It's just the thought of Lavinia being on our side, becoming one of us, acknowledging our superiority–

My blood turns to hot fucking lava.

Accept. Acknowledge. Let it pass!

It's only when she jolts back, smirk vanishing, that I realize how close we've been leaning over the table. Clearing her throat, she looks away. "No."

Before I can do much more than stare at her dismally, the waiter arrives to take our drink order. "Whisky," I say, voice a touch too gruff.

To my surprise, Lavinia looks up at the waiter and says, "Vodka tonic, please."

"You don't usually drink," I say, once he leaves. Remy's been trying to pump her full of illicit substances for weeks now, and Nick's always down to offer her a beer, but I've never seen her take either of them up on it. Looking at the menu, I mutter, "Is the date going that badly?"

"God, no." Her shoulders relax. I'm momentarily fixated on the way her eyelashes look until she ducks her head. "It's been a long time since I didn't need to have my wits about me to survive."

Nodding, I say, "I know the feeling."

"No, you don't." When she glances up, there's a bitter heat in her eyes. "When you're a prisoner being shuffled between shady men who could overpower you with a flick of their wrist, you learn that your only weapon is your mind. You have to keep it sharp at all times, because you never know when..." Her words trail off, but I see it. The same numbness I see in her eyes when she's having a paralysis episode.

My chest feels as heavy as lead.

I drop the menu.

"Because you never know when some guy is going to break into your room and rough you up, right?" I remember that night in the Hideaway's basement with such vivid clarity that sometimes I have to force myself not to call up the memory of being between her thighs. Only these days, it's not her thighs I remember. It's her wet eyelashes as I backhanded her cheek. The scorching fire of hatred in her eyes. The way she looked in that bed, like a wild, caged animal.

She tries to hide her wince, but I still see it. "That, or... something worse."

Grimly, I say, "I doubt anything was worse than what we did to you." I freeze, muscles tensing. "Unless someone else–"

"No," she bursts, eyes wide. "No one ever–" A quick shake of her head. "But there was always the threat."

An uncomfortable stillness settles over us, but I'm too lost in the twist of my thoughts to pay it much mind. Why didn't I ever think to ask her that before? "I did it for Nick, you know." I force myself to look her in the eye. "To become a Duke with him. To be his brother again. To watch his back. I didn't know–"

I stop, knowing that any way I finish that sentence will sound selfish and callous.

I didn't know I'd end up falling for you? As if that'd make it any better.

"I didn't think about you at all, really." My shrug is heavy, defeated. "You were just a Lucia back then. You were the enemy. You were a job." Abruptly, I add, "I shouldn't have hit you like that," and it strikes me as the most ridiculous fucking thing, because really? Out of everything we did to her that night?

"I know." She pulls her hands into her lap, suddenly looking very small.

"Christ," I mutter. And then, "This date really is going that badly."

She offers a strained smile. "Liquor is coming."

"It's just..." When I duck in closer to speak, she reaches out to move the candle, eyes fixed on the flame, even though her head is tilted to hear me. "I was thinking I'd bring you here and tell you I was wrong that night, at the party." Beneath the table, my knee bumps hers and she flinches. Just barely, but enough to notice. I don't let that stop me. Not yet. "And then that shit happened today with Bruce, and I was going to say... things have changed since I did that to you. For me, they have." I wait a beat for a reaction, any semblance of understanding. When none comes, her eyes tracking off to the side, I sigh. "And now, I remember just how much I have to make up for, and it's…" I take a long, bracing inhale. "It's a lot."

She fidgets with the candle, mouth twisting unhappily. "Too much work, huh?"

It's a risk–I've stayed inside my lane so far–but I touch her. Resting my palm over her knuckles, I still the absentminded twirl of the candle. "I'd put in the work, Lavinia." Waiting until she meets my gaze, I add, "Hell, I'd put in twice the work if it meant you'd look at me the way you used to. Remember, that day? When we were on the floor?"

"When you asked me to be your girlfriend?"

"Yes." I was so high on it that I had to go for another run afterward just to wear my nerves back down. There's a reason I pull my hand away, though, dragging my fingertips until the connection breaks. "But I don't actually deserve you. Do I?"

Lavinia watches me closely, carefully, and when her lips part on the crest of an inhale, I just know she's going to agree.

And then the goddamn waiter comes.

We break apart like two criminals being caught in the middle of some heinous act.

Nonplussed, he sets a glass down in front of us both. "Vodka tonic for the lady, and a whiskey for her gentleman."

Lavinia sighs. "I'm not a Lady. But thank you."

The whisky is dark amber, absurdly expensive, the kind of thing one might imagine was aged in the bosom of some luxurious villa, covered in silks, distilled with diamonds, tended to faithfully by generations of virgins, and blessed hourly with smudges of sacred ash on its barrel.

I down that shit in one tasteless gulp.

"You're right." Lavinia says, fingering her glass. "Things have changed. That's what I was trying to say before." She lifts the glass, meeting my eyes over the rim. "I'd never drink in front of someone I didn't feel safe with." Then she tips it back, holding my stare as she takes a long, indulgent sip. I watch, transfixed as she licks the taste of it from her lips. "I don't know what you deserve, Sy. But I know what I deserve, and for once in my life, that's all that matters to me."

I don't need that wry curve of her brow to drive home what I already know.

"You deserve to be safe."

"Among other things," she says, nodding. "Yeah, I think I do."

I give the space beside her hand a longing tap. "I can... be that for you. I can keep you safe." When I look up, there's a warmth in her eyes that I'm surprised to see. It's not quite what it was like before, that day she smiled at me and touched me, and looked flushed and sated and... happy. It's not quite that.

But it's a start.

Clearing my throat, I look back at the menu. "You deserve a good dinner, too."

A loud voice carries from across the room, and I glance over, grimacing when I realize who the voice belongs to. "Fuck, I thought this place had standards." Seriously, this night is doomed.

"What?" Lavinia looks over her shoulder. "Who's that?"

"One of Ashby's little carbon copy fuckboys," I grumble, but before I have a chance to elaborate, he sees me, eyes hardening. Without missing a beat, he strides across the restaurant in my direction, all swagger and cocksure grin. The blonde on his arm is sent to follow the hostess with a hard slap to her ass before Wicker stops at my table. "Perilini. Surprised to see you here. Isn't this restaurant a bit out of your price range?"

Wicker Ashby is a member of PNZ, the Prince's frat, and one of Rufus Ashby's spawns.

Not genetically.

My lip curls distastefully. "Ashby." His eyes flick to Lavinia, but for once tonight, my manners fail. This douchebag doesn't rate an introduction.

Unfortunately, he disagrees. "Whitaker Ashby—my friends call me Wicker. And you're Lavinia Lucia," he says, eyes raking over her.

"I've heard a lot about you." The perfect, sparkling grin he flashes her makes my chest flare hot and possessive. "I've been dying to meet you."

"And why's that?" Lavinia asks, sweetly.

"Because I wanted to see the caliber of pussy that Bruin thought was worth killing one of our men over."

My jaw clenches and the urge to rise out of my seat and pummel this piece of trash is intense.

But no.

I'm not letting this asshole ruin my date.

Sounding bored, I say, "Yeah, you're going to have to be more specific." Even though I know perfectly well who he's talking about. "Nick has a twitchy finger when it comes to the Duchess."

Lavinia gives him a sympathetic nod. "It's a real problem. There have been interventions and everything."

Wicker's gaze moves from her to me. "Forgive me. I forgot with all the hits you take to that big, fat skull of yours, your memory probably isn't up to par. Maybe a name will jog it." His grin turns hard and cold. "Felix Ashby."

"Ah, right," I say, staring mournfully into my empty glass. "Felix. Poor bastard. To be fair, he did insult the Duchess."

"And mistreated his cat!" Lavinia snaps, as if that alone is worth a death sentence. I mean, for her, it just might be. She is Nicky's girl, after all. "He was obviously a piece of shit."

"What's this about, Wicker?" I ask. "Come to issue a threat? A warning? Because you're not the first one to threaten us this week. You're not even the first one to threaten us today. We're fresh out of fucks."

Crisply, he replies, "Like I said, I just wanted to see what drove Nick to murder." He props his hand on the back of my chair while his eyes rake over Lavinia. "The three of you did pluck her out of a whorehouse. She must be fantastic at head for Bruin to be so whipped. I'd have to test it myself to be sure." Pitching his voice to a seductive purr, he adds, "How about you join me tonight, sweetie? Plenty of space for a pretty little slut like you beneath my table."

"What did you just say?" My vision turns red so fast that it's like a freight train slamming into my sternum. I get halfway to jolting to my feet before Lavinia's hand lands on my arm.

"Generous offer," she says, smiling icily, "but we all know there's a reason Princesses are contractually obligated to fuck you guys." Lavinia tilts her head toward me, like she's—very loudly—telling me a secret. "The word around that whorehouse is that East End dick is like getting railed by a soft taco."

Wicker isn't one to get provoked easily. He just shrugs a shoulder, easy as you please. "Don't confuse East End with its blood royalty. The rest of us get to choose our lays. Like your sister, for instance." He lifts his hand, kissing the tips of his forefinger and thumb. "Delicious cunt. Begged me for more."

Something in Lavinia's eyes shuts down, and it makes the storm inside of my chest grow wider, angrier. "You never fucked my sister. I know for a fact."

Wicker casts his eyes around the restaurant. "She here to say otherwise? Ah, that's right." He snaps his fingers, like he's remembering something. "She's gone. Probably deader than a doornail."

"That's enough," I growl, noticing the eyes on us. "Felix fucked around and found out. Don't act like a Prince wouldn't do the same for his Princess. You know, assuming you had the pedigree to be a *real* Royal."

He drags his eyes off Lavinia's chest, and I see something flicker across his face. Anger? Offense? "The Princess would never be in a situation like that in the first place. At a hand-off?" He scoffs. "Our women are treated like queens from the day they're chosen, not dragged around like dogs."

He doesn't mention what happens after that. But Lavinia doesn't miss a beat.

"Until they can't give you an heir, and you toss them to the gutter." She snorts. "Yeah, I met your former Princess that night. Autumn is her name? Used up and discarded at twenty-one. That's the dream, alright."

"You don't know anything about the inner workings of PNZ."

He straightens, expression inexplicably smug. His eyes dart over to where his girlfriend waits. "Gotta go." He pauses and gives me a grin. "Pro tip, Perilini: Always get a booth. It's the best way to get a handjob during dinner." He pauses, doing that annoying finger snap again. "Probably still not enough cover for you, eh?"

He struts off, and I'm left plucking at my collar, the necktie feeling unbearably tight. It's joined by the hard snare of my heartbeat, the hot rush of my blood, and tendons straining with the urge to take a running tackle at his retreating figure.

"I can't do this," I say, the feeling of suffocation surrounding me.

She tears her glare away from him, swinging an alarmed look my way. "Do what?"

"This date." I yank at my tie, loosening it for air. It doesn't help. My blood feels like a living thing, pulsing and energized. "This is a fucking disaster, Lavinia. You know it. I know it. Wicker-fuckboy-Ashby knows it."

She blinks at me. "You want to leave?"

"There's no reason to put us through it. I mean, look at us." I wave my hand over the table. "We're not even compatible—anywhere. We can't communicate. We argue all the time. I can hardly touch you without you flinching. We can't even fuck." My voice clips off and I inhale, trying to calm the stampede of my heart. "I've busted my ass all night to be the kind of guy you deserve, but let's face it. I'm *not*." I stand, grabbing my jacket, and then I shrug it on so aggressively that I'm pretty sure I hear a rip. I reach for the wallet in my pocket to pay for the drinks, but there's nothing there. It's gone.

"Sy," Lavinia says, face falling. "I know this has been a clusterfuck, but don't—"

"Shit." I pat my other pockets.

"What?" Her tone shifts to concern.

"My fucking wallet is gone." Jesus. This is what I mean. Total disaster. *Did I forget it? No.* I put the valet ticket in there when we got out of the car. I bend, looking on the floor, under the tablecloth. Lavinia hops up, and my eyes flick behind her, where I see Wicker in his booth. His arms are extended along the back of the bench, a wide, smug grin plastered across his face.

I straighten. "Motherfucker."

Before I even finish marching my way to his table, Wicker has the wallet held up, giving it a little wave. "Lose something, big guy?"

Anger swells in my chest, and I lunge. Lavinia's hands grab at my jacket in a panicked attempt to hold me back, but we both know she's too small to really do so. I hold back anyway, snatching the wallet from his hand with a sneer. "Gutless, petty theft. You're definitely East End garbage."

"And you're poor," he says, laughing obnoxiously. "It's not like I'd really use your credit card. It'd get declined on appetizers alone." His eyes shift to Lavinia, tongue sucking his teeth. "Date going badly, sweetie? It's not too late to join me. If those bandages on your knees mean anything, I'm betting you know just how to pay your way." He says to his date, "Tiff, scooch over a bit, make room for the Duchess."

"That's it," Lavinia says, pushing past me. She grabs the drink in front of him and tosses it in his face.

Tiffany squeals, jolting to her feet. "My dress!"

"You *bitch*," Wicker snarls, jumping up.

I slam a hand on his shoulder, shoving him back down, and then jerk back my elbow, preparing to beat the ever-loving shit out of him. "*Don't* you fucking dare. If you think my brother has a hair trigger for the Duchess, then you should see how I react."

Wicker's face pales under his tan, and even though his glare doesn't fall, I still see his Adam's apple bobbing with a swallow. Tiffany whimpers, scooching around the booth in a futile attempt to escape.

"Ahem."

A throat clears behind us, and slowly, I turn. A man dressed in a suit stands behind me, nervously hovering. I assume he's the manager and right behind him is our alarmed looking waiter and what appears to be a security guard.

I don't lower my arm, but I hold my fist, waiting.

"Mr. Perilini, it's time for you to leave," the man in the suit says in a quiet but firm voice. "Immediately, or I will call the police."

Wicker's lips tug into the smallest of smirks, and if Nick hadn't just given that speech about putting the frat first, to hold ourselves to a higher public standard, I'd be ruining Wicker's pretty face right about now.

But my stupid brother stepped up, which means I have to, also.

I drop my fist and release him, snagging my wallet in the process. "I'd tell you to meet me outside so we can settle this like real men, but we both know you're too pussy to square up with me."

"Sure," he says, flicking his eyes to Tiffany who quickly re-glues to his side. "Whatever you say."

Security doesn't exactly throw us out. We were leaving in the first place. But we still get an obnoxious escort, the guard nodding to the valet to get our car ASAP. The kid bolts, and I walk over to the brick column next to the valet stand and lean back, sighing.

Closing my eyes, I hope I'll wake up anywhere else.

Lavinia's heels click on the paved sidewalk, and I feel her staring at me. Without opening my eyes, I say, "I'm just not used to this."

"Used to what?"

"Losing." I glance over at her. It's painful to see her. She's so fucking beautiful. So strong. So... everything. I don't know how I didn't see it before. Lavinia Lucia is the perfect girl for me. "Every round I go with you, I end up losing."

She tilts her head, brows pulled together. "When are the three of you going to realize I'm not some prize you can win?"

There's some irony there, given that she literally was our prize for Nick winning his fight against Perez. But I don't argue, because I understand the basic premise of it. We won her body, her title, and the right to call her ours.

Nothing else.

"This was a nice gesture and all, but just out of curiosity," she says, eyes cast down to the knot of my tie. "Are you ever going to actually say the words?"

I know what she wants to hear. It's the reason I wanted to take her out to begin with. The Hideaway. The locker room. That night in my parents' basement. I could apologize for all of that and it'd be easy. Things were different between us then. She knows it. She has to know it.

But how can I erase what I did the night I left?

The pause lingers on, tinged with sadness, and it's heavy with the feeling that this is do or die. A moment where something is either saved or broken.

I shove my hands into my pockets. "You want to know why I've never had a girlfriend before?"

Lavinia rolls her eyes, a flash of annoyance crossing her features. "I know you have *intimacy problems*, but–"

"No, I mean the real reason. The honest truth." It has nothing to do with sex, and from the curious look she pins me with, she's catching my drift. This isn't something I've been able to admit to myself until recently. "My fathers were legends around here. The old guys up at the gym still talk about them sometimes. They were unstoppable forces, respected just as much as they were feared. And then... they fell for my mom." It's always been hard to reconcile the ruthless, tough, hotblooded fighters West End reveres with the two patient men who raised me. "You know better than anyone that you have to be hard as steel out here. The smallest sign of weakness and you get taken to the mat."

Her face clears. "And caring about someone is a weakness."

"I've seen it a million times with other guys. They get a girl, go soft. Even the fiercest fighters–real warriors–get all pussy-whipped and gooey. And I never really got it. Who would want that? I sure as fuck never did." Pitching closer, I peer into her eyes, knowing she must hear the thread of confusion in my voice. "But the weird thing is? Now that I do want it, I don't feel that way at all. You don't make me soft. If anything, you make me want to fight harder. Better. Stronger." My fingers brush against hers. "You're more than a prize to me, Lavinia. To *us*. I wanted to bring you here tonight, to this stupid restaurant, in this stupid suit, with those stupid flowers, because I wanted to show you that I could be... worthy. Of you."

"Sy." The look she gives me is unbearable. *Pity.* "It's just one date."

I smile grimly. "I know. One date against months of evidence that I'm not worthy at all." It was a bad idea. After all we've been through these past few days, this was too soon. Impatient. Impulsive. I guess I really am Nick's brother. But there is one more thing I need her to know. "It'll never happen again, Lavinia. I meant what I said back there. I'll always keep you safe. From others, and from myself." She searches my eyes with an intensity I'm not expecting, but am oddly grateful to see. Intrinsically, I know this is something she's going to hold me to. "Even if you don't want this." I gesture between us. "Even if you don't want me. I'll still keep that promise."

I don't know what she finds in my eyes, but it makes her face soften, head canting to the side. "I already told you, didn't I?" Her smile is small and edged with hurt, but it still makes my chest thump. "There are worse things than being Sy Perilini's girl." She jerks her chin toward the restaurant. "I could be poor Tiffany right now."

I snort, real laughter rumbling around my chest. God, this woman. Knowing I have no right to, I nervously ask, "What does that mean? Are you... mine?"

She steps closer, raising her hand to grip my tie. Then, she arches an eyebrow. "That depends entirely on how this kiss goes."

Slowly.

That's how it goes.

I cup her cheek first, not just because I've seen Nick and Remy do it, but because I want to tip her face up to mine, brush my lips against hers, feel the hinge of her jaw shift as she parts her mouth.

After that it's soft and warm and wet. The sharp edge of vodka and whisky lingers on our tongues, but all I taste is sweetness and a sense of urgency. When I slide my hand around to her lower back, tucking her body closer, something primal yawns itself awake inside of me. It wants to *take*. It wants to spin her around, shove her up against this pillar, and tear this sparkly dress off her.

Accept.

I lick into her mouth instead, biting back the guttural whine threatening to break free from the pit of my chest. Her hand tugs my tie, beckoning me closer, and it roars through me like a wildfire.

Acknowledge.

My dick throbs with want, so hard that I know she can feel it against her belly. But when I tangle my fingers into her hair, I don't make a fist, pulling and fighting. I cradle the curve of her skull and think about that day on the floor. The way she looked at me. Her fingers against mine. The curl of her laughter.

Let it go.

When I pull away, I don't go far, tipping my forehead against hers. I don't open my eyes because I'm not ready to see her answer. I breathe in the scent of her instead, the warmth of her body against mine, the sensation of her fingers clutching my jacket.

If the world ended right now, I'd be okay.

"Pizza." When I blink my eyes open, she's staring back, mouth puckered into a thoughtful curve. "Way better first date food than this fancy crap, don't you think?"

Grinning, I take her hand just as the car pulls around. "Only one way to find out."

7

———

L avinia

When I first enrolled at Forsyth, it became clear that one of the guys would always be close, if not doggedly on my heels. Waiting outside class. Following me to the library. Even with the tracker, they didn't trust me. I had no autonomy, which was fair. I planned to run at the first opportunity.

Back then I'd been forced to comply and pretend we were one happy Royal family. But I'd watch the other frats around campus, putting on a display with their house girls, and think about how controlled they are, how pathetic. Story's Lords follow her everywhere, their bodies inextricably linked. The black cuff wrapped tight around her wrist looked more like a manacle than a fashion accessory. Then there's the Princess, with her shiny hair and perfect features, doted on by three rich boy clones, keeping tabs on their potential heir. Regina, the Baroness, who I only ever catch rare glimpses of, walks around campus with three sentient shadows, her head always cast just slightly in their direction. And I could never forget Sutton, the Countess, wasting away from viper scratch, her shoulders knobby and eyes glazed over and vacant.

All I ever saw were women and their leashes.

I see things a little differently now. These Royal men are given a woman to protect and keep. To produce a legacy. To possibly love. We're the most valuable thing they own, and as much as it rankles my nerves to accept that I'm a possession, after everything we've been through, I'm no longer hostile about their hovering.

There's a target on all of us, all the time, especially if your last name is the same as a King.

Of course, it doesn't hurt that there's a certain prestige that comes with being Royal, something I never experienced as the less-worthy daughter of Lionel Lucia. It's also not a hindrance that my Dukes are ridiculously hot, and one in particular has very recently become my personal orgasm-giving machine.

These things bounce around my mind when we're all finally back on campus. We present a united front, and we are more cohesive than ever, albeit at various levels of functioning.

A bit of the tension eased with Sy after our date, and Remy seems... better. I guess. He stopped puking and has started eating again. His complexion is better, although half of his face is hidden behind a thick layer of blond scruff that he scratches incessantly. His one arm is held back in a sling. The guy they met at the gym didn't push it, but Nick and Sy have. From my reading, it makes the most sense for him to keep it stabilized as much as possible.

But the biggest indicator of how he's feeling is the persistent bounce of his knee and the rapid fire tapping of his marker against the table.

"That's it," Nick snaps, reaching across the distance and snatching the marker out of his ink-stained fingers.

"Hey!" Remy cries.

"Nick!" Sy growls, but it doesn't stop his brother from flicking his wrist, sending the marker sailing across the student center, into a group of students, beaning one right in the forehead.

He snickers, pleased with the accidental bullseye. "Fuck, did you see that?"

"Go get it," Sy says. "*Now*."

Nick rolls his eyes. "No. He'll just start tapping it again, and I just can't fucking take it anymore." He turns a pleading look my way. "Little Bird, I know things have been tense between you two, but maybe if you just gave him a BJ—"

Sy slams his notebook shut. "What the fuck is wrong with you?"

Remy is pointedly quiet, eyes cast down at his blank drawing pad.

"Jesus," I mutter, scooting my chair back. "I'll get it."

Nick bolts up, realizing he's pushed it a step too far. "Christ, just–I'll go."

"No." I press my hand into this chest. "Let me. Sit and think about not being a dick for a minute."

He frowns and pushes my hair off my forehead, planting a kiss. "Fine."

These guys will be the end of me.

I stride over to the group in question. They see me coming. They know who I belong to, and even though they should be pissed, they won't be. Perk of being a Royal.

"Hey," I say to the kid who got hit by the marker. There's a red welt on his forehead. "Sorry about that."

He's younger—probably a freshman—wearing a Forsyth sweatshirt. His eyes are glued to the tattoo on my chest. Well, I'm going to be charitable and assume it's the tattoo, although the shirt Nick picked out for me today does make my tits look huge.

"Uh," he says. "Sure. No problem."

"I'm going to need that marker back."

The kid hands me the marker but I hear a snort of laughter. "Why do you need it so bad? So they can mark you even more?"

I spin, eyes narrowed. "What did you say?"

That's when I see the tattoo on his wrist. A coiled snake. He smirks. "I just figure it's about time they wrote '*Duke's Pussy*' on your forehead and got it over with."

My eyes flick over to the table where each of my Dukes is watching, although we're too far for them to hear the exchange. Lucky for him. Nick is poised, not unlike that tattooed snake, ready to strike at the first sign. But this kid is nothing. He's a fucking freshman pledge. Dirt under what used to be Perez's boot.

"Warren, shut the fuck up," says the kid with the red welt on his forehead. A worry line slashes his forehead. "He's a dumbass, Duchess. He didn't mean it."

"Listen to your friend, asshole." I look up and see Story's approach—a cup of tea in her hand. She's dressed in a short navy skirt and a prim, pale pink sweater set. "This is not the chick you want to fuck with." She smirks. "Not unless you want to end up in an electrified dog crate for three days."

Warren swallows and ducks his head. For now, at least.

She links her arm with mine and steers me away.

"Everything okay?"

I grip the marker. "Sure. I mean, other than the usual."

I have no idea how much Story and the Lords know about everything that went down with the Barons and the hit, but even if they are our allies, we've sworn to keep our mouths shut.

She stops in the middle of the student union. I feel my Dukes' eyes on me like a tangible weight, and across the room, Dimitri Rathbone leans against the wall, his gaze glued to his Lady. "Got a minute?" she asks. "I needed to talk to you about something."

"Yeah? What's up?"

"I'm not sure if you've heard, but every year there's this big charity fundraiser. A fall festival? All the frats cooperate."

"I've heard *of* it," I say, thinking back to the chatter in North Side whenever fall rolled around. "But I've had my doubts about the cooperation aspect."

"Believe it or not, they actually do put the weapons down for the weekend and play nice." She smiles in a way that makes me doubt it's that easy. "That means we have to do the same thing—because we're in charge."

"We?"

"The house girls. We get the glory of organizing set up, games, activities, rides, amusements, food..."

I pull a face. "So, basically the whole thing."

"Pretty much."

"Typical."

"Right?"

Crossing my arms, I can't help but acknowledge this is the absolute fucking worst time for inter-house mingling. "I'm assuming there's no way out of this?"

She shakes her head. "Sorry, it's just something we have to do." Her eyes flick over my shoulder and she laughs. "Wow, he's not liking the two of us talking too much."

I glance over and see Nick staring our way. His jaw is set, eyes narrowed. He's suspicious, which makes sense. The last time me and Story teamed up, things didn't go so well for Nick Bruin.

I turn back to her, eyes rolling. "He'll survive."

Her face turns pensive. "How's that going for you?"

"Me and Nick?" I don't have to look again to feel his eyes boring into me. I used to resent it. Now it just makes me hot between my legs. He's not the only one watching, but Sy has out a notebook, at least pretending not to stalk me, and Remy's focus is completely on not falling apart at the moment. "We're actually..." My shoulders pull up high, arms crossing. "Uh, together?" I brace myself for the disbelief. The disapproval.

Her eyebrow arches. "So he just needed a little tough love, huh?"

"Something like that." There's no judgment in her tone, though. Story is probably the only other person in the world that can understand me falling for a guy like Nick. I'm not exactly sure how far things went for her and her Lords, but I see the cuff on her wrist and the puckered scar lines peeking out of the top of her shirt. "Just tell me what you need me to do for the festival. I'm in."

"I'll text you," she says, drinking the last of her tea and tossing the cup in the nearby trash can. "And seriously, I'm glad you're helping this year. The other house girls…" She scrunches her nose.

I fill in the blank. "Suck?"

She grins. "Pretty much."

Back at the table, I hand Remy his marker. "Thanks, Vinny," he says, tucking it behind his ear.

Nick says nothing about my talk with the Lady, but Sy isn't quite as good at playing it cool.

"What was that about?" he asks.

"The fall festival thing," I say, grabbing my coat. I've got Chem in ten minutes. "Apparently it's part of my job as Duchess to help plan it."

"Bad idea," Nick says. "We don't fraternize with the enemy."

"Yeah, actually we do." Sy stands, picking up my backpack and slinging it over his shoulder. "A few times a year. It's in the charter and part of the deal when you join one of the frats." He gives me an apologetic look. "Sorry I forgot to tell you. Things have been…" He scratches his neck. "Well, you know how things have been."

"It's fine," I assure, even though it isn't. Five Royal women planning one festival? That's a recipe for homicide, the likes of which even the Dukes have never seen. Still, I try to stay positive. "It'll be nice to spend some time with Story, though. You know we're… friendly. Ish."

Sy looks uncomfortable about that statement, but Nick?

He steps next to me, arm sliding around my waist. His head drops, mouth warm against my ear. "Promise me the two of you aren't going to team up against me again."

I hum, leading him away. "We'll see how you behave."

EVEN HAVING to spring up the narrow staircase to reach it, the inert quiet of the room that houses the clock tower's inner workings is a welcome reprieve.

It's a mess when I enter for the first time in a week, parts and tools strewn everywhere, and I spend a long moment looking at it all. What was I thinking, taking this all apart? As if I could fix something this big–this important.

The plan had been to just start over. To take apart the strike train, and put it back together according to the ancient diagram spread out beneath the bare bulb in the corner. But I only got halfway through it last time I was up here.

Steeling myself, I gather my hair up into a ponytail and get to work, welcoming the distraction. Up here, I don't have to pretend I can't see the bulge in Sy's pants when he watches me reach for a glass. I don't have to wonder what crazy thing Nick is going to do next. I don't have to avoid looking at Remy and seeing that flash of memory of Haley on her knees before him. I don't have to think about my father and wonder how he'll strike back at us.

The clock is a mess, but it can be put back together.

Will it work, after?

Maybe.

Maybe not.

It's a long, tedious process, some of the parts looking so similar that it takes me a while to match it up to the diagram on the page. The problem is that I've read the materials, memorized the components, and know how it fits together, but I don't understand it in any organic sense. I know what goes where, but not why, or how it synergizes with the other parts.

I'm almost done–placing the last awkward auxiliary arm–when I hear the door open. I don't turn around, my arm wound so far into the clock's guts that it'd be a chore to start over.

"What?" I ask, straining with my other arm to secure the auxiliary arm with the nut.

"That looks like a good way to lose a limb." The sound of Remy's rough, quiet voice makes my stomach swoop in a complicated way.

"That'd only happen if the clock actually turned." I grunt, reaching around a gear to tighten the threads.

I feel him behind me just as much as I hear him. He has all the presence of a throbbing wound. "These the diagrams?" At my answering hum, I hear papers shifting. "Jesus, these must be a hundred years old." There's a long stretch of silence where I begin feeling the prickling of annoyance. The problem with Remy is that he's so unavoidable.

His energy.

His eyes.

His face.

Satisfied with the tension of the spring, I slowly extricate myself from the mechanics, fingers greasy and smudged, and finally turn to him.

His *body*.

He's shirtless, pants slung low on his waist, and I freeze as I watch him scan the paper. A hand moves to rake his damp hair back, away from his eyes. It's an idle gesture that makes the corded muscles beneath his inked skin shift and flex.

And then he looks up, meeting my gaze. "Do you know what's wrong with it?"

I turn off the attraction like a switch. "Yeah." I drop the wrench into the toolbox. "It's broken."

He blinks. "Oh."

I gesture to the large crank at my hip. "It won't wind. It's like it's stuck or something." I stop short of giving him a demonstration; my small figure struggling comically to push at whatever twisted metal is preventing it from working.

Reaching up to scratch absently at his scruff, he offers, "Obviously I'm useless, but you should ask Sy to try. He's the strongest one here." After a beat, he adds, "Don't tell him I said that."

"It won't matter," I reply, tossing a spanner with the rest of the tools.

His eyes follow the metallic crash. "I've been taking my meds," he says. His brow instantly puckers, like maybe he wasn't intending to.

I wipe my hands with the dirty towel slung over the toolbox. "I know." I've seen the bottles all lined up in the bathroom, sometimes open, sometimes not.

His eyes flash in surprise, the line of his mouth softening. "They're still orange, but I do it." After a beat, he stresses, "I'll keep doing it."

Nodding, I say nothing. It's a constant misery inside my chest to be met with warring absolutes. Part of me still buzzes to life at his attention, while the other half wilts beneath the weight of it. My heart wants so badly to see him like this–alert, clear, rebounding– and it also withers at the knowledge I wasn't enough.

I wasn't enough for him.

Just looking at him makes my throat go tight. "Did you want something?"

It's been an unspoken agreement that we were giving each other space. Sometimes, that night on the cliffs doesn't even feel real, and I find myself relating to all of Remy's doubts about the first time he did it. Other times, I'll look at the scabbing cuts on my legs and remember the words he whispered before we jumped, and it'll be so real that I need to get away, take a breath.

Like now.

He ducks his head, grabbing something from the table beside him. "Give me a hand with this?" It takes me a long moment to realize he's holding the sling and a shirt. "Sy's busy with some lab report and Nick's on the phone with his Pops." His mouth turns down unhappily. "My shoulder's still a little fucked up."

"Of course." I drop the towel and bring up the armor, marching forward to take the shirt from him. It's nothing. This bare expanse of chest? It's just skin. Flesh and bone, nothing more. "You going somewhere?" I ask, keeping my words light and direct.

"Yeah, this meeting thing." He reaches to run his hand through his hair, but then winces at the pain and drops his arm. "Over at the student center."

"Meeting?" I ask, gesturing to his bad arm. He extends it slowly, wincing, and I thread it through the sleeve without even having to touch him. It's a buttondown, so I move behind him, easing the shirt up his shoulder, and then around his back for his good arm.

"Sy found it for me," he explains, words quiet but oddly tense. "It's like... a support group. You know, for... addicts and stuff."

I only pause for a second. "Oh, right." His scent surrounds me like a blanket, muted from what I'm used to. There's no edge of paint or solvent about him, just the masculine spice of his body wash–maybe deodorant. It still makes my belly flip, even though I'm careful not to show it on my face. "That sounds... good."

I don't want to push too hard here, or say the wrong thing. He's like when Archie first came here, skittish and easily startled. I'm glad he's getting help, but with Remy? It's hard to trust anything. To trust him.

I feel his eyes tracking me tenaciously, and every move he makes seems intentionally measured to take as long as possible. He threads his second arm through carefully, even though it's not even injured. I hold my frame, patient and just as deliberate with my movements, mechanically pulling the sides of the shirt to his front.

I'm his Duchess.

This is a duty.

I begin with the lower buttons, pretending I don't hear the slow, growing heaviness of his breath. One after the other, I ascend, hooking button into buttonhole, until my knuckles accidentally graze the hard ladder of his abdomen. Remy sucks in a soft breath, abs flexing.

"Almost there," I say, as if his reaction could be owed to impatience and nothing more.

He responds by bending his head, the tip of his nose grazing along the hair at my temple. "Your color's fading," he whispers, voice like tattered silk. "In your hair. The blue's so pale now. I could re-do it sometime." My jaw clenches, fingers hastening as he inhales. It could just be that he's tired and slumping. He's not even really touching me. Just his breath.

And it's agony.

"There," I say, finishing the third button from the top, just how I know he likes it.

I'm stiffly straightening the collar when his nose trails lower, nudging against my temple, and at that same moment, his hand–the one attached to the *injured* shoulder–reaches up to catch my jaw, lips dragging damply across my cheek.

I jolt back, tearing myself from his grip. All the heat in my blood turns to chill. "Don't." My voice is sharp enough that he flinches, hand still suspended in the air. "Do *not* fucking manipulate me the way you accused me of doing to you." I throw him the sling, watching as he fumbles, the color bleeding from his face.

"I wasn't–" The defense is weak even before it clips off. From the slack set of his jaw, he knows he'd be lying. Remy looks down at the sling, fingers twisting in the material. "So this is how it's gonna be? I can't even kiss you anymore?"

It takes me a long moment to regain that robotic sense of impassivity. When I do, I ask, "Can you do that yourself?"

There's a long pause where we just stare at one another, an understanding slotting into place.

No, he can't kiss me anymore.

Not like that.

Mouth pressed into a grim line, he puts his arm through the sling, fingers tugging it snugly around his elbow. He replies without looking at me, eyes fixed to the clock mechanics looming in the background. "Can you fasten it? Please."

The request is quiet and uncomfortably hollow, and when I step forward to grant it, he doesn't even tip his head in my direction, standing stiffly as I loop the strap over his neck, pressing the velcro down.

"Thanks," he says, turning to leave.

I listen to his retreat, feet trodding away, before I call out, "Remy." Turning, I catch his frozen form, his sharp features cutting a dramatic silhouette in the doorway. "I'm glad you're taking your meds. Just because we're..." I stumble over a word I can't find, because I'm not sure one exists. When have I ever been able to label what Remy and I are to each other, and how would I even begin to find its opposite? I don't try. I glance at the clock mechanics, staring sightlessly at this engine with no spark. "Whatever's happening between us, that doesn't mean I don't want you to be okay. I'll always want you to be okay." I meet his gaze. "Don't ever use that against me."

He steps forward half a step. "I just wanted..." But then he stops, sagging, and turns back to the door. "I just *wanted*. Sorry, Vinny."

I think about it long after he's gone, sweaty and sore, leaning into the crank with all the force in my body as I strain to budge it. My feet slip against the floor, but I plant them harder, shoving, willing the universe to give me this–just this. Even when I know it won't work, I still wrestle with it, throwing everything I have into turning it.

When I leave an hour later, the room is just as silent and still as when I entered.

$$\sim$$

It doesn't actually hit me until I'm stepping out of the shower, eyes falling on the various items surrounding the sink. There's hair gel, deodorant, razors, shaving cream, aftershave–all a manner of male grooming products.

And Remy's pills.

"They're still orange..."

The first thing I do after dressing for bed is go up to my loft, fishing out Sy's journal from beneath the mattress. Whether an intentional gesture or a lapse of memory, he hasn't asked for it back. It's been days since I flipped it open to see the apology he left me in the back, and I don't bother now.

He's hunched over the laptop when I knock on his door frame, buds firmly planted in both ears. Archie is sprawled out in front of Sy's pillow, twisted inexplicably and fast asleep, his little paws twitching intermittently. He sleeps here most nights now, usually coming up to the loft to lay with me in the smaller hours of morning.

When Sy doesn't react, I realize he can't hear me, so I invite myself in.

His head shoots up when I wave my hand in front of him, fingers plucking out both ear buds. "Hey. *Shit.*" He rubs his eyes, leaning back in his seat. There's a sandwich on the desk beside his computer with only two bites taken from it. I know for a fact he made it five hours ago. "I'm so close to being done with this paper," he says, voice rusty.

I grimace. "Sorry to interrupt." All the drama with the Barons, plus the ensuing fallout, not to even mention the fact he was away for a week before that...

I know he's fallen behind.

"No, no." He instantly grabs my wrist, steering me closer. "Trust me, I needed it. What's up?"

I perch on the edge of his desk, ignoring that his blue eyes dip down to my thighs, right below my shorts, and open up the journal. "This."

He blinks at the notebook like he's seeing it for the first time. "Oh."

I have the page open to Remy's color chart. It's not actually in color, which isn't a surprise. Sy isn't exactly the craft project type. But the colors–the words–still correspond to emotions. I hand it to Sy. "You should have this back."

He frowns, glancing into my eyes as he hesitantly takes it. "Alright?"

"No, I mean..." There's a thread of confused hurt in his eyes, and I struggle to explain. "I've already read all of it anyway. You should use it. You should change his pill bottles."

He stares back, confusion capturing his features. "His pill bottles?"

"They're orange, Sy."

He looks down at the chart, comprehension dawning. "You think that makes him, like... reluctant?"

Shrugging awkwardly, I wager, "It's Remy. Lesser things have made him reluctant."

After a pause, eyes scanning the page, he says, "Huh," and then, "Blue bottles, you think? A pill organizer?"

I shift uncomfortably under the weight of his eyes, as if my opinion is important here. "White? Clear? I don't know, just... not orange."

"Or yellow," he muses, reading. It's a while before his eyes wander back up to me, arm reaching out to set the journal on his desk. "You're still mad at him."

I grimace, watching as Archie shifts on the bed. "Yeah. I guess so."

"Any idea how long that's going to last?"

Ducking my head, I answer, "I don't think there's a shelf life on this, Sy." It's hard enough to even put a name to it. Betrayal? Grief? Heartbreak? All of them fit, but none of them tell me what I need from Remy. Something tangible and real. Not skies, or stars, or colors. I can't be Remy's anchor if there's nothing to hold on to.

Sy slips his palm onto my leg, just above my knee. The warmth is light and testing, blue eyes holding mine. "I'm not going to tell you to forgive him, because that's not my place. But I wouldn't be a very good friend if I didn't say this." My stomach sinks, because the last thing I want to hear right now is how it wasn't Remy's fault. "That night I came to save you—when I stole you back from your father—I didn't do that for you."

"You did it because you knew I helped Remy." Maybe the thought should sting, but it doesn't.

"A little," he admits, thumb caressing a soothing circuit into my inner thigh. "But mostly, I did it because I knew if I didn't, he would have gotten himself killed doing it on his own. Because there was no other option for him." Sy nods at the journal. "I've gotten to know you a little bit now, and I'm guessing... maybe after what he did with Haley, you don't feel... special anymore. To him." He ducks into my line of vision, catching my eye. "But Lavinia, that was the real lie—not everything else he showed you. If you can't forgive him for it, then that's your choice to make." Shaking his head, he pulls away, palm dragging over my knee. "Just make sure you're not forgiving the right thing. That's all I'm going to say about it."

He looks frayed around the edges. I'm not sure how much of that is school, or DKS business, or family stuff, or Remy and his problems. He pointedly drags the journal into his lap, covering the growing hardness I catch a glimpse of, and know that some of it is me.

Clearing my throat, I push off the desk, promising, "I'll think about it."

But before I can leave, he swivels in his chair, asking, "Are you going to your loft? To sleep?"

I pause, fingers twisting in the hem of my oversized shirt. It's his. Sy's. A screen print of a longhorn skull is flaked and faded across the front, and as Sy tilts back in his chair, his eyes fall to it. "Yes."

His mouth purses wryly. "Meaning Nick will find his way up there."

My face heats at the acknowledgement. It's been like this all week, Nick coming up to my loft after they've gone to bed, taking off my clothes and fucking me on the mattress. Sometimes slow and gentle, drawing it out. Sometimes fast and loud, like he's been waiting all day, even though I know for a fact he hasn't.

"Probably," I concede, beginning to feel that way myself. Impatient. Anticipating. Excited.

Nick Bruin is a lot of things, and plenty of them aren't good. But this? The way he makes love to me is so damn easy to get addicted to.

I can already feel myself getting wet.

Sy leans forward, elbows propped on his knees, and trains his eyes on his knuckles. "Can I..." His jaw works awkwardly. "...watch?"

My eyebrows lurch upward. "You want to watch Nick fuck me?"

"Just watch," he insists. His eyes are edged with the same mania I see in Remy's sometimes, hands discreetly adjusting the notebook.

I flounder around a response, knowing, of course, that he watched us that day at the river house, when Nick was fucking me out of that... episode. But that was different. We were all sleeping in the same bed and there wasn't exactly anywhere else to go. It wasn't planned that way. If it could have been, it never would have happened.

But I think of it now. Sy tracking us with his hot, blue eyes as Nick peels his brother's t-shirt off me. I think of watching that flush come over his earlobes, the way his eyes get heavy when he's horny—not just physically, but mentally. I think of him seeing Nick push into me, maybe even touching himself to the sight of it, and suddenly, I've gone from wet to *soaked*.

Taking a breath, I square my shoulders. "On one condition." Sy perks and I jerk my chin toward the sandwich. "Eat something, and promise you'll get some sleep tonight."

His confused eyes whirl to the sandwich, and for a second I think he might just cram the whole thing in his mouth in one go. Instead, he nudges it aside, saying, "I'll... make something new. And get plenty of sleep." The bewilderment is still in his eyes when he says, "Promise," but I know he'll keep it.

Over the last few days something is becoming clear; my men need me to take care of them, the same way I need them to care for me. It's not typical or traditional, sometimes it's outright depraved. But it's on our terms, and that means more than anything.

I'm engrossed in a novel when Sy wanders up the staircase an hour later, laptop tucked beneath his arm. Most of the lights are off, but the glow of the city through the clockface and the small lamp that illuminates my little mattress nest are enough. Sy pauses at the top step, staring at me, perhaps waiting for me to call it all off.

I spare him only a glance before returning to my book.

Wordlessly, he settles against the rail that overlooks the living area, opening his laptop. He's changed out of his clothes into nothing but a loose pair of sweats, the screen casting a blue glow over his bare chest. He's close enough–barely five feet from the mattress–that I can see him become immediately engrossed in his work again, fingers tapping away at the keyboard.

It's not long before Nick comes, though.

Unlike his brother, he stalks right up here with the same wildness in his eyes I've come to expect. He's in nothing but a pair of boxers, all of his ink on full display. I know he doesn't spot Sy at first just by the way Nick holds himself, loose and lazy in a way that tells me tonight is going to be of the slow and quiet variety.

When he notices a third presence, he freezes, some of the tension returning to his spine. "Hey," he says to his brother.

Sy closes the laptop. "Hey."

The two of them watch each other for a long moment. Nick's eyes snap to me, then back to Sy, the gesture perfectly clear.

Sy sets the laptop aside and extends a leg, saying nothing.

Nick reaches up to ruffle the back of his hair, which might be the closest to awkward I've ever seen him. "You're staying," he guesses.

Sy's face hardens. "Is that a problem?"

"Depends." Nick looks between us, eyes narrowing questioningly. "Am I still getting some pussy?"

"Jesus." I roll my eyes, closing the book. "Yes, Nick."

He exhales, the tension dropping out of his shoulders. "Why didn't you just say so?"

I'm only half inclined on the mattress, my back propped against the stone wall in the corner, so when Nick bends down to grab my ankles, I know what's coming. I still let out a squeak when he wrenches me down the bed toward him, kneeling between my legs.

He bends over me and I spread my thighs for him, eyes fluttering at the feel of his palm on my temple, smoothing back the hair. "Where were you earlier?"

I skate my fingers along his ribs, resisting the urge to arch up into his body. "Clock."

He makes a dismissive sound, nudging his nose against mine. "When are you going to learn that thing is a piece of junk?"

I chase the promise of his mouth, breathing, "It gives me something to do."

He gives me a slow, wicked smirk. "Baby, I'm right here."

When he finally kisses me, it's downright filthy. His tongue coaxes mine to him, tangling wetly together as he rocks his hardness into my center. He doesn't let his hand slipping up my shirt interrupt it. He pulls and tugs until he can slide the shirt over my breast, exposing me for his greedy palm.

It's only then that he licks a hot path across my cheek to my ear. Gruffly, he whispers, "You really want him up here?"

My fingernails dig into his back at the sensation of his teeth beneath my ear, his thumb caressing my peaked nipple. "I don't mind."

"No?" he asks, abandoning my nipple to tuck his hand between us, dipping into my shorts. "Let's see about that." I welcome the invasion, already knowing what he's going to find. My heart still ratchets up a notch when his fingers meet my slickness. He goes momentarily still, face turning to mine, eyes wide and blown. "God, your pussy's fucking *dripping*."

The truth is, I was already primed for this hours ago. Helping Remy into his shirt, feeling his breath on my face, knowing he wanted me badly enough to leverage his own weakness to get it. Sy's request just multiplied it, and then there was Nick and all his silent intensity, looking ready to eat me alive.

If every day is like this, these men might fucking kill me.

Knowing Sy heard him, I just buck my hips into his hand, unconcerned about giving away my eagerness. It's always dangerous with Nick, predicting how he'll react to something like this. Sometimes he's frighteningly, lethally possessive. And other times...

He pushes two fingers inside of me, the smirk returning. "That get you hot, little bird? My big brother over there wishing he was me?"

"Don't tease, Nick." I grab his face, willing him to understand what this is. Not a competition, or a fight, or some stupid pissing match between brothers. "Not tonight?"

His thumb finds my clit, and he must see the seriousness on my face, because he just plucks a slow, lingering kiss from my lips. "Anything you want."

8

N ick

ANYTHING YOU WANT...

She has to know that by now.

I'd kill for her, die for her, burn this whole fucking city to the ground for her. But all she's asking for tonight is this. For me to pleasure her, share her and show Sy what it looks like when a man does it right.

I could tell from the apprehension in her eyes that she doesn't quite understand this yet. Sy is a part of me, just as much as Remy– just as much as she is. One day, she'll get it. For now, I rear back to slide her shorts and panties off, not bothering to take my time. Beside the mattress, my brother is silent and still, his dark eyes locked on every newly revealed inch of skin.

Don't tease.

Hard to say if she meant her or him, so I cover my bases. Grabbing each of her knees, I spread her thighs obscenely wide, putting her wet pussy on full display for us.

And then I dip down to taste it.

She hisses in a long gasp, fingers tangling instantly in my hair. "Oh, god."

I lick out to catch her slickness, groaning at the taste. Her clit is already swollen, like she's been horny all goddamn day. I flick my tongue against it, catching a glimpse of Sy in my periphery. He has his head tipped back against the rails, watching us through lazy, slitted eyes.

He's squeezing his dick through his sweats.

Lavinia never lets me get her off like this, my tongue flicking wild circuits around her clit, and now is no different. She tugs my hair, begging, "Please, Nick, please."

I'm useless to do anything but obey, licking a sloppy, wet path up her belly, between her tits. "Some day, Little Bird," I wrestle Sy's shirt off her just as her fingers slide my boxers down, my cock springing eagerly from the elastic, "I'm going to make you come on my tongue."

The mattress is old and lumpy, not exactly comfortable on my knees, and every time I come up that staircase to claim her, I find that old fantasy cropping back up in my head; her, waiting for me in my bed. I never ask her to. I wouldn't fucking dare. Lavinia won't ever come to that bed.

Not after what I did to her in it.

So I grab her hip and turn her on her side, facing Sy. When I spoon in behind her, pulling her into the curve of my body, I slide my hand down her thigh and tug her leg up, hooking my forearm beneath her knee to keep her spread.

She's tense at first, not at all as flexible as I damn well know she can be. But then Sy makes a low, gritty sound at the sight, and suddenly the tendons in her thigh go lax, allowing me to slot my dick up against her entrance.

I always love this part. Sliding into her–slow or fast, gentle or hard–watching the slack rapture take her features as I fuck my way inside. Usually, I'd make her look at me, just to bask in my spoils of victory, the sweet curl of satisfaction that she's finally mine.

But tonight, I keep my eyes on my brother's strained face as I position the tip of my dick against her slick entrance. Resting my lips against her sweat-damp temple, I tell him, "She's wet for you, you know." I push in slow and steady.

Eyes fixed to her hole, Sy's jaw clenches so visibly that his teeth must ache. "How wet?"

My own jaw is clenched almost as tightly, holding back the urge to slam to the hilt. "See for yourself." I kick her discarded shorts and panties off the mattress and she whimpers, fingers clamping around my forearm as the motion buries me deeper.

I don't watch him pick them up, shifting my full attention to Lavinia's flushed face. I mouth at the juncture of her neck. "You feel so good, baby."

"More," she breathes, brow knitted together.

I grip her leg and push my hips, sinking into her so easily that I bury a groan into her shoulder. Lingering there, I feel her buck back against me, always seeking more, which is how I feel the new surge of slickness.

Just then, I hear the unmistakable sound of Sy spitting.

Lavinia's pussy flutters around me, a hitched gasp escaping her throat. "Sy…"

"Shit," I grind out, raising my head, which is when I see it. Sy has his dick out, one spit-slick hand squeezing the shaft while the other fists her panties. I drag my mouth over her warm cheek, watching her glazed eyes watch him back. "Just looking at that dick gets you wet, doesn't it?" He always keeps it locked away, like it's something to be embarrassed about. But right now, Lavinia is looking at that thing like she's dying to be the one with her hand around it.

Sy's electric eyes are glued to her, but he lifts his chin at me. "You gonna fuck her, or what?" Glancing up, I realize his hand is gripping his cock, motionless, poised for a reason. So I pull my hips back, dragging my cock away, just to punch it back inside. I push her thigh higher, strangely excited to show him this. My chest burns with too many things to list, but I know pride is one of them.

Look, my body is telling him. *Look at what I got for us.*

Sy's fist moves with me, slow on the backstroke, quick on the upstroke. I've never seen my brother like this before, every muscle in his body tightening as his eyes glow hot for a chick. His nostrils are flared, the line of his mouth hard and angry-looking, and I think I get Lavinia's reservation about the whole thing.

He looks like he wants to murder some pussy.

His eyes are also radiating absolute agony, chest collapsing with the sharp inhale. "You're so fucking beautiful."

"Thanks," I rock into her, indulging in the glide. "I try."

He shoots me a quick, homicidal glare, and it takes some work to keep my stroke up. Guy looks like a wild animal who's afraid of having his kill taken away. It's not that it hasn't occurred to me what's going down here. It's just that I don't give a shit. Lavinia wants my cock, but she wants his, too. I'm his stand in.

If the sight of him matching his fist up to my rhythm isn't enough to remind me I'm still getting the better half of that deal, then the way Lavinia's arm reaches back, fingers winding into my hair, definitely is.

She tilts her head just enough to meet my demand for a kiss, tongue licking out to caress mine. It's not the best angle, but it still makes my balls tighten, even knowing that she's peeking at Sy from the corner of her eye.

I drag another long, slow thrust, watching her eyes flutter. "You feel how wet and primed your pussy is?" I move to whisper my next words into her ear. "I bet if you went slow, you could take him." I keep my voice nothing but the barest breath, the words meant only for her. "Right here, right now. I'd stay and watch, make sure he does right by you."

Something in my brain breaks and rearranges itself at the thought of it. My Little Bird taking that monster of a cock. The look on her face when he pushes it inside. The crush of her brow as she struggles to make room for him inside...

Fuck.

But her lungs seize, and she bears greedily back into my thrust, making her answer clear.

Just me.

I'm not expecting the feeling of disappointment, but I guess I should. Even from the first time, that night in the Hideaway's basement, I've been darkly eager for Sy and Remy to know what I know, to see what I see, to have what I want.

But this isn't about Sy.

Not really.

Lavinia makes a sharp, mournful sound when I suddenly pull back, dick slipping free. The look she shoots me over her shoulder is a mixture of shock, annoyance, and yearning. Nevertheless, she goes easily when I move her legs.

I lay on my back, sideways on the mattress. My feet are pointed at the clock, Sy somewhere behind my head, and when I pull her on top of me, I know they're able to look at each other, face to face.

"Come on, baby." I grab her hips, whispering, "Show him how you'd ride him."

Lavinia's eyes drop down to mine, mouth parting–maybe in surprise, maybe just to say, "Yeah?"

I answer by grabbing the base of my cock, positioning it right at her slick hole. Her eyes shift back to Sy when she finally sinks down, taking me to the hilt, and I should be jealous he's getting that instead of me; the look on her face as she takes me in. The notch her teeth dig into her lip as she adjusts, feeling me so deep. The lazy slump of her eyelids as she relishes it, hips giving a little, testing rock.

Clearly, I'm a saint.

"Fuck," she breathes, rolling her hips to a rhythm. "Just like that," she says to Sy.

I can't see him, but I can hear him behind me, panting like a dog, the wet sounds of his fist on his cock as he matches her speed. "Touch her tits," he says, voice like gravel. When I run my palms up her body, cupping them in my palms, he demands, "Use your mouth."

I push up on an elbow to mouth at her nipple, tongue tracing a slow circle around the pebbled peak. Her fingers wind into my hair, clutching me close, and I don't even have to look to know they're eye fucking each other. I can feel it in the way she's fucking me, hips sliding back and forth, fingers tightening in my hair. I can hear it in his rough breaths, the shifting sound of fabric.

She's fucking him through me.

When I fall back, hands clamped over her flexing thighs, she fucks me like it's some kind of punishment. Eyes intent on Sy behind me, she plants her palms on my chest and bucks hard, making me groan. She doesn't let up, back and forth, up and down, her hips land unforgivingly against mine, and I stare at her in awe. The flush on her face. The wild heat of her eyes. The bounce of her heavy tits. Usually when my Little Bird is on top, she rides me slow and sweet, always demanding my mouth against hers, my hands roving hungrily over her body. Sometimes I'll give it to her fast and a touch too brutal, but I know she likes it most when it's making love—me worshiping her.

I've never been outright *fucked* by her before.

When she comes, I feel it right down to my curling toes, her pussy clenching around me as she cries out. Her hips grind down hard against me, and I'm useless to do anything more than plant my heels, rut up into her, grunt like a savage, and come my goddamn brains out. Behind me, a strained, feral sound comes ripping out of my brother, and I know he must be doing the same.

She collapses against my chest, pressing these sweet little sighs into my shoulder as she comes down. "Thanks for that," she whispers.

"What can I say?" I take back over, tucking her hair back to brush a kiss into her sweaty forehead. "I'm a giver."

Behind me, Sy snorts, but I hear him cleaning up, his breaths evening out slowly. A minute later, he appears above me, looking a lot less tense, and tips his fist out.

I raise my own to lazily bump his knuckles.

His eyes shift to her, softening, before he reaches down to run a hand over her head. "Night," he says.

Both of us want to stay in her bed but not until we're invited. Soon, I think as my brother and I both head downstairs.

Very soon.

I FLIP up my collar to keep the cool air off my neck as I walk across campus. I woke up in the loft next to a shivering Lavinia this morning, trying my best to warm her with nothing but my own body heat and a thin blanket.

Winter's coming up on us like a South Side street dog.

I've just left Remy at his art studio to get to my own class. Sy and I have discussed if someone needs to stay with him, but my brother says no. He's got to do this on his own. Thank the fuck. I'm tired of babysitting a grown-ass man. I prefer problems that can be hit, shot, or otherwise maimed, and whatever demon Remy is fighting, it's not something I can beat into submission. He has to put in the work himself. It won't be an easy road. His family is fucked. His body and brain are a mess, but he's got something others don't.

Us.

Lavinia and Sy are in the science hall. Their schedules align, at least building-wise, and even though he's not in the class with her, I feel good knowing he's nearby. I fight the urge to pull out my phone and look for her on the tracker. This need to know where she is all the time, to make sure she's safe, is overwhelming. It's fucking ridiculous and I resist it.

I've got Lit across campus, although I take my time getting there. My zone of excellence isn't in academia, but I know it's part of the deal and I've got to do it. The good news is my TA is a cutslut and she won't mark it if I'm late.

My route takes me near the athletic complex, and the constant vibe on campus is school spirit and football. Huge orange and purple banners hang outside the building promoting the team. *Football*. What a joke. Helmets and padding? Grow a fucking pair and beat the shit out of the other guy the real way, the *right* way, bare-knuckled and bleeding.

Even I can't avoid the news that the team is struggling without their superstar quarterback, Killian Payne. I have to admit, I'm impressed he gave up a career in the NFL for the position of King. When I worked for Daniel, his son always seemed too egotistical to make the sacrifice, but maybe I was wrong about that. Maybe I'm the one that struggles with the idea of leadership.

It's not my only struggle.

I pull my phone from my pocket and slide my thumb over the screen, clicking the icon to confirm Lavinia's location—

"Bruin."

I pause when I hear my name, eyes shifting to the guy in a basic black suit and aviators. He's older—not a student–and looks like a low-rent cosplay of a secret service agent, so the clothing is a dead giveaway. He's one of Saul's goons.

I barely slow my stride. "What's it to you?"

"Mr. Cartwright would like to see you."

"I have class." I guess college *does* come in handy, because if Saul found out about any of the shit that went down the last couple weeks, I may not make it out of the meeting alive.

His expression doesn't change, nor does his body language. It radiates, 'you're coming with me.'

"He'll get you an excuse."

I glance down at the ring on my finger. Meeting up with Saul without advance notice isn't giving the best optics ever, but like everything else in this world, when do I get a choice? It comes with the territory. The position.

The having of a Duchess.

"Whatever," I say, "let's make it quick."

He leads me back to the main athletic building—the administrative offices that back up to the stadium, Mercer Field, which everyone knows is named after Tristian Mercer's family. Not for the first time, I wonder how much the Mercers know about their little golden boy's exploits. Burning down his King's office building. Programming explosives for the promise of pussy. Tristian's racking up a lot of skeletons around here.

But regardless of the name on the stadium, Saul is the director of this place. Pretty cush job, if you ask me. Big paycheck, big power, eyes and ears everywhere. It's a long way from our janky little West End boxing gym. People can say what they want about Daniel Payne, but at least he did his business *in* South Side, not locked away in the middle of Forsyth proper with all the security campus neutrality brings.

The goon leads me to the elevator, and while he dutifully watches the door, I spend the whole ride up to the top floor openly staring at him. With each floor we pass, I can see the tension in his neck cranking up.

I jerk my chin. "What's Saul paying a guy like you to bum around a college campus?" Guys like him–and me–aren't exactly Forsyth material. This guy runs the book end of Saul's empire. Probably chases down delinquent gambling addicts on the weekends.

The guy doesn't answer, but I still see that tendon in his neck twitch.

I remain motionless, expressionless in that way I've been informed makes people uncomfortable. "Nice. It must be a lot if it buys your silence, too."

Ah, there it is.

His eyes flick to me, narrowing. "Twenty-three."

I whistle. "What's that? Quarterly?" When the guy just stares back at me, I snort a laugh. "Shit, man, that's annual? Are you part-time or something?"

He's looking a little put out now, turning to glare at me. "I'm working my way up."

"Okay," I say, the doubt clear in my voice. "Daniel paid me three times that, plus benefits, the second he took me on."

His eyebrows crash together. "Benefits? What benefits?"

"All the pussy you can eat," I say, even though I never really indulged in it. The only girl in Daniel's brothel I actually wanted was off-limits. When the elevator finally dings, I give him a slap on the shoulder. "Tough luck, chief."

The doors open to an impressive reception area. An attractive woman at the desk barely looks up to say, "He's waiting on you, Neon."

Underpaid Goon—what kind of stupid-ass name is Neon—mutters, "Thanks, Michelle."

I've been in a King's domain before. Daniel's office building before it burned down. The little room Killian now occupies at the Hideaway. The Baron's crypt. But fuck. I'm not prepared for the grandeur of Saul's office.

Saul is one of us. DKS. West End. A Duke, born to fight. You wouldn't know it, though, taking one glance at this place. Sleek chrome and leather furniture outfits the room, while the walls and shelves are a tribute to the history of Forsyth sports. Photographs, plaques, and trophies celebrate the All-Americans, Heisman winners, and various other National Champions the school has pushed out over the years. For all his shortcomings, Saul excels at his job. Finding talent, molding it, harnessing it, promoting it. The players under the Forsyth U banner are just another version of the guns the Dukes sling for him.

Saul deals in weapons.

The furnishings and décor are overshadowed by the glass wall overlooking the massive stadium and expansive green field below. Saul stands next to it, looking down at the grounds crew as they touch up the paint in the endzone. For the first time, I think I finally understand who Saul Cartwright is and what it means to be King. A strange flicker beats in my chest. Sometimes it's easy to forget just how big of a deal this guy is, which is probably intentional. But Saul's just as loaded as the other Kings, running his guns and manipulating the gambling market, all while holding one of the most prestigious positions in Forsyth.

I'm nothing but a name and a trigger finger.

"Beautiful, isn't it?" he says, eyes flicking to the goon. "Wait outside, Neon."

"Good chat, Neon." Flicking the goon a peace sign, I mosey along the length of a sleek credenza, inspecting odd trinkets that aren't quite trophies, but still clearly meant to be awards. A brass tennis ball. A gilded shuttlecock. A silver letter opener in the shape of a miniature hockey stick. "Care to explain why I'm here and not in my literature class?"

"I'd love to," he says, pulling a cigar from his jacket pocket, "but we're waiting on someone else before we get started." My eyes narrow, because if Sy and Remy are about to be hauled in here, then some serious shit must be going down.

Every cell of my body sings with alert.

But when the door swings open, it's not Sy or Remy. It's another one of those badly dressed goons, his hand gripping the bicep of my motherfucking Duchess.

The hand on her is enough to drastically shorten this fucker's lifespan.

The tears streaking down her cheeks are enough to end it entirely.

I take in the scene quickly, noting her hitched breaths and pale face, eyes red-rimmed and panicked.

I swipe the silver hockey stick from the credenza right before I lunge, barreling into the lackey. He slams against the wall with a grunt, eyes wide as I put the letter opener right beneath his eye.

"What," I growl, pushing the tip of the spear into his flesh, "did you do to her?"

He's fast, whipping out a pistol and pressing it against my gut. "I'll do it, Bruin," he says, tone deadly. "I didn't touch her. She just fucking freaked out when we got in the elevator."

My heart pounds in my ears, wondering if I can sink this thing into his eye before he can pull the trigger. But then his words process, and I glance at Lavinia again. She's desperately trying to put herself back together, straightening the short black skirt she'd put on this morning, wiping her eyes with the wrist of her pink sweater.

"Jesus Christ." I blink, nails digging into this asshole's neck. Fuckfuckfuck. "You put her in the goddamn elevator?"

The goon's eyes narrow. "If I'd made her walk all those flights of stairs, you would have seen it as an insult."

From somewhere behind us, Saul clucks his tongue disapprovingly. "Ewing, put the gun down. For Pete's sake, this carpet is Persian. You're not spilling Bruin blood all over it." He sighs. "You too, Nick. Release my man. I prefer his eyeballs in their sockets."

Ewing lowers the gun, and I drop my hand.

Lavinia is already shaking her head when I reach her. "Don't."

I do anyway, grabbing her face and thumbing away the remnants of tears. "I didn't know they were going to do this."

She nods, saying, "I know, I know, just–"

Saul asks, "What's wrong with Lucia? Is she sick?" But his tone isn't worried, it's full of polite disgust. Still concerned about his fucking rug.

"Nothing," I snap because it's none of his goddamn business. I press my forehead to hers and speak low. "Breathe, baby. Take a deep breath and I'll get you out of here."

She nods and exhales a shuddering breath. Her fingers wind around my wrists, gripping tight, like I'm her anchor. She may be right about that. An anchor that's dragging her down.

I'm the one that locked her in that elevator.

"We're leaving," I announce, grabbing her hand. "Whatever this is, we can deal with it later."

"No," Lavinia says, taking another deep breath. "I'm fine." She glances over at Saul. "I-I just need a minute."

"Fuck this," I snap, pulling her into my side. "You want to talk to one of us, you can make an appointment." I turn for the door, but Ewing's massive body plants in front of it, arms straight by his side, gun still in one hand. His expression is blank. This guy clearly gets paid more than poor Neon. "Move," I say, voice low and full of threat, "Or I'll fucking make you move."

"Nick," she says, fingers curled into my shirt, "it's okay."

"He put his hands on you," I argue, wishing like hell I'd brought my pistol.

"I'm not leaving. I don't want to." I look down at her and see it—that stubbornness in her eyes. So *fucking* stubborn. "Please?" she begs, easing me away from the door. "Remember last night? You said–"

Anything.

Goddamn it.

I turn to Saul, trying to tamp down the red-hot impulse to murder someone. "You have five minutes."

"Nick," Saul says, ignoring my time demands, "Lavinia, why don't you take a seat."

Stiffly, I say, "We'll stand."

"Nick," Saul says, voice carrying a heavier tone. A warning. "I'm not here to hurt you or your Duchess. We need to talk, and I'd like to do it civilly."

Lavinia and I share a look. No civil conversation begins with being dragged to someone's office against their will. But I can't go off half-cocked with her in the room. Not while she's in this condition.

I try, "Whatever you need from me doesn't involve the Duchess. Let her go."

"Actually, it does involve her. But you don't need to worry." He walks over to the bar against the wall, uncapping a decanter to pour himself a glass of amber liquid. He pointedly doesn't offer one to us. "Although it stands to reason the hit has made you paranoid."

"I'm not paranoid," I say, realizing that makes me seem more so. "The hit has been handled. Everything's fine."

"It seems to be," he says, gesturing to the slick leather loveseat. Lavinia moves stiffly, reluctantly beside me, but takes the seat next to mine. Saul takes the armchair. "I'm not sure what you did, but it appears all signs of the contract are off." He swirls the amber liquid in his glass. "Bravo."

Lavinia relaxes a little, some of the strength returning to her voice when she says, "Is this about my father? Because if I could get him to back down on literally anything, I wouldn't even be sitting here right now."

I shoot her a dark look.

Well, *that* thought is disconcerting.

"This is about DKS business," he says, tipping the glass to his mouth. "Although it isn't *not* about your father. Nothing can be in this town. You know that."

"Frat business," I repeat, impatient to get her out of here. "What kind?"

Saul gives me a look that says just how much he doesn't care about my impatience. "Each year we have several obligations that require representation by the Dukes and Duchess. One is coming up in the near future."

I clench my fists. "This is about that stupid charity carnival?" I gesture to Lavinia. "The Duchess is off limits. No one approaches her, talks to her, engages with her without coming through me or one of the Dukes. Am I clear?"

He looks up at me, lip quirked. "Didn't like me seeing her weakness, did you? Your 'Little Bird' has a broken wing. A flaw." He tsks. "But you should know by now there's nothing stupid about a city-sponsored networking event, son."

I return his stare evenly.

I'm not your fucking son.

Lavinia cuts in, "Saul—Mr. Cartwright—we already know about our duties for the carnival. I've already begun coordinating with the Lady. I'm prepared to do what's necessary to have a successful event."

He gives her a grin. "I'm glad to hear you say that because you'll have a very specific role to play."

Wringing her hands, she guesses, "What, like I have to man a booth or something?"

Saul looks between us, a low chuckle escaping. "The two of you don't get it, do you? You still think this event is about cheesy carnival rides and inter-house charity." He puts a hand to his chest. "How precious."

"Tick tock," I tell him, voice full of warning. "Say your part, Saul."

"Very well." He puts down his glass only to inspect his cigar, patting his jacket pocket for a lighter. "At the end of the carnival, DKS hosts an annual alumni poker game. These are large donors, you see. Their *generous* support allows us to maintain properties like the clock tower and gym. They also help facilitate our other operations."

This I understand perfectly: operations means guns.

These aren't just alumni.

They're customers.

Saul goes on. "Many of our brothers are powerful members of the community, with roots that run as deep as mine." He presses the trigger on the lighter, torching the end of the cigar as he pins Lavinia with a stare. "And each of them *strongly* dislikes your father."

Lavinia shrugs. "Who doesn't?"

Seeing where this is going, I argue, "Lavinia isn't *his*, Saul. She's ours. She's a Duchess."

"Yes, yes." Saul waves a hand, the ember of his cigar casting a trail. "But they don't see it that way. So you'll understand how a... display of sorts is in order."

"A display?" Lavinia passes me an uneasy glance. "What does that mean?"

He gives her a slow, sleazy smile, jamming the cigar between his teeth. "It means, little girl, that you'll be their entertainment."

That word—entertainment—can only mean a few select things in this town. When it's about a girl, it narrows it down considerably. I shoot up, spitting, "Fuck that."

Saul's still grinning around his cigar, looking disgustingly satisfied. "She'll dance, show her tits, give our brothers a little peek at what's under that hood. She spent two years in a whorehouse. What's a little skin between sworn brothers? Don't you share?"

I can't even let myself imagine it, knowing if I do, I'll lose the already frayed thread of reason that's holding me back from gutting this guy. "If you think I'm going to let a bunch of power-tripping grudgefucks paw at my goddamn Duchess all night, then you're out of your fucking mind!"

Saul puffs his cigar, nodding. "I see that you're worried about her safety, so I'll give you this. You and the other Dukes will be her security."

"I don't think you're understanding me, Saul." I reach down to pull the knife from my boot, voice low and deadly. "The answer is no."

After a short pause, he bursts into a gravelly laugh. "Oh, you've got such spunk, kid." Gradually, the mirth falls away, leaving a ruthlessly pensive expression. "Truth be told, I'd love to meet you in the ring someday."

"*Me* against your washed-up ass? Please." I scoff, eyeing him disdainfully. "You have a beer gut and a bum knee. You couldn't even beat Killer."

"Oh, but I can beat you," he says, raising a finger, "with nothing but my fingertip."

He brings his finger down on the remote control perched on the arm of his chair. There's a brief whirr and then an enormous flat screen appears from behind a wall panel. The picture on the screen is dark and grainy, but I'd know the face anywhere.

Lavinia is spread out on a bed.

A man in a black ski mask is fucking her.

"*No*," she's gasping, fighting, as I punch my hips into hers. "*Don't! Please don't!*"

I grunt, "*Hold her*," and another masked man appears–Remy–climbing onto the mattress and wrenching her arms up.

"I'll scream!" she warns, voice wobbling. "*I'll scream, I'll cut your goddamn throat, you motherfucking––!*"

I slam into her with a deep rumble, remembering all too well what it felt like to finally–fucking *finally*–claim her like this. How warm she was inside. How unbelievably tight. The way it felt to know I was filling her up, making her mine.

I can't rip my eyes away from it.

"The Lucia girl is going to give our brothers a show, Nick." Saul's voice is closer, maddeningly matter-of-fact, and I realize he's climbed to his feet at some point, standing loosely beside me. "Else, I'll have to give them and the rest of Forsyth a show of my own."

When I eventually look away, unable to bear what comes next, it's to the sight of Lavinia on the loveseat with her head bowed. I don't need to see her eyes to guess what she's feeling. This is humiliation to the highest degree. To Saul, I try to keep my voice even, belying the nuclear explosion currently happening in my gut. "Blackmail? Really?"

His eyes swing to the screen. "Oh, it's not just blackmail, kid. This little feature here doubles as a nice, juicy bit of insurance." He straightens suddenly, eyes flashing in delight. In the video, me, Sy, and Remy spread her legs, showing off my cum dribbling out of her hole. "This is my favorite part. Goodness, look at that pretty cunt. Who knew a Lucia girl could be so pink and tight?"

I lunge for him, grabbing him by the collar, his glass falling to the floor and shattering. "This video doesn't fucking belong to you."

"Everything belongs to me!" he snarls back, clamping my wrist in a bruising grip. "This is exactly what I'm talking about. Disobeying orders, making deals with Kings behind my back, telling me what's *mine.*" His nostrils flare wide, eyes burning with anger. "So in case you feel entitled to positions that don't belong to you, consider this, *Bruin.*" He spits my name like it's an insult, full of venom. "If the Lords found out you duped them, they'd kill all three of you. Especially at the agreement of your own King."

I should have known.

All along, I should have known that Saul only let me in to make me fall. The last Bruin. His only competition. I'm not here to be a Duke. I'm here to be his joke. "You ratfuck piece of–"

"I'll do it." Lavinia's voice cuts through my rage like a blade made of ice. "If you let Nick protect me, I'll..." She swallows and I see her in my periphery, trying her best to raise her head high. "I'll *entertain* them."

Saul never breaks my glare, baring his teeth. "Smart girl."

I search his eyes, every muscle in my body poised to tear him apart. "When I came in here, I had this thought that you were smarter than people give you credit for." White hot rage circulates in my blood—pounds in my ears. I twist the shirt, tightening it around his neck. "Obviously, I was wrong, because you just committed suicide," I hiss, then shove him back, where he stumbles into the bar, knocking over the crystal decanter.

Saul violently rights himself, a lock of graying hair flopping into his eyes. "You don't scare me, Nick. Hers isn't the only weakness I've seen this morning. After all, if you're dead, where does that sweet cunt of yours go? To her father? Back to the brothel?" His eyes slide to Lavinia, narrowing. "Maybe I'll just let the alumni have her. Fifty bored, bitter, horny, washed-up fighters just chomping at the bit for a little taste of territorial revenge." His voice drops to a low timbre when he meets my gaze again. "They'd fuck her so much bloodier than you did."

"We're leaving," I say, because I know if I don't, I'm going to stop caring about the fact Payne will kill me when that video gets out.

As I'm grabbing Lavinia's hand, wresting her off the couch and storming toward the door, Saul calls out, "Nice chat, Bruin. To the victor!"

9

L avinia

THE MOMENT NICK steps out of Saul's office, he transforms. I'm not sure which I prefer; the murderous man with the inferno eyes or *this*.

The soldier.

He marches up to the receptionist's desk and evenly asks, "Where is he?"

The woman barely looks up from her phone. "I'm sorry, who?"

"Ewing," Nick presses, spurring me into motion. He can't kill Saul, but one of his henchmen is open season, and right now that's what Nick wants.

When the burly guy showed up to my class and told me to come to the athletic director's office, I knew something was up. I couldn't say no—not as Duchess. Saul is my King and refusing would have caused bigger problems. Maybe not just for me, but for the guys as well. Maybe even the whole frat. So I cooperated, following him across campus, and it was fine, until he made me go in the elevator.

"Nick," I hiss, tugging at his arm. "We're not doing this!"

The frozen, empty look he gives me makes my blood turn to ice. "Wait outside."

There was a time that the void of humanity in his eyes terrified me, and I fight back a shiver at it now. Only it's not the same. Not since that day in the shower, when I cleansed him of Perez's blood. Some part of me knows now that Nick's true nature isn't to kill.

"No." I stand my ground, even though I feel frayed and shaken, exhausted and sore. "I don't know where the stairs are and I can't get into that elevator again." The humiliation of it burns almost as hotly as it did watching that video of me being violated. "Don't leave me alone here," I say, willing to beg if it means leaving this place with both of us whole.

There's a long moment where he just braces his palms against the reception desk, eyes fixed on his white knuckles, and I wait with bated breath. It's not until I reach out, gently touching his shoulder, that he finally moves.

He jerks his head toward the exit sign at the end of the hall, signaling the staircase. "Let's go."

"Thank you." The compromise helps with my nerves, but not the humiliation, burning at my cheeks. I'm familiar with panic attacks. I tried to manage this one, but the instant the doors of that elevator closed it was like my heart was caught in a vise. My chest tightened and my pulse raced. Sweat coated my skin, and I struggled to breathe.

The worst part though, was revealing my weakness. I hate looking weak. I hate not being able to control my body. My fears.

Now Saul holds all of them in the palm of his hand.

Nick pushes open the stairwell door and pulls me with him. Once I'm in the stairwell, he slams the door behind me. "I'll kill him," he says, and I know from the darkness in his eyes, fists flexing, that he isn't talking about Ewing.

He's talking about Saul.

I say the obvious. "You can't. If the Lords find out what you did–"

"I'll talk to Killian,"Nick says, eyes wild. "Make him see that I was doing the right thing."

I flinch at the descriptor–*the right thing*–as if breaking into my room and attacking me was some incredible act of valiance.

Nick sees my reaction. I can tell by the way he goes eerily still, the tattoo on his temple puckering with his grimace. Suddenly, he whirls, kicking the door with the toe of his boot. "Fuck!" he shouts, letting the word echo up and down the cement tunnel.

"They protect what's theirs, Nick." I keep my voice quiet and calm, even though my guts feel twisted into a braid. "And at that point, I belonged to *them*. Even if they wanted to spare you, they couldn't. How would that look?"

"You're not going to do that," he insists, thrusting a finger at me. "You're not Saul's fucking stripper, you're–"

"I'm yours," I say, intending for it to be reassuring.

But it falls flat.

From the coldness of Nick's stare, we're both remembering how I became his. It'd be a lie to say that seeing that video hasn't rubbed the old wound raw, but the truth is, it's pointless. What's done is done.

Nick looks helpless, eyes lost. "I just wanted to get you out of there."

"I know."

More intensely, he adds, "You said it yourself. They protect what's theirs. It's not like I could just walk in there and ask Killer to give me his asset."

"I know."

From the way his eyes flash, he's expecting an argument. "It was the safest way to get you here–to West End–to *us*."

I explode, "I fucking know!" but the anger burns itself out before it can grow into anything he deserves. What's left is an exhausted sense of sadness. I meet Nick's eyes, knowing it must shine through. "Please don't make me defend what you did to me."

"Lavinia…" His face falls, and I don't know what's worse. Me having to defend it, or seeing that flare of guilt in his eyes for doing it.

"Stop," I demand, before the plea can even leave his mouth. I won't be made to feel this creeping sense of urgency to forgive the unforgivable.

Nick, being the irascible martyr he is, raises his chin to add, "The elevator."

My hands shake, but not in fear. It's more like a release for getting somewhere private and finally letting it all rush out. "When that guy came to get me, I should've called Sy. Or said no. I just didn't want to make a scene and didn't realize what was happening until I was away from the class—"

"Do *not* fucking apologize." He rakes his hand through his hair, mouth a tight, angry line. "I'm the one that did this to you. I made your claustrophobia a million times worse."

His admission stuns me, and I grip the railing that looks over the stairwell, like it can hold me up. My issues didn't start with Nick, but he's right. He made them worse.

His eyes roam over me, before he finally snaps, barreling forward to frame my face in his large hands. "Tell me what you want me to do, baby." There's a desperation in his eyes that guts me, because despite how I wanted to use him all those weeks ago, I can't be this for Nick. His compass. His general. His Daniel. "If you want me to kill him–either of them–I'll do it. I'll burn this whole fucking building to the ground. Maybe the video goes with it." He tips his forehead to mine, breath soft on my lips. "*Anything*," he promises, tilting his head. My heart thrums as he leans in, mouth meeting mine.

But it can never be that easy. I see that now. "Take me home," I answer, because for all this strife, for all the wrongs and hurts caused along the way, this is what Nick has given me.

A home.

Nick and I go hand in hand as he leads me down each stair,

through the doors, silent and spent. Thankfully, there's no sight of Ewing as we step into the lobby.

But there is the elevator.

I stare at it, hard-pressed to remember what I must have looked like stepping into it an hour ago. I'd thought to myself that I was going to be brave. I was going to put on an act. I was going to be a Lucia. A Duchess.

And I fell apart the second the door closed.

Nick pauses, looking back at me, and then follows my gaze to the metal doors. I feel more than see him step close, his fingers tucking a lock of hair gently behind my ear. "I didn't know about you then, Little Bird," he says, voice soft as a whisper. "I'd never make you get in there again."

I open my mouth to speak, but the words are caught. It's like I'm in the chest, or one of those nights in bed, when the nightmares paralyze my muscles. Recognition flickers in his eyes, like he doesn't see me, but sees what I'm going through, and his fingers inch behind my neck, massaging the tense muscles.

"Hey," he says, soft and coaxing. "I won't ever let anyone put you somewhere like that again. Understand?"

I look into his blue eyes, the certainty falling upon me like a new, tougher skin. "I know what I want you to do." At his questioning look, I add, "All of you."

"Thanks for coming early," I say, fidgeting in front of the group. "I wouldn't have asked if it wasn't important."

It's an hour earlier than we usually meet to set up for Family Dinner. I'd called Verity and asked for the best way to reach out to the cutsluts. Three seconds later, she added me to the group chat, announcing that everyone needed to be at the gym early for a meeting. Now, we're all here, and I'm standing in front of two dozen women sitting at the tables that will be filled with hungry frat boys in a few hours.

I've never spoken to a group like this before—a group of women who may or may not like me. That was something my sister was groomed to do. Not me. I got the vibe after Nick turned me into my father that most of them had my back. *Most, not all*, I think, eyeing the woman I caught sucking Remy's dick.

Haley is front and center, slinked back in her seat with her arms crossed over her chest.

I've been dreading coming face-to-face with her all day. She's pretty, I'll give her that. Her tits are bigger than mine and her lips are fuller. She's not a natural blonde, cool highlights scattered throughout her curled locks, but I can tell she takes a lot of care with it. She's the kind of girl who spends an hour or more in front of the mirror every day, making every part of herself flawless and beautiful. Just like Leticia.

It takes everything in me not to smack that smug smile off her mouth.

Family Dinner should probably change its name to Family Drama.

This meeting isn't about Haley or Remy, though. It's about setting the groundwork to make this alumni event as painless as possible. So, I avoid eye contact with Haley and start by announcing, "Nick and I had a meeting with Saul yesterday, and he explained that one of our obligations is to... uh," I stumble over the phrasing, eventually settling on, "act as host and hostess of the annual alumni poker game after the fall festival."

A few girls share dark, foreboding looks, and it hits me.

"Oh," I say, surprised. "You're familiar with it?"

One of the older girls, Kathleen, raises her hand. "We always act as servers at the poker game."

But another girl, Laura, rolls her eyes. "Among other things..."

I look between them, wondering, "What does that mean?"

Verity is the one to speak up, shifting uncomfortably. "The alumni are important, so sometimes... some of us will... I mean, not all of us, obviously–"

"We fuck them for money," Haley says, eyes full of challenge.

I'm caught, tangled between abject horror and absolute fury that she has the guts to talk to me like that. I focus on the first emotion, eyes roving around the table. "Wait. You're telling me Saul whores you out?"

Wilting, Verity says, "It's not like that. We're asked to serve, and when the alumni get a little handsy... some of the girls don't mind making a little extra cash."

For a long moment, I'm stunned speechless. This is some South Side nonsense, through and through. If my time at the Crane Motel and the Velvet Hideaway has taught me anything, it's that the kind of men who'd buy a warm hole to satisfy themselves aren't always in the habit of treating women kindly. That's one reason I quietly ask, "Do they... hurt you?"

But the other reason is purely selfish.

Are they going to hurt me?

It's a ridiculous thought, anyway. The Dukes will be my security, and Nick alone would sooner die himself than watch someone hurt me.

This much, I have complete confidence in.

"They're married dudes, trapped in sexless marriages, who are willing to pay for some young college pussy," another girl says. "It's not like they're whipping us."

Kathleen mutters, "Spanking sometimes," and looks distinctly unhappy about it.

Laura, who has always seemed pretty nice, is suddenly glaring at me. "Is that a problem? I thought if anyone could understand, it'd be you. Didn't you spend a lot of time at that brothel in South Side?"

"Yeah," another girl adds, looking offended. "What's it to you, anyway? This pays a whole semester of tuition for some of us, you know. *We* aren't Royal heirs."

Haley snorts a laugh, looking so infuriatingly satisfied that I have to stop myself from flying over the table and bashing her head against it. I hold my hands up instead. "Look, if you want to make some extra money riding their dicks, then that's not my business.

I'm not judging." Several expressions around the table show how unconvincing that statement is. Yet again, Haley's eyes roll. "I just want to make sure it's something you're choosing and not something you're forced to do. So." I square my shoulders, raising my voice. "How many of you *don't* want to be put in that situation?"

Slowly, hands begin rising up, beginning with Verity. One by one, at least half the girls follow, some looking guiltily at the girls who don't. Briefly, I wonder if the cutsluts were ever asked.

I nod, meeting each of their gazes. "You're all off the hook. Don't come."

"But," Katheleen says, looking worried, "it's required. If we don't attend, then we could lose our position. We earned these spots. Someone else will happily replace us."

More calmly than I feel, I say, "Not anymore. That's your Duchess' order, Kathleen. Any consequences arise, and I'll answer to Saul myself. Understood?" At their reluctant agreement, I look right at Laura. "And as you so kindly pointed out? Yes, I am familiar with the workings of a brothel. So I can tell you right now that less girls flouncing around half-naked means anyone interested in making this a business pursuit can raise their worth."

"Really?" Laura asks, shooting an eager look at the girl beside her. "Uh... by how much, you think?"

I falter for a moment, not expecting to be asked such a question. As if my time spent locked inside a whorehouse grants me some supreme wisdom on the matter of selling one's body. Shrugging, I answer, "Honestly? At least twice. If these guys are really as loaded as you say, then they can afford it."

Laura's face spreads into an excited grin. "Hell yeah!"

Verity gives me an impressed nod. "Nice thinking, Duchess."

Still tense, but relieved both halves of the group seem satisfied, I go on. "I'll be honest, though. I'm going to have to rely on your expertise on how to pull this off, because I have no fucking clue what to do."

That gets a few laughs and my shoulders ease. Verity catches my eye and I gesture for her to stand. "There's a notebook in Mama

B's office that should be helpful," she says. "It'll have information about where to rent everything, from the tables and chairs to the poker table tops. The girls who have worked the event before will know the drill."

"What's the drill exactly?" I already know the worst part of my role, but I can't just spend all night topless for these guys.

God, I hope I don't have to.

"It varies," she says. "Girls will have different assignments, like serving drinks and getting them liquored up to bid higher, or drink more. We're just there to get them to spend more money, which is the goal since it all goes to charity."

"Oh!" a girl breaks in, "Remember how that one year the girls all dressed up like devils? They looked so sexy."

"I saw pictures where everyone wore showgirl outfits," Laura adds. "They had these huge feather headdresses. Last year, we were nurses." The face she pulls tells me her opinion on that particular theme. "So many testicular exam jokes."

Verity nods. "We always dress the part—whatever it takes to part these guys with their cash."

"Right," I say, my mind spinning with anxiety. Apparently my ultimate act of degradation will come dressed in a themed costume. Just fucking great. "Okay, why don't we come up with some suggestions in the group chat over the next week, and put them to a vote?" I've tried to avoid putting much thought into what I'll be doing that night. It's a ways off, and the last thing I need to do is dwell on it uselessly. Nick and I agreed that when it comes to Sy and Remy, that same logic applies. We haven't told them–partly to avoid any undue outbursts, and partly because neither of us are sure where Remy's head is at right now.

"All right, ladies!" Mama B calls from the kitchen doorway. "We've got an hour to set up before a bunch of hungry cubs roll in."

The girls hop up, pushing chairs under the tables. I hear a few of the girls eagerly discussing ideas for the poker game. Their energy–the excitement of people who actually get a choice–makes me chafe inside.

It's not the stripping that bothers me. It's been a very long time since modesty was a luxury I had any claim to. It's the purpose of it–the fact that these alumni want to see me debased, sullied. I spent two years under Daniel's watchful eye, dreading the day something like this would come for me. Foolishly, I've begun feeling a sense of security as Duchess, the knowledge that I may have to do uncomfortable things, but never *that*.

"Thanks," I say to Verity as I walk toward the kitchen. "I'll get that notebook from your mom after dinner."

She gives me a relieved grin. "Seriously? Thank *you*. Some of us have really been dreading this, you know. You're doing us a huge favor." More hesitantly, she adds, "I'm happy to help, even if that means you need me there. I don't mind taking one for the team."

There are times I feel bad for Verity. She was born and raised for the position of Duchess but had been overlooked when Nick set his sights on me and decided to claim his position. I can't help but relate to the fact her whole life was turned upside down by one man's decision. *Nick's* decision. But no matter how helpful or willing she is to assist the Dukes, I have to think she dodged a bullet. I'm not saying my Royal blood makes me stronger, but I do think it prepared me for the position. I'm not sure Verity is up to it.

"Don't sweat it." I shake my head, trying my best to hide my own dread. "If the only real impact I can have as Duchess is making sure the cutsluts are treated with respect, then that's all I need."

Passing by us, Laura overhears this, turning to give me a pleased smile. "That's really cool of you, Lavinia."

It's the first time any of these girls, besides Verity, have referred to me as anything but 'Duchess.' It cuts through the grim tension I've been carrying ever since that meeting with Saul, and despite the fact I'm forced to share a space with Haley, I actually find myself feeling lighter, settled in a way I'm not expecting. As we prepare dinner, I can't help but feel as though I have a place here, a new synergy emerging between me and the cutsluts as we pass dishes and stack utensils.

Slowly the guys roll in, pushing through the gym doors and

filling the seats. I keep an eye on the door through the corner of my eye. Although I can't put a name to the feeling that surges through me when my Dukes walk in, I also can't deny its presence.

Anticipation? Relief? Pride?

Their eyes search for me instantly, Nick's shoulders losing some of their tension when our gazes lock. All three of them greet the DKS boys first, slapping palms, bumping fists. Nick has his arms on display despite the cooler weather, his short-sleeved shirt pulled tight over his chest. Sy's dressed in a navy button-down, untucked over a dark pair of jeans, and has his hair pulled back the same way he wore it the night of our date. Remy is in a denim jacket, fists shoved into his pockets as he edges into the fray.

I try not to look at him too much.

Sy's the first to approach me. I'm carrying a heavy pot of meatballs to the table when he walks up, taking it from me. "Hey," he says, eyes cutting to the group before he dips down to give me a kiss. It's quick but no less scorching, his tongue licking out to greet mine. He tastes like mint gum, and I let the frisson of want that's been lingering ever since that night up in my loft pass through me like a bolt of electricity.

"How was the meeting?" he asks. From the pink tinge of his ears, I'm guessing he's noticed some of the people looking at us. Most of the DKS boys know about what Sy did to me. God, a lot of them actually witnessed what Sy did to me.

Now I'm the one whose face is heating. "Good. The girls seem on board."

Nick stalks our way just as Sy's placing the pot on the table, and I give him a smile that feels uncertain.

Nick didn't come to my loft last night.

It was the first night since the river house that he hasn't, and although I waited, I also felt relieved when I drifted off without the intensity of his presence beside me. Watching that video dragged up a lot of feelings that need Olympian levels of compartmentalization.

But if I'm expecting reluctance from Nick, then I'm an idiot. He saunters right up to me, hooks his hand beneath my chin, and takes my mouth in a kiss so obscene and unexpected that I stumble back a step. I make a startled sound, but when he steadies me, wrenching my body up against his, I wind my arms around his neck, welcoming the zeal. Sometimes, my feelings for Nick are so complicated that I forget just how simple the man who causes them actually is.

Nick wants me. That's the beginning and end with him. The blessing and the curse. The rights and the wrongs.

He makes a low, gritty sound when he pulls back–not very far. "Nice dress," he says, eyes dipping down to my chest. "I'll take it off of you tonight." Beneath the devious grin he gives me is a statement I hear loud and clear.

One night apart is his limit.

"Yeah, yeah, you're not coming anywhere near this dress tonight." Beneath my eye roll is a statement I hope *he* hears loud and clear. "It's my only nice Family Dinner dress."

I won't turn you away.

"Oh well." He squeezes my hips tight, getting the message. "You look better without it."

Sy turns to say, "There's garlic bread, right?"

Noticing the hopeful gleam in his eyes, I extricate myself from his handsy brother. "Of course. This isn't my first rodeo with you animals."

I feel their eyes on me as I stroll to the kitchen, but still take a quick peek over my shoulder to see both of their blue-eyed gazes glued firmly to my ass.

The garlic bread is made in batches throughout dinner. Otherwise, as Mama B has made quite clear, the boys would feast on nothing else. As a result, I'm fully anticipating being cub-piled the moment I walk out with it.

But before I even get that far, I hear a voice.

Haley's voice. "This whole thing is such a joke." Her and Laura are lingering just outside. Through the crack in the door, I catch a peek of Haley's arm as she passes Laura a vape pen.

"What's a joke?" Laura asks, hitting the vape. "The poker game?"

"No," Haley says, scoffing. "Her. The *Duchess*. She's the worst person to lead the cutsluts." Haley snatches the vape pen back, voice sharp and bitter. "I don't care what anyone says, she's not one of us. She's a fucking viper, not a bruin."

"I think she's nice." There's a short, awkward pause before Laura warns, "And you better not let the guys hear you say that. Dillon said there was a whole dust-up during that meeting because Bruce questioned her loyalty."

She flips her hair back. "Please. That's all Nick and his obsessive personality. A chance at owning some Count cunt was the only thing in this town off-limits to him. He just wants what he can't have." She hits the vape pen, nodding confidently. "Once he's gotten her out of his system, he'll come back to us. She obviously has no idea how to please a man." My hands are already shaking with rage before the next sentence comes spewing out of her smirking mouth. "Else Remy wouldn't have come to me after the match."

White-hot fury surges through me, and even if I wanted to hold back, I couldn't. I storm through the door. The sound makes them both jump, whirling around to gape at me.

"You would need a dick in your mouth, wouldn't you, Haley?" I fist the tray, heart pumping like an inferno. "Apparently that and my sloppy seconds are the only things that keep it from flapping."

Haley's eyes flash angrily, even though she laughs, straightening her shoulders. "Don't you mean *my* sloppy seconds? Or have you forgotten who had him first? What can I say? When it comes to pleasing your boys, I'm the Royal."

"At what?" I snap, "Taking advantage of guys who are sick and wasted? I guess that's the only way you can get it."

Haley plants her hands on her hips. "Is that what you call it, sweetie? *Wasted*? Because he was 'wasted' all over my tongue until you walked in."

I throw the tray of bread aside, the clatter ringing noisily enough that I know all eyes in the room are swinging on us. "My foot is about to be wasted all over your face."

The room falls to a silent hush.

She surges forward, arms out. "Try me, snake! I'm not some pampered little North Side bitch."

Over the sound of scraping chairs and girls rushing forward, I say, "No. You're just a bottom-feeding slut who doesn't know her place." And then I slam my palm into her shoulder.

Eyes filling with fire, Haley's hand jerks back and flings out, slapping me hard.

Across the tit.

A sharp sting of pain runs along my nerves.

Laura gasps, "Haley! What the–"

But I'm already lunging at her, hand grabbing a thick fistful of her hair, and yanking hard enough that she stumbles. I jam my knee into her crotch, filled with a sick sense of satisfaction at the resulting yelp.

The other girls rush around us, screaming as the fight escalates. Louder, male voices–half of them amused–grow closer.

"Oh, shit!"

"Chick fight!"

"Anyone got their phone to record this shit?!"

"Kick her ass, Duchess!"

Soon we're surrounded, but my eyes are focused on the bitch in front of me. "You don't get to touch my man—ever. *I'm* the Duchess."

She shoves me back. "He didn't care you were his Duchess when he stuck his dick in my mouth." Her lips curve upward. "I've tasted all your men, and one day they'll all come back for more."

This time when I go for her, I don't hold back, slamming full force into her. She falls back, crashing into the table. Her arms flail out, nails sharp, slicing down my cheek. I growl and reach for her throat, but don't make it before I'm yanked back against a hard, solid chest.

The height gives me just the leverage I need to plant my heel into her jaw.

"Ah!" she cries, hands flying up to cover her chin. "Fucking cunt!" Before Haley can lunge back toward me, Ballsack grabs her, wrenching her away.

I don't need to look over my shoulder to know Nick's the one holding me. I can smell his warm scent, see the tattoos on his knuckles, the flash of his gold ring.

"Easy there, beautiful," he says, arms like manacles.

When I do look at him, he's got a small smile on his lips. Of course, he's loving this. I jab him in the gut, trying to work out of his grip.

"Let me fucking go!"

"Can't, Little Bird," he says, tightening his arms. "Haley will rip your goddamn eyes out."

My eyes bug out. I can't even imagine how crazed I must look. "You're worried about *me*? You better be fucking worried about her!" In my struggle, my ass brushes against his crotch and I freeze, shooting him an incredulous look. Is that a–?

Fucking Nick, I swear to God....

"That's enough!" Sy shouts, standing between us. I spot Remy, the cause of this fight, standing a few feet away. He's running both hands through his hair, raking hard, eyes tense and halfway to wild. Sy says, "This isn't how we handle our problems!"

"Oh, bullshit, Perilini." Someone barks out a laugh. All eyes look over to who would interrupt Sy. It's Bruce. "A fist fight is exactly how we'd handle this. Or are you just sexist? Only guys can fight, not chicks?"

Bruce is being Bruce, stirring the fucking pot. But my heart pounds, because all I want to do is show this little cunt exactly *why* I'm the Duchess.

Sy's eyes flick to mine and I plead silently. I need to show these women I can lead them. That we can work together, not tear each other apart. We had a good moment before, all of us on the same page, until she ruined it.

Haley needs to be put down, and I have to be the one who does it.

Recognition flares in Sy's eyes, and he gives me a nod. "Fine. But Dukes don't fight on the fucking dinner table." His eyes flick over my shoulder, across the gym. "We settle it in the ring."

10

R emy

Sy looks pissed when he struts up to me, thrusting a finger in my face. "This is your mess. You're setting up the mat."

Even though he follows me to supervise–something that's always annoyed the shit out of me–I take it like a man, wrenching open the supply closet. Like it's not bad enough that she won't even touch me, that she'll hardly even fucking look at me, now this.

I can't get away from my mistakes for one night.

But that's the thing, right? It was more than one mistake. It was a series of them. The slow slide into not taking my meds. The paranoia. Chasing the mania instead of shutting it down. A million little infractions that snowballed into hurting the woman I love.

Grabbing one of the rolled up mats, I drag it out and across the floor to the ring and pretend like there's not a tiny part of my brain still thinking about bailing out of here and getting high. At least my shoulder is almost better, barely giving a twinge when I heft the equipment out.

Some of the DKS boys watch me and Sy with curious eyes, and it picks at my awareness like a scab.

"They're not used to it," Sy mutters, helping me with the last mat. "Usually, the Dukes are…" He cuts me a dark look as we carry it across the gym. "Well, you know."

"Free to fuck all the cutsluts they want," I conclude, the words tasting sour and gray on my tongue. Glancing behind me to navigate, I add, "But we're not other Dukes."

Sy's eyes harden. "No, we're not."

"And she's not the usual Duchess." I drop my end when we reach the ring, looking around to make sure no one's in hearing distance. "You know what I don't get?" I say, kicking the mat so it rolls across the flat surface. "I'm not trying to rub salt in old wounds or anything, but bro. You seriously fucked her up."

His jaw hardens, eyes fixed to the ties on the mat. "I know."

"No, you don't." Shaking my head, I explain, "Verity had to take her to the clinic. She spent four fucking days locked away up in that loft. Missed some classes, wouldn't even read the books Nick brought her–"

Sy shoots up, snapping, "Get to the fucking point. I don't want to hear that shit."

I peer up at him, knocked off course at the outburst. His fists are flexing, shoulders high and tense. He looks like a man being hunted.

It's not often I see Sy feeling guilty about something.

More carefully, I say, "You caused that, but she's practically forgiven you."

His eyebrows crash together. "And?"

I gesture between us, hesitant to say the words aloud. "You hurt her worse than me."

Sy laughs, the sound low and joyless. "Is that what you think?" At my shrug, he crouches down to where I'm tying a strap. "Remy, come on. Lavinia's practically been genetically modified to have the biggest inferiority complex in Forsyth. Her whole childhood was probably built around it."

My face twists in confusion. "What do you mean?"

He rolls his eyes heavenward, as if he's praying for patience. "I... hurt her, but I did it because I wanted her too much." He glances around before adding, "You hurt her because you didn't want her enough."

I straighten, eyes flying wide. "That's a fucking lie."

"Hey, I know." Sy holds his hands up, palms out, like I've got a gun pointed at him. "I'm not saying it's true. I'm just saying that's how she sees it."

My chest feels like it's been carved out, bit by bit. "She told you that?!"

He sighs, long and beleaguered. "She didn't have to. I mean, dude. She got jealous because you said her sister's skull was pretty. Think about how she grew up, always in her big sister's shadow." He shakes his head, looking tired. "Lavinia's insecure and probably almost as possessive as Nick. I broke her body." He arches an eyebrow. "You broke her heart."

I claw my fingers through my hair, wishing I could feel something other than all this goddamn *gray*. "So fucking tell me how to make it right. What's the secret?"

For the first time in weeks I see empathy on his face. "There is no secret, Remy, and until you figure that out, I don't see anything changing." He feels sorry for me. And Jesus Christ that just makes me fucking furious *and* lights a fire under my ass.

"Strap those down," I tell him, pointing to the edges of the mat.

He whips his head around. "Where the hell do you think you're going?"

Marching away, I answer, "To make sure the Duchess is ready."

I leave him there. I mean, this was his idea. He can set up the fucking ring. I cross the room, pushing the door to the training room open. Vinny is sitting on the table, no longer wearing her dress, but instead, a Friday Night Fury tank and a pair of tight red shorts. She only spares me a brief glance, body stiffening, before she tears her eyes away.

It's been hard to look at her this past week. To see her skin and know I can't mark it. To stare at her lips and know I can't take them in a kiss. To watch her walk, that half finished snake tattoo on her leg taunting me.

I haven't seen color in so long.

Nick is rummaging through a drawer, pulling out a roll of tape. He looks over his shoulder, eyebrow quirking, drawing the tattoo beneath his eye up.

"I'll do that." I hold out my hand.

Tonelessly, Vinny argues, "Nick can do it." The lines of her face are set, hardened in a way I think I'd like to see under better circumstances, and her shoulders squared. A woman preparing for battle.

"I'm sure he can," I reply. "But he's not going to. I am."

It's forceful. Unapologetic. But that's what we are. Vinny and I have never been nice to one another. We've just been real.

Nick tosses the tape to me and I catch it in the air. "I'll be outside," he says, bending to press a kiss to her temple. The glare he passes me on the way out lacks much heat, but I get the message.

Fix this shit.

I saunter over to the table, yanking off a long strip of tape as I search her averted eyes. "Hand?"

The soft, blue vein beneath her collarbone pulses. "Come to tell me not to beat up your cutslut?" she asks, fingers coiled tight by her side.

Ouch. Right in the heart.

Reaching out, I grab her hand, unbothered by the stiffness of it, and drag my fingers over her skin. My canvas. Perfect and smooth and delicate. It's a stark contrast to my calloused, inked flesh. My hands are an artist's tool, a fighter's weapons. When I think of Vinny's fingers, I imagine them caressing my hair, circling my cock, slowly tracing the designs on my skin after a lazy fuck. I don't like the idea of them bruised and scabbed from a fight.

"I came to say that you don't have to do this," I say, running my thumb over a soft knuckle before pressing the tape over it. "She's not really the one you want to hit."

Vinny traps me with her blazing eyes. "If you think I don't want to hit her, then you don't know me at all."

My eyes draw up–not on her, but around her. To the fuzzy edge around her ferocity. I think I might see something, a faint flicker of color emerging, but it fizzles out before I can decide.

I graze my fingers over her wrist and it happens again, the hint of color. She's pissed. At me. At Haley. At the whole damn situation. I don't mention it. I just keep wrapping, gently winding the tape over her knuckles, and hope for another flicker. She shivers and my eyes dart to her tits and her hard, pointed nipples.

"Too tight?" I drag my gaze to her face.

Her breath hitches. "I'm not sure."

I whisper, "Make a fist."

She does and I see that she has enough range, so I secure the ends by tucking them underneath. "If you need to kick Haley's ass, I get it. I'm pretty sure I'd murder any man who touched you that wasn't one of your Dukes. *Assuming* Nick didn't get there first." I swallow. Just like that night up in the clock room, I wonder how I'm going to let her go at the end of this task. It's been so long since I felt her skin against mine and I'm so hungry for it. "Haley's slow," I offer, drawing it out. "She's got shit for stamina. The jogging you've been doing with Sy should give you an edge."

Her mouth pinches angrily. "Remy–"

"But if you're hurting her to get back at me, it won't work. I don't give a shit about Haley." I catch her eye, rubbing the pad of my thumb against the thin skin of her wrist. It's indulgent and unfair, and I don't give a fuck. "Maybe that just makes me a bigger asshole, but it's true. I've already told her–she knows it. That's why she's being such a bitch to you."

"How many?" she asks, another flare of color when she grits her teeth. It's not quite red, but it's also not blue. "Is this something I have to do every week, Remy? How many of those girls out there have you fucked?"

"None," I answer. "None since you. Definitely none that matter."

She turns her eyes on me. "Until the next time you're mad at me?"

I freeze, my face twisting. "Vinny, you know how out of my fucking mind I was." But that's not what I want to say. It's not an excuse. My shoulders sink. "There's this saying–I've heard it a lot in that group Sy sent me to. My issues," shyly, I tap my temple, "my... head issues, you know? They're not my fault, but they are my responsibility. I guess I never really thought about that much." My voice drops. "Not until you."

It's her turn to swallow thickly. "I'm not looking for another apology."

"Good." I tear off the tape. "Because I wouldn't know how to give it." I gave her the sky. I took her to the black and held her stars in my hands, and now black is all I see. "She crossed a line with you, and she has to pay. I get it. But it's not going to change anything." I touch her chin, forcing her to look at me. "Baby, I'm already yours."

She leans out of my touch, sliding off the table. Her face is hard as stone. "You going to do the other hand, or what?"

Deflating, I reach out for her left wrist, searching like hell for another flash of color. "I've given you time. I've given you space. I've given you a complete lack of me. And Vinny?" I meet her gaze, knowing how agonized I must sound. "It's fucking killing me."

"I don't care." She yanks her hand back, snatching the roll of tape, and the furious flare of her eyes makes my face fall. "This isn't a punishment, Remy."

I step back. "Then what is it?"

"It's me," she answers, voice tight, "not ready to jump off that cliff again."

If I were ever a literal person, I might think to tell her that's a statistical improbability. But I'm not stupid. She's not talking about the real cliff.

THE LOWER SEATS are packed with DKS and cubs, cutsluts sprinkled throughout, and there's a strange, hostile energy running through them. Duchess vs. cutslut? Loyalties run thick in West End, but there are rules—some unspoken, some explicit. None of them have the right to touch Vinny any more than the cutsluts have the right to the three of us.

"We should have sold tickets," Nick mutters as we approach the ring. Hands clutching her waist, Sy helps Vinny up on the mat, spreading the ropes to give her space to ease through.

"Keep your shoulders up," Sy tells her, climbing up on the edge to meet her over the ropes. "Watch your feet. And if you can get her into a grapple hold—"

"Choke hold," Nick cuts in, jumping up to lean closer. "Did Sy teach you any leg takedowns?" He glances at Sy. "Any Muay Thai?"

"Would you be real?!" Vinny hisses, whirling to glare at them. "Nails, tits, and hair, guys. This is a chick fight, not one of your macho MMA matches." She reaches up to gather her hair into a tight ponytail, hard eyes flicking across the three of us. "Maybe a few years of being unable to hold my own against men *three times my size* has confused you." She narrows her eyes, challenging. "But I grew up fighting the meanest bitch Forsyth will ever see. That piece of trash over there doesn't stand a chance."

There's a long, desperate groan, Nick's head bowing. "Little Bird, please," he begs, glancing up at her with tortured eyes. "My dick cannot get any harder."

Even Sy reaches down to covertly adjust himself.

Personally, I don't bother trying to hide what she's doing to me, so when I climb up, I rest my elbows on the rope and try, "North Side bitches are fierce, but West End bitches are dirty. She won't fight fair."

"Good." She tightens her ponytail, and even though she's avoiding my gaze, I still feel her next words like a slap across my cheek. "Since when have any of us?"

Haley walks in, some of the cubs letting out loud whistles at her outfit, and this is what I'm talking about. Metallic gold sports bra with criss-cross straps across the back and matching skin-tight shorts get the boys in the stands all riled up. Haley will use that energy. Feed off the colors it gives her. She's a cutslut through and through. All style, little substance.

But Bruce is waiting in her corner, pulling her close to whisper in her ear.

It prompts Nick to grab Vinny by the neck, yanking her in for a hard kiss. "To the victor, baby."

I don't miss her and Sy, giving me a lightning-fast glance.

Fuck.

I'm the spoils.

When Vinny pushes off the corner, hips swaying, arms loose, Sy sidles up to whisper, "I know having two girls fight over you is some bullshit drama that's probably got you all twisted up inside." He cuts me a haggard look. "But is this turning you on?"

I pluck the rope, voice mournful. "Painfully."

He gives me a sympathetic pat on the shoulder. "To the spoils go the victor?"

Vinny reaches the center with a steel spine. Ballsack volunteered to referee, and he stands between the two girls, looking between them dubiously. "First one to cry mercy loses."

The bell rings and he jumps back, which is a good thing because Vinny takes the first swing, fist flying in a blurry right hook. She connects, knuckles slamming into Haley's chin with a loud smack.

Haley yelps, face turning red, and I know what's going to happen before she even lifts a foot. Mouth pulled back in outrage, she lunges forward. It's fueled by anger and hot humiliation, which is made all the more obvious when Vinny smoothly sidesteps the tackle, snatching a fist of Haley's hair instead. She wrenches her head back, jabbing her knee into Haley's side.

The crowd makes a sharp, sympathetic sound.

Sy and I share a look.

"Get up." Vinny circles Haley on the mat, waiting for her to find her feet again. When Haley does, she strikes out wildly, grabbing at the strap of Vinny's tank top. Vinny answers by slamming her palm around Haley's wrist and *twisting*. Even from across the mat, I can see the indents of her fingernails, Haley growling as she punches her palm into Vinny's jaw.

But not before Vinny jams her elbow into Haley's chin.

The *crack* is a sickening sound, Haley stumbling back, and when she recovers, there are tears in her eyes, hot and bitter. My blood rushes at the contrast of it. The way Vinny moves on the mat is as precise as Nick, and as business-like as Sy. I know he trained that out of her. Striking out in anger. Letting the emotion rule you.

But I still see it glowing bright in her eyes when she lunges back, catching Haley in the throat.

Purple.

It blows me back like a gust from a freight train, settling over my skin like static electricity. My lungs stop working, wrung free of air as Vinny bends down, grabbing Haley by the shoulders and dragging her back to the center of the ring.

She wants everyone to see this.

"Get the fuck up," she commands, planting the toe of her shoe into Haley's ribs.

Haley struggles to her feet, expression murderous as she barrels into Vinny's torso, taking her down to the mat. All around us, the cubs and cutsluts are reacting to each hit, each takedown, but uncertain. For some of them, this started as a joke. Two girls fighting, tits flying, bare legs locked. But now they're seeing that it isn't a joke at all.

Haley is West End, but Vinny is their Duchess.

They don't know if it's okay to cheer.

It only takes one more glance–one more bask–in Vinny's purple to spur me into motion.

I climb up on the ropes, yelling, "Are you watching a fight, or jacking off? Come on, fuckers!"

One of the DKS in the back springs up, shouting, "I've got thirty on the Duchess!"

Another scrambles up to take the bet, while the cutsluts to my left begin cheering, "Kick her ass, Lavinia!"

I rally the non-believers as if it were my own fight, watching cubs and DKS–even a few cutcluts–pooling their money for the victor. "She didn't become Duchess because of blood or sex appeal," I bark, gesturing to where she's pelting Haley with a chest-kick. "She fucking earned this shit!"

"Yeah!" Kathleen, another cutslut, jumps up to scream, "Haley fucked my boyfriend, too!"

Despite the speed, everything moves in slow motion, not the fight but the *color*. As the crowd finally shows up, banging their feet and fists with every hit Vinny lands, I finally let myself watch. They're getting gassed out, little locks of Vinny's hair falling in her eyes as she ducks and kicks, cheeks flushed a bright magenta. Blood is covering her mouth, dripping down her chin, but Haley looks worse, eyebrow split, lashes wet, a welt already forming on her cheekbone.

I was right about the stamina, though.

When Haley jolts forward to grab Vinny's ponytail, she hooks her arm around Haley's neck and *drops*.

Haley's body slams tits-first onto the mat.

I can practically hear all the air getting knocked from her lungs, and if that wasn't enough to seal the victory, then the way Vinny plants the sole of her shoe right into Haley's neck, pressing down with all her weight, definitely fucking is.

There's a long moment where the crowd roars, waiting for Haley to concede.

When she finally does, it's with a sharp, frustrated punch at the mat. "Mercy!" she shrieks, then adds with a mutter, "You fucking psycho."

Vinny looks sweaty, winded, and bruised as she releases her foot, eyes finally rising to take in the cheering crowd. The purple in her eyes dims, but never really leaves. It pulses to a beat that I feel in my chest, and when she walks the five paces to the ropes, everyone must feel it, too.

Because they go quiet.

Chest jerking with labored breaths, she calls out, "I know what you all think of me! My blood is North Side, so I'm a spoiled little Lucia, right?" Her mouth pulls into a bitter snarl. "I don't have anything–*anything*–in this world I haven't earned. I don't have a bedroom. I don't have a car. I don't have a fucking family anymore." Her eyes pass over them. DKS. Pledges. Cutsluts. "Maybe I haven't earned your respect yet. Maybe I haven't had the chance to earn your loyalty. Maybe I haven't even earned the right to be in this ring. But these three?" She thrusts her hand out, stabbing a finger in our direction. "I've earned the right to call them mine! And you can fucking spread the word on that to all four corners."

She spits, a glob of blood staining the mat, before marching back to her corner.

Where the three of us are waiting.

Nick is watching her like she just performed some act of divine grace, and Sy... he shines with pride, a smile tugging at his lips as he tosses her a towel. She catches it smoothly, ducking through the ropes, and the thing that gets me–the thing that makes my head fill with a fog of indignant confusion–is that she brushes right past me, not even sparing me a glance.

Why would she fight for me, for the right to call me *hers*, if she doesn't want me?

"Nicky, get some ice," Sy says, eyeing Haley slumped on the mat. "Remy, go check on Lavinia."

I grit my teeth. "She doesn't want–" But his glare is hard enough to make me relent. By the time I jump down, she's already gone, having ducked into the cutslut's dressing lounge.

I'm no pussy or anything. It's not like Vinny's the first girl I ever pissed off on account of my wandering dick. She's just the first one I felt bad about. That's the reason I pause at the door, psyching myself up like I'm about to go eight rounds with someone a lot bigger and scarier.

Flexing my fist, I push the door open carefully, quietly, figuring the element of surprise can't hurt.

What I find inside makes my stomach drop. She's in a chair at one of the vanities, shoulders slumped, back still heaving with hard breaths.

She's crying.

Not like I've seen some girls cry, either. There's no snot or sobbing or wrenching wails. She's just staring down at her taped knuckles, tears tracking like raindrops down her pink cheeks. I stand in the shadow of the hall for a long moment, trying to decide what to say.

In the end, I say nothing.

"Get out," she snarls, her eyes having found me. She reaches up to swipe angrily at a tear, jolting to her feet. "Get the fuck out!"

I step forward, the flash of purple building to a smolder. "Claim your spoils, Vinny." I hold out my arms, defenseless and done. "Hit me, kick me, fuck me, I don't care. But I'm not leaving until you do."

What I get is a hard, jarring shove, her palms slamming into my shoulders. The weak one twinges with pain and it feels good. Deserved. "You're such an asshole!"

I don't disagree, planting my feet for the next push. It comes on the crest of a hitched breath, her face contorted with pained fury.

"I gave you what you asked for!" she screams, eyes wild and wet. "You said there was no going back, and then you–" Her words clip off into a growl, her curled fist banging against my chest. "You lied! *You* did!"

I stay still and expressionless, not needing her to remind me. That night in the rain might as well be tattooed into my flesh, a million pinpricks of light. Sometimes, I swear I can hear thunder in the distance, two celestial bodies meeting, as if we'd given a part of that moment to the universe to hold close, just in case we lost it.

"Once we do this, there's no going back, Vinny. This will make you mine. Not just your body. Not just because you're my Duchess. You understand, don't you?"

I couldn't say the words back then, didn't know how to articulate a request so big and indefinable. I wanted the essence of her. The spark in her eyes. The fight in her heart. The pain of her touch.

I wanted her soul.

"Take it."

Jesus Christ.

Sy was right.

When she strikes out, aiming for my shoulder again, I catch her wrist, surging forward to capture her mouth. She struggles and I clutch her upper arms, swallowing the sharp sound she makes, so quiet and full of despair. I push her back blindly, uncaring of where I'm leading her to, until we hit something solid. The jolt makes her push back, her teeth bearing down into my lip.

The metallic tang of blood just makes me grunt. This is what we are–what we've always been. Words can't fix what I've done. Releasing her arm, I curl my palm around her neck, yanking her closer. Her fist jabs into my side, knuckles punching into the muscle, but she tilts her head, dueling with my tongue as though she'd rather hurt it.

The memory of that morning in my bed, when she bodily flipped me off of her, rings clear in my mind.

If she wanted to get away, she would.

The truth of it makes my blood rush hotter, and when I reach down to grab her thigh, I feel driven by something primal and bigger than either of us. I dig my fingers in and lift her, spinning to dump her clumsily onto the counter of the vanity. Aerosol cans clatter to the floor with hair brushes and bottles of weird, glittery stuff. The sound she makes is rabid, foot kicking out to catch my knee. It makes me stumble into the cradle of her thighs, my hardness crashing into her.

"I was yours, Remy." Her breathless words are punctuated with her fingers, gripping a tight handful of my hair. "But I won't be anymore. Not unless you're mine, too."

"I am," I say, palming her tit aggressively–too hard. "I am, I am–"

It isn't until she pulls hard enough at my scalp to make me growl that I let her go, hands frantically clawing at my belt. The last time I came, it was all awash with green and black and yellow, and I want nothing more than to clean it away with *this*. The blood, the sting, the supernova of purple as she fists my shirt, teeth grazing my tongue.

It all makes such perfect sense to me that my head spins.

Words are colorless. Vinny and I are an arc of lightning in an endless expanse of black. We need the spark, not the void.

I shove my pants down just enough to free my hard, aching dick, and then I'm back to touching her, grasping her, mauling her. Hooking my fingers in her shorts, her body skates across the counter, colliding with mine as I violently yank the elastic down her hips.

She's the one to get them off, though.

She flails out sightlessly, our mouths unwilling to part, and wrenches a single knee up to work them off. Even if I wanted to tease her, I couldn't. Our bodies–our souls–are too magnetized for that.

I slam forward, entering her in one hard thrust.

For a second, everything stands still.

Our mouths hover so close that I can taste her panting breaths, her nails digging painfully into my hip. Her pussy is so tight and wet for me that my toes curl, my hand flying up to catch her chin when she throws her head back. The force of my thrust knocks her back on the counter, skittering away. The purple courses through me, and I curl a forearm around her waist, yanking her back for the next.

Our bodies collide like thunder.

"Do you want to hear it again?" I grunt, thumb digging into the damp flesh of her cheek.

Her face is tense, pinched in rapture, and when I punch forward again, she cries out, low and keening. "Fuck," she spits, nails clawing at my hips. "Oh, *fuck*."

"I love you." I lick the words right into the crease of her lips, lapping up a smear of blood. "That's not a fucking lie." My words come bitten off between thrusts, voice full of red gravel. "It's the truest thing I've ever known, Vinny."

When she finally opens her eyes, I see it all. The ferocity, the hurt, the frantic, reckless want. Her ankles wind around me like a vise, clutching me close as I fuck her in a short, pounding rhythm. "You know what I want," she says, voice breaking on the next slam of my hips.

"Whatever's left of it," I promise, knowing my soul is gray and tattered, "it's yours." It's not what she deserves. I haven't had time to fill it with color again, to show her the beautiful things it can make, if only it has her reflection to fill it. I do it anyway, my cock thickening as I bang her against the vanity, desperate to meet the rising tide.

My orgasm rips through me like a monster clawing itself free, and I hold her close–hard enough to press bruises into her hips–as I mouth my way to her ear. I give her the words she once gave to me so freely. "Take it," I grunt, my cock surging to fill her.

She gasps, her pussy clenching around me as I fuck my cum into her. Biting down on a groan, my hand smacks hard against the mirror. It doesn't stop. Wave after wave of cum, my cock jerking as it feeds it into her, so slick and warm. The only thing that distracts me from it is the sensation of her fingers, fluttering soothingly through my hair.

It feels like it lasts hours, emptying my balls–my soul–into her. Vinny's pussy wrings me of every drop, her hips giving these little, mindless nudges into mine, like she's afraid of losing what I've already given.

When it's finally done, I turn my head to catch a glimpse of her flushed face, prying my hips free of her clutches. She makes a sharp sound, grabbing for me, but I'm already gone.

And dropping to my knees.

Hooking my hands around her thighs, I hitch her closer to the edge, glancing up to watch her heavy, glazed eyes. My lips brush over the star tattooed beside her hip as I count the points.

Real.

All real.

Hovering over the dark ink, I feel it most acutely here, the purple spark illuminating every corner of my mind. Her eyes crash shut, but she writhes eagerly when my mouth ventures lower. Her pussy tastes like heaven because it's *us*. My cum is dripping out, so I lick it up for her, pushing it back inside with the tip of my tongue. It's too much, though—so much that it rushes out, filling my mouth, hot and bitter.

I spring up instantly, grabbing her jaw, working the hinge of it open with my thumb. She stares up at me with a dazed expression, lips parting. When my own mouth opens, the cum streams right into hers and she shudders, clamping her palm around my neck to bring me closer. I taste it on her tongue as I push it inside, needing her to keep it—every drop.

Finally, she swallows.

"Remy," she gasps, chest jumping with desperate breaths. "Please."

The frantic little squirm of her hips sends me back down, my knees protesting as they land hard on the floor. Her clit is so ripe and swollen that I can practically feel it throbbing on my tongue. Any cum that's left between her legs gets fucked back in with my two fingers as I bring her to the edge, tongue swirling wildly around her clit.

She comes with a soundless scream, her whole body seizing as she claws my hair, demanding more.

I feel her trembles all the way down to my marrow.

It's only when she jolts, heel slamming into my bad shoulder—too sensitive—that I fall away, crashing back onto my elbows with an exhausted sigh. She looks like fine art when I raise my eyes, though. Thighs spread, pussy pink and glistening, face red and sweaty.

I've never seen so much purple in my life.

My eyes fall on the star, the memory of tattooing it there fuzzier than I'd like. But I remember the way she looked, so vulnerable, yet so impenetrable as I pushed the needle into her skin.

"Vinny." When her eyes fall on me, soft and tired and warm, I feel higher than any pill could ever make me. "I have an idea."

11

L avinia

REMY and I ride home in the back seat together. Nick and Sy are in the front, and every now and then, one of them will shoot us furtive looks, Nick glancing back while his brother peers through the rearview. There's a low vibration running between the brothers, like they're afraid to ask what transpired in the lounge. Or maybe they already know. These men know one another inside and out. I'm the new one here, learning to understand the shorthand that passes between them. The looks. The gestures.

Like Remy's hands never leaving my body.

Right now, he's stroking my thigh, his green eyes fixed to the patch of skin like he's greeting it after returning from a long deployment in a war. Every street we pass, his fingers change course for a new destination, tickling the thin skin of my inner elbow, caressing the bruises on my knuckles, tracing the edge of my collarbone. It's almost like he needs to learn my body again–making up for lost time.

I let him, because every touch makes me shiver in a new way, even though both of us are fucked out and exhausted when we finally arrive at the tower.

The climb to the top is quiet and slow, but somehow, there's still a restless energy flowing between all of us. It's in Nick's blue eyes when he passes me nearing the party room, his knuckles grazing mine before sliding away.

When we reach the top, Sy lets us in, holding the door for each of us as we filter through. Both brothers watch as Remy hems me in against the arch by the kitchen, caging me with his body.

"Come to my room tonight," he says, forearm resting over my head. He towers over me, lean but muscular, the hem of his shirt rising up to give me a tease of the strip of flesh above his low-slung jeans. As I'm staring at it–*fine*, maybe I've been missing his skin, too–he tucks his thumb into my shorts and circles the pad of it over the star, sending flares of heat radiating outward. "Please?" he adds, quiet and coaxing.

My eyes narrow. "What's this idea of yours?" I ask. Although I'm partly nervous, I also can't deny the part of me that's excited, curious. With Remington Maddox, you never fucking know.

His green eyes search mine, curious in their own way. "I'll tell you when we get there."

In case this idea of his involves more emotionally wrought, athletic sex, I warn, "Okay, but just so you know, I'm gonna need about ten ibuprofen and a heating pad." I wince at a spot on my side. "You were right. Haley's dirty."

"Yeah," he says, dipping his head to lazily lick my lips, "but you're our badass Duchess, and *so much* dirtier."

Across the room, I don't miss the look exchanged between Sy and Nick. They're not happy to have another night without me, but this thing with Remy is fresh and more fragile than ever. I don't know where it's leading, but I know I have to find out.

So I relent, body giving up its tension as he strokes the star on my hip. "Meet you in a minute? I need to change."

His eyes brighten, and it's odd. I've never seen Remy cautiously happy like this. He's always either on or off, all or nothing. Now, however, he whispers, "Okay, Vinny," and slowly drags his touch from me, sauntering away.

After clamping down on the part of myself that wants to chase him, I make a beeline for the spiral staircase to my loft, jolting in surprise when Nick stops me.

He grabs my wrist, pulling me into the wall of his body. "All night?" he asks, eyes hard and unhappy.

Nervous at his expression, I don't bother bringing up that he's the one who stayed away last night. "Nick." I press my palm to his warm chest. "I won," I say, hoping that's enough to soothe this quiet intensity. It's not often that I fight for something and win it, and the truth is, I don't even know what that means yet.

But I want to find out—so badly that my blood is buzzing with it.

Nick holds my gaze, nodding. "I get it. To the victor go the spoils." But then he pitches forward, lips brushing across mine. "You could set an alarm, though."

"Oh, my god." One hand pushes him away while the other drags him back, my fingers twisting in his shirt. "You're being ridiculous. I'm not waking up in the middle of the night to come back out here and fuck you."

It's only when I catch his gaze, seeing the sharp downturn of his mouth, that I realize what this stony, dark expression of his is.

He's *pouting*.

I'm so caught up in the dawning appreciation that when he reaches between my legs, hooking his fingers into the crotch of my shorts, I can't do much more than look up in surprise.

His fingers instantly find my hole, shoulder dropping as he pushes one inside. My jaw goes slack, hands catching his biceps to steady myself, and he freezes.

Nick stares into my eyes, a slow smirk pulling at his cheek. "He already fucked you." At my jerky nod, he groans. "Fuck, I bet it was hot."

Seeing that horny ember in his eyes growing, I bat his hand away. "It was also exhausting, and I'm too sore to do anything more tonight."

His big hands palm my ass, the expression on his face intent. "Tomorrow."

"I know."

He tilts my chin up. "I'm serious, Little Bird."

I see it in his eyes, a promise that might feel like a threat if I didn't know better. A little niggle in the back of my mind wonders how long I could make him wait, but I still agree, "Tomorrow, I promise." This man is hungry for me and now that we've started this up, there's no going back.

His hands slide up my sides until he reaches my breasts and cups them in his hands. "At least send me a picture of your tits. I need something to jerk off to tonight."

I roll my eyes. "I'm pretty sure you can use your imagination."

His eyebrows knit together. "Fuck, you're killing me." He kisses me again, squeezing my tits and running his thumbs over my nipples until they harden into peaks. I know it's an attempt to get me horny for him and it's not going to work.

Well, it's absolutely going to work, but unlike the three of them, I actually have some self-control.

I pat his chest. "Goodnight, Nick."

"Fine." His shoulders drop in defeat, but when I turn to climb the stairs, he brings a palm down hard on my ass, the *smack* reverberating through the room. His smirk shines back at me when I yelp, whirling an outraged stare at him. He shrugs, sauntering backward toward his bedroom. "I'll work off memory."

I flip him off before returning to my task, going upstairs to change. When I come back down in a loose sweatshirt and pajama shorts, Sy is standing at the bottom of the stairs with a glass of water and two familiar capsules.

I stop short, surprised at the thoughtfulness. "Thank you." I pop them in my mouth and swallow them down, wincing when the glass presses against my busted lip.

After taking the glass back, he reaches out, knuckles gently brushing the wound. "You kicked ass out there tonight."

"I learned from the best."

Sy's eyes soften, fingers tilting my head to inspect the scratch on my cheek. "I'm not claiming responsibility for those chick moves, but they were effective enough. You stood up when you needed to, just like a Duke." His eyes dart to Remy's closed door. "You two good now?"

"I think so," I say, following his gaze. "We will be."

"Thank fucking Christ." He looks to the ceiling like he may actually be thanking God. "Not that I think you'll need it, but I'm next door if you need anything, okay?"

"Okay." But he's right. I don't need a protector in this house. Not anymore.

I tap on Remy's door, and he calls me to come in. When I push it open, it's dark inside. It'd be pitch black except for the singular lamp casting a harsh glow on his body. He's sitting on his tattoo table in a pair of boxer briefs, his shirt and pants stripped off. He leans back on his hands and watches as I shut the door, his head cocked back lazily. It's a struggle to tear my eyes away from the tendons in his throat, shifting to the table where he keeps his instruments.

They're all lined up, neat and ready.

"You want to tattoo me?" My stomach plummets at the realization, even though the phantom feeling of his needle ghosts over my skin. The first tattoo he gave me, seared like fire into my shoulder blade, was done in the heat of battle, his body pinning mine to the bed that night at the Hideaway. It's a tattoo that I'm grateful to be unable to see. The second—the star on my hip—was created in a fog of his own delusion, needing a compass to guide him back to reality. The massive moth on my chest took him weeks, hours beneath the heat of that overhead lamp as his green eyes glowed with laser-like intensity. They might vary in pain and intent, but all of them shared a singular thread of unspeakable intimacy.

I don't think I'm ready to go there with him just yet.

"Actually," he says, voice clearer than I've heard it in weeks, "I want you to tattoo me."

I stop short. "You want me to *what*?"

"I'm yours," he explains, tipping his head toward the tattoo gun. "Make your mark. Anywhere you want, anything you want."

Wringing my hands, I start, "I don't know…"

"Vinny," he says, dark eyes capturing mine. "No one's ever tattooed me before. No girl, not even another guy. This is all mine." He dips his eyes to his body, to the intricate designs over his chest, arms, torso. "But now it's yours, too. So go ahead. Pick a spot."

Reluctantly, I step forward, eyes roving his skin. His chest and arms are pretty covered, and I can't imagine adding anything to them. "I'm not good at drawing," I worry as I walk closer, getting a good look at his neck.

He tilts his head, putting his neck on display for me. "Then I'll draw whatever you want."

Anxiously, I round the table, realizing now why his back is a wide, muscular swath of unblemished skin. Unthinkingly, I reach out to run my fingertips over his spine, watching as his skin erupts in goosebumps.

"Fresh meat back there." He twists his head, raising an eyebrow. "Can't reach it myself. You should take it. Make it yours."

Shyly, I confess, "I like it like this," running my palm down his shoulder. Some of the hardest moments during our time apart were watching him do pull-ups by the windows in the living area, just as fascinated by the wiry, shifting muscles as turned on by them.

So I keep going, rounding the other side of the table pensively.

In the end, it's incredibly obvious. "Lay back," I decide, watching as he situates himself on the table. I bite my lip, not missing the significance of this. Remy's where I usually am, laid out for me like a canvas, hands tucked behind his head as he waits, looking as comfortable as I've ever seen him.

Until I reach for the waistband of his boxer briefs, tugging them down.

He yanks his arms back down to his sides, abs flexing and tense. "Uh," he says, suddenly pale. "Shit, yeah, I guess you would want to do it there." He stiffens as I tug, revealing a soft patch of pubic hair. "Makes sense–dibs and all." His eyes drop to the slow reveal of his long, half-hard dick, brows crushing inward. "Just your name, right? What's 'Lavinia', like seven letters?" His voice pitches higher and higher, and then chokes off as I peel his boxer briefs down his legs, his green eyes flying wide. "You're not going to do your last name too, are you? Because it's not like there are that many Lavinia's in Forsyth. If you think about it, initials would work just as–"

"Remy," I say, throwing his underwear aside. "Relax. I'm not going to tattoo your dick."

His head thumps back, body sagging in relief. "Oh, thank *fuck*. Not saying I wouldn't take it like a man, because–"

"Right here," I say, thumbing a section right between his dick and hip.

"Yeah?" He eyes it curiously, some of the color returning to his face. "Like yours, huh?"

"Yep." It's in the same place as my star, but on the opposite side. "So..." I look around, wondering what to do next.

He stretches out, gesturing loosely to the table. "Gloves first, then wipe the skin down," he instructs, green eyes following me as I ready the area. The sanctity of the routine washes over me. It's something I've never done, but I've avidly watched Remy perform dozens of times, both for me and other people. Choosing my ink, adjusting the lamp, seeing the design in my mind and imagining how it might look on the skin.

By the time I'm ready, the heavy tattoo gun clutched in my hand, Remy looks relaxed, eyes hooded as he watches me with a silent intensity. When I pause, hand inching to his cock only to gently prod it toward his other hip, it twitches in interest.

Remy grins. "You remember, right?"

Nodding, I press the trigger on the gun, carefully dipping the needle into my ink. "Stay still," I whisper, poised over the area. Before the needle touches him, however, I glance up, feeling skeptical.

He never even asked me what I'm going to draw.

It could be anything.

But he doesn't ask. He doesn't even look concerned, forearm tucked behind his head as he waits, eyes dark and penetrating. He twitches at the first touch of the needle. I don't stop, because I understand it's not pain, but merely surprise, his body greeting the sensation with a little *hello.*

I'm positioned right over his thigh, my elbow held awkwardly to avoid grazing his cock as my wrist works the gun, when he touches my hair. Gently, he winds a lock around his forefinger, the weight of his eyes on my every move.

"Is the light always this bright?" he asks in a bizarrely slurred voice.

I dip the needle again, glancing up at his dazed expression. "Yes."

There's a beat where nothing but the buzz of the tattoo gun surrounds us, his fingers pulling shivers from my scalp as he strokes the hair. Softly, he offers, "Maybe I'll blindfold you next time."

The needle pauses over his skin, but I recover quickly, hearing the statement for what it is. I know from reading Sy's textbooks that someone with Remy's condition might be prone to making promises they can't keep later.

This isn't a promise, though.

It's a dream.

I hear it in his voice, the wistfulness of wanting everything to be better, and that's the only reason I agree. "Okay."

I get lost in the task for a while, letting his gentle caresses of my hair lull me into a singular focus. Even though the design is small, I can still feel the responsibility of it heavy in my chest. This is something he'll have forever, my victory immortalized inside his skin. Maybe this new leaf he's turning won't last. Maybe he goes off his meds again, or falls back into Scratch, or just gets sick of wanting me.

But this moment, the knowledge that at one time, we fought for it, will last until his decay.

I'm already mostly done when I glance over, startled by the sight that greets me.

His dick is rock-hard.

I look up into his hooded green eyes, exasperated. "Seriously?"

Remy chews his bottom lip, bucking his hips ever so slightly. "Never knew it was like this," he rumbles, his cock giving an enthusiastic twitch, "feeling someone else do it to me."

I cut my eyes at his dick again, watching a thin pearl of precum fall onto his belly. "Just a little more."

When the needle touches his skin again, he lets out a deep, gravelly groan, cock surging. "Fuck." His fingers twirl my hair, a stark contrast to the urgency of his voice. "Is it as purple for you as it is for me? Every nerve in your body begging to be touched?"

I can feel his heel behind me, grinding hard into the table. "Yes," I answer honestly. "But this needs to be sterile. No shenanigans." He looks like he might argue, but then the room goes silent, the tattoo gun ceasing. "There," I say, carefully wiping down the skin.

"Already?" He pushes up on his elbows to finally look, his eyes so glassy that he might as well be half drunk. He stares at the shape for a long moment, fingers reaching out to ghost around the red edges of the crescent moon.

A somberness falls over us like lead gossamer, and I know we're both remembering the sky that night.

"When we jumped," he whispers, looking transfixed, "I wasn't scared. I knew I couldn't be, because I had you with me." His eyes jump to mine, brimming with energy. "I wanted to be strong for you, Vinny. Like Nicky and Sy. Like steel. Like a Bruin." He touches my face, fingers tracing a tender scratch beneath my temple. "I wanted to hold on to you, Vinny, but the river tore us apart. I knew where you were, even in the dark. My guiding star." The curve of his grin is mocking and bitter. "But when it mattered, I couldn't hold on."

I search his eyes, knowing he's not only talking about the river. "The first thing I saw from the water was this moon," I say, eyes fixed to the new ink beside his hip. "And then you were there, dragging me to the shore. Because stars guide the way, but moons—they wax and wane, always revolving." I pitch closer, willing him to hear me. "You *were* strong, Remy. You were lost in the darkness, but you revolved back to me when I needed you. You saved me from drowning."

But he's clawing his fingers through his hair, face lined with misery. "My colors didn't come with me. They got so lost in the pills and the black, and now I can't make anything."

"Hey." I tug his fingers away from his hair, wincing at how hard he's pulling. "Hey, it's okay."

"No, it's not." He shakes his head. "I let you go."

The red rimming his eyes makes my chest throb. "I didn't hang on, either," I insist, remembering how impossible and hopeless it felt. "The current was stronger than us."

He gives the tattoo another assessing stare, knitting our fingers together. "Not anymore." When he meets my gaze, his eyes are as bright and alive as the moon. "I won't let you go again, Vinny."

I don't forgive easily. Not my sister. Definitely not my father. But I've made exceptions before. The man in front of me deserves some grace and as long as he's willing to try, I'm willing to give it to him.

As MUCH AS I love the library, and yes, the scent of paperbacks is as warm and comforting as a pumpkin spice latte in early fall, sitting at a table in a 4th floor study room with the other house girls takes away the charm.

The door is closed for privacy, but a glass window spreads across the front wall, giving all five of us the sporadic view of passing students. The itchy feeling on my neck, the tension around us thick enough to cut with a knife, tells me this is good. If any shit goes down, there will be witnesses.

"Is everyone clear on their roles?" Story asks, looking around the table. She's spent the last ten minutes detailing our responsibilities.

Once again, I have both Verity and Story to thank for not looking like a complete idiot in front of the other house girls. Turns out, Bianca, the former Duchess, was the primary organizer of this event last year. Verity had all the details in a notebook stashed in Mama B's office, although I feel that same twinge of guilt, knowing she only had it because she was meant to be in my place.

Regina nods, her long, glossy black fingernails clicking over the keyboard on her phone. She's quiet, barely saying a word, but she's also not disagreeable about anything. Maybe she's never allowed to be. Then again, maybe she's just pissed at me for orchestrating the hostage thing between Sy and Maddox. I'd called Ballsack myself, using Nick's phone, and made sure the whole plan went off without any harm coming to her.

"*Make sure Regina knows,*" I told Ballsack, "*that this was my idea, and that she has my word as a Royal that we won't hurt her.*"

Looking at her now, the way she pointedly avoids my gaze, maybe that little tip-off didn't gain me as much civility as I'd hoped. After everything I've learned about the Barons over the last few weeks, from the night in the crypt with Nick to learning the truth about Maddox, the more curious I am.

"Do you think Autumn has the details from last year?" Piper, the Princess, asks from the seat next to mine. She looks like a neurotic Barbie doll. Massive chest. Tiny waist. Chestnut hair pulled up into a tight, slicked-back, fluffy ponytail. Not exactly sure how she's supposed to get a baby past those narrow hips. "My time is pretty limited right now and the last thing I need is more stress."

Stressed is exactly how she looks, eyes going constantly to her phone. The crown ring on her finger gleams silver every time she smooths back her hair, something a Princess is only given when she conceives.

As much as I want to know about the Baroness, I'm perfectly fine staying in the dark about the Princess. What I do know is that the role is coveted. Girls all across Forsyth, from freshmen to post-grad, all pray for the chance to produce the next PNZ heir. But if Wicker Ashby is an example of the kind of fuckboy pedigree that comes with the opportunity, then God help her.

"You can try," Story says, frowning at the mention of last year's Princess. I remember Autumn from the night Felix was killed, and I rescued Archie from that shithole apartment. "I know she's still local." Story shifts her focus across the table. "Sutton, we good?"

I stiffen to realize Sutton is staring vacantly at me from across the table, her fingers either scratching at the scabs on her forearm or twisting in the necklace around her neck. She hasn't spoken since she got here, although she did kick the leg of my chair on the way to her seat.

"Sutton," Story says again, this time louder.

The Countess' eyes snap up, making the rings underneath more noticeable. "Yeah. Beer and food. Whatever."

The rest of us exchange wary looks. Beer and food are mandatory for any successful event, but for a crowd of college students? It's an absolute necessity.

"If you need some help," Story says in a forced, polite tone, "I'm sure we can adjust the plan."

Sutton's eyes flare with anger. "What I need is for someone to rein in her psycho boyfriend."

I look around the table. To be fair, any one of us can be accused of having a 'psycho boyfriend', but when her eyes snap to mine, it's clear who she's talking about. *What* she's talking about. Although we also all know there's zero actual proof Nick killed anyone. Thanks to the fucking Barons.

"North Side is crumbling, you'll be happy to know." Sutton gives me a flat, humorless smile. "Charity work isn't exactly a priority to us right now."

"Why?" Regina snaps, abandoning her phone. "Because the drug trade is more profitable?"

"Fuck off, Elvira," Sutton says, but doesn't deny it. She shifts her gaze back to me, clearly not finished, and flashes a winning smile. "Duchess, you're on rides and entertainment, right?"

I nod, not sure where this is going.

"Well, you should probably switch jobs with the Lady," she gestures to Story, "because last year, Bianca lost her deposit from all the blood and semen she and her Lords left in the goddamn fun house."

I had actually seen something about that in the margins of Bianca's notes.

Story's cheeks turn red, and she stands, slamming her palms on the table. "You're lucky that blood didn't belong to *your* psycho boyfriend! After what Perez did to me, he deserved worse!"

Sutton and I hop up at the same time, her to lunge over the table at Story, me to stop her. The Princess cowers in her seat, hands clutched over her flat stomach, while Regina slinks back in hers, eyeing the show.

"Look," I say, voice low. "Perez was living a reckless life, and it finally caught up to him. It happens and you know it." Looking around the table, I lock eyes with the other girls, adding, "It could be one of ours someday, and we know that, too." Ignoring how my stomach churns at the thought, I lock eyes with Sutton. "I'm sorry you lost someone who belonged to you, Countess. But North Side isn't my concern anymore, so if it's crumbling, then it's up to you and whatever's left of my father's degenerate lapdogs to fix it."

For the first time since the meeting started, I see a small glimmer of recognition in her eyes, and it legitimately startles me. Sutton is in deeper than I ever knew, pumped up on Scratch and barely functioning. Her fingers drop to her neck, scratching red streaks in her pale skin. "I'm not dealing with a bunch of traitors and whores," she says, turning abruptly and walking out of the room. "I'm out."

The room is quiet for a moment until the Princess sighs. "Does that mean one of us has to deal with the booze?"

"I'll do it," Story says, still glaring in Sutton's wake. "Us whores have whorehouses, and the Velvet Hideaway already has a liquor license."

"I'll help," I offer, edging away from the table. The less time with these girls, the better. "I need to get everything together for the alumni poker game, anyway."

Regina and Piper hop up and quickly leave, probably hoping they don't get roped into more work. I gather my things while Story's phone buzzes and she shoots off a quick text.

"Hey." I reluctantly stop her before we leave the room. "Should we.. do something about Sutton?"

Story's head tilts, brows furrowed in confusion. "Why would we?" she asks. "She doesn't exactly pose much of a risk without her attack dog."

I shrug, balancing my notebooks. "I don't know. Maybe because my family is part of the reason she's... like that."

She doesn't look any less confused. "Like what?"

Awkwardly, I reply, "Addicted to Viper Scratch. Countess to a dead Royal. Victim of a crumbling territory?"

Story deflates, eyes sympathetic. "You were right before, Lavinia. North Side isn't your problem any more than it's mine, or Piper's, or Regina's. Take it from someone with some pretty heavy baggage in this department." She gives me a significant look. "Your parents' sins aren't yours to answer for. North Side is going to sink or swim, and I think both of us agree which option we're rooting for."

"I wouldn't say I'm rooting for it," I say, although the denial is weak. At Story's baffled expression, I try to explain. "Look, my sister could have been her. Hell, I could have been her."

Story argues, "But you aren't. You're you. Duchess to three chaos goblins, leader of cutsluts, the hot talk of West End and apparently a pretty scrappy fighter to boot." She pauses, eyes narrowing. "Until I take your ass down on Screw Year's Eve, that is. I *am* the reigning bitch."

I bark a dry laugh, following her out. "Oh, Lady. I'm going to make you eat those words with so much Jell-O."

She glances at me over her shoulder. "Hey, we could always throw it. Give them a show and make out at the end?" Her wink makes me laugh a little more genuinely.

"I can't decide which of my Dukes would have an aneurysm or cream their pants."

Story shoots me a wry smirk. "Well, we both know where on that spectrum Tristian would fall." She jabs a thumb toward the elevator, where I'm only now noticing her Lord, Killian Payne, is waiting. "That one, however..." She rolls her eyes.

I eye him. The bulking mass. The crazy laser-eyes he has for her. The aggressive, borderline-hostile posture. "He's the psycho boyfriend, huh?"

She walks backward, smiling. "All day, and definitely all night. Later, Lav!"

"Later," I say, but the second she turns, I bring a palm down on her ass, fighting a smile at the scandalized look she throws at me.

"Traitor."

"Whore."

She flips me the bird as she saunters up to Killian, whose crazy laser-eyes are very close to jumping right out of his sockets. He looks between us before finally pinning her with a stare, hauling Story into the open elevator. I can't hear what he says when he ducks down, whispering into her ear, but before the doors slide closed, I catch her deep, scarlet blush, his hand reaching down to grip a hard handful of the ass cheek I just whacked. Right as the doors meet, I see a flash of his kiss, just as aggressive as the rest of him.

Twenty bucks and my pistol says they're going to fuck in that elevator.

A flicker of emotion sparks in my belly at the thought.

Envy.

Not because of the sex. God, no. I have three men fulfilling every desire I could possibly dream up. No, I'm envious of the fact she stepped into that elevator without falling apart. Just watching the doors shut makes my heart hammer anxiously and a sheen of sweat coat the back of my neck.

Maybe that's why I asked her about Sutton. Story was right about us both wanting to see North Side fall, but I still carry a part of it inside me, like a festering infection. Until I get rid of it, North Side will always carry a part of me, too.

My phone vibrates, jarring me from my thoughts.

Nick: You done? Just saw Sutton storm out the front doors.

Lav: Yep.

Nick: Hurry.

Rolling my eyes, I head toward the emergency stairs, moving quickly. I'm perfectly aware that Nick is starting to lose patience with our time apart. I keep expecting him to start shit with one of the others, because recently–if briefly–Nick had me all to himself, and now he has to share. But it's not like that.

It's like *this*.

I start to text him again, to let him know I'm on my way down, when the door to the stairwell opens and I'm pulled inside.

"Beat you," Nick says, arm sliding around my waist.

"Jesus, you scared me." My shoulders loosen a little, but my heart hasn't settled from the surprise.

"Sorry," he says, not looking sorry at all. "Time's up."

My pulse thrums as he leans in, mouth meeting mine in a sharp, bruising kiss. The split in my lip is still tender, but I hardly feel the throb when he coaxes my lips apart, sliding his hot tongue between them.

Being with Nick is always a swooping thrill, like dropping from the highest point of a rollercoaster for the very first time, and I'm just happy to be along for the ride. The feel of his hands on me, the pressure against my tense muscles, and the invasion of my mouth is all secondary to what's driving it. The growl I can feel building in his throat, the way his hands keep moving from my tits to my ass, back to my face, like he wants to consume me all at once–it buzzes with a frantic need.

Nick once said no one could ever want me as much as he does.

That's exactly how being with him feels.

It makes my prior anxiety slip away, hot arousal taking its place. I groan in approval, arching into his body, and he hums in response.

"You missed me too, didn't you?" he asks, tipping my chin up to mouth at my throat.

"Yes." I flatten my hands on his chest, running them down to the hard muscle of his abdomen. I stop at his buckle, panting as he sucks a painful bruise into my neck, and then begin clawing it open. Tugging at the waistband, I shove my hand inside to reach for his cock, finding it hard and radiating heat. "And this," I whisper, stroking the length.

He shudders, forehead landing on mine. "Shit, Lavinia." His cock swells in my hand, sparking warmth in my lower belly, but nothing is hotter than the way he's looking at me, hooded and desperate.

I touch the sticky precum gathering on his tip, spreading it messily over the head of his cock. "I want to feel you in me, Nick."

My request triggers something. I sense it in his rippling muscles, his clutching hands, the way his pupils blow wide, leaving nothing but the barest ring of blue. His face goes hard and intent, and then he's grabbing the hem of my skirt and yanking up the fabric.

My breath catches as he wrenches my panties aside, eyes boring into me as his fingers trail over my clit. "Oh, fuck," I breathe, knees wobbling.

"This," he rumbles, fingers finding the slickness building in my folds, "is never off limits to me. You're mine now, Little Bird. Do you understand what that means?"

I nod absently, fervently. He could ask me to magically grow a third tit and I'd probably agree when he's looking at me like this, so unbearably intense. But when I say, "I understand," I'm telling the truth. Giving myself to Nick wasn't something I did lightly. A person doesn't chain themselves to an atomic bomb without considering

the ramifications. "You don't want a third of me," I say, driving this home. "You want it all."

The lines on his face slowly ease, punctuated by my measured tugs on his cock. "So long as we're clear." His mouth crashes against mine, a groan reverberating between us, and I forget to consider how there simply isn't enough of me to go around. Instead, I get lost in his rough whisper. "Fuck, I love how wet you get for me. Your pussy knows who it belongs to, doesn't it?"

Liquid heat pools between my legs and he tears his mouth away, spinning me around to bend over the rail. My ass juts out, pressing against his crotch.

"Hold on to that railing, Little Bird," he tells me. I comply, wrapping my hands around the cool metal, listening to the sound of his zipper lowering. A second later, I feel the sticky tip of his cock slotting between my legs. I spread open, giving him access to my entrance, where he nudges at my pussy. "That's my girl."

My back arches and his hands grab my hips, lifting my body as he guides himself inside with a quick, impatient punch.

"*Ah!*" I gasp, surging forward. The rail hits my abdomen, and my knuckles turn white against the black painted metal. I relish the feel of him inside, the push of his cock expanding against my walls. I look over my shoulder and beg, "Deeper."

His hand shoots outward, wrapping around my neck, tilting my face so he can kiss me. His tongue burns hot in my mouth as he rocks his hips, dragging his cock out before slamming in again. "What did you two do last night?" he asks.

Biting down on a cry, my body jolts with another thrust. "We fucked."

"Where?"

"At the gym," I answer.

A gritty rumble escapes his throat, and then his hand dips down, fingers trailing down the cleft of my ass. "I meant *where*," he says, fingertip pushing into the rim of my asshole.

I freeze, eyes widening. "Not *there!*"

Dragging his hips back, he drives me into the rail with another slam of his hips. The force of our bodies meeting sinks the tip of his forefinger into my ass, making me hiss. Nick's breath washes over the shell of my ear. "You know he wants it, don't you? This pretty little ass of yours taking his cock."

"He's mentioned it," I say, feeling Nick swelling inside me, his fingertip teasing at my rim.

He can feel me, too. "Fuck," he groans, slamming a hand over mine on the rail. "Your pussy's getting so wet for this. You'd like it, wouldn't you?"

The truth is, if Nick had asked me that ten minutes ago, I would have said no. Now, I'm spreading my thighs for him, neck straining as I gulp in large, hungry breaths. "Deeper," I demand, shoving my hips back. It makes his finger sink inside my ass, my belly erupting with rabid flutters. "Oh, god, Nick..."

His breath is just as quick and stilted as mine, and he lets loose a deranged rumble into my ear. "You better come fast, Little Bird, because I'm not gonna last much longer."

The command spurs me on, and I bear down on his cock. It's his turn to gasp, and he pours all of that desire into the slam of his hips, fucking me out of any other emotion that isn't about him. My pussy clenches, tightening its grip around his cock. True to his word, the instant the orgasm rips through me, Nick grabs onto my hips and drops his forehead to the base of my neck, shuddering to his own release.

I cling to the railing, legs wobbly and numb. Without removing his cock, he wraps his arms around my body and kisses my neck. He asks, "That's all you did? Just fucked at the gym?"

He almost sounds... disappointed.

"No," I answer truthfully. "I tattooed him, and then we went to sleep."

Nick's breath stutters, arms tightening. "He let you–you inked him? Like, real ink, not a marker or–"

"A real tattoo," I confirm, still winded and dazed. Fucking Nick Bruin is better than I imagine what it's like to take Scratch. My muscles are loose, my breathing unsteady, not out of panic but exertion.

He kisses me again and pulls out, immediately dipping his fingers between my legs to catch any cum dripping down my thighs. I squirm against him as he pushes it back inside, fingers warm in my pussy.

"He's never let anyone do that before," he says, fucking his cum back into me. On one of these finger thrusts, he catches another drip and gently eases it into my asshole with his finger. When I tense, hissing his name, he just coaxes me back down, sliding the tip of his digit past the ring of muscle. "I want one," he says, voice husky and dark.

It takes a moment to get my jaw unlocked. "One what?"

"A tattoo," he answers, voice lost in thought as he fingers my ass. "You should mark me up, Little Bird."

I finally wiggle my hips, nudging his hand away. "You're jealous of the weirdest things, Nick Bruin." Maybe that's a part of why we work–two youngest siblings grasping for what we're owed.

He watches me with dark eyes as I shimmy my panties back up, stepping forward to hem me in against the rail. "I'm drawing a line," he says, eyes glued to my mouth. "I sleep where you sleep. Pick a bed–I don't care whose. Mine. Sy's. Remy's. Sleep in the Archduke's little kitty bed for all I care, but I'm going to be there with you." His mouth hovers over mine, blue eyes pinging back and forth to capture every inch of my gaze. "Understand?"

I understand.

And more than that?

I'm thrilled.

12

S ^y

"YOU WERE RIGHT." I glance over at Lavinia as I shift gears, her eyes tracking a raindrop's descent on the passenger window. It's barely more than a sprinkle now, my Trans-Am rumbling like an animal beneath us.

"Of course I was," she says, turning to blink at me. "But what specifically was I right about?"

Trying to keep my attention on the road, I answer, "The pill bottles being orange. I've been putting them into a white organizer, and I think it's helping." Remy never told me he was struggling with it, and just because I'm determined to let him stand on his own two feet doesn't mean I haven't been keeping tabs. He's taken his medication every day, faithfully. But some days he's been lingering in the bathroom longer than others.

It's hard not being the shadow looming behind him all the time. Two straight years of schedules, check-ins, and hovering is a hard habit to break. It'd be a lie to say I don't lay awake some nights, wondering where he is, how he's faring, when he's going to need help next.

"Good." Her mouth tips up into a pleased grin. "That's... good." She tugs down the hem of her skirt, seeming distracted, but I can't really blame her. I'd sprung this trip on her from out of nowhere, catching her just after class. "Where are we going?" she asks, surveying the landmarks.

"Do you trust me?" I glimpse at her, knowing it's vague and pushy. She might think it's a fun surprise and then get really fucking disappointed.

Although her eyebrows pull together in curiosity, she replies with no hesitation. "Yes."

My chest thuds harder at the easy agreement.

So I keep on the path, heading to the outskirts of town, toward the grassy hill that overlooks Forsyth. She shifts in her seat, drawing my eyes to her legs. The bandages on her knees are gone, but the wounds are still a vivid, half-healed pink.

When she realizes where we are, she looks from the window to me.

"You brought me to the cemetery?"

I don't answer, turning into the narrow drive. Like the rest of the town, it's divided into four quadrants, with the crypt looming ominously in the middle. In some ways, it's safe to say the roots of the Royal houses start here, running deep from the decayed bones of our ancestors, generations of Royalty, to the rest of the town. The ropy vines run like a current, spreading down the streets, connecting businesses and communities, all leading to a breeding ground at the University.

I drive slowly, passing the different sections, marked by stone walls or wrought iron barriers. I come to the junction of north and west and stop, idling. To the north, it's impossible to ignore the large marble Lucia family stone in the distance marking her ancestors' plot. It's too far away to see from our foggy windows, but I know from my earlier visit that her mother's name is engraved in the white surface, along with dozens of other distant relatives.

To our left, on a slight hill, is an arch made of iron, the name 'Bruin' curled across the top. Next to me, Lavinia is uncharacteristically quiet. I turn, the leather creaking under my movements.

"I know what it's like to think I've lost a brother," I begin, remembering there was a time I'd stay awake worrying about someone other than Remy. It was both better and worse with Nick. I didn't see him enough for certain fears to take hold, but the unknown was almost harder, the possibilities of what he'd be doing in South Side endless. "I didn't—but if I did, I know I'd want to bring him home." I look out at the gravestones. Some are tall and regal, monoliths to honor Royalty like her. Others are simple and squat, some just flat and flush with the earth. There's no equalizer greater than death. "Or as close to it as possible."

"This is about Leticia," she guesses, following my gaze.

"This is about you." I take my hand from the gearshift and place it over hers, resting on her knee. "You don't have to be a psych major to know there are five stages of grief. You really didn't get a chance to process your sister's death, and we can't—" I stop, not wanting to make this moment about Leticia's murder. "I don't know who killed her, but I can do this for you. I can help you lay her to rest." I look between the family crests. "If that's what you want, you can pick which ground you want to lay her in."

A flicker runs across her expression. I've seen it before. It's the panic of having a voice. Whenever Lavinia is given a choice, she freezes for a moment, uncertain of how to decide.

I wait patiently.

"That's not her home," she says quietly. "Leticia wasn't a Bruin."

"No," I agree, thinking of my old friend. "But she was Tate's, and Tate was ours. Her parents took mine up on the offer to have her buried here, so she'd be with friends." I grip the steering wheel with my left hand, knowing this must be overstepping. "If you think that's what she was to Leticia–a home–then we can bury her there. But, if you think it's what your sister would want, we can place her next to your mother instead." I look to the North, knowing it's a bit riskier, disturbing Lucia soil. Not that it matters. I might not belong in that section of the cemetery, but Lavinia and her sister do. I'll fight for their right to be there if I have to.

She thinks for a long moment, eyes focused on the marble headstone signaling the short life of Emily Lucia. "No," she says with an exhale. "You're right. She deserves some peace. Something my father could never give her. This is..." Her fingers wind in mine. "This is right. Isn't it?"

I gaze into her questioning eyes, giving a nod. "I think so."

I'm prepared. While Lavinia is wrapping her sweater around herself, I get out and round the back of the car, removing a small, watertight box from the trunk. The skull, the only remaining part of Leticia we have, is securely sealed inside. I pluck out the bouquet of flowers resting next to it, and when Lavinia appears, I hand them to her.

She takes the flowers, pressing her nose to the petals. "Blue again," she notices, eyes soft and somber.

I scratch my neck, gesturing to them. "Remy said I should." Idly, I wonder how long it's going to take him to realize that blue means something more to him than just calm and trust.

Last, I grab the shovel.

"So we can just... dig?" she asks, looking around. We're alone, the sky gray and wet, casting the cemetery in a cold shroud of mist. No funerals or visitors today.

"You can if you pay off the caretaker." I close the trunk, assuring her, "The family knows. Dad, Pops, and Mom are all good with this."

She frowns, hugging herself against a gust of wind. "They're really okay with a Lucia crashing your family's eternal life?"

I tighten my hold on the box tucked under my arm. "They're okay with Tate being with someone she loved," I venture, which is mostly the truth. The other part is that they know Lavinia must be more to us than a mere Duchess if I'm willing to go to all this trouble. I gesture toward the iron gate in the distance, ducking my head as I walk. "My parents don't buy into this bloodline thing the way other Royals do, Lavinia. Tate was our family, just like Remy is."

When we arrive at the graves, I find her there. *Tatum Grady*. Her headstone is a smooth black granite, etched with the date of her birth and death. I stare at it for a long moment, thinking of the last time I was here, six months after her funeral. Nick was gone. Remy was barely himself. I was bruised and swollen from the fight I'd just won at a random bar, drowning my misery in a bottle of shitty malt liquor. Everything was so fractured and hopeless back then, and I find myself wanting to tell Tate everything.

This is Lavinia, I want to say. *She put the parts of us we couldn't find back together.*

But when I glance over, she's staring at Tate's grave with a pale, drawn expression. "This is her?"

I nod, nudging the ground beside her grave with the tip of the shovel. "I was thinking here. They'd be close."

Lavinia's throat jumps with a swallow and she crouches, fingers plucking a single blue flower from the bouquet. I watch silently as she places it on Tate's headstone, the mist clinging to her powdery blue hair like glitter. "Thank you." At first, I think she's thanking Tate, but then she looks up, meeting my gaze. "And thank them for me, too. Your parents."

Clearing my throat, I shrug. "You're welcome." I don't tell her I'm doing it for Tate as well, because I'm not sure how to explain it. Tate and Leticia had something. Maybe she felt the same way about Leticia as I feel about Lavinia, and it cuts at my mind that Tate hid it from me–from us. Whatever she needed, some facet of trust that wasn't there, I figure I can give her this. Some small, ultimately meaningless gesture of acceptance.

She's silent as I dig, my shovel cutting into the earth. I'd waited until a day like this, the ground wet and soft after a night of rain, to finally come out here. It helps that things back at the tower are more settled, Remy attending his classes and support group, while Nick tends to higher stakes DKS duties. This is exactly what I've needed. Something real. Something useful.

It's been a long time since I didn't have someone else to worry about.

The mud clings to my boots, and halfway through, I strip off my jacket and overshirt, handing both to Lavinia before returning to the task. I'm hit with the sudden curiosity of what they may have been like–Lavinia and Tate–if they'd ever met.

The thought is both tragic and terrifying.

When I'm done, I stab the shovel into the mound of upturned dirt, turning to her.

"This should be deep enough."

She hasn't said one word and I search her eyes, wondering if I'm fucking this up. It's still a mystery to me how Nick and Remy can just... *be* with her so easily. Every time I try something like this, my palms sweat. My chest feels too tight. My mind runs a mile a second, always questioning.

So when she begins trying to open that box, I jolt. "You don't have to–"

Her eyes fly to mine. "It doesn't make sense, does it? She was such a bitch to me, but... I can't do it." Her fingers unlatch the box, revealing the skull inside. "I can't just leave her in this box."

My heart falls into my stomach as I watch her crouch down, placing the box on the dirt. "I'm sorry. I wasn't thinking." A fucking cemetery. Really? Bring the girl with pathological claustrophobia to a place where all the bodies are in boxes. *Real smooth, shithead.* Sighing, I offer, "You're giving her something she never gave you. But..." I hold her eyes, almost unable to bear the strange, panicked misery swimming within them. "Boxes aren't always bad, Lav. It'll protect her."

She glances down at the skull, teeth worrying at her lip. "You don't think it's cruel?"

"The things that were done to you..." I stall, trying to find the right words. "Leticia probably had her own demons."

There's a moment where she just stares at the skull. And then, "Leticia had the chance to take her freedom. Maybe if she'd had someone to protect her like I do, she would have kept it." Slowly, she closes the box. "You're right."

Still, she springs up, like she might change her mind at any moment. That's the only reason I act swiftly, lowering it into the hole.

Brushing my hands off, I ask, "Do you want a minute alone? I can go wait in—"

"Stay." Her hand clamps on my forearm. "Please."

Like there's any fucking way I could say no to her. "Of course."

"When I was ten," she's staring down at the box, clutching the flowers to her stomach. For a second, I'm not sure if she's talking to me or Leticia, her face so set and blank. "Dad put out two tables across from one another. Each filled with duplicate weapons. Pistols, revolvers, shotguns, and a box of mixed-up bullets. He stood at the end, set the timer, and told us the first one to get each one fully loaded with the right bullets would be the winner." Her voice catches, eyes sliding away. "You won. *Of course*, you won. And I spent the next twenty-four hours in the chest." Her brows pull together, eyes beginning to brim with a shiny wetness. "For a long time, I thought that was your fault. But now I understand that, like me, you were just trying to survive. While he was breaking me down, he was building you up for a life just as miserable."

When a tear finally spills over, she angrily swats it away. I pull a handkerchief out of my pocket, pressing it in her hand, and she stares at it in surprise before going on.

"With all the lies and secrets and competitions, we never had any hope of being sisters. *Real* sisters. I always figured that made us less like family, but here's the thing, Tish. No one in the world could ever understand what it was like to grow up as a Lucia but the two of us. Maybe that's the realest sisterhood of all." She chuckles darkly. "It took me a long time, but I realize now that's why Dad pitted us against one another. Because he knew that together we were stronger than him." She shifts, her shoulders squaring. "But what he didn't understand then, and doesn't under-stand now, is all the abuse, the challenges, the belittlement... it *did* make me stronger, Tish. Strong enough for the both of us." Her hand finds mine, cold fingers threading through mine. "I'm sorry I never got to meet Tate. I'm sorry you had to run away and didn't feel like you could come to me for help. I'm sorry that our father is a sociopathic monster who cares more about money and power than his own family." Her tears fall faster now, and she makes no attempt to stop them. When she speaks next, it's full of resolve. "We *will* find out who killed you and Tate, and we'll make them pay. But I promise you, big sister, Dad is going to find out just what kind of Lucia girls he's raised."

She inhales deeply, and I press a kiss to her temple, my own throat feeling tight. "That was perfect."

In the middle of the graveyard, a murder of crows surveys us from the crypt as we cover the box with layers of dirt, their caws setting our rhythm. When there's nothing left but a mound that doesn't quite fit back in, Lavinia bends, resting the bouquet of flowers on the soft soil. When she straightens, she leans into me, and it doesn't matter that I was the one who did all the physical labor.

She's the more exhausted of the two of us.

Wrapping my arms around her body, I tuck her into me, ignoring the way her little body is shaking. "You're right, you know," I say, watching as the crows depart, their wings flapping in the mist as they fade into the distance. "All that pain and suffering made you strong. Probably the strongest woman I know, and hell, I know Mama B."

She takes a deep breath, her back expanding against my forearms, and then tips her head back to meet my gaze. "Thank you for doing this for me," she says, eyelids fluttering when I thumb away her tears. "I've been trying to find out how I could forgive her, and now…"

"I know," I say, thinking of Nick and all the hurt he's caused. "Family can feel like that sometimes."

"Sometimes," she agrees, ducking her head as she wipes her face.

I take her hand and lead her down the path to the car, clutching my jacket and the shovel awkwardly in front of me. The mist is lifting now, a single ray of anemic sunlight limping through the clouds overhead as I open the door for her.

I have a stern talk with myself, jaw tight as I stand over the trunk, breathing hard. Our eyes meet in the rearview mirror when I slam the hatch, and I don't think I've ever felt so bare, my nerves zinging as I hobble toward my door, wrenching it open. When I drop into the driver's seat, Lavinia turns to me with shrewd, assessing eyes.

"You know, you're not too bad at this boyfriend thing," she says, giving me a soft, tired smile.

I don't know what it is. Maybe it's the emotional upheaval of the last hour, and trying so hard to hold it together. Maybe seeing Tate's grave dug up too many memories. Maybe when Lavinia looks at me like this, it just makes me feel like scum.

Either way, I can't hold it in anymore.

"I'm fucking terrible," I burst, fisting my jacket as I lift it off my lap. I point to the obscene bulge hiding beneath. "Would a good boyfriend get a fucking boner at a funeral?"

Her eyes drop to my crotch, narrowing. "Well... I've read that emotional stimuli can–"

I don't let her finish. "I lied to you, Lavinia."

A little of the reclaimed brightness fades in her eyes. "About what?"

I open my mouth, but the words are lodged in my throat. It's a struggle to speak, not for any physical reason, although I'd blame it on that if I could. No, this is something I've held onto for so long that saying it out loud—acknowledging it—admitting it, feels like pushing a boulder up a mountain.

Clutching the steering wheel so hard my knuckles turn white, I train my eyes ahead, too cowardly to look her in the eye. "I talk about being in control all the time, feeding you that bullshit about not being able to stop myself once it gets past a certain point." In my periphery, I can see her watching, her gaze like a painful point of heat on my face. "But it's all a lie. The truth–the real truth I haven't had the guts to face–is that I like how it feels to lose control. To punch someone in the face. To win. To claim." I finally turn, finding the courage to meet her confused stare. "I could have stopped that night, Lavinia. I just didn't want to."

It sounds bad when I've spoken the words, somehow worse than the revelation felt in my head, and that's saying a lot. It's the reason I left that night, turning my back on her, Nick, Remy, and DKS. Running away. I couldn't face the truth of it, which is that I had something *so fucking good* and I ruined it with this creeping, writhing selfishness inside of me.

A shudder runs through her, and I stiffen, preparing myself for the tears. The screams. The slap. The kick. I'd deserve it.

Instead, she laughs.

It's a quiet, mirthless sound, her mouth twisting into a wry purse. "Yeah, Big Bear. I know."

"You... know." I repeat.

She shrugs. "Did I ever for one second buy that you have some uncontrollable beast inside of you?" She gives me an obvious look. "Not even remotely. I guess I was just waiting for you to figure it out yourself."

Lamely, I say, "Oh."

That's the response to my big confession? The open admission to my greatest flaw? *She knows?*

Quieter, she adds, "I can see it in your face, Sy. I can feel it on your skin when you give in, sparking like electricity. You do have control, but you love losing it. Being selfish, letting go, taking something for yourself... it's a rush." Her eyes drop to her lap. "It's how you escape your box."

It's probably the most scared I've ever felt, realizing Lavinia Lucia knows more about me than I do myself. "Well, shit." I run my hand through my hair. "Guess that wasn't such a revelation then."

Now I feel like both an asshole *and* an idiot.

"But it's a revelation to you," she says, reaching out to curl her palm over my strained knuckles. "I don't need an apology, Sy. Trust isn't built on expensive dinners and pretty words. Those aren't what I've been waiting for. All I've needed is *this.*"

I swallow thickly, hypnotized by her flowery scent. "Really?"

She looks at where her thumb is stroking over my fingers. "It's easy to blame your weaknesses on something you think is unchangeable. A sickness. A biological flaw in how your brain is wired. But Sy, you're not Remy. There's nothing wrong with you that can't be changed."

The words strike a chord that guts me, because she's more right than she knows. Watching Remy these past two weeks has made it painfully obvious that it wouldn't matter anyway. Even with his disorder, he still fights, and anyone who fights still has a chance of winning.

I have no excuse.

"And you believe I have?" I ask, heart thudding hard. "Changed?"

She doesn't answer.

Not with words.

Suddenly, she's climbing over the gearshift, my hands flying up as she straddles my lap.

"What are you–?" My words are cut off with her kiss, lips eager and demanding against mine.

My dick is hard—it has been since she kissed me. With one hand I push her hair back over her shoulder, thumb stroking the column of her neck, and with the other I extend the seat, making room for the two of us. Her hips rock forward, and I groan. We're so close, noses an inch apart, and I see the want in her eyes. The *need.* But...

"Lav."

Two spots of color rise on her cheeks, tongue licking out to wet her lips. "I can't fuck you right now, because it'd probably take a lot of time and practice and patience."

"I know," I say, grimacing from the feel of her pressing down on my cock. "I'm not–you don't have to–"

She plucks another long, wet kiss from my lips, whispering

against them. "That doesn't mean I don't want you." But she takes it further, grabbing my fingers and pushing them between her legs, beneath her skirt. I go where she leads, following far enough to reluctantly tuck my fingers beneath lacy elastic.

I bite out a low, "Fuck," chasing her mouth when she leans back to give me more room. My girl is wet, slick under her cotton panties. Shuddering, I yank them aside and finger her folds, asking, "Like this?"

She lets out a hitched breath, nodding, and I surge forward, capturing her lips with mine. Our tongues slide together, and I feel it, burning beneath the surface like napalm.

God, I just want to let go.

I settle for pushing stiltedly at her sweater, asking in a gravelly voice, "What are the rules?" She helps me lift the sweater over her head, brows crushing inward when I begin palming hungrily at her tits, daring to hook my fingers in the top of her bra, fisting. My breath comes so quick and loud that I feel the tips of my ears burn in embarrassment. "You have to tell me. How far?"

She pauses for a second, staring at me with heavy, sex-fogged eyes, and it just makes it all so much worse.

But also so much better.

"I want to ride your cock," she finally tells me, pushing higher on her knees. Her eyes are dark and full of want, and when she tugs at my shirt, I'm powerless to do anything but tear it over my head. "I want to feel you against me."

I reply unthinkingly, breathlessly. "Yeah, baby, I want that, too." It takes me a long moment to realize why she's hovering there, and I jolt in surprise as I get with the program, reaching down to tear my belt open. I watch her carefully as I pop the button, shoving my jeans down my hips, but she doesn't look afraid.

She glances down at it and licks her lips.

"Shit." My cock jerks eagerly in my hand, and I grip the base, hissing as the tip grazes her inner thigh.

It isn't until she contorts herself, working her panties down her legs, baring her pussy beneath her skirt, that I realize where this is going. It's an agonizing tease. Even the radiating heat of her is enough to make my cock give a surge of precum.

Her lips fall to my shoulder, hot and unbearably sensual, but it's the scrape of her teeth that sends a wave of blood to my cock.

I pull aside the cup of her bra and drop my mouth to her nipple, licking and sucking, tugging at it until her back arches, driving her pussy down. She said *against*, not *in*, and despite the tease of it, I'm more than willing to make that happen. I guide my cock across her folds, spreading her wetness from front to back.

Her shoulders jerk with a shudder, voice low and strained. "Do that again," she says, and I rut up against her, realizing my dick is long enough that it nudges at her backside. She *mewls*. "Yes, *that*. God, Sy, your cock." She gasps, looking overwhelmed and almost as tortured as I feel. "I can feel you everywhere."

Her praise spurs me on, and I grab her ass, spreading her cheeks wide enough to bury the sensitive tip in her soft, sweet flesh, hitting her clit to tail.

Fuck.

Her cunt is like slick, liquid fire against my cock, and I grip her hips hard just to keep her still.

"Wait," I urge, mouthing against her warm cheek. "Let me feel it..."

If I were a better man, I'd look back on that night at the party—my first time being inside a woman—and feel nothing but disgust because of the way I behaved. I'm not a better man, though. With my cock nestled in her folds, her hips making these little hitching rolls against it, all I feel is disappointed that it couldn't be good. Our breaths have fogged the windows, her forehead tipping to rest against mine, and I can see how we're supposed to be. Me and her, not her and Remy, or her and Nick.

Lavinia and I were made to be like *this*. Tender and careful, her hips rolling against mine in a slow rhythm. Her tits rock with every thrust and her nails tug at the hair at the base of my neck. There's a sense of inhibition, something that's never transpired between us. Trust? Grief? Abject horniness? There's no lesson here. No justification. I want her and she wants me. Whatever emotion she's riding, I chase it, matching her pace, her movements, her desire.

Do I want to fuck her?

Hell yes.

So badly that my bones ache from holding back.

But more than that, I want this to last. I want her in my bed every night. I want her warm body pressed against mine. I know if I hurt her again, I'll lose her forever, so everything I do is about making her feel good.

Making her mine.

"Jesus, I'm not gonna last," I say, dropping my forehead to the crook of her neck. "You feel too fucking good."

She tugs my hair, forcing my eyes back to hers. "Don't hold back. Let go, Big Bear."

The command to unleash ripples through me. My hands clamp around her hips but it doesn't still the shudder running down her spine, or the muscles in her thighs from clamping around mine. I fall with her, exploding in the narrow channel between her legs, the hot, sticky cum binding us together.

The air in the car is hot. Sweaty skin. Shuddering breaths. It should be stifling but I feel like I'm gulping in fresh air for the first time in my life.

It's the result of letting go. Revelation.

It's the embodiment of us.

13

L avinia

"JUST, UH, SQUEEZE IN THERE." I pant, stretched to my limit. Sy grimaces, a bead of sweat trickling down his temple. "Can you reach?"

"If I shift like this, I can." His body moves like a contortionist. The problem is his size, obviously. That's always the problem with Simon Perilini. He's just so fucking huge. "Okay wait," he grunts, moving one last time. "How about this?"

"Yes! Oh my God, yes!" We grin at one another. "Okay, now just move your fingers a little..." His fingers flail around. "Almost, yes! That's it. Right there."

As his grip finds the right spot, I also get in position. Our gaze holds as I silently count to three and we move at the same time. He wraps his massive hand around the old crank handle as I flip the lever across the room.

The old metal wheezes to life.

Sy's muscles bulge as he gives it his all, the cog turning with a grinding noise as the mechanisms spin. Remy had a good point before about Sy being the strongest, and I see that strength now, his body rippling with it, eyes narrowed in determination. His white tank doesn't leave a lot to the imagination, and I get a little dazed as his biceps swell and shift. It's a struggle to move my gaze to the pendulum hanging down the center of the tower. I wait for the connectors to trip it off, to force them to swing but—

"Ugh!" I groan. "Are you fucking kidding me?"

Sy deflates while his chest heaves from exertion. Wiping the sheen of sweat from his forehead, he offers, "Want me to do it again?"

"No." I slump against the wall, resisting the urge to kick the closest thing. "Something's still wrong, and I don't want to force it." I point to the system overhead. "When you crank that, this whole section should connect into this other part, which should then propel the ropes that hold the pendulum, which *then* should make the hands move."

I thought if I got Sy to turn the crank, everything would get moving. But it only partially worked. I eye the area I'm convinced is the culprit. I searched high and low for the nut I finally got to fit, but now I'm not so sure.

Sy eases himself out of the tight area he had to wedge into in order to reach the lever and holds up his oily hands. "Well, I can say for certain we definitely used enough lube that time."

Remy pops his head through the door, gaze pinned to my face. "No luck?"

Shrugging, I answer, "Some. Sy got the crank to work, but it trips up around here." I point to the area I'm pretty sure is the problem, but my attention is diverted by the pull of Remy's shoulders as he slips into his motorcycle jacket. "What's up?"

"I'm headed to my meeting," he says, green eyes trained too intently on zipping up his jacket. "Just, uh, wanted to let everyone know."

He's been good about this. Communicating his comings and

goings. At first I thought it may be a good way to keep us from asking questions, but now I suspect having another layer of accountability makes him feel more secure.

Whatever he needs, we're happy to give it.

Sy dusts off his hands. "Cool. I think we're just going to stay in tonight." His blue eyes sweep to mine, face carefully blank. We talked about it yesterday, the drive home from the cemetery somehow both relaxed and buzzing with the tension of what comes next for us.

Nick announced this afternoon he has some business to take care of, and Remy has been going to meetings pretty consistently, so we saw the opportunity coming. It gives Sy and I a few hours to work on our other project.

"Definitely," I agree, not sure why my cheeks feel warm. Sex in this house is no secret. Their need for me, and frankly my need for them, is pretty well known, but it still feels strange to be so open about it. I give the lever a casual tap. "Just a quiet night at home alone."

"Sure, Vinny." Remy snorts, flashing me one of his panty-dropping smirks. "You keep pretending like you're not a screamer."

"I am not!" I shout, grabbing the first thing I come in contact with—one of the clock repair manuals—and toss it in his direction.

He snags it out of the air and tucks it under his arm, giving Sy a lazy salute. "Save some for me, brother."

"Hey, give that back," I demand, but Remy just grins and ducks back down the staircase. I throw my hands in the air. "Fucking *guys*, I swear!"

Sy stalks up, following my gaze, and says, "Forget him." Bracing his forearm on the low-hanging rod above my head, he reaches out to graze my hip with his greasy fingers. "Let's go make the most of a quiet house." Even though he's towering over me, hemming me in, his blue eyes simmer with playful anticipation. "You think we'll both fit in the shower?"

Nothing with Sy Perilini is an easy fit, but I strain up on my toes to press a kiss to his sweaty neck, delighting in the way those bulging muscles of his go tense. "I'm willing to give it a try."

~

Spoiler: We need a bigger shower.

I try not to stare.

I swear, I do.

But Sy scrubs the shampoo through his hair, and he doesn't even pretend. He let me wash first, content to lean back against the wall and watch, his fingers reaching out to occasionally catch my hip, steadying me as I navigated the tight space.

"Jesus." His eyes slither up and down greedily, pausing darkly on my tits. "You have the perfect body, you know that?"

My cheeks have probably been red since Remy left, but I still feel a flash of heat rising to my face. I'm not used to having Sy like this. In the past, everything sexual between us was aggressive and rushed, or tense and full of shame.

Now, the low-burning heat builds between us differently.

I wait until he bends his head back, rinsing out the suds, to dip my gaze low, landing on his long, half-hard cock. "You're not so bad yourself."

He lifts his eyelids enough to catch sight of me, and even that's enough to make a shot of lust zing right to my center.

Sy slams the shower off a second later, either not noticing the couple suds still trailing down his shoulder, or just not caring. "Let's go."

We don't bother dressing after we dry off, my quick footsteps following Sy's long stride through the main living area toward his bedroom. For once, we don't see Archie on the bed when we step through, giving the bed a long, considering glance.

"This isn't..." I begin, unable to deny the thread of nervousness taking hold. "This doesn't mean we can—"

He stops me with two fingers on my chin, turning my gaze to his. "I know the rules," he says, clutching at the towel slung low on his waist. "This is just... training." A drop of water falls from his hair to his cheek, rolling toward his mouth, and I reach up to thumb it away, captivated by the texture of his lips.

"Okay." I don't tell him I trust him, because the words aren't enough. Instead, I drop my towel, holding his eyes as I lower myself into his bed.

His eyes darken as I spread myself out for him, my nipples already peaked from the air against my damp skin. Sy eases his head to the side to crack his neck, restraint visible in the tendons there, jaw hardening as his gaze assesses the expanse of my skin.

"Okay," he says, dropping his towel.

His cock is already rock hard.

He climbs over me, eyes fixed to his destination, which is why I don't startle when his mouth descends onto my breast, lips opening to greet my nipple with his tongue. I arch into the warmth and he makes a low, rough sound, moving to the other breast. He palms me while his tongue explores the flesh, occasionally tracing over the dark lines of my tattoo.

I can feel how much he's enjoying it, the lines of his face growing harsher and hungrier by the second. The possibility of him losing control in the heat of passion worries me, but not more than the thought of me doing the same. This isn't a rowdy party downstairs.

This time, I'd give in willingly.

But that's not what we're here for.

So I do the only thing I can. I grab his hand, pull it between my legs, and wait.

"Fuck," he sighs, fingers curling, but not in the good way. Suddenly he's stiff, tense. "Maybe we should—"

I spread my legs wider, rocking my hips and clit against him.

His teeth clench, eyes sliding closed. "Lav..."

"I want it, Sy," I say, coaxing him with another buck of my hips. "Touch me."

Pausing, he reaches up, rolling my nipple in his fingers. "Like this?" A sharp thrill rushes down my spine, but I don't lose sight of the objective.

"No," I tell him, making sure I'm absolutely clear. "My pussy. My cunt. My cum pocket. My flower. My tunnel of love. My lady garden—"

His eyes fly open, jaw going slack, and then he starts to shake, laughter seizing him. "Your *lady garden*?"

Rolling my eyes, I say, "Whatever. I read *a lot* of romance novels back at the Hideaway." Romances where the hero always knows exactly what to do with his woman's secret pleasure zone. How the fuck did I end up with one so broken? "Sy, come on. If we're ever going to get past this, then you'll need to touch me."

The mirth fades from his eyes, and they grow dark, grim. "What if I hurt you again?"

"You won't," I say, fluttering my fingers through his hair. Before he can argue, I add, "And if you do, I'll say so and you'll stop." I hold his eye. "Right?"

His eyes soften with a sorrow I'm still unused to seeing. "Of course, I will." Quietly, he adds, "Lav, I promise."

"Then there's nothing to worry about." I lie back, spread my thighs, and press his hand between my legs again. That alone is enough to send a zing of pleasure through my limbs. "Tend to my lady garden, Big Bear. Cultivate that flower. Plant those seeds. Fertilize my—"

When his mouth crashes into mine, it's clearly just a way to get me to shut up, but I embrace it, parting my lips so I can taste his tongue.

The tension melts away and his ministrations turn diligent—worshipful. This time when he teases me, it's the right way, the way we worked on before 'the incident.' He rubs delicious circles into my clit, thumb pressed in exactly the right spot. My hips rise, desperate for more and he gives it to me, shoulder shifting to give him more access.

Sy kisses me absently, his mind clearly focused on the route of his fingers, sliding through my slickness. Every time my own fingers skate up his arm, his ribs, the broad expanse of his shoulders, his muscles flex into the touch, almost like it's just instinct to chase it down. I've noticed his reaction to my touch for long enough to understand what it is.

Sy is used to being hit, used to being the one doing the hitting, but this? The way my palms smooth down his back, the tickle of my fingers at the top of his shoulders, how my touch lingers greedily...

It makes my chest hurt to wonder how long he's been starved of gentle touches like these. There's an unspeakable power in the way I can make him shudder with nothing but a brush of my fingers over the nape of his neck. I watch his eyebrows crash together mid-kiss, and then suddenly, he's gone, sliding down my body.

His face hovers between my thighs, and when he finally dips down to press a long, wet kiss to my clit, his blue eyes never leave mine. The whimper that punches from my lungs sounds pained, but in truth, it's anything but. Weaving my fingers through his curly hair, I watch, captivated as he gathers my wetness with the point of his tongue.

It's impossible to forget who he is–Simon Perilini, undefeated fighter, a man strong and violent enough to take down anyone in Forsyth–but right now, he's licking my pussy with such a slow, careful intensity that it makes my body fill with liquid warmth.

It's like straddling a bomb.

"Oh, god," I gasp, fingers clenching in his hair. "Don't–don't stop." My hips chase his tongue, eyes locked on his as he brings me steadily, unforgivingly to the edge of annihilation.

It's a battle to watch his face as I come apart beneath his mouth, my eyes wanting nothing more than to slam closed as I ride the wave of ecstasy. The flash of wicked satisfaction in his eyes is enough to hold me there, trapped beneath the glow of it as he holds my hips down.

He claims his victory with a sharp, pleased rumble against my clit.

When the arch in my back falls, my body collapsing bonelessly into his mattress, he doesn't shift away. I'm too blissed out to really pay much mind to what his fingers are doing, but in the back of my brain, I know they're exploring me. My pussy is slick, wet and loose, and he pulls back far enough to look at it, his finger slowly descending.

His finger brushes the entrance, stalling there. A flash of trepidation crosses his face before he finally shifts his shoulder, sliding a long, thick finger into me.

I suck in a breath.

Freezing, his blue eyes jump to mine, throat jumping with a swallow. "Good?"

"Easy peasy," I reply, brain clearly befuddled from the orgasm.

After a second of hesitation, he drags the digit out and back in, eyes pinging back and forth between mine and his own hand. Sy approaches most things with a sense of aggressive curiosity. It's one of the aspects of his personality I can relate most to, and it's on full display here, his head dipping to observe the way I look as I take him to the knuckle.

It's with that same air of investigation that I begin feeling the teasing pressure of a second finger. Slowly, carefully, he slides it in along the first, brow furrowed as he meets my gaze.

"Now?" His voice has dropped to a low, rough octave that sends a shiver through my spine.

I spread my thighs wider for him. "You've seen your brother's dick, right?" I hold up three fingers to indicate size. "I can take more, Sy."

He looks at my pussy skeptically. "Are you sure?"

I rock my hips, taking the two fingers in deeper, whining at the feel. "Please."

The expansion of his chest on a long inhale isn't the only sign this is affecting him. His stiff cock bobs heavily between his legs when he shifts, a trickle of eager precum dripping from the head. "Here goes," he says, the tone full of warning.

He pushes in the third, and yep, like everything else with Sy, his fingers are big. Thick. Blunt. Long. Three fingers are more like four, and this time I feel the stretch. But I force myself to exhale, to let the burn dissipate, my body adjusting for him.

He pauses, eyes watching mine. "Lav?" This time, I hear the strain in his voice.

"Yeah, like that," I tell him, hips rising off the bed. He takes the bait, following my rhythm, fucking in and out until the burn has transformed into a toe-curling enjoyment of the fullness.

"Damn, you've really come a long way." Sy and I both tense, our gazes whipping to his open door. Remy's body forms a casual slant against the jamb. He's shirtless, arms crossed, eyes hooded as he observes us. "You don't even look like you want to kill her. I'm proud, man."

Sy stiffens over me, hand pulling back. I grab his wrist, keeping him from leaving me.

"Don't stop on my account," Remy says, eyes blazing as they trail over my naked body. "I've been here since she came her brains out on your tongue, but if you'd rather I leave…?" He jabs a thumb over his shoulder, eyes questioning.

Sy gives me a quick look, his cock pressing against my thigh. There's a question in his eyes, and I know he'd tell Remy to get lost if I asked him to. But I also see a thread of relief there, understanding that it might make this easier, knowing he has someone to be accountable to.

"Then stop hovering in the doorway," I tell Remy, watching some of the tension in Sy's shoulders unwind.

Remy stalks to the bed, replying, "If you insist." He's never looked more menacingly feline, the ink on his skin shifting with his every movement. His jeans are slung low on his hips, giving me a peek of the crescent moon I'd tattooed there, and when he eases down on the edge of the bed, I mourn the loss of it. He asks, "What do you think?" and palms my inner thigh, peering down for a look. "Can you take four, Vinny?"

I nod, pushing past the tickle of uncertainty in my belly. "I want to try."

He turns his gaze to mine. "I was hoping you'd say that." When he reaches up, finger tracing my bottom lip, there's a spark of hunger in his eyes that momentarily consumes me. He uses it to push his finger past my teeth, wetting it on my tongue. That flinty need in his eyes burns brighter when I close my lips around his knuckle, sucking. Briefly, his eyelids flutter. "Good girl."

He pops his finger out, slick with my saliva, while Sy shifts to give room. Watching the two of them, both their attention fixed to my center, might be even hotter than what comes next. There's a nudge of pressure as Remy prods his way in, thumb giving my clit a soft, idle stroke as he breaks through the resistance, sliding into my entrance alongside Sy's fingers.

Remy moves slowly, deliberately, widening me with every inch. "Breathe," he says, reaching up to stroke a warm palm over my breast. He glances at Sy. "You, too."

We both inhale and exhale at the same time, and that simple move allows Remy to push in deeper.

"Oh, *fuck*." I bite down on my bottom lip at the intensity of the utter fullness. "That feels so–it's so much, but–so good."

Ignoring my incoherent rambling, Remy says, "Look at this." The words are spoken in a tone of awe as he and Sy watch my hole take them in. "I've never seen a pussy so pretty, Vinny. You're getting so wet for us." He shifts his eyes back to me, bending to push a slow, lascivious kiss to my throat. "I knew you could take it, baby."

I'm not sure which one of them curves the finger that brushes against the magic spot inside me, but the gush of resulting heat makes me clench around them both. "That," I gasp, white spots popping in my vision. "Whatever *that* is, do it again."

Remy chuckles as he pulls back, eyes brightening in a way I haven't seen in weeks. He does it again and my body turns to jelly.

Sy looks at Remy, face set into a contemplative scowl. "How are you doing that?"

Remy smirks, and under normal circumstances, he might take the opportunity to tease him. Tonight, he doesn't.

Remy pulls his finger out, nudging Sy's wrist. "Turn your hand so your fingers are–yeah, exactly. Feel around a bit. Curl a finger here and there, but not too much. Wait until–" The sparks explode again and I keen, head digging back into the pillow. Remy laughs. "Bullseye."

While Sy is mastering the art of my G-spot, Remy shifts closer, his touch grazing lower and lower, until...

My hips lurch when he makes contact, his fingers pushing at my other entrance. The garden's back gate. I remember Nick's words to me the other day in the stairwell.

"You know he wants it, don't you? This pretty little ass of yours taking his cock."

"Sy can have that." Remy's voice comes hushed and full of gravel. "But I want this. Please, Vinny?"

I nod, unable to formulate words. Pleasure skates up my spine, the combined sensations–three fingers in my pussy, one entering my ass–are enough to meld my mind. Remy's gentle, exploratory, coaxing his way inside patiently. A fresh layer of sweat breaks out on my skin as he rubs and teases me, finger still slick from my wetness.

It's deliriously intense, and for a moment, I get this surge of confident knowledge that if someone doesn't put a dick in me soon, I might actually fucking *die*.

"Fuck, she's close," Remy says, sliding his finger in and out of the ring of muscle. "Feel her clenching?"

Sy grunts next to him, pushing his three fingers in deeper. "She's fucking soaked. Do you think this will–"

My eyes crash closed as Sy curls his finger, the orgasm abruptly within reach. Paying no mind to how crazed I must look, my back arches, hands clawing wildly at the sheets. I chase their fingers like a woman possessed.

"Holy mother of Christ." My eyes fly open and I see Nick's shadowy profile in the doorway. His hand is already fisting his erection through his jeans.

"Nick," I gasp, face twisting in the sweetest torture. "Please..."

I don't know what happens from one moment to the next. I just know that one second I'm feeling relieved–so relieved, because Nick would never leave me a writhing mess like this–and the next, he's above me, tearing at the button on his jeans, shirt already lost somewhere on the floor.

Nick takes his cock out of his pants, eyes already blown to black. "God, what the fuck are you two doing to her? She looks like she's about to crawl out of her own skin." The question is rhetorical, because Nick bends to get a very thorough look at exactly what it is they're doing. Once he does, he reaches up to stroke the hair off my temple. "Have they let you come at all?"

"Yes," Sy says defensively. "I got her off."

Nick nods, eyes lazily moving to Remy. "And you?"

Remy's finger wiggles, still buried knuckle-deep in my ass. "I'm here for support. Just helping stretch her out."

That's all. A twinge of delicious tension shoots up my spine as his finger presses deeper in my ass. I moan in pleasure and Nick's hand drops to my jaw, thumb grazing my chin.

"You getting yourself ready for them, gorgeous?" At my nod, his cock gives an aggressive twitch. "So fucking perfect."

The compliment sends another surge through me like a jolt of electricity.

Having the three of them like this—well, it used to be my biggest fear. Now my whole body sings at the feel of their hands on me, inside of me, all at once. The hard press of Sy rutting against my leg, Remy lips leaving wet, searing kisses along my inner thigh...

And Nick.

God, the way he handles his cock. It's both graceful and barbaric. The hard line of his tattooed chest rises and falls as his fist glides over his length, thumb running under the dark red head, brushing past the spot I know drives him wild.

My breath catches, the sensations too intense to fight. Every inch of my skin, inside and out, is hot and tight.

In my periphery, I see all three of them share a look, and then everything happens at once.

Sy curls his fingers again, hitting that delicious spot inside of me.

Remy thrusts deep into my ass.

Nick flattens the tips of his fingers over my clit, pressing.

"Oh, fuck!" I cry, hips shooting off the bed. If I didn't look possessed before, then I know I do now, body shattering into a million pieces as it twists and bucks, seizing painfully against the slam of pleasure that overtakes me.

It goes on for a long time. So long that when Nick kneels next to my head, depressing the mattress with his weight, I'm barely coherent. He tilts my face toward him and runs his fingers along my throat. "Give me your tongue," he demands, voice hard and urgent.

I flick it past my lips and Nick's hand slides behind my neck, holding me up. A desperate noise comes from the back of his throat as he pumps one last time, bringing his cock to my mouth and coating my tongue with his salty release.

The sounds that follow come from Remy and Sy, both groaning through their own orgasms before I feel them falling back on the mattress.

I'm in a daze after that, the throbs coming from my pussy, clit, and ass merging into one satisfied thrum. I only know Nick's the one who turns me to my side because his scent is suddenly all around me, his bare body tucking me against him. In front of me, there's another one–Sy, going by the sheer heat radiating off of him. I know Remy can't be far, because the fingers that rest on my hip, touching the star, can only belong to one man.

I'm filthy inside and out. I'm stretched. I'm defiled.

But most of all, I'm theirs.

I CAN'T REMEMBER EVER SLEEPING SO soundly, and when I wake the next morning, it's to find my limbs are twined with Nick's. Behind me, Remy's face is burrowed in the back of my neck. For a few long moments, I indulge in the warm tickle of Remy's breath on my nape, the steady rise and fall of Nick's chest against mine, the way he looks when my eyes blink open, face slack and yet somehow still lined with an inexplicable hardness.

I don't feel Sy, though. His presence, his heat, his breaths–they're absent in a strangely obvious way. It's the only reason I lift my head, craning my neck to seek him out. I don't catch a glimpse of his bronze skin, but I do smell the tantalizing waft of coffee, and then his distant, aggrieved voice.

"I told you, no more people-food!" he's hissing. "It upsets your stomach, and no one else cleans the litter box!"

I laugh quietly, trying to keep from jostling the bed. Listening to this six-foot-four, two-hundred-and-twenty pound fighter, spar with my floof of a kitten is the best part of my day.

"Little Bird," Nick's rough, slurred voice suddenly rings out. "You keep shaking the bed like that and I'm gonna have to pin you down." His lips move, but the rest of him still looks peacefully inert with slumber.

"Sorry," I whisper, brushing the hair off his forehead. "Your brother and Archie are at it again."

The corner of his mouth tugs up into a small, soft smirk. "I think we both know who will win whatever fight they're having."

His erection stabs at my lower belly, but for once he doesn't make a move. He just holds me, eyes still shut. If it weren't for the changed rhythm of his breathing, I'd assume he fell right back to sleep.

"How'd the meeting go last night?" I ask, reaching up to snag someone's discarded shirt–Remy's from the rich cologne scent of it–off the headboard. As much as I'd love to stay in bed all day, we all need to be on campus in the next hour.

"Good," he mutters, arm clamping hard around my waist to hold me down. "Perfect. Flawless. I'm a god among mere mortals."

I slide up to sit against the headboard, easily escaping his grip, and his resulting groan makes me grin. "Modest, too."

"What happened last night?" Remy shifts, drawing my gaze to him. His mussed hair lays over one eye, and when I reach over to sweep it away, it squints up at me, green and annoyed. "What meeting?"

"Just a little product demonstration." Nick frowns as I slip the shirt over my head, covering my tits. "Standard Duke stuff."

Remy rubs his eyes, pushing up onto an elbow. "What does that mean?"

Nick sighs. Aware that we're not going to let him go back to sleep, he opens his eyes and begins, "After that bullshit with Saul, I'm looking for new customers. *Non-alumni*." Nick and I share a significant look. It'd been his idea, and although I doubt it'll make much of a difference, having a backup cash cow to milk isn't the worst idea.

"You're doing *what*?" I look up and see Sy in the doorway. Archie is lazily draped over his arm, unconcerned by the suddenly tense set of Sy's posture. "Alone?"

Nick waves dismissively. "It's fine. Ballsack and Porterfield were with me." Sitting up, he scrubs a palm over his face.

Sy's forehead creases in astonishment. "Ballsack and Porterfield? Are you fucking with me right now? You're setting up meetings and carrying product around town–*Saul's* product–to find customers outside his system?" His eyes, having grown exponentially bigger, eventually bug out. "You could have been ambushed!"

Nick's eyes roll. "We weren't. I did my due diligence. Give me some credit here."

"Are you hearing this?" Sy's eyes pin behind me, on Remy.

"Yeah, I hear it." Next to me Remy shakes his head, raking his hair back. "Nicky, this sounds pretty fucking foolish, even for you."

"Foolish?" The corded muscles in Nick's neck tense and he glances at me. "Do you want to tell them or should I?"

"Tell us what?" Remy sits up now, the sheet pooled around his waist barely hiding his morning erection. He looks between us. "Fuck. What now?"

Sy is wearing the same expression.

Dread.

Clearing my throat, I give Nick one last bracing look before explaining, "We were called into Saul's office the other day to discuss the alumni poker game. You know, the one after the festival?"

Nick snorts. "You're worried about ambushes? Well, he had a goon waiting for me on campus." He jerks his chin at me. "And fucking Ewing pulled her out of class and hauled her in with me."

Well, there goes breaking it to them slowly.

Every muscle in Sy's face hardens. Before he can speak, Nick holds up a hand. "You may want to put the kitten down. It gets worse."

Sy puts the cat on the bed, muscles already rippling as Archie makes a nest in my lap. I'm grateful, because after we take turns explaining what went down in Saul's office, from the elevator ride to the big blackmailing video reveal, and then the specifics of the entertainment I'm supposed to provide at the poker game, Sy reacts by slamming his fist into the bedroom door.

"I'll kill him," he says, voice dripping with rage. "I will fucking kill him before I let anyone touch you. Do you understand?"

I jump up, stepping over Nick and grabbing Sy's arm before he can do any more damage.

"There's no need to kill anyone." I square my shoulders, forcing him to look at me. "I'm a Royal woman, Sy. I was born and bred into this fucked-up system, and trust me when I say if this is all I have to do, then I'll still make it out of this thing luckier than the rest."

Flinty-eyed, Sy explodes, "How can you be okay with this? Letting that fucker parade you around like his whore?" I know somewhere deep down that this anger isn't directed at me, but I still clench down on a flinch at the word. *Whore.* That's exactly what Saul wants everyone to see me as, and hearing it barked from Sy's mouth cuts at something in my gut.

Sy sees.

He always sees.

His face falls, and he surges forward, taking my face in his hands. "I didn't mean it like that. You *aren't*–no matter what happens. You're ours." Slowly, he repeats, "You're ours, and he's using you to punish us." The cast of guilt over his features isn't new. I've seen it ever since the morning in the belfry, when he came to apologize for hurting me.

This is one more thing he'll need to atone for.

"Then don't let him win," I reply, the words sounding far more simple than the reality.

Sy's face twists. "How are we supposed to just... do nothing?"

"He agreed that we can act as her protection," Nick cuts in, glancing from his brother to Remy, "so that's what we're going to be. Nobody touches her. Nobody even fucking breathes on her."

Remy makes a skeptical sound. "You're really going to let a bunch of old fuckers put their eyes on your girl?" He shakes his head. "No way. This'll be a fucking bloodbath."

Nick snaps, "You think I want to? If this were just about what I want, Saul would be in a shallow grave somewhere. And then what?" He gestures to Sy. "I'd get my brother killed. I'd get you killed. I'd get myself killed. God only fucking knows what happens to Lavinia." He glances at the ring on his finger, like he's trying to remind himself of his role. "As leader of the Dukes, I can't make rash decisions. That's why I'm coming up with a contingency plan. Finding new customers. Making connections and hopefully a few deals. Expanding our territory so we're not held hostage by that blackmailing asshole." He looks between his boys. "He found a weak spot and I'm patching it up."

"That's very mature of you." Sy grimaces down at his bleeding knuckles. "But I still want to kill him."

"Get in line," Remy says, still looking tired. "But, as much as it hurts to say it, Nicky's right. We have to be smarter than these guys. Fucking *Kings*. They don't use brawn to get what they want. They use their brains, their power, and money. If Nicky is going to be one of them one day, he's got to start thinking like them—like my father."

The words hang heavy, because it's the closest any of them have come to saying it aloud.

One day, Nick will be King.

To become King means taking down Saul.

"Shit." Sy drops to the bed, rubbing a hand over his face. "God-damn it."

Listening to them talk, I know they're right. It's how I would suggest dealing with my own father. The Kings raise these men to be soldiers, not leaders. Why? Because they're terrified they'll lose their throne. Nick said something else that tugs at me, something that makes my palms sweat and my stomach churn. Something I've been thinking about since we left Saul's office.

"It's time for the other plan, Nick," I announce. Six eyes shift my direction, and I know I don't look like much. Just a girl in nothing but an ill-fitting shirt, bluffing with a raised chin. "Saul saw me have a panic attack after being forced in the elevator by Ewing. He knows my weakness too, which is worse than the blackmail. I have to face this head on." I look between them, steeling myself. "Will you help me?"

14

N ick

Sometimes it's handy to have a brother who's studying psychology. It's not like I don't understand the word–desensitization–but he's the one to explain the process.

Later that evening, he does.

"The point of exposure therapy," he says, nodding to the elevator door beside him, "is for a subject to gradually experience their fears in a safe, controlled environment. The idea is that avoidance nurtures phobia, so what do we do instead?" Sy raises his eyebrows. "We face it, head-on."

Remy shrugs. "Kick it in the teeth."

I add, "Make it your bitch."

"Exactly," Sy says.

But when we all turn to look at Lavinia, she doesn't look anywhere in the vicinity of bitch-making. She's as far away from the elevator as she can be without just completely leaving the room, leaned back against the kitchen counter, arms crossed tightly.

Her shoulders hitch up closer to her ears. "So you're saying I'm going to have to go inside there." It's not really a question. More like she's trying to convince herself. She swallows, throat jumping. "All alone."

I take an involuntary step toward her. "Who the fuck is saying that?" I whip a glare on Sy. "That's not a part of the deal." She's the one who wanted to do this—it was her idea—but fuck, my Little Bird looks like she may puke, and I don't exactly feel much better.

Sy shakes his head. "No, I actually think it's best that you're not alone. If you panic too much, you could hurt yourself. One of us should be with you in the car while the other two are at the top and bottom floors." He lifts an eyebrow. "This isn't about torturing you, Lav. It's about making you comfortable. One step at a time."

"Okay." She doesn't look or sound okay, but sure, *okay*.

"Where do you want me?" Remy looks up from where he's sitting on the floor, body curved over a sketch pad.

Her face scrunches up like this is the hardest decision of her life. "Um..." she reaches up, rubbing the back of her neck in a strangely aggressive way.

When it's clear she can't answer, Remy offers, "How about I wait for you up here?

"Right, right," she says, face as ashen as I've ever seen it. "Good."

Sy must sense the moment is spiraling, so in the least pushy voice I've ever heard he asks, "We'll go slow. You control the pace, even if that means you can't get in." Gently, he asks, "Are you ready to start?"

"Yes," she says, even though her head gives a definitive shake.

"You want me in the elevator, or up here?" I ask. We already talked about it. We're going to let her have the choice on who goes in the elevator with her. She may tell me to fuck off, and it's not like I don't deserve it. I'm the one who locked her in there as punishment. We've all noticed the wide berth she always takes around that door, as if some part of her is always innately aware of the threat of it. Sighing, I add, "It's up to you, Little Bird."

She shifts her weight back and forth, eyes jumping from me to my brother. It won't bother me if she picks him over me. I can deal with it. I think.

Finally, she meets my gaze, nodding. "I want you with me."

Fuck fuck fuck.

Responsibility.

Knowing it's cowardly, I ask, "You sure?"

"Yes." This time she looks like she means it, squaring her shoulders as she straightens, locking stares with Sy. "And you'll be downstairs, right?"

My brother whips out his phone, thumbing it open to reveal the stopwatch screen. "For as long as you need."

But even after all is said, nothing gets done.

Lavinia stares at the elevator across the room, body frozen.

Sy clears his throat, shooting me and Remy a look before approaching her. "Hey, it's okay if you can't go in. Just try to step as close as you feel–"

"I'm going to do it," she says, voice both firm and uneven. "I just need a minute." Closing her eyes, she inhales deep, unmoving.

So we wait, me and Remy sitting against the wall on either side of the elevator while Sy rides it down. Each clang and whir of the car, no matter how distant and muffled, makes her flinch, but she doesn't open her eyes, brows creased in concentration.

I try not to count the minutes it takes for her to actually cross the line between the living room and the elevator. It's only seven. We've already eaten dinner at the gym and tended to our business for tomorrow's Fury. The four of us can stand here all night, if we need to.

As we wait, the sun begins dipping lower through the clock face. Remy and I share the occasional skeptical glance before he returns his attention to the sketch pad. Sometimes, my eyes follow, narrowing questioningly at what he's drawing. It looks like mechanics, all hard lines and confusing circles–nothing like the colorful chaos I'm used to seeing from him.

In between picking at a scab on my knuckles and wondering if we have enough beer stocked for tomorrow night, Lavinia's eyes suddenly fly open. "Okay."

Just like that, she's marching for the door to the elevator, spurring me and Remy into a flurry of motion. He shoots up and slams the button, the door rolling open, but I'm the one to wrench the metal gate aside, revealing the badly lit interior. If I'd had time to prepare, maybe we could have spruced it up. New bulbs. Air freshener. Liquor. *Something.*

It takes everything in me not to just pick her up and show her I can fix this, but she walks right inside, spine rigid.

Never missing a step, she turns, striding back out.

"Alright, so basically, this is fucking crazy." Her eyes are wide and already growing wet. "That elevator is a million fucking years old. What if it dies? What if it's like the clock? Everything around here is ancient and broken!" She flails around, gesturing wildly from me to the elevator. "We're going to get stuck in there, Nick! We'll be trapped, and before too long, all the air will get breathed up, and then–"

I grab her shoulders, giving her a soft shake. "This hunk of metal has survived decades of rowdy frat boys, Little Bird. It's unstoppable."

She breathes hard, clutching at my shirt sleeves. "Nothing is unstoppable!"

"I am," I tell her, chasing her gaze when she rolls her eyes. "I'd never let anything hurt you, and you know it. There's a door," I point up, into the elevator, indicating the emergency hatch eight feet up. "If we get stuck–and we won't–I'll haul your perfect, tight, fuckable ass up there and carry you out on my own back. You got me?"

She holds my stare, some of the wildness in her eyes easing. That's when Remy swoops in, scooping her into his arms. "Come on, baby. Deep breaths." She breathes, although I'm not sure how deep it goes. "Can you close your eyes for me?"

She looks wary—but he rubs her back and slowly they flutter shut. "Good girl." His hand wraps around the column of her neck, and he ducks his head, whispering into her ear. "I want you to think about the two of us on that cliff. Think about how that was the scariest fucking moment of our lives. Think about how certain we were, Vinny. If we stayed, we wouldn't be here now. But we jumped. We pushed past the fear and took that step off the edge, because we needed to survive, and somehow–some way–that made us bullet-proof." He makes wide strokes with his thumb down to the hollow of her neck and shoulder. "But the truth is, fear wasn't how we ended up there. I had a weakness and everyone saw it." Remy's eyes flit to mine, hardening. "Our enemies have weaknesses too, but we have something the rest of them don't."

Lavinia groans. "If you say 'each other,' I'm going to barf."

Remy pauses, mouth twisting. "Well, I was going to say... a massive stockpile of ammunition and the heaviest balls in Forsyth." Her lips twitch and he grins, tucking a lock of hair behind her ear. "The point is, our weaknesses will tear us apart faster than our enemies will. It's why we have to fight it. Get stronger. Better. Harder. The rest of them don't have the guts for that, Vinny. They're not like us." Brushing a kiss against her temple, he adds, "They're not survivors."

It may be the most coherent thing I've ever heard Remy say in his life, but he's right. Our weaknesses will be our downfall. Not just the Dukes, but us—the four of us. Sy's weakness is the reason he hurt her. Mine was the reason I sent her back to her father.

But Lavinia's may be the worst, because anyone can use it against her, and I won't let that happen.

Not even if I have to go down stopping it.

A tear runs down her face and Remy thumbs it away. "You're right," she says, exhaling slowly, evenly. "You're absolutely right."

She steps past me and walks right in, head bowed.

Sharing a nervous glance with Remy, I follow her, stepping into the small box. Immediately, I can feel the waves of panic rolling off her. It's an energy that buzzes like a warning, an animal caged, her body strung so tight that she flinches at the mere sound of my foot touching the metal. The pink in her cheeks from a moment before is gone, although it seems to have traveled down her throat in red streaks. Tears well in her eyes and she gulps for air.

"What if I can't do this?" she whispers, hands latching onto my chest.

"Hey." I smooth down her hair, tucking her gingerly into my chest. "Everything is fine. I'm here. Remy is a few feet away," I nod out the open door, "and Sy's waiting downstairs for you. Do you want to go to him?"

In all my life, I'll never comprehend how my brother became anyone's pillar of comfort, but I know that's what he is to her. Warmth and reassurance. Strength and security.

She nods, but her throat bobs as she tries to catch her breath. "What if the lights go off? What if we can't get the door back open? What if—"

Her panic is making me panic, and *fuck*, I'm not even afraid of elevators, but she kind of has a point about this tower being older than dirt. I glance at Remy. "Dude—"

He narrows his eyes at me and mouths, "*Distract her!*"

"Baby," I say, running my hands down her back, "none of those things are going to happen."

"But—"

I cut her off with a kiss that's gentle, less demanding than usual. She's still crying, and I've got to give her the chance to breathe.

Her jaw relaxes, and I feel the muscles in her back ease.

"Better?" I ask.

Her eyes flutter open, eyelashes wet. "Yes."

Searching her eyes, I ask, "Ready to shut the door?"

Her eyes dart to Remy, who's still standing just outside the elevator. "It can't be me or Nick." He jerks his chin at the gate, telling her, "You've got to be the one who does it, Vinny."

The sound she makes is strangled and full of dread, but she lifts her trembling hand, giving the two of us one last nervous look. Her whole body vibrates as she wrenches the gate closed, slamming it hard into the frame.

Then she punches the button–violently, like it deserves to feel pain.

As the door slides closed, I feel her heart against my chest, pounding like a jackhammer, and do the only thing I know I'm good at. Taking her face in mine, I kiss her again, drawing her attention away from the walls literally closing in. Seeing her like this makes my chest hurt. This is a girl who kicks fuckers in the face, looks Kings in their eyes and dares them to try to break her, keeps going even when she's held down.

I won't let this take her away from me.

The car moves with a lurch, and she whimpers in my mouth. "Nick!"

"You've got this, baby." Gathering her trembling body closer, I ask, "You want to know what my biggest fear is?"

She gasps, burying her face into my neck. "W-what?"

Solemnly, I answer, "Crickets."

She doesn't relax, but her exhale is definitely edged with exasperation. "Stop."

"Hey, I'm dead serious," I assure, stroking my fingers through her hair. "Menacing little Geppetto freaks. Always hiding, but screaming so you'll know they're there, jumping around, even though they can fly, and they'll never let you forget they *can* fly, because those disgusting wings of theirs flap around like–"

Ding

The doors slide open with a rusty grinding sound, and then Sy is there, yanking the gate open. I get a flare of envy when Lavinia leaps at him, Sy catching her with both arms like he was anticipating it, but it melts away just as quickly as I watch her gasp into his neck, chanting, "I did it, I did it..."

My brother's always been good at helping others train, so he doesn't even look awkward when he cups the back of her head with his big palm, saying, "Nice work, Lucia."

I hold the door, feeling so tense that I need the break, too.

He glances at me to ask, "All good, brother?"

Giving her a worried look, I shrug. "I told her about the crickets."

Sy snorts, ducking his head to catch her gaze. "He never did get over that thing in second grade. How about you?" He brushes her hair back, searching her eyes. "Status report, Lucia."

She shakes her head, a little of the color coming back to her cheeks. "I fucking hate that thing."

Sy nods. "I know."

Inhaling deep, she seems to rally herself, spine stiffening. "And I have to ride it back up."

"You're sure?" I ask, but this time it isn't cowardice that's driving it. Seeing the spark of victory in her eyes, I want her to know–to feel, without any doubt–that this is all her.

She glances at the doors leading outside, and then to my brother. "Losers aren't allowed through the doors, right?" The smile she gives is watery and weak, but it makes something inside of me unwind at the sight of it.

Sy gives her a slow, stony grin. "No losers here."

Squaring her shoulders, she finally lets him go, turning to me. "Okay," she says, sounding far more convincing than she had upstairs. "Let's do this, Bruin."

Sy grabs my arm to hold me back as we watch her enter the elevator again. In a low voice, he says, "Help her keep her breathing under control. In through the nose—out through the mouth. It's okay to distract her from intrusive thoughts or panic." He gives me a longer, considering look. "The cricket thing was a nice touch."

I flip him off as Lavinia begins clutching for me, dragging me back to her. "I've got this."

The ride back up is a little easier.

Her body still trembles, strung tighter than piano wire, and she's still making these little gasping whimpers, but I get halfway through a story of my harrowing second grade cricket war before the *ding* sounds.

This time, I'm prepared. The door slides open and I instantly roll her out of my hands to Remy, who steps in the elevator the second he can.

Then he grabs her hand and shoves it down his pants.

"What the fuck?" I snap. *Jesus.* I kept my dick completely out of this.

"Just showing her a touch point," Remy explains, ducking his head to watch her fingers trace the crescent moon tattooed beside his hip.

"That helps?" I ask, both confused by this ritual of theirs and annoyed that I'm not a part of it. I've got tattoos for days.

"Yeah," she says, looking up at him. My Little Bird looks wrung out and halfway to falling apart, but she doesn't. She firms her jaw and says, "Because I know he'll find me."

"Always." He brushes her hair off her face. "Are you okay?"

She shudders an exhale. "Yeah, I think so. It's... a little easier?" She doesn't sound convinced, but she sounds like she wants to be. So when she pulls away, shaking out her arms, I already know what she's going to say. "Ready for the second bout?"

THERE'S something satisfactory about seeing a douchebag get his ass kicked, even if he is DKS.

It would feel even better if I was the one pummeling Bruce in the ring, but Wicker Ashby is surprisingly agile. Especially for a fucking lacrosse player.

It's the second fight of the night, a sophomore cub, Kaczinski, having already won the first. Bruce, who's currently getting his ass kicked, is my undercard. I'm up next, and the room is abuzz with anticipation. Mine will be the Dukes' first real fight since our probation expired, and I'm lucky it's me, because all three of us are itchy with the need to punch someone.

"Yeah!" Lavinia cheers when Bruce takes another hit, then

freezes, looking up at us to weakly add, "I mean, *oh no*, get him, Bruce."

Remy looks at me from where he's leaning against the railing, and we share a smirk.

Maybe make that all *four* of us.

Seems like I'm not the only one willing to let Bruce get his ass handed to him.

PNZ is notorious for recruiting pretty, rich fuckboys, but despite all the jokes and insults about them being pampered little pussies, they're more than a nice trust fund. A Princeship might necessitate some form of blood lineage, but getting into the frat is somehow both easier and harder. Their skills run the gamut, because Ashby doesn't care about specialty like the other houses do.

He's a collector.

Only the best and brightest for his house. The future surgeons. The law majors with the highest promise. Engineering majors with a focus on security. CS majors who dominate hard enough that their op-sec is absolutely fucking bulletproof–something that used to drive Daniel Payne up the wall. They are undoubtedly the cream of the Forsyth crop, and I'll give Ashby this much–it's smart. For all the Princes might be about kicking out more Royals, he's not building a family. He's building an empire, and he pulls the brightest stars from the frat right into it. Saul has Neon and Ewing. Lionel Lucia has Cash Mallis. Daniel Payne had *me*.

But Ashby doesn't recruit Forsyth's garden-variety goons, and despite the fact he raised the man in the ring–even gave him his own last name–that's exactly what Wicker Ashby and his two brothers are.

Recruits.

No one has ever been fooled. These three were chosen not by blood, but because they excel at something. God only knows what. Whatever it is, Wicker has a hunger in his eyes that I haven't seen since my time in South Side, and it makes me more alert.

His two brothers, hovering just outside the ropes, watching him fight, aren't much better.

Lavinia leans into me and follows my gaze to the hulking one. He's got the hood of his sweater pulled up over his head, so I can't see his face, but I know it's his brother, Lex. "Is it weird that sometimes I feel better knowing Leticia, and I weren't the most fucked up sibling group in Forsyth?"

I throw my arm over her shoulders, wondering, "Are you talking about me and Sy, or Ashby's Powerpuff Boys?"

Her mouth purses in this insanely sexy way that always makes my dick twitch. "I'm talking about the farce of it all." Loosely, she gestures to them. "The Prince tradition being all about blood links when their own King's sons are adopted."

Remy's head whips around. "Wait. You're telling me they're not his real sons?"

"Dude," Sy says, fixing him with a look. "Pace is half black."

Remy waves a hand at me. "So? Like you're as white as your brother?"

My eyebrows rise. "He's got a point, Brown Bear."

Sy shakes his head, pinning his gaze back to Bruce's beatdown. "Let's face it. He calls them his sons, but they're really just glorified employees."

Remy turns to the ring, looking at Wicker a little more thoughtfully. "Princes get so hard about their paternity machine, I guess I just assumed." And then, "How the fuck did Ashby become King without a blood heir, anyway? What a hypocrite."

Sy shrugs. "Something nefarious, I'm sure."

Lavinia looks between them, balking. "You don't know, do you?" When the two of them just give her blank looks, Lavinia tuts. "Ashby *did* have a son. He died when he was little, just after Ashby became King."

Already knowing this, I mutter, "Cancer or something."

"I know he's a total prick and all," she says, frowning, "but I always thought it was really sad. Don't you think?" She adjusts the strap on her top—a drapey thing that covers all the good spots while teasing me with the possibility underneath. There's plenty of exposed skin, and I can't keep my hands off her.

I tug her closer, not liking that she's looking at those three. "Sad for a normal person, sure. For a Prince, it's catastrophic. And for their King?" I let the silence speak for me.

Peering at her, Remy wonders, "Obviously Nick has a pocket full of Forsyth chatter, but how do you know all this?"

Scowling, she explains, "Oh, my father never missed an opportunity to gloat about that. He drilled our superior lineage into us whenever possible. Sadly, his own Royal spawns didn't come equipped with dicks."

Remy raises his beer, saying, "And we thank god for it every day," and rests his hand on her ass, fingers sliding down to toy with the hem of her skirt. "Not everyone can be pure-bred studs like me and Nicky." He shoots Sy a look. "No offense, brother."

Sy, distracted with the fight, answers with a quick, absent-minded, "None taken." His hands are coiled around the railing with a white-knuckled grip, but he pries one away to gesture angrily toward the ring. "I kept fucking telling him he needed to work on his cardio!" His eyes narrow, assessing every move. No matter the beef between him and Bruce, DKS losing even a single fight is an abomination in his eyes. He leans over the railing and shouts. "Block him! Use your legs!" When Wicker's left hook lands, Sy drags a palm down his face. "Jesus Christ, I can't believe he's getting his ass kicked by an East Ender with manicured fingernails."

While Sy spits curse after curse, I lean down to brush a kiss beneath Lavinia's ear. "That shellacking will make my victory even sweeter. Everyone loves a comeback, and I already know how I want to celebrate it."

A loud shout comes from across the balcony, drawing our attention. Obviously, we're not the only ones enjoying the beat down. The Kings' box is across the gym from us, but near enough to hear their ruckus. Tristian Mercer leans over the railing and shouts, "Ashby's manicurist can fight better than that!" making Sy thrust out a palm, as if to say, *See?!*

Killian and Dimitri laugh. The Lady rolls her eyes, but they all look like they're having a great time.

Saul is sitting in the best seat in the section, alone, a sour expression on his face. Like Sy, he's not pleased with the impending defeat. They bet so much money on every match, I can't imagine what kind of hit his wallet is going to take tonight.

The thought almost makes me want to throw my own.

Almost.

Not quite.

"Lionel's a no-show," Sy says, nodding over to the Counts' empty box.

"Good," is all Lavinia says, voice hard and toneless. All of my sources say Lionel has gone underground, probably licking his wounds from the failed hit, not to mention being down two daughters and his best Count. Also noticeably absent is the Baron King.

No—*Maddox*. Remy's dad. The guy who'd dragged my best friend away in high school. The boring stiff all the whores at the Hideaway used to dread giving head to.

That's still going to take some getting used to.

I know Ashby is here, though. I saw him earlier, on my way up here. I scan the gym now, wanting to catch a glimpse of his satisfied expression before I wipe it off his face with his best Prince's loss. It takes a few minutes to find him, but when I do, he's by the judge's table.

Standing next to him, dressed in all black, her shirt cut low and in boots so high the heels look like weapons, is Mama B.

I watch as the two have an interesting exchange.

Huh.

"Hey." I nudge Sy with my elbow and he reluctantly tears his eyes away from the shit show on the floor. Quietly, I ask, "That's weird, right?"

He looks to where I'm gesturing, forehead scrunching. "That they're talking? I don't know, man. All these people go so far back, we'd need diagrams to connect all the lines."

True. Our parents and their muddied relationships with all of the Royals is evidence of that but— "Look." I lift my chin, jolting him. "He just touched her."

Sy's shoulders tense. "What, like he hurt her?"

"No. Like this." I turn to Lavinia, who's sipping a beer of her own, and rest my hand on her shoulder. Slowly, I drag my fingertips to her wrist.

She turns to face me. "Hey. What's up?"

I smile. "Nothing."

"Okay, weirdo." She rolls her eyes and refocuses on the match.

I look back at my brother. "See? It's weird."

He shakes his head, but at that moment, Wicker gets a final hit, knocking Bruce flat on his ass. I guess what Wicker lacks in power, he makes up for with speed and stamina, because minutes later, he's gotten the best of a DKS. The floor turns into utter chaos—upsets always do. The Princes and their sorority girls explode into excited, inebriated celebration, while the DKS boys and the cutsluts throw cups of beer and trash on Bruce's dazed body.

"Shit," Sy hisses. "Come on, Remy, we better get down there." He palms my shoulder. "And you and Lavinia better hurry up and get your ass dressed, wrapped, and in that ring. Don't leave these animals without entertainment for more than thirty minutes. They'll tear this place apart."

I give a lazy salute, knowing it's enough time for the boys to get another beer, but not long enough for people to get restless.

I grab Lavinia's hand, but she's the one pulling me down the stairs.

"Hey, what's the rush?"

She tosses me a glare over her shoulder. "You've got people down there waiting, Nick, and despite your earlier show of supreme *modesty*, I'd personally feel better if you went into the ring prepared."

I scoff. "Thirty minutes is plenty of time to take off my clothes and get taped." I'm already warmed up, having spent a couple hours on the bags before Bruce's bout began.

Crisply, she says, "Yes," and then arches an eyebrow at me. "But is it enough time to do all that *and* eat my pussy?"

I stumble a step, but she doesn't wait, meaning I have to sprint to catch her wrist, tugging her faster toward the locker room. "Fuck *me*, Little Bird. You can't just say shit like that in public. My poor dick's going to pop right through my shorts."

She's been on a tear ever since the elevator last night, high on the conquest of riding the elevator through four whole trips. The energy rolling off her ever since just makes me want her more, and I practically ply myself to her ass, navigating us through the wild throng.

The main hallway is crowded, and possessing the whiff of something that isn't conducive to seductive oral shenanigans, but we wrinkle our noses and power through.

Until I slam into someone.

"Coming through," I explain, impatient and annoyed.

The guy turns to narrow an eye at me from beneath his raised hoodie, but I just keep plowing on by. I'd stop and deal with it but... pussy, motherfucker.

A man's got priorities.

I turn down the back hallway, toward the training room, but there's someone blocking the door.

Is everyone in this building a cockblocker?

It wasn't in my plan to take Lavinia into the locker room, and I don't really feel good about it now. Too many bad experiences for her in there, and the last thing we need is her reliving the memory of Remy's mindfuck. However, needs must.

But before we even turn the corner, I hear a voice that makes me tense.

"To the victor, go the spoils. Isn't that how your Dukes play this game?" When he comes into sight, I see Wicker, shoulder propped against the wall. His body is slick with sweat, a towel draped around his neck. Beads of blood drip to the floor from a hit Bruce managed to land, and he's still catching his breath. Wicker tilts his head, smirking. "Well, I won that fight, Red, and you're the prize I want."

I can't see the girl's face, but when she speaks, I recognize the voice in a heartbeat.

"You're on the wrong side of Forsyth to claim any," Verity says, voice dripping with disdain.

"Rumor is, West End's cutsluts get mounted like bitches," he shifts, moving to cage her against the wall, a hand on each side of her head. "I could fuck you until you scream."

The cutsluts know how to handle themselves but Verity isn't like the rest of them. She's sweet. Soft. And this prick would fucking tear her apart.

I curl my fist, stepping forward to break it up, but not before Lavinia does.

"Hey!" she shouts, charging toward them. "Get away from her, asshole!"

Shit.

There goes my pussy feast.

Wicker glances over at my girl, a smug grin already plastered on his stupid face. His eye is swollen, and I see now that the blood is coming from his knuckles. I can feel the post-fight adrenaline running through his system and it makes my fingers twitch toward the gun against my back.

"Oh, the Duchess," he says, eye-fucking her. "Ready for that threesome yet? Obviously, if I'm going for this one over here, I'm not in a picky mood. I can mount you both like bitches."

"And I can tell the future," I say, jaw hardening as I step in front of her. "Ask me what happens in five seconds?"

Wicker's eyes dart down to where my hand is tucked beneath my shirt. "Ah, Dukes. Never travel anywhere without that piece on you, do you? An observant man might call that cowardly."

"That man might observe his brains splattered on the floor." Smiling coolly, I add, "A lot like his cousin."

Any teasing nature drains right out of his eyes. "Look at you, Bruin. You've barely been in the belfry three months, and you've already caught probation and implicated yourself in multiple murders. Yeah, you run a real tight shipwreck." His lip curls pompously. "Pathetic."

"You're the pathetic one," Lavinia grinds out, and it's only then that I feel her hand clutching mine–the one reaching for my gun. Her fingers clamp like claws around my wrist. "There's not a woman in this gym who'd willingly fuck you over what we've already got." Snapping forward, she grabs Verity's hand and tugs her away from him.

I give my most polite 'you just survived murder' smile. "I'd stick around and kick your ass the way Bruce should have, but I'm saving my energy to take down your reigning Prince."

Wicker snarls, "I'd wipe the floor with you, Bruin," and I step closer, ignoring the hand tugging hard at my shirt.

"I know what you are, Wicker. More importantly, I know *who* you are, and where you come from." Up close, I can see the flash of split-second panic in his eyes, but it's gone just as quickly as it came.

"You don't know shit."

I search his face, trying to figure out what it is about him. It's something just beneath the surface. He tries hard to hide it, and most of the time, I'm betting he does a pretty convincing job.

It only takes a couple seconds for me to find it.

Desperation.

I grin wider, showing my teeth. "Too bad you don't have the title that earns you the chance. Featured matches are for Royals only." Coolly, I add, "*Real* Royals. Not cheap knock-off orphans of Roy–"

As expected, he lunges, meeting the force of my palms as I slam him back toward the wall. It'd probably be a nice fight too–a better warmup than hitting the bag could ever be–but then his King steps into the hallway.

Ashby pauses, looking between the four of us, and Wicker suddenly goes rigid. His dad's eyes pass right over him though, landing on Verity. "Whittaker," he says, not sparing me a second glance. "I came to tell you what a good fight you had, but I see you're not quite finished with the last round."

Wicker raises his chin, shaking out his fists. "Just playing in the dumpster a bit."

Ashby gives Lavinia and Verity a cold grin. "Excuse my boy. His appetites are legion." He shifts his gaze from the women and raises his hand, two fingers extended in a small wave. "Come, Whittaker. Since you won the fight, you're invited to my box as my personal guest."

Wicker's shoulders ease, but his smug expression stays firmly in place. "Perfect. I'll have an excellent view of you getting demolished on the mat."

It's an empty threat, but Wicker Ashby isn't my concern. I have a bigger prince to ruin.

Once they're gone, Lavinia turns to Verity, frowning. "Are you okay?"

"Yes." Verity exhales. Despite the bluster she'd shown before, her hand gives a tremble when she lifts it to tuck her hair behind an ear. "Thanks for stepping in. That was getting... intense."

Lavinia holds her gaze, her words strong and clear. "I've always got your back, Verity. I'd never let anyone fuck with you and the other girls." She shoots me a pointed look. "And neither would your Dukes."

It's only then that I let my gun go, flexing my tense fingers. "Never."

15

L avinia

THE GIRLS and I all must look ridiculous as everyone begins the walk from the gym to the tower, arms wrapped around ourselves, huddled close for warmth. It's late, but the boys' rowdy celebration pings off nothing but empty warehouses and vacant buildings, so Nick and Sy just grin, leading the pack toward the tall building a few streets over.

I find myself staring at it in the distance, my neck craned up as the darkened clock face grows closer and closer. Odd to think there was a time I stood here on the street, right in front of it, so intimidated by the sheer enormity of it that my stomach roiled.

Now, the sight of it unwinds me.

Home.

One by one, we all pack through the doors—the Dukes and I first, then Kaczinski, tonight's other winner. He whoops as he comes through, slamming palms with a few other DKS boys, then they all head up the stairs.

I hang back to wait for my guys, engaged in an idle discussion about holiday break with Laura. She plans to drive south with one of the other girls to see a concert, but it doesn't really mean much to me. What am I going to do, go home for Thanksgiving? Christmas?

Yeah.

Fat chance of that.

I'm caught in a thought loop of mashed potatoes and murder when Sy suddenly shoots forward, blocking the doors.

Planting a palm on each side of the entry, he asks, "Where do you think you're going?" He leans forward, posture both casual and threatening. "You know the rules."

I feel the sudden tension more than I see it, an uneasy hush falling over the foyer as everyone cranes their necks to watch.

"You can't be serious," comes a sharp voice I recognize all too well. *Bruce.* The only parts of him visible through the blockade of Sy's body is the curled fist at his side. "The only reason Kaczinski won was because I've been training him!"

Sy's broad shoulders twitch in a shrug. "He won. You didn't. You're a legacy, Bruce, you know the deal."

Laura shoots me a dark look, whispering, "Here we go..."

Behind me, Kathleen clucks her tongue. "Boys are such babies, I swear."

Bruce snaps, "This is fucking bullshit!" and then peers around Sy, revealing a bruised, swollen eye that fixes on Nick. "You're going to let him do this, Bruin? You're the one wearing the ring. You make the rules!"

Nick doesn't even look at him, shoulders pressed back against a pillar as he shrugs. "I've also got a victory."

"You already got your ass kicked once tonight," Sy adds, jerking his chin out toward the street. "Walk it off somewhere else before you get another one."

One of the DKS guys must approach Bruce from outside,

because we suddenly hear an exasperated, "Come on, dude. It's one party, you'll live."

Over the last few weeks, Bruce has become a major pain in the ass. Outwardly defiant to Nick's leadership, hostile about my position, and well, that showing tonight was just embarrassing.

"I'm a senior," he shouts. Sy moves just enough that I can see Bruce out on the sidewalk, face red with an unattractive blue vein throbbing on his forehead. "Like you said, I'm a fucking legacy, Perilini. I have just as much right to be in there as you do."

"That's right." From my vantage, I only catch the knot in the back of Sy's jaw hardening, but I can perfectly imagine the daggers he must be glaring into Bruce's eyes. "You think I'd have the disrespect–the fucking dishonor–to walk through these doors after a loss? Then you don't know shit." Like me, he's probably remembering that beating he took from Saul's goons. We didn't spend three days holed up in the Crane Motor Inn like fugitives for some entitled shithead to question Sy's loyalty to traditions.

But Remy's the one who says it, back stiffening as he saunters to the door. "Sy's never broken the Dukes' tradition. Not *once*. And he sure as fuck isn't about to break it for you."

Bruce's mouth curves into an ugly, bitter smirk. "Not once, huh?" His eyes flick to me, making my own narrow in response. When the other guy goes to tug him away, Bruce shakes him off, turning his head to aim a glob of spit at the sidewalk. "Fuck it, then. Your parties have sucked ass since day one, anyway." With a final flip of his middle finger, Bruce ambles away.

"Coming through!" Ballsack and Porterfield push through the crowd, carrying the keg from the back room. The guys already went through one, and that doesn't include the punch Kathleen made in a giant paint bucket or the row of shots lined up on the bar reserved for the winners.

That's where Nick is now, leaning against the bar with a bag of ice in one hand and a shot in the other. He catches my eye from across the room and gives me a wink before swallowing it back.

Even though I'm stone cold sober, the lick of heat in my belly makes me feel like I'm the one that just took the shot.

"If you'd told me three months ago that you'd tame all three Dukes, I wouldn't have believed it." Laura follows my line of vision. "But you did it. I have no idea how."

I shift uncomfortably. "Tame seems like a little bit of an exaggeration."

Across the room, Remy waves the winner of the first fight, Kaczinski, over to the chair to get his victory tattoo. He's loose in a way I haven't seen him before. The glint of wildness is missing from his eye, but it's replaced by a clarity so intense that when he catches my gaze, I feel trapped, my skin suddenly tight.

"I don't know," she adds as I take a sip of beer, "taming one bear isn't easy, but three? You must have a magic pussy or something."

I choke on the beer, first in surprise, then on a laugh. When I recover, I say, "It's not like riding their dicks is a chore," and the admission is made so casually, so unthinkingly, that my stomach seizes in shock.

I wait for the wave of shame, as if I'm betraying myself by confessing something like that, but it never comes. It's just the truth. These men are mine now, for better or for worse, and I've already had their 'worse'.

No one deserves their 'better' more than me.

"I bet it isn't." Her eyes flick to Sy, who's over by the door talking to a group of guys. From their strong gestures, I'm guessing they're reenacting some prior fight. His cheeks are ruddy with the flush of liquor, and all I can think about is getting him naked. Again. "But you're the first to tap that, so bravo."

'Tapping' isn't quite what's happening, but I'm not telling Laura that. We're getting closer, spending time every night warming up my body and stretching me out. Although, ever since Remy showed Sy how to curve his finger to find my G-spot and turn me into a puddle of liquefied heat, it's hard to get him to focus on anything but that.

I glance at Laura, trying to decide if I need to handle another jealous cutslut, but she's making eyes at Ballsack across the room. I tip my drink toward him. "You guys have something going on?" The thought all at once warms and terrifies me. Ballsack is a nice guy. Loyal. Sweet. He deserves someone who'll be good to him.

Laura looks like she wants to eat him up. "Some girls won't waste their time on recruits, but what can I say? I like the ones that need a little breaking-in."

The way she and Ballsack exchange a long look makes me believe her. Even more so when a few seconds later, she pushes her empty cup into my hand and says, "Later, Lavvy. I'm going to go find a dark corner and ride his face."

"Bring him back in one piece?" I call, looking down at her discarded cup. Nick catches me just as I reach the trash can, intending to toss it in.

"Babe, you know we have recruits to clean up." Taking the trash from my hand, he drops it right onto the floor like the slob he is. "Besides, I have another job for you. Much higher priority."

My eyes narrow as they dip down, watching his thumb work the button on his jeans. "That's not a job, Nick. It's a career."

His mouth curves into a wicked smirk. "Oh, Little Bird, you should know by now that fucking me is pleasure, not work." He leans in and licks the seam of my lips, pushing his tongue into my mouth. It tastes sharp, like tequila and fire, and he uses it to speak against my lips. "I need my victory ink."

"And you want me to watch while Remy does it?" I ask, trying to figure out what he wants. It doesn't help that his hand is creeping up my shirt, fingers running along the underside of my boob.

"I want *you* to do it."

I blink slowly, trying to find my bearings. "Do what?"

"Ink me." I pull back but his hand splays behind my back, holding me tight. "Like you did for Remy."

I loosen as it dawns on me. "Oh my god, you really are jealous!"

"Fuck yeah, I'm jealous. I want your mark on me, Little Bird. Somewhere special." He releases me and again goes for his pants. I expect him to show me the same spot I gave Remy the moon, but instead, he reveals a smooth, hairless swath of skin above the cock that's currently straining against the lower part of his jeans. "Right here."

I gape at the skin. "You already shaved?"

Shrugging, he answers, "Of course. In the shower, before we left for the gym earlier."

So he's been planning this. I shake my head, trying to dislodge the question of just how far down that goes. Instead, I ask, "But what if you didn't win?" Only it's a stupid question, and the sarcastic tug of his brow is more than enough to drive that home.

"Come on," is all he says.

"You're ridiculous."

Tipping my chin up, he stares at my lips, licking his own. "No, ridiculous is when I considered having you put ink *on* my dick. You know, so I could see it every time I fucked into you." He says it so seriously, as though he's considered this in a very careful, scientific way. "It would have been hot as hell, but let's face it, there's no way I'm going sexless long enough for it to heal, so obviously that's off the table."

"Obviously," I say, not hiding my sarcasm. "So instead, you just want me to mark you *above* your dick."

"Exactly." He tugs his pants back up but doesn't button them. "I'm the victor, Lavinia. These are my spoils." He tilts his head, and even though I know the glare is playful, it still sends a shiver down my spine. "You wouldn't deny a Duke his spoils, would you?"

Some girls would suspect a gesture like this is bogus. A way of over-compensating for a wayward eye or to prove something. Nick doesn't need to give me grand gestures, though. His whole existence is proof of his commitment.

But maybe he needs a gesture from me.

"Okay," I say, just as coolly as he'd requested it. "But Remy needs to supervise, and it can't be anything too involved, because I'm not an artist. At all."

He grins, eyes darkening. "Don't worry, baby. The design I want is so easy, you could draw it with your eyes closed."

That's easy for him to say, but I let him lead me across the room to where Remy has his things set up. He's just finishing up with Kaczinski, who hops out of the chair, showing off the broken crown tattooed on his forearm to his friends.

"You ready?" Remy asks, putting away the dirty needles and opening a package of sealed, sterile ones. He lost his shirt somewhere in the last five minutes, and the curve of his bare shoulder blade distracts me as his back curves over his large box of supplies, green eyes darting up to meet ours.

"I'm going to do something a little different this time, Rem." Nick spins the chair that Kaz was sitting in to face Remy. It's adjustable, and he shifts the lever, dropping it to a reclining position.

Remy observes this with a suspicious stare. "Different how?"

"Little Bird." Reaching up, he tugs his shirt over his head, revealing his chest and torso, the muscles sharp and toned and wallpapered with Remy's designs. "She's going to ink me."

Remy's rolling eyes land on me. "He got jealous, huh?"

I don't respond, because when I turn around Nick has dropped his pants, lowering his shorts until they're just covering his junk. He leans back, spreading his legs on either side of the seat. With his hands, he makes a motion over the hard V muscles flanking his lower abdomen. "Right here between the cum gutters."

Needless to say, his cock bulges against his cotton shorts.

It's instantly obvious that everyone, male and female, is turning to watch my man put his body on display. Cheeks heating, I suggest, "Maybe we should go upstairs."

Nick follows my gaze around the room, an impish chuckle escaping his throat. "Who's jealous now?" But he doesn't shrink away from the attention. If anything, he leans into it, grabbing my hand to tug me closer. When I duck down, close enough for him to speak into my ear, he whispers, "I want everyone to see."

Remy drags his chair over and places it right in front of Nick, "Here you go, Vinny." I'll basically be positioned between Nick's legs, trapped by both of their hot, piercing gazes, only then Remy is the one to sit in it.

Spreading his legs, Remy pats the chair, beckoning me.

Inhaling, I work myself in between them, tingling at the feel of Remy's warm hands on my hips, guiding my ass right up against his crotch as I perch over Nick's. Remy's smooth, beer-laced breath brushes over my ear. "Good?" he asks, a box of sterile gloves suddenly appearing in my lap.

No, I should say. There's no way I'm going to be able to focus with Nick's dick in my face and Remy's pressing against my ass. I'm pinned right between them, the skin on the back of my neck prickling with sweat, and it's all I can do not to squirm around, feeling my own building wetness.

"How do you do this?" I ask Remy, even though I don't mean to.

"Tattoo someone?" Remy asks, sounding confused. Only then he hooks two fingers around my hair, brushing it over my shoulder, and he must see the ember of heat in my eyes, because he laughs, low and teasing into the juncture of my neck. "Yeah, it's a lot of nice skin for you, huh, Vinny?"

Nick's eyebrows pull together in confusion. "What?"

I shoot Remy a warning look–*Don't*–but he pretends to not see it. "We're getting her horny." Ignoring my outraged expression, he says to me, "I'm always horny when I put ink on you. All that purple and red... it just makes it better. You'll understand the next time you see it, all healed and waiting for you." His fingers reach up, brushing the top of my cleavage where the moth rests. He whispers, "Then you'll feel how much it's yours."

I shudder at the feel of his lips against my ear, trying to get myself together. Nodding, I pull out two latex gloves, giving in to the impulse to squirm–right up against Remy's dick.

He grunts, holding my hip. "You thought about getting it on

your dick, didn't you?" Remy asks Nick. To me, he says, "Prep the space, baby," and hands me an antiseptic wipe next.

Nick shrugs a shoulder, forearm wedged behind his head. "Thought about it, but—" I swipe the cold cloth over his skin and he hisses, belly sinking.

"Healing time," Remy says, finishing his sentence. "Figures."

Sy wanders over just as I'm blowing over the antiseptic on Nick's skin, watching the ripple in his abs. I don't even know how the hell, but like Remy, and now Nick, Sy has lost his shirt, too. "What's going on?" he asks, tipping a beer bottle to his lips before passing it to Nick.

"Getting my victory tat." Nick grins down at me, eyes heavy and glazed as he takes a drink from the beer. "Lavinia's doing it."

He rolls his eyes and raises his eyebrow at Remy. "He got jealous. I told you."

"You *told him*?" Nick says, passing the beer to Remy next. "You're talking about me behind my back like little bitches?"

Sy shrugs. "Anything I say behind your back, I'd say to your face. I knew you were going to get jealous when you saw Remy's tattoo. You're such a spoiled little shit."

"Whatever," Nick says, his bitterness only lasting a moment. "You ready, Little Bird?"

I pick up the tattoo gun, comfortable with the weight of it in my hand these days. "You never told me what you want me to put on you."

Flippantly, Nick says, "It'll be easy. No templates. No drawings. I just want two letters in your own handwriting." His fingertips trace over the area. "L.B."

Face growing hotter, I realize, "For Little Bird."

His eyes hold mine for a heartbeat, the muscle in the back of his jaw ticcing. "Yeah, for Little Bird."

I scoot the chair I'm sharing with Remy close enough that it's touching the front of Nick's, all of our legs cramped and tangled, yet somehow fitting perfectly. Leaning forward, I use the hard, flat plane of his lower abdomen to keep my hand steady.

"Is this good?" I ask, looking over my shoulder at Remy.

He assesses the space, "A smidge to the right."

"A smidge?" Nick asks, but I do as he suggests and Remy nods.

"That's centered."

My hair falls forward and Nick reaches down to tuck it behind my ear. A shiver runs down my spine. Voice strained, I say, "*Nick.* You can't touch me while I'm doing this."

"No?" His eyes drop to my chest. That chill made my nipples peak.

"Not if you want it to look *legible.*"

Remy's hand gathers up my hair, giving me a full view of Nick's bare abdomen as he watches me. "That better?" Remy asks.

"Yeah, thanks."

Nick says, "So *he* can touch you?"

I swear to God. "Nick."

He licks his bottom lip. "Go ahead, I'm ready."

It's almost an impossible task to be this close to him, to smell him, the soapy scent from his post fight shower. The hint of tequila when he breathes. The warm heat coming off his skin. I force myself not to look at the way his cock swells under the thin fabric of his shorts, or the goosebumps rising off his skin when the needle makes contact. I give him what he wants. The L and B, a stamp of ownership over his most important organ, in handwriting that's entirely my own. There's part of me that knows this is deranged, that no normal girl would tie themselves to a man like this—to *men* like this.

But since when have I been normal?

By the time I finish the last loop on the B, Nick's cock is hard as nails, the head almost pushing out of the elastic of his boxers near his hip. I pull back a bit, the buzz of the gun finally ceasing, and place my palm right over his hardness, the motion full of cool nonchalance.

Nick spits a low, "Fuck," and bucks into it, but I'm already pulling away.

Sy's rough, quiet voice rings out. "So you and Nick are definitely fucking tonight."

When I look up, his hooded eyes are assessing us, taking the bottle of beer the three of them have been passing around in the same circuit the whole tattoo. "Him, too?" he adds, tipping the neck of the bottle toward Remy.

He's just as hard against my ass as Nick is in front of my face. "Maybe," I say, feeling Remy grinding his boner into me.

There was a time such a declaration would make that old, familiar bitterness fill Sy's eyes. Now he just watches us, not even bothering to hide the bulge in his own pants. "You could do it in my bed."

Nick looks up from his new tattoo to share a glance with Remy, and then me. I let him decide. Nick is the victor, and he was right before. The spoils are his to claim. If he wants me alone tonight, then that's what I'll give him.

"You know me." His dick gives a frighteningly obvious twitch. "I'm always down to put on a show."

"Porterfield!" Sy suddenly barks, downing the rest of the beer in two gulps as the recruit makes his way over, winded and covered in a cutslut's dark red boa.

"Yeah, boss?"

Sy pushes the empty bottle into Porterfield's chest. "You and Ballsack are on closing duty."

REMY'S always had this way of kissing me. It's not just his tongue and greedy lips, or the way his hands grab two big handfuls of my ass as he slams me up against the wall. It's something distinctly spiritual, like he's gathering me up into his own gravity, consuming me, body and soul.

When I manage to find my vision, his eyes are all I see, piercing right through me as he slips my panties down my thighs. It's dark upstairs in the main living area. Remy barely got through the door before descending on me like a prowler. Somewhere behind us, I can vaguely hear Sy and Nick, breathing and shifting, the sound of fabric hitting the floor, but all I can really absorb is the brush of Remy's fingers between my legs, gathering my wetness.

His tongue traces my lips in the same path his fingers take, slow and teasing, the hint of a threat in the way he hovers around my entrance, tongue poised to push through my parted lips.

The second he pushes inside–fingers, tongue–I let out an agonized keen, arching into each penetration, already desperate for more. He pins me there as his free hand reaches for the button on his pants, clawing it open and shoving them down.

It's always more frantic with Remy since that night on the cliffs, and tonight is no different. He hoists me up and I cling to him instinctually, my legs winding around his hips.

From behind him, Nick snorts. "Everyone's always acting like I'm spoiled, but look at me, letting him take first dibs, even though *I'm* the vict–"

I gasp loud and sharp as Remy enters me, his green eyes boring into mine as he sinks to the hilt. I say his name, and he hooks a hand beneath my chin, holding me still as he kisses me, deep and commanding. It's both better and worse than it used to be with him. Better, because it's so electric. Worse, because it's so consuming. My lungs burn with the need to breathe, but the fire between my legs won't let me, Remy's cock dragging away only to punch back into me.

It takes me a long time to realize Sy is talking. "...take her into the room. Come on." Remy's body stiffens suddenly, and Sy adds, "Chill out. Just get her into the bed. *Christ*."

There's a low, mournful sound, and I'm surprised to find it's coming from me. The thought of losing the fullness makes my thighs clench around his waist, but Remy has no intention of abandoning me. He just hooks an arm around my back and wrenches me close, carrying me effortlessly toward Sy's bedroom. Every jostling step he takes pushes his dick a little deeper, and I hang onto his neck and savor it.

That's when I finally catch sight of Nick and Sy.

Both of them are already stark naked, erections bobbing heavily between their thighs as they follow us. Nick reaches down to fist his when our gazes meet, raising his chin.

"Don't come until I tell you to," he says in a spine-chillingly sinister timbre. "Understood?"

Feeling dazed and too horny to think about how annoying that'll be, I nod, mouthing idly at Remy's salty neck. "Okay, Nick."

I'm so fixated on watching their bodies that I don't even know we've arrived until Remy abruptly lowers me onto a soft mattress, following me all the way down.

His dick never once slips out.

"Where were we?" The impish smirk he gives me tells me how proud he is of that fact, but then he's curling a hand behind each of my knees and shoving them *up*, bending me in half as he thrusts impossibly deeper.

I claw at his shoulders, trapped between his body and the bed as he pistons his hips, driving back into me with a hard, jarring thrust. "Oh, fuck," I gasp, staring down my body at how close we're pressed together. Remy's looking too, and I know he's seeing the same things.

Our tattoos—moon and star—meeting the way they were always meant to.

"Get this off," I hear, and then hands appear from over my head—tattooed knuckles, must be Nick—tugging at my top. Remy's mouth descends to my breast the moment it's uncovered, Nick wrestling the top up my arms and over my head.

While Remy sucks on one nipple, Nick fondles the other, pillowing my head on his thigh. I turn my head and see his cock, hard and waiting for me, the letter's LB emblazoned right above the root, but he doesn't tell Remy to hurry.

He says, "Fuck her hard. Get that pussy nice and wet for me. That feel good, baby?" Nick says the last part while stroking my hair back, and I look up into blazing blue eyes.

"Nick," I moan, biting my lip hard as Remy buries a grunt into my neck. "Can I... come? Please?"

Completely stone-faced, Nick wraps his hand around my calf, bending me further for Remy. "Not yet."

Remy fucks me like he has something to prove–not to Nick, nor to Sy, who I can feel on his back beside us, watching–but to himself. He fucks me like he's telling himself it's okay to lose control here, his cheeks growing red as he grunts, slamming me into the bed.

I feel him swell inside of me, but even if I didn't, the way his face hardens, brows crashing together as he stiffens would be enough to tell me he's coming. I wind my fingers into his hair and ride it out, thighs clenching uselessly as I desperately try to take every drop of him into my body.

"Fuck," Remy growls, lips dragging wetly across my mouth. "So much blue..." He kisses me then, slow and slick, his cock growing soft inside of me as he palms my breast, drawing it out.

Nick eventually reaches the end of his generosity, disappearing from behind me only to round the bed, kicking at Remy's ankles. "Enjoy your afterglow after rolling ten inches to the left."

Groaning, Remy rolls away, leaving me cold and squirming. Nick is already kneeling up onto the bed though, blue eyes dropping to my thighs as he flips my skirt up, baring my used pussy.

He fists his cock, saying, "Come look," and it isn't until Sy appears, sitting up to peer between my legs, that I realize who he's talking to.

Biting my lip, I spread my thighs for them, knowing my face must be magenta. Expecting the wave of hot humiliation, I find nothing but a low, simmering arousal in its place as Sy and Nick stare down at me, stroking their cocks.

"Jesus, Remy," Sy whispers, wetting his lips. "That's like a gallon of jizz."

Fingers touch my chin, Remy turning my face to meet his slack gaze. "I save it up for her," he says, pitching forward to give me another slow, sensuous kiss. While I'm wrapped up in that, Sy takes my skirt off. I don't need to look to know it's him. I can tell just from the warmth of his fingertips, the roughness of them, the awkward skitter they make over my thighs as he pulls the skirt off.

But the tongue that descends on my clit is all Nick. It makes me jolt, and when I whip my gaze down, Nick stares up at me with a warning look, licking out to caress my folds.

"Now?" I ask, already on the edge of begging for my own orgasm.

Nick shakes his head, tongue sweeping back and forth over that bundle of nerves. "Not until I say," he replies, dipping to lick a hard stripe from my entrance to my clit.

All of Remy's spent cum is gathered on Nick's tongue.

"Hey!" Remy makes a low, frustrated sound. "Give it back to her, Nicky."

Nick's eyes flick to his, then back to mine, and suddenly he's surging up, pushing the cum into my mouth with a filthy, slippery kiss. It tastes just like Remy, sharp and hot, and I take it back with an aggression that startles even me, curling my hand behind Nick's neck. I hold him close as I suck Remy from his tongue, chasing every last drop when Nick rears back.

"It's my turn," he says, jerking his chin at Sy. "Get on top of him."

Sy tenses as I turn, slinging a leg over his hips to straddle him. "Nick," he hisses, hands steadying my hips as I push him to lay flat. "Come on, don't be an asshole."

"You wanted a show," Nick says, moving to get behind me. Planting a palm between my shoulders, he pushes me down, until I'm on my hands and knees, hovering over Sy's naked body. "Front row seats, big brother."

Sy's throat jumps with a swallow, but I can see his pupils blow wide as his gaze wanders down, settling heavily on my breasts. His voice comes rushed and strained. "Fuck, Lav, I'm not going to last long enough for him to even get inside–"

But he's cut off by my sharp cry, Nick having already lined himself up, entering me with a slow, powerful thrust. I tip my hips up to him, taking him as far as he can go, and Nick grips the back of my hair with stinging pressure, releasing a barely-restrained rumble.

"Goddamn, you're wet," he growls, hips rocking into my ass. Sy's staring into my eyes with a dazed expression, watching me take his brother's cock, and it makes me clench around the fullness. Nick says, "He's not the one fucking you." Any plans I might have to dip down to kiss Sy are wiped away by Nick's gruff, commanding voice. "Look at *me*."

Pushing up, I twist to meet his gaze, but Nick's already yanking me up against his body, hand gripping my chin for a sloppy, unco-ordinated kiss.

He never even closes his eyes.

"That's my good girl," he says, pushing his hips into mine. When my mouth drops open in ecstasy, he takes the opportunity to slide two of his fingers through my lips, the pads salty on my tongue. After a moment, he moves his gaze to Sy. "You want to know the best part about fucking her?"

Sy's expression shutters, eyes fixed to the way my mouth is wrapped around Nick's fingers. "What?" he asks, voice curt and cold.

Nick smirks. "The look on her face when she takes your cock? It's as close to being powerless as she'll ever let you see her." He turns, lips grazing over my cheek as I tip my head back on his shoulder, moaning. "That's the secret, you know. It's not flowers or fancy dates. It's seeing her like this and knowing the value of it. Respecting it. Waiting to be given something instead of just taking it by force. It took me a while to get it, too."

I look down at Sy through heavy eyelids, Nick hard and full inside me, and see the moment it finally clicks. Nick knows. He knows the same way Sy now knows, and how Remy beside us came to understand it, as well.

I've never given myself to anyone the way I've given myself to these men.

Nick finally relents with his teasing, grabbing my hips and punching into my body with a relentlessness that makes me fold.

When I bow my back, desperate to get more of him, Sy's hands are the ones to find me, framing my face as he rises to push a kiss to my mouth. It's slow and sweet, a stark contrast to the jolts of my body as his brother fucks me hard, knocking me and Sy together in an unforgiving tempo.

It's a battle not to come, my fingers twisting frantically in the sheets as each slam of Nick's hips sends my clit grazing against the hard shaft of Sy's cock. The only thing that staves it off is opening my eyes to meet Sy's, letting myself get lost in the ocean of blue.

Nick feels animalistic when he comes, slamming into me with a snarl as his cock surges. For a long moment, everything goes still as he fills me up, pumping me with slick heat. I feel the tension draining out of him with each jerk of his cock, even though my own muscles are still coiled tight, clit so sensitive that a strong gust of air could probably send me over the edge.

"Nick," I rasp, rocking back into him. It sends my clit skating over Sy's length and I shudder, forehead dropping to Sy's sternum. "Please..."

Nick's hand caresses the curve of my ass as he pulls out, saying, "Remy. It's time."

My brain is so hyperfocused on my aching core that it doesn't even occur to me it could be time for anything else but a nice, hard orgasm.

And then Sy lurches up, saying, "Hey! What the fuck?"

"Stay still, fucker." Remy's voice is low and strained, and when I finally lift my head to see what's going on, he's wrestling a pair of cuffs around Sy's wrists, the chain threaded through a slat in the headboard. With one last grunt, Remy closes the cuff, backing away from the bed with a glare. "Jesus, try to get a brother laid and how does he repay you?"

Sy stares over his head at the cuffs, tugging futilely. "This isn't funny," he barks, swinging his glare on Nick, who's currently wiping off his dick with one of Sy's towels. "*Nick*. Take them off."

"Nope," Nick replies, tossing the towel aside. His face is flushed nicely, eyes soft in that special post-fuck way. "Here's the thing, big brother. Our girl wants your dick, and you obviously want to give it to her, but all you've been doing is getting hornier and hornier."

Flopping back to the bed, Remy kicks up a knee, already looking half asleep. "We're here to make sure you lay that pipe responsibly."

I look at Sy, who's finally stopped struggling against the cuffs, and I imagine it. Taking his cock. Sinking down. Watching the look on his face when he can't move.

Unthinkingly, I grind down, pussy clenching on the emptiness Nick's left me with.

Sy tenses, eyebrows knitting together. "Yeah?" When he speaks, I know it's only meant for me. "This is doing it for you?"

I nod, rocking my hips. "Do you...? Want to?"

"So fucking much." Raw heat flickers across his face, that look he gets right before he succumbs to the thing he loves the most, losing control. This way we can both get what we want.

Finally.

SHE'S A GODDESS.

I've never seen anything so sexy in my whole goddamn life, Lavinia straddling me as her pussy, slick with cum and her own hot arousal, grinds across the length of my dick. It's not just her pussy, though. It's her tits, supple and full, right in front of my face. It's the notch her teeth dig into her lip as she rocks against me. It's the way she gazes down at me, so full of raw *want* that it makes my toes curl against the instinct to shove my hips up.

"Lav," I pant, wanting to reach for her face, but feeling the cuffs restraining me. "Please."

Her mouth parts on a moan, because of course she'd get off on me begging for it. Tied up. Helpless. So horny that my dick surges with another stream of precum. My secret is that it doesn't matter how she takes it, only that she does. She can tie me up, make it hurt, bring me to the edge of insanity and shove me off the peak, and it'd all be the same to me, so long as I get *inside*.

I rush out, "I'm ready when you are," but when I shift, bracing myself in anticipation, my wrist snaps, the chain to the cuffs jangling against the bed frame.

Remy snorts. "I bet you are, champ."

"Shut up," I hiss, then turn back to her. "You're in control, baby."

"You say that," her eyes cut to Nick, "but someone won't let me come."

Nick sprawls next to me, head down by my feet, his gaze firmly on Lavinia's ass. He extends a finger to skate teasingly around her ankle. "Thought you should save it. Let him feel it when you clench around him." He looks at me and smirks. "Happy birthday."

Lavinia freezes, gaping down at me. "It's your birthday?" A flustered look comes over her face. "No one told me it was your birthday."

I attempt a shrug that probably looks like a spastic twitch. "It's not until tomorrow. I never make a deal out of it."

"I didn't get you anything," she worries, and I raise my head to fix her with a long, significant look.

"Lavinia." My eyes dart downward, to where her pussy hovers over my cock. "Trust me, this beats any present I've ever gotten, or ever could get."

She blinks. "Oh." When she rises up, my cock springs with her. We're both wet, drenched in our own arousal and the sticky residue left by both Nick and Remy. My brother may play it off like this is all spontaneous, but Nick wouldn't give his victory fuck up for just anything. If this is my birthday present, then that means he's done his research. The hornier she is, already fucked open by both of them, the easier it will be for her to take me.

Hopefully.

"You scared?" I ask. She's got me nudging at her entrance, and I force my hips to stay on the mattress. Someone should probably tie that part of me down too.

"No. Not scared." She bends forward, kissing up my chest, tongue lathing over my nipple. "A little nervous, I guess."

I grasp the chain of the cuffs with my fingers, the grip so tight it stings. "I'll be good." I mean it wholly, but I still shoot Nick a quick, desperate look.

Don't let me hurt her again.

Nick locks his fingers around her ankle and lowers his chin in a nod.

A shiver rushes through me as she ascends, tongue painting a hot path to my throat. "Just working up to it," she whispers, pussy dragging over the head of my cock.

I strain upward to plant a kiss on her throat, sucking a bruise into her pale flesh. "Feed me your tits," I tell her, dying to get them in my mouth. She grabs them both, squeezing them together and leads them to my hungry tongue. I suckle her, listening to her moan as I tug her nipples into hard peaks.

She rises up, grinding her pussy against me again. Her eyes flick to the chain binding my wrist, mouth turning down. "I wish you could touch me."

The air escapes my lungs in a hard, painful gust. "Fuck, babe. I want to touch you, too." I give Remy a pleading look. "Maybe–"

"Nope." Remy sits up, his own cock already stirring to attention again. "I've got this." He moves behind her, his hands sliding around her chest, palming her tits. "That good, Vinny?"

It's infuriatingly unfair, but the burn of envy is eased by the sound of her hum when she reaches between our bodies, fingers sliding enticingly over my shaft. I feel the warm heat as her lips spread apart, welcoming me in her folds, and I know instantly that it's worth it.

"Take him slow, Vinny," Remy says in her ear. His eyes are closed, his mouth sucking at her neck. He tweaks her nipple, and she bucks forward, taking the head of my cock with her.

A breath gets caught in my throat as I hold her gaze, feeling the resistance on the tip of my cock. Her hips give a little testing rock, which is all the warning I get before my dick finally spears through, the head slotting right inside her entrance.

Lavinia tenses, lips parting with a gasp. Her palms land flat on my chest, fingers splayed over each of my pecs. "Oh my god, you're–"

"Fuck," I growl, jaw clenched painfully. She's hovering on her knees, the tip of my cock disappearing into her hole, and it feels like silk, liquid fire. "Fuck, fuck, *fuck*."

Her eyes widen, and she licks her bottom lip. "It doesn't hurt. I think... I think I can take a little more." My fingers scream in protest as I brace for it, the chain digging painfully into my knuckles as she gives another careful rock, sinking another hard inch of me into her slick pussy.

"How the fuck," I snarl, slamming my head into the mattress. "How the fuck do you feel this and not instantly come your fucking brains out?" From the distant, low chuckles, I can assume Nick and Remy understand this question is meant for them.

Remy's the one to say, "It's just experience, bro. We all bust our nuts too early the first few times."

I can't tear my eyes away from my own dick to see how honest he's being. She's so tight, but so much more pliable than the last time. That night, I think I probably felt it, the way I tore myself into her. The whole experience was always knitted up in that sense of wrongness. Right now, it's the complete opposite. She squirms to make room for me, but it's there–a place for me inside of her. I can feel it, and all I want is to *thrust*, shove my hips up and pierce right through the resistance, sheathing my cock in all her warmth.

I resist the urge, my muscles so tense that I can feel them vibrating with restraint. Sweat begins beading on my forehead. "Lav," I grind out, watching her sink down another slow, agonizing inch. "Say something. Are you... is this...?"

"I'm okay," she says, even though the words are spoken through a series of panted breaths. She touches my jaw, stroking day-old stubble with the pad of her thumb. "Are you? You need to relax, Sy. You're going to pass out or something."

"Yeah," Nick says, "you're not the one taking that thing. Ease up a bit."

I shoot him a glare because he doesn't fucking get it. There is no easing up when it comes to this. Only then, Lavinia tips down to kiss me, and it's so gentle—so achingly sweet—that my muscles begin unwinding. I fall into the sensation of her lips, her hair tickling my neck, her pussy fluttering around the head of my cock, and the next rock she gives, taking another thick inch of me, doesn't even make me clench against the instinct to slam upward.

I take it with a long, tortured groan. "Your pussy's so fucking good," I say, licking the whisper into her mouth.

Nick shifts on the bed next to me, his eyes trained on her pussy while his hand fists his cock. "God, look at you taking him. You're doing so good, Little Bird. Just a little more."

'A little' is an exaggeration. It's barely halfway. We may be past the 'just the tip' phase but nowhere near fully inside. I understand that may not happen this time. I'll take whatever she can give me.

But instead of pushing down, Lavinia rises back up. Panic washes over me, but before I can react to the loss of heat, she comes down again, harder than before. My cock slides in deeper, balls twitching as her walls cover me in warmth.

Remy soothes her groan by stroking her hair, whispering, "Don't force it, Vinny." His hand disappears behind her, and then I feel his fingers scissoring around her folds. Belatedly, I realize he's checking her for tears. For blood.

"Is she…?" I don't breathe again until he meets my gaze.

Remy dips his chin in a nod. "So far, so good."

Lavinia's fingers descend next, my stomach flexing at the feel of her brushing my shaft. Her eyes go foggy as she touches the place where we meet, and I realize she's measuring, seeing how far she has left to go. "Oh," she breathes, eyes snapping to mine. "That's… deeper."

Deeper than the last time.

More than she's ever taken.

Victory sparking in her eyes, she clamps her teeth into her

bottom lip, rises in a slow, slick drag, and dives back down, taking so much of my dick that my thighs clench in shock.

"Babe, you keep doing that and—"

Shit.

She does it again, her hips rising in a long, torturous tug, and then sinking back slowly. Remy's hands are on her hips, but they're not guiding her. I can tell, because gradually, he pulls them away, as if he's been waiting to catch her falling off a bike and suddenly realizing she doesn't need the support.

My eyes fly frantically from her pussy to her hooded stare. Every time she drops back down, taking just a little more of me, I'm hypnotized by the way it looks, the space between us disappearing inch by inch. Somewhere in my brain, I try to reconcile what I'm feeling with what I'm seeing. My dick is inside there, through her belly, buried into her sweet, wet cunt, and I want nothing more than to tell her to stop.

I want to stay inside her forever.

"Don't come," she begs. "Not yet."

My ass flexes in time to her rhythm, and when I speak, it's in a voice I hardly recognize, deep and slurred. "I won't." It's a promise I don't know if I can keep, because the truth of what's happening is almost as hot as the act.

I'm getting fucked.

My eyes rise to Nick and Remy, even though it's not like last time. I don't care that other people see–that they *know*. This is about me and Lavinia becoming what we're meant to be. Nick and Remy aren't my audience, they're my compass, and right now I need them to tell me if this is right.

Both of them are watching her pussy, though.

Remy's leaning back, ducking his head to see it from behind, and I can't even imagine how it must look. "Fuck," he breathes, running a finger around her tight, stretched hole. "Your pussy's taking him so good, Vinny."

Nick's eyes are glazed and almost black as he touches her thigh, desperate for a better look. "Get your phone," he tells Remy. "Take a picture so they can see later."

I start, "You don't have to–"

But Lavinia's only protest is to look at them over her shoulder, saying, "No faces."

Remy's already fumbling for his discarded jeans, pulling out his phone and bending to get a photo.

"I can take more," she says, teeth baring down on her bottom lip. "I just... let me just..." She shifts, changing the angle, falling forward and trapping me with her dark eyes. With one roll of her hips, I sink in farther than before, watching as her jaw goes slack. "Oh God, right *there*."

Her eyes, which had been locked-in on me, flutter shut. That simple act sends a jolt through my heart. She trusts me.

Behind her, Remy is snapping a photo of her pussy, but all I can focus on is the way she looks, forehead creased in abandon as she writhes to take more of my dick. Carefully, I plant my heels and give a small, measured nudge with my hips, bracing myself for disaster.

But when her eyes fly open, she just says, "Yeah, like *that*."

"Yeah?" I give another testing buck, not trying to drive myself in deeper, just wanting her to feel me here.

She makes a low, keening sound, bearing back into motion, and behind her, Remy spits a soft curse. The urge to come is over-whelming—the need to touch and make this good for her more painful than the ache in my balls. She deserves it.

She deserves the best.

My eyes drop from her, down to Nick who is watching this with sharp intensity. Our eyes meet and I jerk my chin.

He doesn't miss a beat, licking his thumb and leaning between us. He swipes the pad over her clit, rolling it in a slow circle. I don't just see her react; I *feel* her, the muscles lining the walls of her pussy clenching around me. My hips rock up, and she drives down to meet me. Nick must do it again, because this time she cries out, one hand thrusting in my brother's hair as the other claws down my chest.

The rush of feeling her tighten around me, all the way around me, eclipses all other moments. "Oh my god, Sy," she pants, eyes snapping open and meeting mine. "I'm coming."

She doesn't have to tell me, because her back straightens at the same time her pussy strangles my cock, gripping me like a goddamn vise. I lurch forward, the thread snapped, my orgasm unleashing like a detonated bomb, but then slam back, forgetting my restraints.

"Fuck!"

Lavinia falls forward, hair tumbling over her shoulder, her hips convulsing. Her mouth meets mine, tongue pushing between my lips. Her nails dig into my chest, but nothing matters but the sensation of her pussy milking my cock.

Nothing matters but her.

She finishes her kiss, the same time my cock stops twitching inside of her, and I gaze into her eyes.

"I love you," I say, not caring if the guys hear me. Not caring if she says it back.

I just want her to know.

"Look at me." My mother reaches for my face, twisting it back and forth as if she's searching for something. We're in the kitchen, just the two of us. Nick, Remy, and Lavinia are in the other room with Dad and Pops.

"Ma." I grab her forearms and gently force her to stop manhandling me. "Jesus, can't a guy just get a drink?"

"Something's different." She frowns, twisting to grab my hand, and I cringe as her eyes zero in on the marks around my wrist. "What happened here? A fight? Oh, Simon..."

"No, I'm not fighting again!" Breaking away, I stick my head in the fridge, originally planning on grabbing a bottle of water, but *fuck*. A beer seems like a better idea. In moments like this, I understand what it must be like for the guys and Lavinia to live with me. The hyper-analyzing is annoying as fuck.

I stand, slamming the door, well aware that my cheeks are flushed. I grab the bottle opener off the counter and pop the top. "If you *have* to know, Lavinia and I…" I swallow the rest of that sentence along with a gulp of beer.

She turns to smooth out the icing on my birthday cake, eyebrow rising. "You know the rule, sweetheart."

'If you can't talk about sex, you're not mature enough to engage in it.'

That just about sums up life with a mother who's a sex therapist. "We had sex," I blurt, hand clenched around the bottle of beer.

She looks at my wrist, brows hiking higher on her forehead. "Adventurously, it seems."

Shaking my head, I explain, "No, I mean… we're together. She's my girlfriend."

Her eyes flick toward the living room where Remy's excited voice carries as he describes something enthusiastically. "And your brother and Remy?"

"She's their girlfriend, too." I swallow, picking at the label. "Our Duchess. You know how it is."

Mom's good at keeping a straight face. The job requires it, but a mix of emotions runs through her eyes at the announcement. "Are you sure? Because managing this type of relationship isn't for everyone."

I rake my fingers through my hair, already regretting this conversation. "I know things didn't work out with all of your… Dukes." God, this is weirder than telling her I lost my virginity. "But that's the thing. I get it now, that this isn't something that comes easily. I fucked up with Lavinia–bad, and more than once–and we still worked through it. She's the right one," I tell her, feeling this from the bottom of my soul. "For *us*. She gets Remy. Like, really gets him." I snort. "And God, Ma, she might be the only person in this world who can actually handle Nick."

That makes her expression ease, because I know these are her real questions. Nick, Remy, and I aren't normal men. We're a mess–always have been. "And what about you?" she asks.

"Me?" I rest my elbows on the counter in front of my birthday cake. It's red velvet–the same every year, just the way I like. "I gave her my journal," I whisper, keeping my voice low. When I glance up at my mom, she's frozen, searching my eyes. I've never let anyone read my journals before. "I know I don't talk about it much, but I think... I think I was really messed up when I met her." Lavinia dragged me from the edge of a place so filled with anger that it was eating me up inside. She showed me patience and care while dragging me out of that dark place of doubt and rage, over and over. She taught me to understand myself, and that women weren't my problem. *I* was the problem. I could tell Mom all of that, but I don't, because in the end it's shockingly simple. "I love her. She makes us... better. Connected. Not new or different, just..." I struggle to find the word I'm looking for.

My mom knows, though. "A family."

Something in my shoulders unwinds at the realization. That's it. "Well, she needs that just as much as we do, because her own family is fucked all to hell."

She frowns at my language but asks, "And you're sure she can get past the things you had to do to get to this place?" She pulls the collar of her shirt to the side, revealing the puckered brand right above her heart. Although she normally hides it, it's been a presence our entire life. I don't—no, *can't*—think about what she went through to get it. She lets me look at it for a brief moment before covering it again, saying. "Some things can't be undone, Simon." It's the first time I've ever heard her mention her past with my fathers in anything but a happy light.

"We didn't brand her," I say quietly, squirming under the weight of her stare. "Remy marked her with a tattoo. That was enough."

Her head snaps back in surprise. "And Saul is okay with that?"

My lip curls. "Saul doesn't get a say in how we manage our Duchess."

"Hm." The corner of her eyes crinkle with skepticism. "Well, you never know, I suppose. Maybe things will be different for you."

"They will be." I say this with absolute conviction. "No one is going to hurt her again. I wouldn't let them, and neither would Nick or Remy." I don't say that the three of us are willing to give everything for her, but from the worry in my mother's eyes, she still hears it.

"That's what I'm afraid of," she says.

Before I can find a way of reassuring her, Nick struts in, loose and easy in a way our mom probably hasn't seen him since high school. When he passes her, ducking in to press a quick, affectionate kiss to her temple, I wave my hand.

See?

She twists to give him a long, considering look, Nick opening the fridge to grab three more beers. When he turns, he freezes, looking between us. "What?"

Mom says, "Nothing," and fidgets with the cake, but Nick narrows his eyes at me.

"Motherfu–" he swallows the curse. "You told her, didn't you?"

I glare at him. "Like you can judge." He nearly shouted it from the rooftops when he lost his virginity in high school. All it got him was a lecture from mom on communicating his intentions to young girls who are prone to romantic attachments and a trip to the pharmacy to buy condoms with Pops. At least I don't have to go through that.

"All he told me is that you're happy," Mom says, adding a wink.

My brother's eyes meet mine, and as unfamiliar as the term is to us, she's right. We are happy, and I plan to do everything I can to keep it that way.

"Mom said dinner will be ready in ten minutes," I say, walking into the living room.

Nick's showing Pops the gun he got from Maddox. "Do I want to ask how he got it from you?" Nick asks.

Pops handles the gun reverently, running his thumb over the design etched in the side. The Bruin 'B.' He answers with a pointed, "Do I want to ask how you got it back?"

Nick pauses before sinking back into the couch, crossing his arms. "Touché."

As curious as I am to know the answer to that question, I know it's futile. Nick and Lavinia have been pretty quiet about what transpired in the Baron's crypt. "Hey." I look down at Remy, nudging him with a loose fist. "Where's Lav?"

He twirls his marker around his fingers and jerks his chin toward the stairs. "Washing up, I think. Want me to find her?" I shake my head before the seed of eagerness in his eyes can grow. Normally, Remy loves chatting with our dads, so I know it's not the company. It's her. Lavinia.

All three of us are hooked.

The house isn't big, a modest two-story bungalow with a basement. By the time we were in middle school, it was clear two growing boys, along with two adult men, were not going to fit in the current footprint. Instead of moving, they blew out the back of the house and the attic. They used our old rooms to build a large ensuite and then expanded upstairs for me and Nick.

I jog up the stairs, noting that the hall bathroom light is off, door open. I peek my head into Nick's room, but it's empty. I look in my old room next, finding her standing by the dresser, looking at a photo of me and Nick standing on the edge of a dock. I was about fourteen, Nick thirteen. We're posing like Mr. Universe, puffed out chests, straining to produce biceps. We were scrawny little shits, but Dad and Pops had recently agreed to workouts.

"Hey." I lean in the doorway, thinking that fourteen-year-old me would have absolutely fucking died at the sight before me. A hot girl in my childhood bedroom. "Dinner's almost ready."

"The Perilini-Bruin boys. Heartbreakers from the start." She turns from the photo and sits on the end of the bed, eyes assessing the space. "It smells like you in here," she says, running her hand over the quilt.

Her skirt is short enough to expose the lean line of her thigh. And the low scoop of her shirt... well, someone should have suggested a sweater. "I was just here a few weeks ago, I doubt my mother's washed the sheets yet."

When I left. When I hurt her.

"No." She shakes her head, a smile flirting at the edge of her mouth. "It's a different smell. You, but... more boyish."

"More boyish?" I ask, stepping into the room. I like the look of her on the bed, a million teenage fantasies colliding.

She hums thoughtfully. "Yeah, kind of a mix of sweat, hormones, and cheap body spray."

"Aside from the body spray, how is that different from now?" Birthdays always make me ruminate on the fact I don't feel any differently, but this one especially. I'm still a jumble of exposed nerves and hormones when I'm around this woman. My cock incessantly hard. *Painfully* hard at the moment.

She stands, never breaking my gaze as she closes the gap between us. Hands flat on my stomach, she pushes up on her toes, pressing her nose into the crook of my neck. "Now you smell like a man," she whispers, inhaling.

If I thought it was hard to keep my hands off Lavinia before, actually sinking my cock into her has made it substantially worse. I clench down on a surge of instant, consuming lust, but can't fight the impulse to grab her hips, turning to catch a whiff of her hair. "I've worked a lot on my self-control the last few months, but you keep sniffing me like that and I'm going to come in my pants."

"Or you could come inside *me*." She slides her hand lower, cupping my erection. "We can be quick."

I give a strained laugh at the lie. The truth is, sex between the two of us might never be quick. There will always be prep work and patience. It's odd to think there was a time that reality would have brought a sense of bitter disappointment. Now, I imagine spending an hour working up to getting my dick inside of Lavinia and shudder at the prospect.

The ache in my balls is already returning. "Two things will happen if we're not downstairs when my mother calls us for dinner."

Her hand gives a torturous squeeze, lips brushing against my jaw. "Oh yeah?"

Struggling to find my voice, I rumble, "First, she'll send someone up here to find us. Second, it'll be Nick, and he will lose his goddamn mind if he thinks I'm fucking you in my childhood bedroom before he does."

She pulls back, eyes growing wide. "Oh my god, you're right. He'll *hound* me."

"Like a dog."

"Fine," she says, but even though her lips turn down, I can tell she's trying not to laugh. "We'll go eat."

This is how I end up sitting through an entire dinner, surrounded by my family, with a throbbing boner.

"Granted," Remy is saying, recounting the events of last night's fight, "this Prince was built like a bus ticket–"

"Aren't they all?" Dad says, laughing. Remy laughs along, but Nick and I share a look.

The Princes are getting bigger and stronger as the years roll by.

Remy goes on, "So Nick absolutely mollywhops this guy, right in the jaw. And you know Nick. He's boasting the crowd up like he does, pretending like he's above it all."

Lazily, Nick cuts in, "I am above it all," and Lavinia rolls her eyes.

"Please, you love the attention," she says.

"Speaking of," Nick says, pushing back his cleared plate, "any heads up on this alumni poker game Saul has directed us to host?"

There's no missing the look exchanged between our parents. Abruptly, the whole vibe around the table sours.

In a not so subtle way, Pop rests his hand on mom's and

squeezes it. "How about you two ladies—sorry, *Duchesses*—take a break." He gestures to the messy table. "We've got this."

"Thank you, honey." Mom stands and gives both of her husbands a kiss on the cheek. She looks to Lavinia and says, "Let's get out of here before they change their minds."

"Grab the plates," Dad says, reaching for the empty platter and starting for the kitchen.

"We don't keep things from her." I follow, carrying my plate and my mother's. "Whatever you have to say to us, you can say to her."

"Vinny's tough," Remy adds, shoving the last roll into his mouth before stacking the basket on top of an empty bowl.

"That's obvious." Dad pushes his chair back. "But the life they lead, being a Duchess…" He goes unexpectedly quiet, his long dark hair shielding his expression.

Pops is the one to explain. "She needs someone who can relate to her situation just as much as the three of you do."

That statement sits uncomfortably in my chest.

"Which is exactly why we need to know what we're getting into with this poker game," Nick says.

Pops snorts and turns on the faucet, shifting it over to hot. "You mean the one we haven't been invited to since we dropped DKS?"

There are rules in the fraternity. If you drop, like our parents did, then that means you're no longer affiliated in any way. It's full-on persona non grata. A former member can no longer attend events, receive any perks, or wear letters or symbols associated with the fraternity. But this is Forsyth, where allegiance runs deeper than a pin or ring. The brand on my mother's flesh tells that story just as much as the blood that runs through Nick, Lavinia, and Remy's veins. Still, I know our parents were ostracized when they chose one another over Royal life.

Dad opens the dishwasher and starts rearranging the plates, but abruptly freezes, jaw dropping in horror. "Who put this pot in here?"

"I did," Pop snaps. "It's fine."

"This is hand-wash only!" Dad barks, thrusting a finger at the pot. "And it takes up too much space, anyway."

Fighting over the dishwasher is a lifelong struggle with these two. Both think they've figured out the key to maximum arrangement. Whatever talk she must be having with Lavinia isn't the only reason my mom happily escaped from cleanup.

"Jesus," Nick says, swiping the pot from Dad's hand. "*I'll* wash." He shoots me a look. "You dry. Remy, you put up the leftovers. You two sit down and drink a beer."

Dad and Pops both look impressed. It's the first time they've seen Nick wearing this new leadership skin. It suits him better than anyone expected.

I grab the dish towel off the rack. "So," I start, trying to get this back on track. "The poker game?"

"Right," Dad says, taking a seat at the kitchen counter, while Pop grabs two beers. "I don't know what to tell you, son. Other frats gather alumni together for homecoming or a family weekend. DKS has always had our poker game. As it grew, it seems like Saul decided to link it to the fall festival. A lot of local families come out to that anyway—"

"Because it's a good place to be seen," Pops adds, sitting next to him, sliding the beer over. "The media is there. Politicians. Saul likes that attention, but really what he wants is to remind everyone that West End is still open for business. *His* business."

Dad's eyes dart between us. "But you boys already figured that out, didn't you?"

"It's not the business part that worries me," I say, that flicker of possessive anger sparking in my chest. "He's making Lavinia the night's entertainment."

Pops freezes, the beer halfway to his mouth. "You pissed him off, didn't you?" After a moment of obvious silence–Nick can't spend time with anyone and not piss them off–Pops deflates. "I've tried really hard to hold back on the 'I told you so,' but Nick." He levels my brother with a hard look. "I told you so."

"You can always walk," Dad says. "We did."

I chuckle, the sound dark and mirthless. "You 'walked,' huh? Because that's not the way I hear it."

Pops' eyes narrow. "And just how do you hear it?"

A lot was happening that night I met with Maddox at the Underworld, so much that I didn't have time to dwell on what he told me. That doesn't mean I forgot, though. "Word is, you lost the loyalty of the frat."

Nick watches our fathers closely, expression hardening at the look they share. "Hey, fuck that. Don't just leave us in the dark."

Pops sighs, avoiding Nick's glare. "You know your grandpop died when we were Dukes." Grandpop was his grandfather, our great-grandfather.

My back goes ramrod straight. "You're not saying Saul–"

But Pops shakes his head. "Saul didn't kill him. Your grandpop had been dying for years with lung cancer."

Dad pipes in, "We all figured he'd go once Davis was in the belfry."

"And we were right," Pops says, the dullness of an old grief filling his eyes. "In fact, we'd only been in for a couple months when he kicked it. I never wanted to be King. You all know that." Finally meeting Nick's gaze, he adds, "But grandpop was always good to me, and I wanted to honor him. Do right by him. Do things just the way he taught me." He lifts the beer to his mouth, giving a bleak smile. "Saul had other ideas."

Dad stresses, "Bigger ideas," and I take a guess.

"Business ideas."

Pops gives me a slow nod and begins massaging his knee. It's an old training injury that always seems to flare up whenever he needs a fidget. "West End's always had the gun trade locked down, but it wasn't always about running them, you know. We're built differently than the other Royals." He jerks his chin at Remy, and then Nick. "We're fighters. Our weapons are our bodies and our cunning, and we're good at knowing how to use them–*when* to use them."

Dad snorts. "A Count, a Baron, a Prince, a Lord... none of them are going to match a Duke on pure physicality alone. They need guns to beat us."

"So," Pops says, watching Nick with shrewd eyes, "what does a fighter do to ensure a victory?"

It takes Nick a second to answer, comprehension dawning on his features. "You monopolize all the guns."

Pops tips his beer at Nick. "Exactly."

"But where we saw strategy," Dad says, eyes growing dark, "Saul saw business potential. Your grandpop was sitting on a stockpile that could have earned West End a fortune."

Pops grabs his knee, leaning forward. "I don't need to ask you to imagine what that would be like—Forsyth stocked to the teeth with West End guns." He gestures broadly. "You're living Saul's dream out there, boys."

Anger flickers in my brother's eyes. "So you just... fucking *left*?"

"Hey," Dad snaps, because as much as he and Pops bicker, no one jumps to his defense faster. "No one *just* leaves the Royalty, Nicky. Especially not when they're about to become King."

"There was a vote." Pops' voice is low and toneless. "That's how it's done in the belfry. You know that."

Dad adds, "Saul campaigned the frat. Davis promised a future of the status quo, which was more about community and building up the gym than power, but Saul was offering a way for West End to earn money hand over fist."

Pops rests his head back against the cabinet, eyes faraway. "DKS chose Saul."

I share a look with Nick, because this is news to us. We've always been told it was a choice. That the three of them packed their bags and gladly left the Royalty behind them. It can't all be a lie, only now I'm realizing it wasn't as easy as they made it sound.

Because I'm looking into my Pops' eyes, and somewhere beneath all the resentment and stubborn conviction, there's a wound that's never quite healed. Maybe Davis Bruin never wanted power or legacy, but he wanted to do something right. Something good. Something worthwhile.

And Saul Cartwright took it from him.

There's a crash, Nick dropping a coffee mug into the dishwater. He clutches the counter, shoulders forming a taut, tense curve over the sink. "Do you have any fucking idea what it's like out there?" he asks. Turning a glare onto our father, he keeps his voice low and measured, but so full of venom that it makes me jolt to stand between them. "West End was yours. You should have fought for it."

Pops jumps off the counter, his knee injury forgotten. "You think I didn't fight?" he asks, mouth pinched into an angry grimace. "You asked how the Baron King got that gun, so here's the truth. I went to all of them–the Kings of Forsyth–hoping for one goddamn promise of support." He tilts his head in that special, menacing way that comes with the Bruin genetics. "Do you know what that masked asshole told me?"

Remy's the one to answer, the words quiet and grim. "Death is business." He shoots me a look, because my fathers might not know Maddox's true identity, but we do. "More bodies, more money."

Pops gestures to Remy like it's the most obvious thing in the world, and I suppose it is.

Dad clutches his beer, staring sightlessly at his knuckles. "The other Kings liked Saul's pitch. They lapped it up, Nick. They were all too happy to see West End in his hands, however bloody they might become. They wanted the firepower."

"More than that," Pops raises his chin, "they wanted the war."

The words ring with a frightening clarity, because it all makes perfect sense. The Barons wanted the business. The Lords would have wanted to build their own arsenal to protect their land and women. The Counts would have needed the enforcement. And the Princes...

They wouldn't have settled for anything less than the best of the best.

"Well," my laugh is clipped and full of bitterness, "they got it."

Some of the fire bleeds from Nick's eyes, but he doesn't look any less tense about the revelation. "Even if we wanted to walk, we don't have that option," he says, turning his focus to the dishes. Steam runs from the hot water, but he runs his hands underneath anyway, his fists clenching at the burn.

Remy snaps the lid on a glass container and admits, "He's got us by the balls."

Nick and I shoot him a glare. "Dammit, Rem–"

But it's too late.

"I see," Dad says, and it's clear from his expression that he does. They both do. They don't have to know the specifics of the video to understand that Saul has leverage on us, and that's why there's no walking away from this one.

"You don't need to say you told us so." I ball the towel up and toss it on the counter. "Again."

They don't have to. It rings in the air. This is what they were always warning us about. Living this life... the danger was never about how it would hurt us. That's not how people like Saul come at fighters like us. It's always about how it will hurt the people we love. People like mom.

Like Lavinia.

But that's the thing about the belfry. Our fathers wouldn't understand it, because they never had it. We're not fractured like they were. We're three Dukes and a Duchess, the way grandpop always knew it had to be. DKS finally has someone to get behind. The Bruin in the belfry finally has a house he can count on.

And if the Kings want a war, we'll give them one.

17

L avinia

I'M NOT sure where Sarah is taking me, but I know better than to push back when my boyfriends' mother wants me to go with her. Although, the abrupt way we left when talk about the poker game came up gives me a clue.

She leads me to the back of the house. At the jagged turn of the hallway, I get the sense a few walls have been knocked down. That's confirmed when she enters a large ensuite, which is beautiful, but out of place in an older home. I hesitate outside the door, but she beckons me in, stopping at an antique apothecary chest. While she opens drawers, pulling out a small box and a bundle of dark blue satin, I survey the space.

The room is a nice size, with the bed taking up the majority of the space. It's massive, and for a second, I get caught up in imagining the three of them in there, all wound around each other like my Dukes were with me this morning.

I've heard of some Royal women whose relationships with two or more of her guys extended past their tenure in house leadership. Story and her Lords weren't the first, and they won't be the last. But that's usually just horny college stuff. Guys getting off on the thrill of sharing a girl. Girls getting off on the thrill of being shared. I've never seen a relationship like theirs last this far into adulthood. Marriage, houses, kids, careers.

I think about how Sarah sleeps with two men—and I sleep with three.

How did they make it work?

She passes the bed for a set of French doors, opening them to reveal a deck that overlooks the sloped backyard. "Let's get some air," she suggests, beckoning me through the doors. Once we're out there, the space illuminated by a string of lights, she gestures to a couch, eyes wistful as she stares out over the yard. "Manny built this about ten years ago. I'm sure you'll come to see that Perilinis are very handy."

The cushions are soft and I sink into them, feeling awkward. "Oh, I know. Sy's been helping me with a project."

She takes the bench seat across from mine. There's a table between us, or what I think is a table until she flips a switch and fire ignites from the top. "It's a little chilly. Do you need a blanket?"

"No." I warm my hands over the firepit. "I'm good."

She sets the two items she's retrieved from the apothecary chest on the seat beside her and flips open the box, removing a rolled joint. Sarah's eyes assess me carefully. "I hope this is okay."

I straighten. "Sure."

"Usually I just take an edible, but when the weather is nice, I like to sit back here and relax." She flicks the lighter and burns the tip. The red ember glows when she takes a drag. "Want a hit?"

"*God*, yes." I lean over and take it, securing the thinly rolled joint between my fingers. I take a drag, feeling the burn in my chest, and my slight cough makes Sarah grin.

"First time?" she asks.

"Sarah." I stare at her. "I'm North Side."

She laughs, watching me take another hit. "I guess you'd know a thing or two about it then."

Inspecting the joint, I say, "Ironically, growing up, my father didn't allow drugs in the house. I guess after my mother OD'd, he figured he'd keep me and Leticia away from the garbage that killed her." I arch an eyebrow. "Until we'd eventually need to organize the mass sale of it, that is."

Sarah nods, bending to take the joint from me. "But you kids always find a way, don't you?"

Shrugging, I exhale, watching the plume rise into the evening sky. "I know the guys used to keep weed and stuff in the tower, but ever since Remy got clean, so have we."

"Ah." She gazes at the joint thoughtfully before taking another drag. "That's good to hear."

As she passes it back, I take the chance to say what's been on my mind for a while. "Can I ask you a question?"

She doesn't even pause. "Of course, but let me warn you. If you want to know how to balance the sex drive of three young men, I may need a glass of wine to go with this."

"Um..." That is *not* what I wanted to ask, but fuck, maybe later. *After* two glasses of wine. "Actually, I was wondering about Saul. Did you ever... love him?"

"No," she says with zero hesitation, barking a harsh laugh. "We had some good times, and I accepted him as my third Duke, but I'm not sure it's possible to love a man like Saul. I know for certain he's incapable of loving anyone but himself."

I think about how bitter Sy was when they first won me from the Lords. He loathed me. He was *terrible* to me, but I saw his love for his brother and Remy. I knew he had the capacity for it. We just had to tear down those walls.

Sarah takes another slow drag and hands the joint back to me. "Not that any of it was easy. Back then, Davis and Manny wanted two things: to fight and fuck. It was fun, but later, they saw I wanted more. To have a career, to build a family." There's a dread in her eyes that startles me to see. "Saul always wanted one thing: Power, by any means necessary."

"Sounds familiar," I say, thinking of my father.

She lifts her feet, resting them on the edge of the pit, warming them. "But we tried to make it work, and for a while, we did." A nostalgic smile pulls at her mouth. "Saul was handsome and a strong fighter. On campus and at the gym, we made it seem like everything was fine. We put on a show. But back at the tower," she waves a hand, "he wasn't involved in our relationship at all. After a while, he didn't require much from me—sexually speaking. Turns out, he had incredibly specific desires, and I didn't check the boxes."

"Wait." I pause with the joint suspended halfway to my lips. "Is Saul gay or something? Is that why he doesn't have a Queen or any kids?" Saul has always been a strange Royal outlier. Ashby doesn't have any blood heirs either, but that's a special circumstance. To have a child and lose it so young...

But she shakes her head. "Oh no, not Saul. He's bolted very firmly to the zero on the Kinsey scale." Her expression turns pensive. "It might even be one of the reasons I specialized in sex therapy. I suppose you could say his predilections fascinated me. I wouldn't call Saul deviant, just... very particular. Nothing about me fit what he wanted." She spins her wedding ring around her finger. "Specifically, I wasn't a Royal daughter or a sweet, compliant virgin."

My eyebrows shoot up. "Seriously? Saul's forever alone because he's just a big, throbbing Royal cliche?" But then I think about what Story's told me about the Kings' plans for her. She was meant to be their asset until she ran away, leaving me in her place. She was *it*. A sweet little virginal Royal daughter-not by blood, but who knows? Maybe she was close enough. I look up at Sarah in shock. "God, he really is, isn't he?"

She shrugs. "I thought we'd reached an agreeable place in our relationship. He had the status to get ahead. I had two men that I loved and who worshiped me in return."

I take another drag before passing the joint back over the table. "I hear a 'but' coming."

She gives me a tight smile. "It was little stuff at first. He was dismissive to me. Demeaning. He wanted me to treat him like a god while he acted like I was dirt on the bottom of his shoe. He trivialized my academic drive. While Davis, Manny and I were taking classes and partying, Saul was making plans."

My muscles ease, the cannabis seeping into my bloodstream. "What kind of plans?"

She tips her head back, exhaling a long stream of smoke. "Business plans. Social plans. Setting the frat up for his takeover. For instance," she says, giving me a significant look, "the alumni poker game."

A shiver runs up my spine. "Oh. That."

Nodding, she explains, "Gambling and tradition have always been West End vices, but it was Saul's idea to turn the annual poker game into a networking opportunity. Suddenly, it wasn't just a fun night to catch up with everyone and lose all their money. He's the one who came up with the idea of having the cutsluts provide entertainment." Barking a sour laugh, she adds, "Hell, he's the one who came up with cutsluts. Him and Mama B."

"Really?" For some reason, a part of me had always figured the cutsluts were an institution as old as the clock tower itself, only now that I think about it, it makes sense.

"Oh, yes," she says, flapping a hand. "Of course, there were always gym girls milling around. They just gave them a name. An identity. A purpose. I'm sure he pitched it to Mama B as the most feminist thing she ever heard."

I give her a doubtful look. "And now he basically wants me to be one." Leaving out everything relating to the blackmail, I explain that Saul wants me to be the entertainment.

"He wants you to perform," she clarifies, going quiet. I don't like the sting of pity in her eyes, but even worse is the tug of confusion in her brow. "I doubt Saul's ever ordered a Duchess to do that before. You understand that, don't you? It's not your duty."

Shifting uncomfortably, I say, "He's my King now. My duty is whatever he says it is." She knows this is smoke and mirrors, surely. I'm Lavina Lucia. I don't take orders from just anyone.

Not unless they have something on me.

"Lavinia…" From her pause, I get the impression she's choosing her words very carefully. "You're a Royal daughter. The exact thing he's always wanted."

"I'm not sweet or virginal," I point out, scoffing.

"Still," she says, reaching out to place her hand over mine. "You're not safe with him. From one Duchess to another, I need you to know that."

I raise an eyebrow. "It'd take a truly stupid girl to think she's safe with any King, let alone one who's competing with her father." More thoughtfully, I add, "I don't trust Saul, but I trust Remy and your sons. They'll protect me."

There's a light in her eyes that dims with each passing word, until finally, she leans back, taking a steeling breath. "I have a question for you, too. Normally, this is something I'd ask them directly. I don't like secrets, Lavinia." Her mouth flattens to a tense line. "Unfortunately, Nick does."

Squirming under the weight of her gaze, I already know I won't betray Nick—not even to his mother. Still, I answer, "What do you want to know?"

She watches me intently, her words quiet and solemn. "Does my son intend to take Saul's crown?"

I lock up, feeling foolish. If she brought me out here and got me stoned just to interrogate me about Nick's plans… "I don't know," I answer, unable to blame her. "Maybe."

She gives a slow, heavy nod. "I was afraid of that. Maybe I've always been afraid of that."

"Would it be so bad?" I wonder, searching her expression. Pretty Nick Bruin, King of West End, the way it should be. Yeah, Nick has issues, but he's no Saul Cartwright. He'd do right by our house. "To the victor go the spoils," I remind her. Nick would have power, prominence, opportunity. There's not a lot of that out there for a guy with his background. Men with facial tattoos don't become CEOs.

She gives me a slow, sad smile. "And to the defeated go the casket."

I feel my face harden. "My Dukes don't lose."

"I hope you're right," she says, eyes tired and damp as she reaches for the bundle of blue silk beside her. "But just in case you're not..." She flips the fabric up, revealing a curvy, silver spike. No—not a spike.

A *snake*.

It's about ten inches long, and I'm so enthralled by the glint of the fire catching on the scales that it takes me a long moment to recognize what it is.

A hair pin.

"It was your mother's."

My eyes fly to hers, heart skipping a beat. "What?"

Sarah extends it to me, explaining, "I guess you can say she loaned it to me. It was after one of Davis' matches."

I reach out, fingers hovering over the pin, before plucking it from the satin. It's heavy and solid, shiny and– "Shit," I hiss, pricking the pad of my fingertip on the spiked edge.

Sarah nods. "It's a weapon just as much as an ornament." She gestures to my hair, which I'd pulled up into a loose bun for the night. "She wore her hair like that a lot."

I've seen photos, my mother's long, blonde hair twisted up into a bun, usually with one of these stabbed through it. The hair pin *is* an ornament, delicate and feminine, and I feel my world reorient itself as I imagine her having held this in her hand.

"She loaned it to you?" I press, trying not to sound accusatory.

She winces. "I meant to give it back, but it wasn't too long after that we left the belfry for good." Sarah nods at the pin. "The night she gave it to me, Davis was fighting her Count. Not your father," she's quick to add. "But it was a rowdy crowd and some of the Kappas were out for blood. I'm sure you can appreciate that the wardrobe of a Royal woman isn't always conducive to concealed weaponry." She smirks at the comprehension dawning on my face.

"This is a weapon a woman can wear with anything," I realize.

"Yes," she agrees, watching me intensely. "Or nothing."

I shudder to imagine the situations my mother–or even Sarah herself–must have found herself in back then.

I guess I won't have to imagine for long.

Reluctantly, I confess, "I've... never had anything of my mother's before. Anything worth handing down went to my sister, and Lucias... well, we aren't much for sharing." Tearing my eyes away from the silver, I look up, meeting Sarah's gaze as I spear the pin through my hair. "Thank you."

She responds with a tight smile. "I know my boys would do anything to protect you. I also know they've been one of the things you've needed protection from."

Frowning, I say, "Things are different now."

"I've seen." She doesn't look relieved. If anything, the crease of worry in her forehead deepens. "But Lavinia, some things about my sons will never change. I promise you, I've tried. These... personality traits might make them good Dukes, but I suspect they don't make them easy to love."

I hesitate, unsure I can tell her what she wants to hear. The way I am with my Dukes... it's still new. "What are you getting at?"

"I just hope," she says, eyes dipping down to her wringing hands, "if you're ever put in the position, you'll protect my sons the same way they'd protect you."

When it finally hits me, I jolt. "Of course I would." As much as I want to feel insulted by the implication I'd let them die, I know Sarah couldn't understand. She looks at me and sees the same broken, bitter girl who was sitting in the clock tower before the Baron's equinox party.

"I can't help them, and to be perfectly honest, I don't want to." I looked her in the eye that day, telling her nothing but the bare truth of it. *"You seem like a nice woman, but you need to know this. Your sons are fucking terrible."*

In the glint of the string lights, I can almost imagine Sarah as she used to be. Young and commanding, beautiful and strong–just like my mother. Her eyes sparkle as she smiles. "You really are the perfect Duchess," she muses, the praise warming me in a way I'm not expecting. "Sometimes I think that's why they keep the families competing, you know. A Lucia girl in West End? No one would have entertained it, but here you are, getting ready."

I blink. "Getting ready for what?"

"To become a Queen." Her eyebrow arches meaningfully. "*Maybe.*"

The words bring me up short. I've thought about it before, back when I was nothing but a prisoner. The thought of using Nick's position as Bruin to climb my way to a place where I'd have the power to fight back was enticing. But now the reminder makes my stomach flop uneasily.

If Nick becomes King, that's what I'll be.

His Queen.

I've spent my whole life trying to escape a box–my father's chest, the Hideaway, the elevator. Maybe Sarah managed to make it out, but I'm not a Bruin. I'm a Lucia. I'm North Side.

Where I come from, Royal women always end up in a box–dead or alive.

⁓

"KILLIAN CALLED me into his office after we broke into the Hideaway and tagged Lavinia."

I freeze just outside the kitchen, overhearing Nick's words. Sarah had sent me down to pilfer a couple pieces of birthday cake, the weed making us maudlin and hungry, but I pause, straining to hear the conversation.

He goes on, "For a second, I thought I was busted. Fuck, part of me is still surprised I walked out of that whorehouse alive. Killian might be a jock, but the guy isn't exactly stupid."

"And these are the Lords," Sy stresses. "Not exactly forgiving of being double-crossed."

"But you're still alive," Davis says in a confused tone.

Nick explains, "Saul and the Lords have massive beef. Something major went down, but Killian Payne wasn't in the position to handle it himself. Not when he was newly anointed and scrambling to get a foothold in his father's Kingdom. He needed someone he trusted–more than Saul, at least–to head up the Dukes and take him out. I'm a Bruin. Killer knew I had a ticket in, and he wanted to use it."

Manny sounds incredulous. "You're saying you manipulated Killian Payne–a rival King–into giving you their asset?"

Nick's voice rings out defensively. "I didn't manipulate. I just... maneuvered things. Strategically."

"Jesus Christ, Nick," Davis groans. "What the hell were you thinking?"

"He wasn't," Sy mutters, but Nick cuts in.

"Saul wanted revenge on the Lords. The Lords want revenge on Saul. I wanted Lavinia Lucia." There's a long pause–probably all of them figuring out what I already know. Nick's problem isn't that he fails to think things through. It's that he's so good at thinking things through, he can turn bad ideas into weirdly brilliant ones. He scoffs. "Guys. It was a win-win-win."

"And now it's a cluster fuck-fuck-fuck," Remy says, voice garbled in a way that suggests he's in the middle of eating something.

"Let me get this straight," Manny says. "The Lords gave you Lavinia in exchange for your position in the belfry, which would be beneficial to them."

"Yes."

"But they only did that in light of your... uh, initiation ritual," Manny stutters, which is reasonable. Not many initiation rituals include breaking into the basement of a whorehouse and assaulting their prisoner.

Then again, this *is* Forsyth.

Maybe they do.

Davis says, "So this video..." and I feel my face instantly flare with heat. I'm definitely not stoned enough to survive hearing their fathers talk about that video. "It's hard, indisputable proof that you knowingly, *deliberately* betrayed the Lords."

"And," Manny adds, "if Saul were to show it to Payne, they'd come after you."

Sy's the one to answer, the words low and harsh. "Best case, we'd start a massive war with the only house who's ever shown a willingness to ally with us. Worst case, they'd hunt us down like dogs in the street."

There's another beat of silence, and then Davis speaks, the words full of defeat. "Then Remy was right. He's got you by the balls." There's an anger in his tone that surprises me to hear. It's not anger directed at Nick, nor does it seem directed at Saul. Davis sounds more angry with himself than anything. "I should have—"

Ding!

I stiffen, fumbling my phone from my pocket to silence it, but I know it's already too late. The kitchen has gone pointedly silent. I read the text notification without really intending to, my face burning in embarrassment at being caught.

And then I see the message.

It's only four words—barely a sentence—but it might as well be a sledgehammer with the way my chest caves.

"Vinny?" Remy calls out. "You out there?"

Swallowing, I tear my eyes away from the screen, shuffling slowly into the kitchen. Davis and Manny are on the counter, Remy and Nick at the table, Sy standing in the middle of it all with his hands buried in his pockets. The birthday cake is a gruesome carcass, but even if it weren't, I've lost my appetite.

"Story just messaged me." I hold my phone up, clearing my throat. "It's the Countess."

All of them are staring at me, but Sy's the one to speak, lip curling in distaste. "Let me guess. Another depressing revenge scheme is brewing in North Side."

"That'd be red." Remy's up in an instant, searching my eyes. "This is green."

Clutching the phone, I explain, "She OD'd this morning." The words fall with all the grace of a boulder. "She's dead."

~

THE CAR RIDE home is quiet. Remy sits next to me in the backseat, strangely still. He's not moving at all, other than to rub his thumb in an idle circuit against my knee.

"Are you okay?" I ask him, after meeting Sy's eye in the rearview mirror.

"Yeah." His inked fingers lift my chin. "Are you?"

It's not like I have the right to be anything else. Sutton was an enemy. Her boyfriend was killed by one of *my* boyfriends. My family did this to her. My father's Viper Scratch. His Count's recklessness. My Duke's revenge. It's like my name is all over this, but in all truth, I barely knew her–never wanted to.

Still, something dark gnaws at my chest as we arrive back at the tower, and by the time we reach the main floor, it hasn't gotten any lighter.

It's not just about Sutton.

It's about my sister's skull, the only part of her that this town spat back out, sitting in an unmarked grave. It's about the woman who sat across from me an hour ago, asking me to save her sons. It's about the woman who once loaned her a weapon, even though they were rivals, because my mother knew something I'm only just figuring out.

Royal women are *women* first and *Royal* second.

Remy and Sy both disappear into their rooms, but I stand beside the couch, watching as Nick methodically unties his boots. I'm not sure what makes the question break free. I just know that it emerges like a hiccup, unstoppable.

"Would you let me leave?" I ask.

His back is curved into an exhausted bow as he leans down, forehead creasing. "What?"

"If I tried to run again," I clarify. "Would you stop me?"

Nick's fingers go still for the briefest moment, tangled in the laces, before he yanks them harder. His reply comes low and harsh. "Why would you ask me that?"

My eyes narrow as I watch his stiff, jerky movements, palms prying the boot from his ankle. "Why aren't you answering?"

His eyes fly to mine, flinty and hard. "Why are you pretending you don't already know the answer?"

My breath escapes in a punch of shock, although I don't know why it should. He's right. Some part of me has been aware of this, too cowardly to face the truth. "So I'm still your prisoner."

"You're my girl!" he snaps, bolting to his feet. He extends an arm, jabbing a finger toward my loft. "I told you that night, there's no going back for me. You heard me–I know you did. So why are you bringing this up now?"

For a moment, his reaction renders me speechless. His nostrils are flared, shoulders tensed into a hard line. When I finally find my voice, I say, "I thought things had changed." That's the crux of it. I was arrogant enough to think I was different–that there's a happy ending in this for us.

I was right, I think.

We all end up in a box.

His eyes widen in disbelief. "Look around you. Everything has changed!" He gestures broadly, and at first, the glint of frenzied rage in his eyes throws me off. "I'm not here for me. I'm not out there in Northridge chasing down rich kids because I give a shit about their pussy Preston turf wars. I'm not standing up and leading this frat because it's some fucked up dream of mine." He stabs a finger in my direction, insisting, "I'm doing this because it's what *you* want me to do. And now what? You want to leave me?"

Suddenly, all the fury and weirdly intense panic make sense.

I lunge forward, taking his face in my hands. "Nick, no. I didn't say I wanted to leave." He's so tense that he barely budges, not lowering his chin when I strain up, pressing a kiss to his stiff jaw. "I just need to know I could."

His blue eyes dart down to mine. "You want to test me? Fine." Jabbing a fist into his pocket, he yanks out a pair of keys, shoving them into my palm. "It's got half a tank. That should get you out of the state."

I blink down at the glimmer of silver in my fist, confused. "So you would let me?"

"I didn't say you couldn't leave Forsyth." The response is rough and curt, but I hear with a crystal-clear clarity the words beneath them.

You just can't leave me.

"You'd come with me," I realize, chest thudding painfully as I meet his stony gaze. "Even after everything you've worked so hard to build. Sy, Remy, your parents–" My words bite off, because Nick loves them. I've seen it, felt it. He left them once, and maybe he had a good reason, but it cleaved a part of himself away. There's only one response to this that rings true. "Nick, that's crazy."

"Of course it's fucking crazy!" he explodes, the words hurled so viciously that they might as well be fists.

I couldn't stop the flinch if I tried, stumbling back in shock.

His furious grimace plummets away, leaving a miserable, pleading expression in its wake. He drags both palms down his face. "Goddamn it, Lavinia. I've always been straight with you. I've never dressed this up into something it isn't. I know you hate hearing it, and god knows you'll never fucking say it back, but I still lay it out there." He waves a slack hand between us. "I love you. To other guys, that means rainbows and fucking sunshine, but to me, it looks like this." He holds out his arms as if presenting himself. The aggressive posture. The inked skin. The scars.

Take it or *take it.*

I deflate, wrapping my arms around myself. "You don't understand. You've never had all your freedom taken away. Sometimes... the way you are with me..." I choke up, unable to tell the truth of it. Nick's love can be scary. It's been a long time since he locked me up and threw away the key, but I can't shake the feeling that he'd do it again if it meant keeping me.

Nick knows, though.

"Freedom?" A wretched breath of laughter tears through his throat. "You've got to be fucking kidding me. I'd follow you anywhere, put a gun to my head and pull the trigger, leave my family, my friends, my whole fucking world if you asked me to. But even after all these years, you still think the way I love you makes you a prisoner. When are you going to get it?" His jaw tightens, and he reaches up, tucking a lock of hair behind my ear. "You're not shackled to me, Lavinia. I'm shackled to you."

The defeated frustration in his eyes makes my stomach drop. Unthinkingly, I reach for him. "Nick, I didn't mean–"

This time, he's the one to flinch, turning away with a bowed head. "I'll sleep in my room tonight," he mutters.

He's already slammed the door by the time I manage to process the enormity of that decision. Nick has been a chain around my neck since the first night we met, an obstacle between me and freedom. Standing here alone, I realize that somewhere deep down, I've been waiting around for him to give it back to me.

But maybe Nick's been waiting, too.

A Queen would take it back herself.

18

R_{emy}

"Fried chicken!" I snap my fingers, feeling restless in a way that chafes at me. "*That's* what it is."

"That's what what is?" Dusty, the leader of this group of freaks, looks up from the cup of coffee he's pouring. A deep line of confusion scars his forehead. "Chicken?"

"Can't you smell it?" The room they gave the students for the NA meeting is down in the basement of the student center, two floors below the various restaurants circling the main area. One is a fried chicken chain and I swear the oily scent has seeped into the walls.

He sniffs the air, contemplative. "Yeah, kind of."

I scratch my head like a bad habit, nails digging painfully into my scalp. "Fuck, now I'm hungry."

"This will have to work for now." Dusty hands me the paper cup of coffee and says, "Stop scratching."

My sense of smell is back–apparently also my appetite. Thank fuck. Among the other side effects of my bender, I felt my muscle eating away at itself. Unlike Nick and Sy, who are genetically predisposed with a six-pack of abs and magically ripped, I have to work on keeping bulked up. I'm too tall, too lanky, too slack on my fighting physique.

There are other things I've noticed getting better. My hands are less shaky. I was able to ink the guys after the Fury the other night. There's still the occasional tremor, but it feels good to be able to hold a pencil and pen. Losing the ability to create sucked.

And almost losing my best friends and Vinny...

Let's just say I understand the concept of rock bottom a little better than I ever wanted to.

"Hate it here," I mutter, eyeing the yellowing walls and flickering lights.

He gives me a disgruntled look. "It's a support group for addicts. No one likes it here, kid."

"Not the group," I reply, grimacing at the grungy carpet. "The building."

Humming, he stirs a sugar packet into his styrofoam cup. "Too institutional for you?" Dusty knows a little about my background at Saint Mary's, which always makes my muscles tense to think about.

At some point, the university couldn't deny the high level of substance abuse in the Greek system. The local and campus police can only cover up so much. So the Kings made a concession. This fucked up little group, complete with a certified counselor, is meant to clean up the destruction left in the wake of Lionel's drugs. Dusty is a haggard fifty-something South Side expat, and if it weren't for the way he commands the group with a quiet wisdom, one could miss entirely that he's the one running it.

He's wearing an Iron Maiden t-shirt.

I always tread a little carefully with him. Metal tees or not, counselors are just a few steps away from therapists, and therapists can be bought. "Not really," I answer, trying to put my finger on why the building bothers me. "It's yellow," I say, pointing at the anemic fluorescence overhead. "And it's old, but not *old*, you know? There's no history or heart here, it's just a room beneath the ground. Every breath we take is filling our lungs with vermillion and dead birds."

He watches me with a blank expression taking this in. I brace myself for the usual bullshit psych jargon I'm used to being assaulted with. Dissociation. Sensory issues. Med balances. Brain chemistry. Experiments. "Son," Dusty sighs, bringing a firm hand down on my shoulder. "That's some weird-ass nonsense. Shut the fuck up and take a seat."

I blink. "Oh." And then, "Yeah, okay."

"Looks like everyone's here," Dusty says, walking over to the circle of chairs. "Why don't we go ahead and get started."

I take a seat, even though it kills me. For some reason, I have the urge to walk. Run. Fight. Fuck. Jesus, just *something*. I settle for the sketchbook I balance in my lap, flipping it open to the clock diagram I've been working on for Vinny. Dusty is okay with me doodling during the meeting, probably because it gives me something to do with my hands that isn't starting an epic round of contagious, neurotic scratching. It's never bad until I'm here with the others. Just watching them scratch makes me want to, and watching me scratch makes them want to.

We're a fucking sideshow.

It's better not to make too much eye contact with them, anyway. We're not just a bunch of junkies. We're also all aligned with the Royal system in one way or another. Everything about this set up feels like a cliché. The dingy room, the circle of chairs, the participants reluctantly avoiding each other's stares while taking a seat. It's usually a rotation of six or seven people, most sent here directly by their frat's leadership, who'd rather their guys get clean than maintain some flimsy pretense of stability. It's kind of profound, when it doesn't make me want to punch someone.

It's mostly guys. There's an LDZ sitting across from me who compulsively bounces his knee up and down. There's a Beta Nu who I'm always assessing, wondering if my father has this guy in his sights as another Baron. There are two sacrificial Kappas, pledges to the Counts, who were clearly sent to pretend they aren't the problem. Fuck, one of them sold me a hit of Scratch last month.

They're not the only Kappas who have made an appearance, though. A couple weeks ago, Sutton herself showed up, greasy hair pulled back in a ponytail, pupils solid black. Her skin was so gray that she barely looked alive, and I sat as far away from her as possible, cringing against the energy pulsing off her in erratic, yellow-green waves. Obviously, she's not here tonight, but that doesn't mean her presence isn't felt.

Everyone knows she's dead and exactly what killed her.

"We all know the rules," Dusty says, but then stops, his intro interrupted by a loud, jarring slam of the door. It's a heavy metal thing that all the regulars have learned to ease shut. The guy standing frozen beneath our glares isn't a regular, though.

It's Lex Ashby.

He doesn't look much better than Sutton did the last time she came. His skin is pale, dark bags beneath his eyes, and even though he's dressed like an Ashby in his preppy white button-down, the arms are viciously wrinkled, as if he's been pushing them up and down his forearms all day. His dark hair is winning a war with whatever product he'd slathered it with this morning, some locks sticking up while others flop limply against his forehead.

His gaze skitters over us skeptically. "This where all the junkies meet?"

"It's the twenty-first century, kid." Dusty nods to the empty chair next to mine. "We prefer to be called the pharmaceutically disadvantaged."

Lex hesitates a moment, his hands curling into fists, but eventually stalks toward us, lowering himself woodenly into the silver folding chair next to mine. I shudder at the orange radiating off him, not-so-subtly scooting my chair a few inches to the right.

"I'm Dusty, the head junkie," he says in his rough voice. "And you're...?"

"Lex," the guy mutters. After a moment, he adds, "Recreational junkie."

"What's your house alignment?" Dusty seems to know a lot about senior Royalty, but he knows fuck-all about our generation. To him, we're all the same.

"Psi Nu." Lex raises his chin, eyes flashing with that patented East End arrogance. "I'm in my senior year of pre-med."

Dusty gives a low whistle. "Tough workload."

Lex barks a mangled laugh. "Yeah, it is." He tips forward suddenly, scrubbing two palms down his face. "I don't have time for this shit."

Dusty shrugs. "Then we don't have time for your shit. If you don't want to be here," he thrusts a thumb over his shoulder, "then leave."

Lex drags his hands down his face, bloodshot eyes rolling. "I can't. I'm here on orders."

"From your King," Dusty guesses.

"From my father."

"He wants you to get clean?" Dusty shares a look with a few select group members–me included. "At least you've got that. My old man wouldn't have cared if I died in South Side's slimiest gutter."

Lex gives Dusty this long, disparaging look, like he's the dumbest man alive. "It's not like that. Ashbys don't do this frilly kumbaya bullshit."

This doesn't faze Dusty at all. "Well, as long as you're here, you might as well get acquainted with the rules." He spins a finger. "Everything said in this room is confidential. All the inner-frat rivalry is left at the door. Nothing in here can be used against you. Who knows? You may actually embrace our frilly kumbaya bull-shit–find an unlikely ally or two." He pauses, but it's crickets in here.

We play nice, but nobody's walking out of here friends. There's too much spilled blood.

Dusty shrugs it off. "Why don't you tell us a little about yourself and how you got here?"

Lex shifts, eyes tightening. "Can someone else talk?"

"They can, but they won't." Dusty gestures to Lex. "Not sitting in front of a King's son who's only here to listen."

Lex's eyes flash angrily. "I'm not here to gather intel. I don't even qualify to become a Prince!" When it's clear no one gives a damn, he makes a low, frustrated sound. "I'm taking the MCAT this spring," he starts, jaw tense. "Between finishing my pre-med classes and studying for the exams, the schedule is kicking my ass. I started taking a little bump here and there, just for concentration. Then I needed it to stay awake–alert. I guess along the way, a few things started slipping. Not my grades, but... other stuff. Family stuff."

Dusty watches him carefully. "And your family is important to you?"

Lex gives Dusty a stiff, grim smile. "My father has high expectations." I'd love to throw stones, but my glass house is a massive hotel and built by a man I didn't even know had a secret identity until he tried to kill my girl.

Shit, we're all so fucked.

Snorting, I mutter, "I hear that," and Lex turns to stare me down.

"Your father's Timothy Maddox," he says.

"Yeah," I answer, just as aggressively.

"What does he do when you screw up?"

Shrugging, I say, "Tries to lock me away in a mental hospital." At the resulting hush, the LDZ giving me a bizarre look, I defensively add, "It only worked once."

Dusty cuts in, "And what does yours do, Lex?" But Lex's mouth presses into a flat, tense line.

He doesn't answer.

Dusty tries a different tack. "So this is new for you? Using drugs to cope?" He has this way about him, where he asks these fucking intrusive questions, but you feel compelled to answer.

"Not exactly," Lex eventually admits, brows crouched into a low scowl. "I partied like everyone else. Typical college stuff. A little weed. Some coke. Ritalin when I needed to focus on a big exam." My eyes follow his gaze down to his hands. His fingers are slim.

Elegant. The kind best served for skilled work. Similar to my own—artists' hands. But also like my own, I see the small tremor running through them. "My dad didn't even start caring until he had something for me to–" His words bite off, and I can practically see the gate closing, eyes going shuttered. "Whatever. Here I am."

Dusty must sense that Lex has given everything he's willing to part with. "Thanks for sharing, Lex. I'm sorry you had to meet us on such a shitty day, though." His bushy eyebrows twitch as he looks over the group. "I know gossip travels fast through Forsyth, but I wanted to make sure everyone has heard about Sutton." The majority of the room nods, although one of the Kappas noticeably stiffens while the other stares hard at the floor. "I've been told there's a memorial service on Wednesday." He gives a low, sarcastic chuckle. "Obviously, showing up for that may not be wise, but if anyone would like to say something, go ahead."

The room is quiet enough to hear a pin drop. I'm not sure if it's because of the harsh reality that any of us could have the same happen to us, or if no one wants to poke a viper nest. I use my thumb to smear the pencil shading on my paper and keep my mouth shut.

Dusty takes the reins, gazing thoughtfully into his cup of coffee. "I've gotta be honest, fellas, it's hard watching someone lose the fight, no matter who they are." There's a weariness about him that makes me wonder how many members of this little sideshow have died over the course of him leading it. "Everyone here loves their war between east and west, north and south, cops and dealers. We accept the casualties, because there's nothing we can relate to more than having a flesh-and-blood enemy to strike out against." Dusty shakes his head. "But when the war is inside of us–when we're the victim of our own battle–suddenly, it's incomprehensible. Does that seem right to you?"

The resulting silence grows tense.

"Sutton was a bitch," the Kappa says suddenly. All eyes jerk to him. A small smirk plays on his lips. "Kind of like an older sister who kept everyone in line. She liked to bake. Cookies mostly, but she also made these amazing cupcakes. She only made those for the Counts on their birthday."

"Losing Perez fucked her up," the other one says. His linked hands are balled into tight fists—his knuckles raw and scabbed. I watch him out of my periphery, eyes trained carefully on my sketchbook. I feel his gaze on me, though. The accusation. We took Perez from her—from them. "Shit's dark back at the house. The old man is pretty much MIA. He even gave his dog to Lars. He's keeping Amos at the Kappa house."

No Perez. No Countess. No Lionel. He's right, North Side is a fucking disaster. But the viper scratch is half the reason I'm here. Half the reason we're *all* here.

I tap the pencil eraser on the paper in a fast drumbeat, and I don't really understand why, but I'm struck by the impulse to dig up something nice to say. "Sutton was always a, uh, fierce contender at Screw Year's Eve wrestling match. She gave it her all."

"Hell yeah she did," the Kappa says, nodding a little. "She almost took the Lady down."

The LDZ snorts. "*Almost.* Story's ruthless. Anyone that can hold their own against her deserves credit."

Go figure—we can all agree on one thing: hot girls Jell-O wrestling in bikinis is a good time, no matter where they fall on the compass. I'm struck by the image of Vinny this New Year's Eve, slicked up and rolling around in a barely there bikini. My dick twitches. Jesus. After watching her take down Haley, I have no doubt our girl will win the crown.

That seems to break the gloom, and everyone tosses out their favorite badass Sutton moment. It's trite, but what the fuck can we do? Wallow in the bleakness of it all? Everyone here is tired of pain and depression. Sutton was a bitch who probably did a lot of fucked up shit, but haven't we all?

None of us want to be remembered for our worst moments.

∿

THE TOWER IS quiet when I get back, Sy's door hanging open. I don't think twice about barging in, pencil still fidgeting between my fingers. I pause at the scene that greets me, though. Him and Vinny are already in bed, her in a tank top and pink lace panties, him shirtless, laptop propped open on his thighs. She's sound asleep, curled into his side. Between their feet, Archie is tucked into the nook their ankles have made. He opens one eye at my entrance, checks me out, then lazily lets it fall shut.

The room smells like sex.

Sy looks up, noticing me at the door. "Hey, man," he says quietly. "You just get back?"

I stretch my arms over my head, grabbing the top of the door frame. "Yeah."

"How was the meeting?" He's not supposed to ask, but I know he can't help it.

"Fine. Solid six." It's a lower number than he's been used to hearing lately, and it makes him frown.

"Just fine?"

"Another day, you know." I shrug, but then add, "They talked about the Countess."

"Oh." His eyes flick behind me, across the tower to Nick's door. We both know Sutton was a junkie long before Nick killed Perez. And that Perez was living the kind of life that *gets* you killed. But still... "I hope you didn't get much blowback."

I shake my head. "Not really." I want to say some other things. About how the Counts are legitimately falling apart, or how Lex Ashby showed up looking like a hot mess. But I don't want those assholes talking about me outside of the group, and I keep my word to extend the same respect. "Is this a post-fuck cuddle?" I ask instead, nodding at Vinny.

Sy looks down at his laptop, and I grin, watching the tips of his ears go pink. "We didn't... do *that*." Quieter, he adds, "Not without you or Nicky."

Him and Vinny are still gun-shy about full-out fucking, I see.

"And where is our brave leader?" I wonder, twisting to stare at his closed door.

"Out," Sy says, not looking happy about it. "Things are still pretty tense." He dips his eyes to Vinny in an obvious gesture, but it's not necessary. We both heard Nick yelling last night, his door slamming. She slept up in her loft, the message loud and clear that she wanted to be alone.

A ball of tension in the back of my neck unwinds seeing her in Sy's bed again. Whatever happened between her and Nick, it doesn't extend to us.

"Remy," Sy says, giving me a long look. It isn't until he jerks his chin toward my hand that I realize I'm tapping my pencil against his doorframe.

I curl my hand into a fist. "Oops."

"What is it?" he asks, moving to shut his laptop. "You're agitated at a six head-check."

"Nothing," I say, and there used to be a time Sy would pry it out of me until my teeth ached from gnashing them. These days, he just shrugs and diverts his attention, reopening his laptop. Groaning, I relent, "Jesus, man, I need something to fucking *do*."

His forehead creases. "Don't you have a piece due for art history?"

I pull a face, amending, "I need something *interesting* to do. Nothing is holding my attention." I gnaw at my lip, ignoring the worry that crosses Sy's face. This has always been the beginning of a cycle for me, kicking around for something to get lost in and always finding the worst goddamn thing. I raise my chin. "Let me tattoo you."

All the soft concern on Sy's face slams into a scowl. "No."

"Please?"

"You know I don't do that random ink shit," he insists, resting a palm on Vinny's head. "I get a tattoo when I win a fight. That's it."

I arch an eyebrow. "I can put Vinny's initials on you, like Nicky did."

"Fuck that," he says, even though I see a flare of intrigue in his eyes at the thought. "Go tattoo Nick."

"He's gone," I whine.

"Then tattoo Lav."

I look at her, all smooth and serpentine, her legs soft and begging to have that snake tattoo filled in. "No," I sigh, deflating. "Vinny's art, bro. I can't just put something on her all slapdash and shit. I need time to plan a worthy piece."

Sy's eyes narrow in outrage. "But you'd put something on me all slapdash? Fuck you."

Shrugging, I don't deny it. "Hey, I don't look at your skin when I'm getting off." But then I pause. "Although, the way we've been sharing Vinny lately, you and Nick *are* getting kind of unavoidable."

I see the sock he chucks at me coming a mile away, and I easily bat it to the side, chuckling.

When the playfulness fades away, a seriousness fills Sy's eyes. "Remy, are you going to–"

"No," I say, unequivocally. "I'm done with the drugs."

His eyes grow tight. "If it gets that bad, I'd let you tattoo me. You know that, right?"

I grip the door jamb, nodding. "Yeah, Sy. I know." After an awkward beat, I say, "I'll leave you alone so you can get that finished."

He searches my eyes, which is something that used to piss me off, always feeling analyzed. Now, I just meet his gaze back, challenging him to find something.

Finally he rubs his eyes. "Yeah, this fucking paper is driving me crazy." He looks back at the screen. "Careful with the cat when you come to bed. He gets so fucking territorial."

Feeling a bit lighter, I toss him a salute. "I'll be in later. Something I've gotta do first."

I think about stripping down and climbing in with them now. The invitation was a deliberate message. *Stay close.* My cock twitches at the idea of waking Vinny up and using her to help get the empty feeling out of my gut, but she looks peaceful. *They* look peaceful, so I keep walking.

I grab the pack of cigarettes off my bedside table–*smoking*, the lamest of vices–before heading upstairs, passing the loft, and climbing the staircase to the clock room. Vinny's clock pieces are spread out across the floor like a complicated puzzle. I step over them, knowing if I fuck up her organizational system, she'll get pissed.

Although… there's something about her when she's riled up—cheeks pink, eyes shining bright. It's why Nicky fucks with her so much. He likes it when she fights back. Scratch that—he *loves* it. The first time she kicked him… well, that was the day he locked in on her for life, imprinting like an animal to its mate.

But even Nicky wouldn't touch her clock pieces. He's a possessive, horny fucker, not a dumbass.

I climb the ladder in the corner easily, lifting the hatch and pushing myself up onto the stone of the belfry. For a long second, I just tip my head back, letting the cool gust of night air embrace me.

Finally, *sky*.

It's dark up here, but the city provides enough light to navigate around the pillars to an archway overlooking the campus. I hop up on the ledge and fish a cigarette out of the pack, feeling fifteen again, and then light the tip, inhaling.

Clouds cover the night sky, obscuring the stars and moon, but I feel the vibration of our town: the horns honking in the distance, the neon lights over on the Avenue. Sometimes it's weird to think about Lionel Lucia's failsafe lurking beneath those streets. Beneath this very tower. A viper hidden in the brush. A glow of red-orange-yellow illuminating the landscape. Forsyth becoming the hot ember on the end of the universe's cigarette, burning lower and lower with every pull of its lungs.

I'm not sure how long I'm mulling over it, rolling it around like a filter between my fingertips, when the creak of the hatch shatters the stillness. Vinny's pale hair appears first. Her body rises next, Sy's hoodie hanging over her shoulders, the hem almost grazing her thighs. My heart skitters at the sight of her, thinking about those pink panties, about *her*.

"You're awake." I hop down, reaching my hand out, helping her off the ladder.

"Thanks." Her eyes dart down to the cigarette–my second one. "Everything okay?"

There's no mistaking the worry in her voice. It's fair. I don't fully remember the day she found me up here, carving up my skin. The memory exists, but it's shadowy, like it's lost in fog. More feeling than imagery. I know I scared the shit out of her, though. I also know she saved my ass.

"I'm fine. Just getting some sky. Those meetings happen in the ground, you know?" But even as I assure her, my fingers are pushing up the hem of the shirt, my thumb seeking the star. This time though, her hand does the same, dragging down the waist of my jeans to find her matching moon. Goosebumps rise on her skin and I edge closer, scenting her hair. "You cold? We can head back down."

She shakes her head. "Between Archie and Sy, sometimes it feels like I'm sleeping next to a furnace." There's a long pause where she watches me, searching my eyes a lot like Sy did earlier. When her lips part, there's a tremor in her voice. "Why did you come up here, Remy?"

It's impossible not to see the fear lining her eyes.

"You heard us talking in his room," I realize.

She rushes to say, "I wasn't eavesdropping. I was just in that place." Deflating, she adds, "You know the one." That just happens to Vinny sometimes, getting trapped somewhere in the purgatory between sleep and wakefulness. Whatever this thing is with Nick, it must be serious. She hasn't had an episode in a while.

"It's been nice having Sy back," I say, tipping my head back to look into the clouds. "When I got out of Saint Mary's, he started treating me like his patient. Suddenly, it wasn't cool to fuck around with him anymore. Everything I did had some kind of deeper meaning to him, like I was some kind of puzzle he had to figure out." When I glance down, she's frozen, her knuckles warm against my belly. "It's not that I didn't understand why he was doing it, because I did. Sy loves me. I never once resented that, but I just... really fucking needed a friend. Instead, I became his burden." Reaching up, I cup her cheeks in my palms, impressing the words into the wind between us. "I don't want to be that for you. You don't need to save me all the time, Vinny."

Her lips twist into a small, rueful smile. "I don't think that's something I get a choice in now."

It's the first time I've seen it in weeks.

Blue.

It surges through me like liquid warmth, driving my mouth to hers in a slow, reverent kiss. Her fingers tangle in my shirt, tugging me closer.

"Then maybe let me save you back sometimes," I say, thumbing at the worry line in her forehead. "What's going on with you lately?"

Her eyes flutter open, still dazed from the kiss, so it takes her a moment to answer. When she does, it's with a pensive frown. "Would you... let me leave?"

"*Let* you?" I snort. "Woman, if you wanted out of here, I'm pretty sure there's no power in this tower that could stop you."

She tilts her head. At first I think she's being coy, but then I realize she's baring her neck–her ear. "Nick could," she argues, and then it hits me.

The tracker.

"Ah."

Her mouth twists unhappily. "He's mad at me for asking."

I press my fingers to the spot, eyeing the scar left from the first tracker. I stand by my earlier statement. Maybe there was a time when Vinny was a prisoner here, but if she wanted out, she'd already be gone. "This is Nick we're talking about. Rail him tenderly and he'll fall over himself to forgive anything."

She sighs. "Weirdly, I think that'd just make everything worse."

I think carefully about my words, knowing that she's still waiting. "I'd let you leave. I know what it's like to belong to you, Vinny." I press our hips together, knowing the moon and the star are aligning. "Going back to how it used to be would be the same as losing you, anyway." Tipping her chin up, I force her to meet my gaze. "Do you want to leave?"

"No." The answer is instant, punctuated with a strained, pleading expression. "But I don't want me and Nick to end up like Perez and Sutton."

Scoffing, I reply, "That'll never happen. For one, Nicky's not feeding you drugs on the reg. For two, Perez never loved that girl. But most importantly," I squeeze her hips, "Perez and Sutton didn't have me and Sy."

She gives me a skeptical look. "So you're saying if Nick ever tried something crazy, you and Sy would stop him?"

"That's exactly what I'm saying." I list off on my fingers, "Nick and I will keep Sy from going too far, Sy and Nicky will keep my head straight, and me and Sy will keep Nick from caging up his Little Bird." Shrugging, I conclude, "We're a bonafide system of checks and balances, babe. It's why you can't have just one of us."

Her brow creases with a thoughtful frown, her big eyes searching my face. "Oh." Just like that, her expression clears, a brightness filling her eyes. "Thank you."

"For promising to kick Nicky's ass?"

This time when she smiles, it's a soft beam of blue. "For saving me."

"Yeah, I'm really carrying you three lately."

I herd her over to the window and stand behind her, bodies close. I hold the cigarette up to her lips, but she shakes her head. "No thanks. The nicotine will give me a buzz, and I'll never get back to sleep."

She's got a point, so I take one last drag before stubbing it out on the granite wall.

"At night like this," she says, leaning into me, her hair smelling sweet and flowery, "it's hard to remember how fucked up Forsyth is. That there are monsters lurking in every corner."

"You see that?" I say, pointing to a streetlight three blocks over. "I flipped my skateboard on the curb and had to get six stitches in my knee." I shift my gaze, turning it toward the line that separates West and North. "That's where I bought my first dime bag, from a guy named Pee-wee."

"Aw," she says. "I knew him. He was nice, actually."

I grunt, eye scanning the city, pausing on a three-story brick office building. "That's my old orthodontist office."

"Hey!" she twists her neck to look at me. "That's my orthodontist office too."

The idea of crossing paths with a younger Lavinia, fresh-faced with a mouth full of metal, makes my heart kick with a thud.

"I guess good dental care crosses lines in Forsyth." I bend down and kiss her, palming her ass under the shirt. Her panties are cotton, soft, and I pull them aside and slide my finger into the warmth of her cheeks. "I've been a good boy, right? Going to meetings. Taking my meds. Eating your pussy on the regular."

Her lips twitch, but she nods, solemnly. "A very good boy."

My other hand travels up her shirt, tweaking her nipple. "I think I should get a reward for all that good behavior."

Her eyebrow arches. "What kind of reward are we talking about?"

I meet her eyes. "The thing I've been wanting since that first day we watched Nick destroy Perez in the ring together." My dick goes hard just talking about it. I've been obsessed for months. Dreamt about it. Drawn it. Jerked to it. "I want to bend you over–be the first one in there." I press a wet kiss along her throat, keeping my voice quiet and silky in that way I know makes her shiver. "Nicky had your pussy, and you and Sy... you guys had all kinds of firsts. I just want to be the first one to fuck that tight, pretty ass." I tug on her earlobe with my teeth. "Please, Vinny? I'll make it so damn good for you. I promise."

I accentuate the request by stretching her cheeks and running my knuckle over the sensitive opening. She shivers but doesn't pull away, instead pushing back against the pressure.

Doesn't seem like a *no*.

"Yeah?" I ask, licking her lips apart. "You want it?"

Her eyes are heavy, shining with want. "I think–yeah."

Fuck.

Yes.

Running a hand up her back I turn her towards the arched opening, the yellow lights of Forsyth twinkling below us. Hooking my fingers in her panties, I hastily pull them down her thighs, bending as she steps out of them. I think about tossing them over the edge, some poor recruit coming across them in the gutter next weekend, but find I can't do it.

I cram them into my pocket instead, blood buzzing with anticipation. It's the exact feeling I've been frantically searching for all day. The swoop of thrill in my gut. The burst of colors around here, purple and blue and white. The rush in my veins. The tingle of pinprick stimulation as I cup her round asscheek in my palm, squeezing.

"Here?" she asks, the question carried on a soft gust of wind.

"Here," I confirm, unzipping my jeans. Nudging my nose into the scar below her ear, I whisper, "What good are wings if you can't see the sky?"

There's a stretch of silence, and I worry at first she won't allow it. But then she turns, just far enough for me to make out the curve of a smirk. "Maybe I'm a bat."

"No, you're not," I say, reaching between us to pull out my dick. "You're a raptor. No–a dragon." When the cold air bites at my overheated skin, I mutter a relieved, "*Jesus.* My dick was about to drill a hole out of there." I move quick, slotting it in the heat between her thighs, but I find she's already slick, sticky in a very particular way I've become familiar with over the past few weeks. My eyes narrow. "Sy said you didn't fuck."

Her puff of laughter is amused but strained, thighs widening for me. "It doesn't matter how he finishes. He always finds a way to get it in there."

"Yeah?" I ask, balls tightening as I whisper into her ear. "He finger his cum into you, Vinny?"

She shudders, nodding. "He—we like that."

I groan, giving my dick a slow thrust through her folds. "You've got the best pussy out there, baby. Always so fucking wet and warm."

I slide my fingers between her legs, gathering her wetness—and whatever Sy's left for me—then bring it up to her hole, getting her ready. Her back arches, putting that pretty, perfect ass on display. "That's it, baby. Open up for me."

My fingers are slick, and I push one in, loosening her up. God help me if I tear into her. Nicky will lose his shit, and Sy? I have no interest in taking a beat down. After everything she's been through, I'm willing to get her good and warmed up before staking my claim.

"How's that feel?" I ask, wincing at the throb in my balls. Vinny's gotten good at knowing what she can take. She has to, being Sy Perilini's girl.

"Good," she breathes, glancing over her shoulder. I wrap my hand around her throat and pull her back, kissing her hard as I push in a second finger, stretching her out. She keens against my tongue, rocking back. "God, yes. That's good."

I should probably draw it out longer, make her nice and loose for me, but it's only a couple minutes before I ask, "You ready for me?"

She nods, and my dick lurches forward, desperate to feel her around me. The sound she makes when I fuck my dick abruptly into her pussy is full of shocked awe. "Remy…"

My own jaw clamps down on the wave of pleasure, feeling her so tight and wet around me. "Just getting my dick wet for you, baby. Better than spit." In my eagerness, I pull out too fast, soothing her mournful groan with a kiss. If I stayed in her pussy, I'd probably come in two pumps, but I've been waiting on this for too long. I'm gonna make this last. Slowly, I pull out my fingers and replace them with the tip of my cock, nudging at her entrance. "You tell me if it's too much," I say, voice rough as gravel. "I'm not Sy. I can stop."

I think.

"Remy," she says, hands gripping the granite ledge, "no offense, but after taking Sy's cock, I feel like I can handle anything."

That's all the permission I need, and I hold on to her hip as I push through the resistance, feeling the tight ring of muscle relent as my head pops through. "God*damn*." I pant hard into the nape of her neck, feeling her tense around me. It takes every ounce of control not to punch in. "Take a breath, Vin. You've gotta let me in, baby." Her inhale is followed by a shallow exhale, so I curl my arm around her, dipping between her legs to brush my fingers over her clit. The distraction works and her muscles loosen, the next careful rock of my hips sliding another thick inch of my cock into her. I shuffle my feet, nudging closer. "That's my girl."

The sensation is unreal; warm, wet, tight. It takes every bit of focus not to shoot into her with the first pump, but I drag back out, gathering a shallow, careful rhythm. With each thrust, she takes a little more of me, these sweet little aborted cries writhing their way from her throat.

"Touch me," she pleads, grabbing my hand and shoving it back between her legs.

It's hard to focus on anything that isn't the tightness of her ass around me, but one glance at her slack face, brows pinched in rapture, drags me back to the moment. I rub her clit in a circuit that matches my hips, lips dragging over her ear. "You know the only thing that would make this better?" She doesn't answer so much as she moans, fingernails digging into my wrist as I rub her. "Sy or Nick... right here." I punctuate this by trailing my fingers through her folds, nudging at her entrance.

"Oh, fuck," she gasps, clenching around me. Vinny's body is small, but she's more sturdy than she was when we brought her here. She takes me punch for punch, meeting the gradually more pointed collision of my hips against her ass.

The cool night air is no longer an issue, both of us hot, skin growing damp and sticky. I curl over her back, needing to be closer, wanting to smell her, feel her, hear her little pants as I continue to play with her clit, working her body into a heated frenzy. It's torture to stave off the creeping promise of my orgasm, but I do it. I gnash my teeth, press my forehead into the back of her neck, and fuck her with rapidly dwindling restraint.

Her cries grow louder, carried away by a gust of wind that scatters her mewls like ashes around the burning city below. I hear her climb in the sound, feel its grip around my own cock, see it in the tremble of her white-knuckled fingers, scrabbling against the stone.

"Give it to me," I grunt, snapping my hips faster, harder, fingers rub-rub-rubbing.

I know when we're at the peak–that deliciously dangerous second before the plunge to ecstasy–because she gulps in a loud gasp of air and clenches around me, body seizing.

I can feel her flying as she comes around me.

Slamming into her, I whisper the words that always seem to break free just before I fall. "I love you, Vinny." The orgasm bursts through me with a strangled grunt. I bury it into her sweaty neck, cock filling her ass with wild, desperate surges of come.

She leans back, lifting her eyes to meet mine. "I love you too."

I don't pull out, not right away, wanting to stay in the warmth of her for as long as possible. I came up here tonight feeling restless and anxious. That's gone, replaced with satiety that only comes from being in alignment with my girl.

19

L avinia

"Hey," I say, knocking on Mama B's door. "You have a minute?"

She flinches, head whipping forward, and given the way she quickly clears the frown on her face, I realize I've caught her in a moment of deep thought. A ledger is laying open on the desk in front of her, the old kind with rows of numbers jotted down in ink. Fight stats, bookie numbers, who knows what else. I've come to learn that Mama B is the record keeper and historian of the DKS gym. There's nothing that goes on here that she doesn't know about.

That's why I hold out the clipboard I've been carrying around for the last week, clearing my throat. "Sorry to interrupt. I just wanted to see if you could take a look over my checklist for the festival and poker game. I think I have everything in place, but I figured it would be good to have someone double check."

Homecoming starts tomorrow, first with a parade, followed by the football game, and then finally the carnival. There's no Fury this week, the carnival and poker game taking prominence. All of my focus has been narrowed down to the event–*both* events–and I've spent every moment outside of classes procuring everything on the prior Duchess' list. A better woman could say that dedication is because of the sheer nature of the responsibility, but I have more than one reason to throw myself into a productive distraction.

The biggest one is named Nick Bruin.

He hasn't said more than two words to me since our fight.

"Sure," she says, scribbling down a last number and shutting the ledger. She takes the clipboard, giving me a scrutinizing stare.

"The extra items on the list are because Sutton had already backed off her obligations," I say, wringing my hands. "But the rest of us are splitting the work."

She nods, skimming the list quickly. "All of this looks good, except..."

Ugh. "Except what?"

She hands me back the clipboard. "The beer truck kegs are fine for the festival, but not the poker game. Bottles only—high end."

Worrying my lip between my teeth, I explain, "I'm already pushing the budget on the alcohol. Saul sent a list of top-shelf to stock the bar with, so I figured I could save a little by ordering a few extra kegs from the festival vendor."

"Make your cuts somewhere else, but not with the booze." She looks me up and down, assessing me closely. "Nor the entertainment."

"I'll see what I can move around," I say, hugging the clipboard so hard that the corners dig painfully into my breasts. "And I'm well aware of my entertainment obligations."

She leans back, arm draped over the arm of her chair. Even after getting to know her better, I find the woman intimidating. She carries herself with absolute confidence—not like she's surrounded by two dozen young cutsluts with perkier tits and tighter pussies. She's the queen bee around this place, which makes no sense, when one considers she doesn't have a drop of Royal blood running through her veins.

"You're pissed about the show, aren't you?" she asks, tapping her long nails on the edge of her desk.

"It's humiliating," I admit. I gave the cutsluts an out. They don't have to participate if they don't want to. But I don't have that choice. Duchess' duty. "Saul's only making me do it because—" But I clamp my mouth shut.

Mama B's eyes narrow enough for me to know she sees through my silence. She may not know about the video or *why* the video is a powerful piece on the chessboard between my Dukes and their King, but she doesn't need details. She understands this world.

"You're right," she says, filling in the gap. "It doesn't matter if it's humiliating, demeaning, or degrading. Your King gave you a command." She tilts her head, a calculating look crossing her features. "And you're actually going to do it, aren't you? You're going to parade that prissy ass around the stage for a bunch of stuffy bruisers who'd give their left nutsacks to leave a handprint on it, and you're not even going to put up a fuss." I stiffen, expecting her to ridicule me for it, maybe even rub my face in it. Instead, she gives me a small, but no less severe grin. "I respect that, Lucia." She stands from the chair and rounds the desk, walking to the door. "Come on."

She strides past me on boots with five-inch heels, heading toward the cutslut's lounge. None of the other girls are around, just a few guys working out in the gym. In the lounge, she passes the lockers and vanities, pulling out a ring of keys from her jacket pocket, which she uses to unlock a closet against the back wall.

"I'm sure we can find you something in here." She glances at me over her shoulder. "No need to spend your own money for one night. Mama always does her girls up right."

In the closet is a row filled with outfits, although the descriptor seems like a stretch. Nothing in that array of lace and silk could be described as actual clothing.

Lingerie is the better word.

"This is for *under* my costume, right?" I ask, shifting anxiously.

Mama B rolls her eyes. "Jesus, girl, stop acting like you're some kind of delicate flower. We all know you've got three rowdy Dukes railing you balls-deep every night." My jaw drops, but quickly snaps shut. Mama B notices, though, putting a hand on her hip. "Listen, Lavinia, you're a beautiful woman. Hot. Sexy. And you're being asked to flaunt that for the DKS alumni for a couple hours. Yes, it'll be demeaning, and maybe a lot of these assholes have got it out for you on account of your last name. But you've got three protective daddy bears to keep you safe." She gestures to my body, voice flippant. "All you need to do is show a little skin, make your father's enemies horny, take a little of their shit, and then you can go home and take your frustration out on your men."

"I'm not a prude—"

"Good." She pulls out a red lace bodysuit and holds it up to me, turning her head in assessment. "Try that on."

I look around, but there's no partition for privacy. I know the other girls always just change in front of their lockers, but still. Like a prude, I blurt, "Here?"

She gives me a wry look. "Honey, you think I've never seen a pair of tits before?" Reaching up, she gives her own breasts an embellished squeeze. "Try it on. Let me get an idea of what will look best."

Boundaries. None of these people have them. I rest the lingerie on a chair and quickly undress. Mama B flips through the rack while she waits, the scrape of the metal hangers against the bar the only sound in the small room. I get the bodysuit on—I mean, if you can call it that. It's made of sheer netting that does little to hide anything. The majority of the fabric is around my neck and the long row of buttons lining the back.

"A little help?" I ask, turning my back to her.

Mama B faces me and nods approvingly. "Good. You've filled out since you first got here."

I clamp down on a rush of embarrassment. "Being out of captivity will do that to a girl."

Her long nails graze my skin as she fusses with the buttons. "You saying Delores didn't feed you?"

"She did." God, the last thing I need is for Mrs. Crane to catch some gossip that I'm badmouthing her. Although, to be perfectly frank, her cooking left a lot to be desired. "I just didn't have much of an appetite back then. But the boys like me a little meatier."

She snorts and spins me around. "I bet." Instantly, however, her nose wrinkles. "Aw, hell. Makes your tits look flat. Take that off."

Irritation, along with the humiliation of being treated like a Barbie doll, flares in my chest. "Would you be so blasé about all of this if Saul was making Verity entertain these assholes?"

Her jaw tightens, and I can see that I've struck a nerve. She plays it off well enough, turning to pull out another set—this one leopard print with fur trim. "Lucky for her, she's not a daughter of Royalty. Saul Cartwright wants nothing to do with her."

I can't tell if she's pissed about this or not, but I think back to what Sarah said about Saul not being interested in her either. I remove the red number and reach for the leopard print. Jesus. "Well, she's a virgin, so she's halfway there." Mama B throws me a wide-eyed look, and I explain, "Verity told me she saved herself for the Dukes—if they chose her for Duchess." I wiggle into the leopard lingerie, which I realize makes me look like I'm cosplaying as a cat. "Nope. Can't do it," I say, peeling it right back off. I've just handed Mama B the outfit when a thought pops into my mind. "Wait, is Verity Saul's daughter?"

Her head snaps back in shock, face twisted in outrage. "Hell no! Him and I might fuck occasionally, but that's just gravity, Lucia. Even a snob like Saul has basic needs. Sometimes I'm able to meet them, but Saul would sooner lop his own dick off than stick it in a woman who wants a baby." She gives me another surly look. "Verity's father was a useless deadbeat who's currently dead as a doornail."

"Okay," I concede, raising my palms, "all of that is beside the point. If Verity was asked to do this, would you be in here playing dress up with her?"

She levels me with a look that's both hard and convicted. "Sweetheart, I don't know how it's done in North Side, but around here? If your King calls your daughter into service, you better have her waxed, trimmed, buffed, shined, and her asshole bleached to the heavens before personally delivering her to his doorstep, wrapped up in a bow." Her eyebrow arches. "But why would Saul be interested in my girl when there's a Lucia sitting right in front of him?"

I tense, taking a frilly black babydoll number from her outstretched hand. It's not a good feeling, knowing that no matter what I do or who I become, the last name of the man I hate most will always define me. "That doesn't repel you?" I mutter bitterly, slipping the sheer fabric over my head, my shoulders, my tits. "A King is only interested in daughters from other Kingdoms for one reason. He's obviously looking for some poor girl to abuse, like that's the ultimate shame to her father, not to mention–"

"Stop," she snaps, and for a moment I see a crack in her finely honed armor, eyes ringed with panic. After a pause, she looks me up and down, quickly composing herself. "That's... far too cute for you. These men will be expecting a Duchess, not a Princess. Take it off." I keep my mouth shut as she cards through the rack in search of something less cute. "Around here," she says, not turning to look at me, "we like to give our girls a purpose that isn't just spreading their thighs. Saul has a position ready and waiting for any West End girl." She plucks something off the rack, staring down at it for a suspended moment. "Just look at Tatum."

My head snaps up. "Tate? The guys' Tate?" Mama B looks flippant when she hands over a black corset, too distracted with rifling through a box of garter belts to notice the doubt on my face. "Because from what I hear, she didn't seem like the type to buy into all this King stuff."

She produces a pair of thigh-highs, saying offhandedly, "Saul wasn't Tate's King. He was her employer." Catching the look on my face, she explains, "The kids in West End do that sometimes. He pays well for certain jobs, and while I'm sure you can't relate, financial desperation has a way of making anyone reevaluate their stance on the Royalty."

I roll this over in my head as I try on the outfit, barely seeing it. "Do the guys know about this?" I finally ask, standing still as she assesses the bustier.

"Ask them," is all she says, holding up the garter belt to my hips. She nods in approval. "This is the one. Not too sweet, not too trashy. It suits your personality." From the sly smile she gives me, it's hard to believe I'd ever seen that split-moment of dread in her eyes. "Your Dukes will love it."

Forsyth goes all in for homecoming weekend. Orange and purple are blanketed over every column and staircase. There are events and activities across campus, but it seems like it's all just preliminary for the final party on Saturday night.

On the outside, homecoming feels like wholesome fun: the parade, the football game, concerts, and parties. But in the bright glare of the carnival rides and games, under the squeal of children stuffing their faces with cotton candy, it's impossible to forget what's coming later tonight.

"So this is what living in a parallel universe looks like," I say, handing Story the money from the beer truck.

She jots the amount down on a receipt and zips up the money bag, securing the built-in lock. "What do you mean?"

"Killian and Sy have been competing in some kind of strong man contest for the past thirty minutes." From what I can tell, the challenge is to see who can hold the most weight on their body for the longest period of time. They're each standing on a massive, novelty-sized scale up on a stage, and every five minutes one of the volunteers hangs another weight over their taut biceps. They're currently breaching the hundred-pound mark. "And no one has pulled out a knife yet."

"Killian doesn't use knives," she says absently. "That'd be

Dimitri. But yeah, somehow, one night of the year, they manage to play nice."

The crowd growing around the two guys gets bigger the more weight is added. Kids seem to love the display the most, cheering on the guys when another five pounds is added.

"Who's ready for the final test?" the volunteer asks the crowd.

"I'm ready," Killian says, his grin smug. The Lords' King is massive. Fit as fuck.

But there's no one in this world more competitive than Simon Perilini.

"You got this, baby!" Story shouts. He hears her, looking up and over the heads of the spectators, winking at his Queen.

The whole crowd, Sy included, watches as the volunteer adds more weight, the scale inching up another twenty pounds. That's when my Sy jerks his chin. "Keep going."

Killian rolls his eyes, but Sy takes on the extra weight. Ten, fifteen, twenty more pounds. The increase is evident when Sy's face turns red, and the tendons in his neck bulge.

He won't just last the longest, he'll have the most weight.

"Hey, beautiful. What'cha looking at?" Remy appears at my side, grabbing a beer off the cart. When he spots the competition, he shakes his head. "There is literally no such thing as a challenge he'll pass up, is there?"

I take in his outfit. With his normal attire of worn jeans and T-shirts, Remy is the kind of man you forget is wealthy, until he shows up like this. A pale green shirt that pulls the color from his eyes, black jacket and pants that look like they were sewn to fit his body. Even the tattoos peeking out of his collar and shirt cuffs aren't enough to dampen the masculine elegance of the look.

A tremor shoots through my body at the memory of him taking me up in the bell tower last night.

"That beer isn't free, you know," Story says, interrupting my ogling and shooting him a glare.

His eyes narrow in return, and he takes a long, slow sip. "Hey, don't get bitchy at me because your man is about to lose."

"He's not going to lo—"

Remy tips his cup at the stage and Killian explodes in a loud groan before dumping the weights to the ground. A bell rings and Sy, with a cheering crowd of delighted observers, is confirmed the last man standing.

"Hell yeah, brother!" Remy shouts, raising his beer in the air. "To the victor!" It's as much to congratulate his best friend as it is to rub it in Story's nose.

Story sighs. "If you'll excuse me, I have an ego to patch up. Later, Lav." She rolls her eyes and walks off, money bag tucked safely under her arm.

"And that's how you suck in a new generation of DKS," Remy says proudly.

I see that he's right. A slew of kids crowded around both Sy and Killian are eagerly demanding autographs and fist bumps. Fuck. Are we in a cult?

But as the excitement dies down, Remy and I grow quiet, unable to avoid the tick of the clock. The game starts in an hour.

Drawing my eyes from the spectacle, I ask, "Have you seen Nick?"

Remy shakes his head, gazing soberly into the crowd. "No, but he's around here somewhere."

"How do you know?"

He gives me a look and reaches out, taking the pen I'd placed behind my ear earlier. "Because you're here, and because you need him. It doesn't matter how mad he is. He'd never abandon you."

When he takes my hand, I let him, staying still as he turns my wrist up, uncapping the pen with his teeth. He only says that because he's not aware of how it feels to have Nick refusing to speak to me—look at me. He wasn't just mad at my question. He was hurt. He didn't storm out of the tower or go down to the Hideaway to drink and fuck away his upset. He got quiet.

It's scared me more than anything he's ever done.

The tip of the pen tickles on my wrist, but I stay still, watching his face more than what he's drawing. I'm not sure if it's the sex or the company, but Remy's been sleeping better since we began joining Sy in his bed every night and it shows on his face. From this close, I can make out the faint spattering of pale freckles over the bridge of his nose, a feature that had been lost to his sickly pallor before. I give in to the urge to touch them, running the tip of my finger from brow to nose tip.

His eyes raise to mine, and he pulls back, capping the pen.

The letters 'LB' are inked into my wrist in elegant, swooping calligraphy.

"You know what that stands for, don't you?" he asks.

Rolling my eyes, I blow over the ink. "Yeah, yeah, I'm his Little Bird."

"And?" There's a stretch of silence where he just watches me, as if he's willing me to come to some conclusion about Nick's inside jokes regarding jailbirds. Finally, he smirks, folding my fingers into a fist. "It also means 'pound'."

Behind Remy, I see Verity strutting up, her red hair shining in the flickering lights. She's agreed to fill in for me while I go get ready for the poker game.

"You're early," I say, trying to pull some semblance of normalcy over my expression.

"The girls are all getting ready in the tent," she says, nodding toward the west end of the grounds. "I figured you might need a little extra time to prepare."

My stomach flips. The truth is, I'd rather stay here all night, watching the pretty lights and happy, clueless people. But she's right. I need to get my head in the game.

"Story knows you're filling in," I tell her, handing her the clipboard. "All the other details are on here. Sorry for dumping this on you."

She gives an easy shrug. "Hey, you're giving me an out from working the game tonight. I owe you one—possibly five." More solemnly, she adds, "Good luck."

Remy takes my hand, and we walk like a funeral march over to the tent set up at the back of the grounds. A few of Saul's men stand outside, already on duty. It strikes me that one reason Saul wanted the event connected to the festival is that there's an understood truce between the frats. The game attracts the most powerful men connected to the Dukes. Alumni with deep pockets. It'd be the perfect opportunity to make a move. I know more than anyone that there's no such thing as guaranteed safety, but this may be as good as it gets.

But it makes me wonder about what Mama B mentioned this morning. I haven't had the chance to ask about it, so wrapped up in my duties here. Sy's been unusually quiet today, just as preoccupied with planning the event as I've been. Nick's MIA, and Remy...

I glance over at him, the way he watches his feet as we walk like he's lost in thought. Maybe he's mentally preparing for the night ahead, or maybe he's wrestling with something worse. He's been so clear-headed and present lately, and I hesitate at the thought of drudging up a trigger.

Still, he's my Duke, so reluctantly, I begin, "Remy..."

"He's going to come," he says, looking up at me.

"Oh." I blink, realizing he thinks the worry in my voice is about Nick. "I mean, I hope so, but I kind of wanted to ask you something about... Tate."

Remy comes to a slow stop, giving the guys guarding the tent a furtive, assessing look. He meets my eyes with a curious tilt of his head, keeping his voice low. "What is it?"

Taking a breath, I ask, "Did she ever work for Saul?"

Remy scoffs, his answer immediate. "Nah, she didn't even know Saul. None of us did—not until we got into Forsyth. Why?"

"Mama B says differently." Feeling annoyed by the eyes on us, I lean closer, smelling the sharp scent of his cologne. "She told me Tate was working for him."

Remy snaps back to stare into my eyes, searching. "No chance. She would have told us." The words are spoken with a certainty that his green eyes lack, and I practically see his mind kicking into overdrive.

"Sorry I brought it up," I rush out, not wanting to burden him with something unfounded. "I know tonight is hard enough without filling your head up–"

"Vinny." He hooks a finger beneath my chin, raising my gaze to meet his. "Remember what I said to you last night?"

How could I possibly forget?

"You don't need to save me all the time..."

I exhale, knowing he's right. Remy might need a doctor, but it's not going to be me. Letting the tension fall off my shoulders, I try on a coy grin, fluttering my eyelashes. "That you wanted Sy or Nick to fuck me at the same time you did?"

His eyes darken, a smirk flirting at the corner of his mouth. "That," he says, leaning down to brush his lips against my ear, "and that I love you."

Lucias have never been the type for sentimentality. Before I came to West End, I'd never heard those words said to me before. For a long time, they made me feel uncomfortable, panicked, and maybe deep down, painfully unworthy of them. Now, they warm me from within, an odd sense of calm soothing over the tight boulder of alarm in my gut.

I turn to brush a kiss against his clean-shaven jaw, whispering, "I love you, too."

He pauses just short of pressing his mouth to mine, eyes zeroed in on my lips. I understand why. It'd be easy to get lost in each other right now. To forget what we have to do. To let our guards down and indulge in this feeling, so raw and enticing.

Sighing, he links our fingers together and jerks his head toward the tent. "Whenever you're ready, Duchess."

Taking a bracing inhale, I nod, leading us to the looming tent. I scowl at Saul's goons, Neon and Ewing–the guy who took me out of class. Neon opens the flap to the tent when we approach, but he's stone-faced, impervious to our arrival. Even when Remy empties the last bit of his beer an inch from Ewing's feet, and says, "My bad," neither of them blink.

We step inside and I'm shocked at the size of the room. It's an elaborate set up of professional gaming tables, a full bar, and a stage along the back wall. I don't miss the stripper pole affixed to the center of the stage, all looming and gross.

We had nothing to do with his part of the setup. It was spearheaded by someone in Saul's office. He made it clear what our roles are tonight: hosts and their sacrificial lamb.

We cross the room, to the flap that leads backstage—the dressing area. I'd already put my things here earlier. Remy bends and gives me a kiss, tongue slipping between my lips, hot and possessive. "Just a few hours," he whispers, eyes intense as they hold mine, "and we'll be out of here."

He'd agreed to tend the bar. Sy will act as general security. And Nick, if he shows, will be the host to match my hostess, socializing and networking. My stomach flips with apprehension.

What if he doesn't show?

Remy turns his gaze toward the back of the tent. "I should probably go get behind the bar and learn how to make douchey drinks." He dips his fingers under my waistband, giving the star a reassuring little rub before reluctantly dragging himself away.

It takes everything in me not to clutch for him.

We've all got a part to play tonight, I need to go get ready for mine.

I spend the whole time getting dressed lost in a stupor of worry. Nancy, one of the older cutsluts, wordlessly steps up to lace my corset for me. While I gather her hair into a tight, high ponytail, Laura kneels down to snap the back of my garter belt into my thigh highs. It's an odd unity here, each of us helping the other without even having to ask. There's a station for hair straightening, and then a station for hair curling. Greta and Lucy are the two cutsluts who make a circuit around the room, painting a glittery card suit below each girl's left eye. Laura is the Ace of Diamonds. Greta is the Nine of Hearts. Nancy is the Jack of Spades.

I'm the Queen of Clubs.

None of us miss that the symbol looks like a bear's paw printed on my cheek.

I save my hair for last, gathering it into a high bun, and then reach into my bag to pull out the hair pin Sarah had given me. The nervousness in my belly flares up at the thought of bringing a snake into this place, but when Laura watches me stick it through the center of my bun, she grins.

"Dope pin, Lavvy."

Shrugging into my short satin robe, I say, "Thanks," some of the tension falling away.

It helps that the first person I see when I step out of the dressing room is Sy. He's across the room, changed into a black suit with a white button down. His eyes find me like a magnet, sweeping across the room and coming to a hard stop on mine. His jaw goes tight as he looks down, getting a good look at my outfit before I close the robe. His hands are shoved too deeply in his pockets for me to see it, but I can perfectly imagine how tightly he's curling his fists right now.

It's at that moment I realize that we've been put in an impossible situation. It's not just me that's on display. It's my men, hot-blooded and possessive, short-fused and cornered. Seeing me like this? It'll take a miracle for the four of us to get out of here alive.

I tug at the satin trim on the robe, my throat suddenly tight.

"Don't fidget." A hand falls over mine and I look down. The fingers have the letters D-U-K-E inked across them, a heavy gold ring glinting from the ambient light. "Don't ever let them see you squirm." My movements still under his touch, but when I look beside me, my breath gets caught somewhere in my chest.

Nick is in a suit, just like Remy and Sy, the top three buttons on his shirt hanging open, revealing the tattoos inked on his muscular chest. Clean-shaven. Hair slicked back. Blue eyes flick to mine, but I don't see anything in them, the patented mask firmly in place. Nick, the soldier, has always been expressionless, cold, and lethally mechanical. I've been dreading the return of this part of him ever since he killed Perez.

"Nick," I start, but before I finish, he removes his hand.

"Come on," he says, voice smooth and measured. "Let's get this over with."

When he strides into the fray, it's with an energy I'm unfamiliar with. His posture and expression... it doesn't repel in the way I'm used to. It attracts. Three business men are drawn to him instantly, taking his tattooed hand in firm grips.

I realize this isn't the soldier I'm seeing.

It's the Bruin.

It's a *King*.

20

L avinia

"Be a sweetheart and grab me another bourbon," comes a grating voice from the table I pass. The guy is old. Balding. Drunk. Also, his hand is on my arm.

I smile down at him, trying not to bare my teeth. "Let me find you a server," I say. "I can have one of the girls get—"

"I'd rather you do it," he says, tone laced with a hint of warning. "That's not a problem, is it, Duchess?"

I'm already fed up with hearing that tone. *Duchess.* They say it like it's a joke they're on the butt end of. It's said spitefully. Hatefully. But I'm Lavinia Lucia, and I grew used to being in the presence of a man's hatred long ago.

"Of course not, Mr. Richmond." I take the glass from him and pry my arm away from him. "I'll be right back."

I turn my back to him and feel the sharp sting of his hand coming down on my ass. My spine goes rigid as the table erupts into boisterous laughter, and it takes everything in me not to turn around and smash the glass on his forehead. But, in the split second I'm trying to make my decision, my eyes land on Nick across the room, and I think better of it.

He's leaning against the end of the bar, a casual smile plastered across his pretty mouth. I don't miss that he's speaking with Carmine Ledbetter, distributor of military grade AK-47s. He's networking, doing his job, and *fuck it*, I can do mine too.

It's been two hours since the tent flaps pulled apart and the space filled with loud voices, cigar smoke, and unrepentant testosterone. Poker chips clink as the gamblers toss them on ever-growing piles. The dealers–people Saul hired–do a good job of upping the ante, reminding everyone the proceeds go back to the frat.

With a smile plastered on my face, I keep an eye on everything, although things seem to be running smoothly. The cutsluts work the room like pros, serving drinks and flirting with the alumni who seem pleased with their skimpy outfits and attention.

The entire time I feel awkward and out of place. I don't know how to be a hostess. I wasn't raised for this role. Leticia had that honor. Standing by my father's side during his business dinners and the occasional cocktail party was something she excelled at.

I didn't realize it was a skill I'd need in my wheelhouse.

Approaching the bar, I sidle up next to Laura. She's in the red bodysuit I'd tried on with Mama B–the one she said made my tits look flat. Laura's tits are at least two cup sizes bigger than mine, though. They look fucking amazing. She's turning to leave with a tray full of liquor, the red diamond on her cheekbone shimmering in the light, when I catch her eye.

"Everything okay?" I ask.

She pauses mid-stride, the liquor shifting in the glasses. "The dumbass at table four just offered me a hundred dollars to sit next to him. He said I was his 'good luck charm'."

My nose wrinkles. "You know you don't have to."

Scoffing, she says, "Please. I've done so much worse than sit around and look pretty for cash." She rolls her eyes. "I mean, one summer I worked at a Taco Bell for minimum wage."

Well, that puts things in perspective. "Okay, just let one of the Dukes know if he gets too handsy."

"You got it, girl." She blows me a kiss and strides across the room in six-inch heels without the slightest wobble.

Embracing these little trips to the bar has been the only thing that's made the night bearable, my eyes fixing on Remy as he pours a row of shot glasses for a group of younger alumni. I push the empty glass over to him when he's done. "Bourbon for the perverted geezer at table three."

His green eyes instantly zing toward table three, jaw shifting irritably. "If he left a handprint on your ass, I swear to fucking god, I'm going to cut his goddamn hand off." So I guess he saw everything. *Great.* Grabbing a bottle off the top shelf, he unscrews the top, asking, "You're up soon, or what? Sick of watching this shit."

Knowing his frustration isn't directed at me, I take a deep breath. I've been trying not to think about it, even though my eyes are constantly drawn to the stage in the middle of the room, that silver pole sparkling in the lights. "I'm sure they'll tell me when." I peek over my shoulder and find Sy manning the bank, exchanging money for chips as the men get drunk and looser with their wallets. He feels my eyes on him and glances up, looking me over like he's assessing me for damage. "How about you? Doing okay back here?"

"Well, the prospect of this being my future is depressing as fuck," he says, filling the glass. He tilts his head, eyes sharp. "Do you think if Nicky becomes King we can abolish this fuckery?"

Now that's an idea. "I don't know. This *is* the Royalty. It's probably written in blood somewhere that this shitshow has to keep going, no matter what."

We share a dark, mirthless laugh, because what else can you do? None of us were cut out for this kind of charade.

"Discussing blood doesn't seem like the ladylike thing for a night like this, does it, Ms. Lucia?"

The hair on the back of my neck prickles at the sound of his voice. Remy's smile falters, lips pressing into a tense line, and we share a brief look.

Good thing I'm not a Lady then.

Saul lifts his chin. "I'll take a glass from my personal bottle, Remington." Remy seems to understand what this means, and he reaches under the bar for a bottle of whiskey with a blue label. Remy pours it into a glass and Saul says, "Make that two. One for Ms. Lucia."

I keep my eyes trained to the pervy geezer's drink. "I'm not drinking."

"I thought maybe you'd like a hit of liquid courage before your debut," he says, leaning in to whisper in my ear. "I can smell your fear from here. I don't really care if it's real or not. The alumni are eating it up with a spoon."

Instead of tossing that two-hundred dollar glass of whiskey in his face, I square my shoulders and walk away, carrying the drink back across the room. It's obvious in the last ten minutes the energy in the room has changed. Too much booze and money. Too many men. Saul's right. The clock is ticking, and the bead of sweat sliding down my back confirms it.

I'm going to be grinding on that goddamn pole soon.

"There's that slippery snake," I hear at the same moment a hand reaches out. I'm yanked down into a lap, my ankle twisting at the sudden fall. The move is so abrupt that it takes a moment to process that it's Bruce who has his arm latched around my waist.

"What the fuck are you doing?" I say quietly, eyes darting toward my Dukes. Sy is busy counting money, Remy is suffering through Saul, and Nick... I don't know where he is. This table is tucked against the back wall of the tent–not exactly the most visible spot.

"Thought you may want to meet my family," he says, baring his teeth in a savage grin. Bruce has this weird little mole beside his nose, and from this close a vantage, I can see a single hair poking out from the middle. It moves when he talks. "You may not realize it, but the Oakfields have a long legacy with DKS." He nods to an old man with a weathered face and thinning hair, who's eyeing the four cards in his hands. "That's my Grandpa," he says, running his sweaty hand down my arm. "He was a Duke back in the day."

"Great." I clench up as his hand travels lower. "Let me go."

"No can do, *Duchess*. I know you have no choice but to play nice tonight." His eyes flick around the room. "*All* of you do, and I'm going to make the most of it." His hand slides under my robe, rough against my thigh. "That's my Dad over there..." he nods to a man across the table, leaning back and smoking a cigar. "Also a Duke."

I keep my voice even, even though it's strained. "Lovely."

Fingers inching higher, Bruce shifts his attention to the guy next to us. He's only a few years older, and the striking similarity can only mean one thing. "And this is my brother, Brice."

"Of course," I say, scoffing.

"Why do you say that?" his brother says, grinning as he lifts his glass to his mouth.

"Because only rapists are named Brice."

Brice barks out a laugh, but it doesn't reach his eyes. Gesturing to me with the glass, he asks, "So this is the Count cunt you've been telling me about."

Bruce grins back, holding me tighter. "The very one."

"I see what you mean," Brice says, looking me up and down. "I hear you've got some kind of magic pussy. You know, good enough to convince Dukes a Lucia is worth fucking." He leans forward and reaches out, ignoring my flinch as he tugs at my bottom lip. "You're right, Bruce. She would definitely look better with a dick in her mouth."

I jerk away from his touch and go to stand. "Okay, I'm done." But Bruce yanks me back down, hand moving between my thighs. I'm only wearing lace panties under this robe, and I clamp my legs together to fend him off. Stiffly, I hiss, "Let me go, Bruce."

"Did you know my brother was a Duke, too?" His fingers stab between my legs, working against my muscles. "Every male in my family, for generations. Everyone but me." His fingers inch higher and I grimace, feeling his obvious erection pressing into the back of my leg. "You know why?" Across from me, Brice's grin slips away, and I fight off a gag at the scent of alcohol from Bruce's breath on my ear. "Because Nick fucking Bruin showed up."

"Yeah," I say, fighting to get away, but his grip is solid. "He has a way of doing that." Except right now. Where is he? Does he know I'm being manhandled by this asshole? I could yell. Shout. Make a scene.

The worst thing–maybe even worse than the way Bruce is forcing his fingers between my thighs–is the little niggle of worry in my mind that says Nick doesn't care anymore. Maybe the fight was the last straw. Maybe the man who would have once done anything to keep me safe has given up on loving me enough to make a fuss.

That thought settles in my gut like a smoldering bomb. Regardless, it's with confidence that I add, "They'll kill you." They will, but the threat falls flat. Bruce knows as well as I do that if I fuck up this night, they'll be dead first. Saul and the Lords will see to it.

"Then I may as well make it worth it." Bruce pushes me off his lap, but before I can even get my legs beneath me, his brother plants a hand on each of my shoulders, shoving me to my knees.

Right between Bruce's legs.

"Remember that blow job you weaseled out of before?" Bruce says, looking deceptively loose as he thumbs open his pants. "You better open wide, slippery snake, because it's time to pay up."

"Fuck you," I spit, elbowing Brice in the shin. He barely even moves, laughing as Bruce grabs hold of my chin, working my jaw open.

"God, you're going to look perfect with my cum dripping down your chin." Bruce's eyes are glazed with the booze and lust, but beneath it, I see a murderous spark, jaw tight as he unzips.

I look around, desperate to find help. Not all these people are bad, I reason. They can't be. This isn't a room full of rapists and abusers. They aren't Counts.

But I make eye contact with one guy–a forty-something VIP–and he just smirks, jabbing his friend with an elbow. I hear laughter, and their words might be muffled, but I catch enough to make my blood turn to ice. *"Count, North Side, whore, traitor, on her knees where she belongs..."*

Soon we're surrounded by horny former frat boys, blocking me from the rest of the room. "Is this part of the show?" one guy asks, pulling out his phone.

Another executive-type comes up behind him to say, "Finally. Was starting to wonder why I bothered dropping seven grand on this."

The walls close in on me. Brice's grip tightens on my shoulders, Bruce reaching into his open pants, eyes glinting with an evil I've never seen. Not at the Hideaway. Not in the tower. "First," Bruce says, voice gruff, "you're going to take my cum. Then my brother is going to drag you out of here, and trust me. What he'll do to you will make you beg for my cock again."

A deep feral scream rips from my throat as I jerk away from Brice and reach to the back of my head. The hairpin slips from my hair, the weight perfect in my hand, and I slash out, the razor-sharp tip slashing satisfyingly across Bruce's cheek.

There's a split moment of stillness where the red burbles up, blood appearing as if from out of nowhere, and then Bruce reaches up to touch it, fingertips coming away crimson. "You fucking bitch!" he shouts, blood racing in fat streams down his cheek. His arm jerks back, fist curled, and I know how hard he can punch. He's one of the best fighters in the frat. He swings, fist barreling toward my face, and I brace myself for the hit.

It never comes.

His arm is stopped mid-swing, his elbow twisted back. I don't even hesitate. As soon as he's restrained, I spin around, stabbing Brice in the thigh. He releases a pained snarl, but instead of reaching for the hairpin, he lashes out at me, palm slamming like fire into my cheek. It knocks me to the side, the bloody pin still clutched in my fist as I topple over.

The sound of a gun's hammer cocking plunges the space in a frozen silence.

"Touch her again," Nick says, the barrel of his gun pressed to

Bruce's temple, "and I'll spray your whole family with your brother's brains—assuming he has any."

I gaze up at him, palm pressed to my stinging face. The anger rolling off Nick isn't just something you can feel. You can see it, a low hum vibrating across his skin.

Nick Bruin is looking for a reason.

Any reason.

Bruce's family must see it too, because suddenly, everyone's pulling out a gun, Brice's hand forming a tight fist in my hair. There's something cool against my temple, and I know immediately that Brice has a barrel pressing into me.

"Let him go," Brice barks, and all around us, more guns are coming out, one by one. Even the geriatric Duke—class of 1958—who had to be parked at the blackjack table with his walker, tugs a pistol from his jacket.

Fucking West End and their fucking guns...

"Gentlemen," comes a voice that's far too friendly for the standoff, Nick's eyes flicking from me to Brice's gun. "If those guns are loaded, then you're breaking an unspoken rule of the event. If they're *not* loaded, then you just look ridiculous. Either way," Saul breaks through the throng, assessing the scene in front of him, "this is unseemly."

"It's going to get bloody," Nick grits out, and from Bruce's wince, he's driving the barrel in harder, "unless this sack of shit lets her go."

Saul looks first at me, then at Nick, his nostrils flaring as he flicks a hand. "Put your guns away." When no one moves, he snaps, "Right fucking now!"

Brice is the first to move, and I gasp in relief as the metal disappears, the hand in my hair giving me a sharp shove before he steps away. Nick moves next, hurling Bruce into the table as he lowers his gun.

I feel a soft hand on my arm, but flinch, slashing the hair pin in that direction. "Whoa," Laura says, hands up in surrender. "It's just me."

"Sorry," I say, cradling my cheek as she helps me stand. That's when I see both Sy and Remy at the back of the room, Saul's security restraining them both. From the way their shirts are mussed and tangled, they tried fighting back, too.

Both of them are ashen, watching me with wide, panicked eyes.

I want nothing more than to run to them—to Nick—but then Saul lets out this curt, irritated sigh and says, "Ewing, I've had enough of this." Jerking his head, he orders, "Head across the park. Get Payne. We'll put an end to this now."

"No!" I shout, tearing away from Laura. Every eye in the room snaps in my direction. Including Nick's. Approaching Saul, I beg, "Please don't," lowering my voice to a strained whisper.

Saul narrows his eyes. "Why shouldn't I? I made my demands perfectly clear. The two of you were to act as hosts. You were to provide entertainment." He looks around at the blood and the toppled table top. "As thrilling as this has been, it's not what you promised."

"I-I'll do it," I stutter, untying my robe. "I'll go dance. Right now."

Saul looks unimpressed, mouth pinching in distaste. "You think these men came here for some amateur striptease, Lucia?" Gesturing to the crowd, most stopping their games to spectate, he says, "Not good enough."

My stomach roils, and I swallow down the taste of bile. "I'll undress," I offer, voice wobbly and thick.

"Like fucking hell you will," Nick spits, surging forward. Neon grabs him, yanking him back. Nick could easily break out of his grip, but he goes stock still instead, jaw hardening.

I can't see it, but I'm willing to bet there's a gun in his back.

The last person I'm expecting to speak is Bruce's father. "I wouldn't write the night off just yet, Saul. We were already having ourselves a nice little show. I say we finish it." His beady eyes lock on me, mouth twisting into a demented smile. "The Lucia bitch should get on her knees for my boy."

"Fuck that!" Nick's eyes meet mine, full of an anger that I'm not used to seeing on him, always so composed and cool. But there's also a shrewd sort of panic in them, and I know he's thinking fast, sizing up our options. I see the moment something sticks, his eyes sliding to the side to meet Sy and Remy's. Whatever passes between them, it makes Nick's expression firm out, his voice rising to address the room.

"Who would you rather see Lionel Lucia's daughter on her knees for, boys? Some random DKS?" He raises his chin, peering out over the men. "Or a true, full-blooded Bruin."

There's a hush of silence, and then the room erupts into disgusting, excited murmurs. A man by the roulette table cups his hands around his mouth to shout, "Show us what it's really like up in that belfry, Bruin!"

But Bruce shoves forward toward Nick, his face sticky with smears of blood. "Why? So she can manipulate you even more? Face it, Bruin, you've been playing all sides for a long time now. One day you're a soldier for South Side, the next you're worshiping Count cunt. You're no better than a goddamn whore, looking for a warm place to land." He spits a glob of blood at Nick's feet. "Prove to us that you're really a Duke."

"You're questioning my loyalty?" Nick says, holding Bruce's glare. There's murder in his blue eyes, but Nick just nods, breaking away from Neon to march up to me.

I gasp when he grabs me by the throat, shoving, guiding me to the stage like his palm is a collar. I grab onto his arm and struggle to keep my footing, the alumni we pass smirking at us the whole way.

They don't know that Nick's fingers are loose.

If that wasn't enough to signal what this is–a show–then the look on Nick's face when we dip behind the curtain seals it. He releases my neck, breathing hard as he turns my face, assessing the damage from Brice's hand. A lock of hair has fallen into his eyes, enhancing the unhinged look I see there.

"I have seventeen rounds in my mag," he says, glancing toward the room. "Remy has twelve. Sy probably carried lighter, but he's a good shot and he's better with his hands–"

"What are you talking about?" I struggle to keep my horrified voice to an urgent whisper. "Nick, if someone shoots, this place will turn into a bloodbath."

He fixes me with a bright, belligerent glare. "What are we going to do, sneak out? I'm not going to make you their whore!" He wrenches me closer, his face twisted with fury. "They don't want to watch you suck a dick. They want to watch someone fucking ruin you!"

My stomach sinks at the realization he'd rather we shoot our way out of here than put me on my knees.

The bloody hair pin clatters when I drop it. Reaching up to cup his face in my hands, I say, "I know." Staring into his eyes, I make sure he sees the honesty in mine. "Baby, I don't care."

He tries to turn away, eyes shuttering. "Lavinia–"

I pull him back to me, adding, "I'm sorry." My eyes swim, but I don't make an effort to blink back the tears. "I'm sorry I doubted you, and I'm sorry that I'm asking you to do this." I search his dark eyes, feeling a pang in my chest. "I know what Daniel used to make you do in the pit."

He grabs my wrist but doesn't try to pry me away. He just touches it–holds it–his answer gruff. "This isn't about that." His thumb presses into the letters Remy inked there hours ago. *LB.* The same letters Nick asked me to tattoo on his own flesh. Suddenly, Remy's question flutters back to me.

"You know what that stands for, don't you?"

At the time, I didn't understand the way he looked at me, as if he was waiting for me to understand something. And now it's finally dawning on me.

LB doesn't just stand for Little Bird.

They're initials.

Lavinia Bruin.

"Then listen to me," I say, chest aching with this new knowledge. "If I'm the reason you don't want to go through with it, then you're an idiot. Because I trust you, Nick Bruin. And because..." My breath hitches, the words vibrating through me just as surely as my own pulse. "And because I love you."

His chest goes still, and even though the harsh lines on his face remain, his eyelids fall closed. There are three hard breaths, and then a mangled demand.

"Say it again." He sounds *gutted*.

This time, it's easier. "I love you," I say, straining up on my toes to brush a soft, tentative kiss against the tense line of his mouth. "I love you, Nick."

He snaps into motion like a loaded spring, grabbing my head and crashing our lips together. It hurts–the clash of teeth, the bruising pressure of his fingertips, the cartilage of our noses colliding–but I wouldn't have it any other way.

Loving Nick Bruin *should* hurt a little bit.

He breaks away with a low grunt, lashes fluttering open to reveal blazing eyes. "I'll have to make it convincing. That doesn't mean–"

"I know," I assure him, touching the hard plane of his chest. "Don't hold back. I can take it."

Nick releases me, backing up against the curtain. "So can I," he says, reaching up to thumb my lipstick from his mouth. "Remember the first time we met?"

A slow, mischievous grin rises to my lips. "Are you sure?" I ask, bending to adjust the strap on my shoe. "It might hurt."

"Oh, Little Bird..." He spreads his arms, smirking back. "Wouldn't be any fun if it didn't."

21

Nick

THERE'S A SAYING: what you fear is what you create.

I know I created this moment. Because why would something so good, like hearing Lavinia finally tell me that she loves me, be tainted by being forced into this position?

It's like the pit all over again, except this time I've brought *her,* my Little Bird, with me.

But no matter what I do, the fights I win, the men I kill, I will always be this man. Except now I'm also the man Lavinia Lucia loves. And that, *that,* is what drives me when the sole of her strappy high-heel meets the center of my chest, sending me stumbling from behind the curtain.

It's been a while since Lavinia kicked the shit out of me.

I think I might have missed it.

She comes barreling at me and I grab her easily, hauling her up onto the stage with a showy sneer. The alumni jolt into action, ready to take her down, but only for the amount of time it takes me to dump her in front of the pole. I know it wasn't intentional, but she looks the part, eyes still wet from her apology, two perfect mascara streaks running down her pink cheeks as she spits a sharp, "Fuck you!"

Looking out over the tables, I see all the guys perking up in excitement, scooting their chairs closer. One of them barks, "Make her pay!"

"She'll get what she deserves," I promise them. I flick Sy and Remy a look as I shuck off my jacket, hoping they see this for what it is. Since they don't exactly have the best track record, I'm relieved when the tight, furious scowl on Sy's face smoothes into a stoic expression.

Remy's eyebrow twitches.

They know what's going down.

Thank fuck.

When she goes to cower away from me, she trips on her heels, and it's only then I notice the slight limp. That didn't happen from the kick. One of those fuckers hurt her, and now I'm going to have to reinforce that.

"Strip her down, Bruin!"

"Show us her tits!"

"Bend her over, Bruin! Fuck her like a Duke!"

"Shut the fuck up," Remy roars, his voice cutting through the mayhem. I realize that he and Sy have positioned themselves at the edge of the stage, Neon and Ewing between them. They know better than to try to stop this—none of us can at this point—but they'll let me and Lavinia do this our way.

I raise my hand to her, flicking my finger. "Off."

She scowls out at the men as she grips her robe, parting it only a scant few inches. I can practically hear every man in the room breathing more quickly as she reveals a glimpse of the bustier beneath, taking her sweet time actually taking the robe off.

Pretending to be fed up, I lurch forward and grab it, yanking it forcefully off her shoulders. The robe flutters to the floor, revealing her pale, perfect skin, and the most dangerous black lace and satin I've ever seen.

"Finally!" Someone whistles, and it doesn't matter that they're being lied to here. The thought of them all getting off to the way she's holding herself, reluctant and tense, still makes me want to give that seventeen-bullet strategy a try.

My eyes flick to Sy. "Give me a chair." There's a moment where I'm sure he's going to chuck it at me, knock me out cold, but he grabs one of the folding chairs from a nearby table and tosses it up to me, not saying a word. I yank it apart, placing it a few feet away from the stripper pole. I sit, nodding to the DJ behind the stage. "Play something for the Duchess to dance to."

A slow beat comes out of the speakers. It's sexy, pulsing. After rolling up my sleeves, I make a motion for him to turn it up louder, engulfing us in the throbbing sound.

Sending her a hard, cold stare, I command, "Dance for your Dukes."

She doesn't make it hard for me, turning instantly to the pole, which is a kindness I doubt I deserve. Back in the pit, Daniel always made me be as physical and hands-on as possible. Much like Lavinia, those girls all knew what they were getting into, but unlike her, they weren't always acting scared of me. Most of them just *were* scared of me.

I don't need to tell her what to do. It's like the music does something transformative, drawing us into a separate world. She tugs at the garter belt around her waist, as if she could cover up the enticing peek of her tiny black thong, but then wears it like a second skin, turning to show the room her two round ass cheeks.

Any concerns of me not getting hard during this vanish. My cock leaps in my pants, pressing against my zipper as she trails her fingers down the shiny pole in the center of the stage.

She takes a slow, sensuous spin, and the men in the room erupt into rowdy, dirty cheers.

"That's right, Lucia," one of them belts out. "You're our bitch now!"

I crack my neck, holding myself back, but Lavinia doesn't look fazed at all, turning to nestle the pole between her ass cheeks as she drops, thighs spreading obscenely. She pops back up just as quickly, spinning to pop her hips in time to the beat. There's a controlled grace to her movements, like a fighter in the ring. My eyes are drawn to how long her legs look with the garters holding up her stockings, then up her body to the sliver of flesh between her panties and corset. *My* flesh. My gaze continues to the taunting swell of her tits, pushing out of her top. I thought this would drive me fucking insane, knowing all these men are seeing my girl like this.

But part of me just wants to smirk.

Yes.

That's mine.

I sprawl a leg out, giving my cock a little room to breathe, but it doesn't help. Her eyes drop down between my legs, to the bulge created by her, and her tongue darts out to lick her bottom lip.

Fuck me.

I can't tell if it's the thudding bass coming from the speakers or my pulse pounding in my ears, but my cock twitches in time to her sways and bucks. Lavinia continues her performance, wrapping her palms around the pole and grinding against it.

Shooting Remy and Sy a look, I realize we're all sharing the same hungry sense of bafflement.

Where the fuck did this vixen come from? Survival? Instinct?

When she gets close, I grab her by the wrist and yank her over, tired of watching. She falls toward me, crashing sideways in my lap, and I place my hand on her tit and *squeeze.*

"Just pretend it's you and me," I whisper, keeping my gaze fixed to hers. If I lose her, we're fucked. My inked knuckles disappear under her hair as my hand tightens on her shoulder.

The nod she gives me is so small, no one would notice.

I shove her roughly to her knees, hearing her startled cry, but knowing it's not real. The real Lavinia wouldn't sound so cowed. She'd spit in my fucking face.

Raising my chin, I call over the jeers of the crowd, "Ready to see a Lucia take a Bruin cock?"

The old guy from table three–the one who'd smacked her ass thirty minutes ago–belts out an excited, "Make her choke on it!"

Lavinia looks up at me from between my thighs with shiny eyes.

"You and me," she mouths, and something passes through us. It's an understanding we built during all those late nights in a shitty motel room. It solidified that night at the Hideaway, when she agreed to let me fuck her to lessen her value to the Kings. And it imprinted on our souls when she locked me inside a cage of her own, wanting me to feel the same pain I'd inflicted on her.

Lavinia and I understand one another, and right now we both understand we need to get out of here alive.

That time in the pit taught me what people like this want. They want their sex dirty and raw, their women stripped down and degraded. But I don't plan on treating Lavinia any different than I would if we were alone. She's mine. Her mouth, her tongue, her body.

She's mine, and these Royal assholes need to understand that.

I run my hand across her shoulder, skating up her pale neck, all the way to her mouth. When I thumb her bottom lip, her tongue darts out, licking the pad and sending a sharp zing to my balls.

It's never been difficult getting hard for this girl. Not when she's looking at me like this. Not when her hands are pulling at my belt and lowering the tines of my zipper. Not when her fingers graze my shaft. I give into the moment, groaning. "That's right, baby. I've wanted this for so long." She leans into my hand and I run my thumb up and down the column of her throat. "Put your hands on me."

Pausing only enough to make it seem like reluctance, she reaches into my pants and touches me, her slender fingers cool against my overheated flesh. I hiss as she pulls me out of my pants, my cock swelling against her soft, trembling palm.

I've fucked Lavinia a lot these past few weeks. Hard and soft. Fast and slow. Quiet in the dark of her loft, and loud in the echo of the Forsyth University Library's emergency stairwell. She's even tasted me, those red lips of hers slick against the head of my cock. But she's never—not once—gotten on her knees to suck my dick like this.

When she releases me, my cock bobs painfully against her chest, brushing the sticky tip across her soft skin. The contact elicits a shiver, from the top of my spine all the way to my balls. Her jaw loosens, pink tongue peeking out to take a tentative swipe over my tip. The surge that runs through me is more intense than the electrical current in that cage.

"Shit, she likes it," comes a voice from the crowd that filters through the music. Another remarks, "Of course she does, Eugene. She's a Lucia. She's a *slut*." My jaw tenses, but I remain still as her hand fists around my base, jerking fast. Too fast.

I take in her tense shoulders, her perfunctory moves. This won't do.

"Slower," I demand, raising my voice so they'll hear it. I wind my fingers in her hair, yanking her hair back. She cries out, then takes a breath, before her hand moves again, finding a good rhythm. "That's better."

I lean back, relishing the feel of her hand on me. My balls tighten, clear precum weeping desperately from the head. Fuck, if she doesn't stop, I'm going to come like this. We're here, and we're going all the way. Clamping my hand over hers, I say, "Enough. Open your mouth."

She doesn't skip a beat, and that's when I notice how flushed her skin is, all the way down to the swell of her heaving tits. Lavinia is turned on, probably almost as much as I am. Her tongue unfurls, wet and pink, giving me space to slot my cock against the warm surface. She closes her mouth around my head, giving it a little suck.

"That's right." I yank her forward, pulling at her hair, and thrust my hips at her face, fucking in deep. She gags around my shaft, startled by the invasion, but I told her I wouldn't hold back, and I don't intend to. I drag her off my dick by a fistful of hair, barking, "You're not wet enough! Open."

Unblinking, she drops her jaw, looking so open and trusting that my stomach flips. Bending over, I hook a hand beneath her chin, aiming for that pink tongue of hers, and spit. The crowd erupts and I bring her back to my cock, feeding it to her with a grunt.

Lavinia's mouth is warm, *perfect*, and when I thrust again, fucking into her throat, the men around us go wild. It's an ugly thing, the looks on their faces, all gnarled and hateful and probably hornier than they've ever been in their pathetic little lives.

Her hair falls in her face, sticking to her stretched, shiny lips. I brush it back, wanting so badly to feel her tits, to push my fingers into her tight pussy. But Lavinia isn't coming on this stage. Not in front of these assholes. They can have this ugliness–this *lie*–but I won't allow them to bear witness to something so sacred.

I give her head a few more forceful tugs before leaning back and letting her draw her own rhythm. She curls a hand around my base and bobs, tongue gliding up my shaft until it reaches the head. She gives it a ball aching, suction-fueled tug.

"Keep that up," I rumble, voice low, "and I'm gonna blow."

She looks up at me, eyes watering, cheeks pink, but I see something in them. Lavinia Lucia is a fighter, and she's fucking fighting for me and my boys right now, down on her knees.

She's not a Duchess.

She's a goddamn Queen.

Suddenly, I just can't take it anymore, shooting to my feet as I grip my cock. "You want to know what a Bruin's Duchess looks like?" I shout, fisting the top of her hair. My eyes pass over Remy and Sy, who are standing between us and the crowd with squared shoulders, ready to fight if they have to, and then the men in the crowd. They're on their feet in anticipation, phones pointed at us as they record a Bruin jacking off over the heir to North Side.

And then, with a hard grunt, I come.

The first thick ribbon lands on her cheek. She flinches but

doesn't move away, eyes fluttering closed as the second surge lands on her nose, down her mouth, dripping toward her chin. I exhale as I shoot on her forehead, the glob of cum dribbling into her eyebrow. I paint her with it, long slashes of jizz trickling toward her neck, and the crowd erupts in a victorious roar.

It takes me a second to catch my breath, dragging the back of my wrist over my sweaty lip as I watch her rest back on her haunches, cracking one eye. There's a glob of cum racing toward her mouth and she meets my gaze, lips twitching up into a lightning-fast smirk.

Her tongue darts out to catch it.

It strikes me then, why I've known from the first second I saw her that Lavinia is it for me. She's not just a fighter.

Lavinia is a *victor*.

LIKE AFTER EVERY BATTLE, we celebrate our wins.

And that was a major fucking win. Saul thought he could break us down, force our hand. And sure, things escalated in a way I didn't anticipate but, in the end, the Dukes flipped off Saul Cartwright. With both fingers.

Tonight, we celebrate with pancakes, because fuck, I'm starving.

"You hungry?" I ask Lavinia once we reach the car. There's an exhaustion running between us, but when she looks at me, there's a warmth to her smile that takes my breath away.

Lavinia loves me.

Me.

"I could eat," she says, leaning into Remy's side. She's got his two-thousand dollar jacket wrapped around her shoulders and that sexy outfit underneath. Her hair is a mess, and her makeup is smeared, but none of that takes away from how fucking beautiful she is. All of us are wrinkled as hell, and beside the tender bruise forming in the middle of my chest, Sy has a welt forming on his jaw and Remy's wrists are raw and scraped from being held back by Saul's goons.

The only one I care about is the girl in front of me. I touch her chin. "You sure you're okay?"

It's a loaded question. Is she okay with what just happened? With me coming on her face in front of a group of DKS? With the way things are between us? Despite being hungry, part of me wishes we were already back at the tower, piled into Sy's bed. These last two nights without her have been complete shit.

"I'm..." she bites down on her bottom lip, squirming beneath my gaze. The antsy energy about her makes sense. She probably just wants to get the fuck away from here, too. Finally, she answers, "I'm fine. I promise."

"I have a question," Remy asks, giving her a long, considering look. "How did you learn to dance like that?"

"Seriously," I say, thinking about how easy she made it look. Our girl has secret talents. "What's up with that?"

She shrugs, cheeks going pink. "I learned it when I was at the Hideaway."

Sy goes eerily still, fists clenching. "I thought they never put you to work."

"They didn't," she assures, eyes rolling. "But I needed to stay active, and Auggie's not going to let an investment go to waste. She had a few of the girls come down and show me some of their routines. It kept me limber, and... also, you know. Just in case they decided to send me upstairs..." She makes a vague gesture that doesn't make Sy any less inclined to unclench his jaw.

Remy, however, brings his hand together in a clap. "Remind me to send Augustine flowers." He opens the door and slides across the back seat, but when Lavinia goes to follow, I grab her hand, stopping her.

"You were so fucking good," I remind her, kissing her the way I wanted to during the show. It's long and slow, hard and deep, and when I pull away, she sends me the kind of smile I spent two years desperate to see.

"So were you," she says.

Remy's hand latches around her waist, pulling her inside the vehicle.

"I'm going to get, like... three sides of bacon," I tell Sy, after I slam the back door, securing both Remy and Lavinia in the back. "And I don't want any of your shit about nitrates."

He shrugs and opens the driver's side door. "Hey, it's your colon." He looks over at me when I get in, the interior shrouded in darkness. "The Diner?"

"Yes," Remy calls from the back seat. Sy starts the car, shifting it in gear. We pull out of the parking lot and I flip open the glove compartment, rummaging around in the dark.

"Hey, Little Bird," I pull out a pack of wipes, "you need to wipe my cum off your—?" I turn in my seat, the sentence stalling at the sight of Remy's tongue lathing over her chin, already doing the job. I arch an eyebrow. "Guess not."

Lavinia's head drops back, giving him room to suck a mark into her throat. But then, in a quick motion, she slings her leg over his lap, straddling him.

His eyes widen. "Fuck yes—magenta." Pushing her hair out of her face, he springs up to lick into her mouth. She shrugs her way out of her coat, moaning as he slips his fingers between her legs, voice rough. "Goddamn, you're soaked."

She turns her head, catching my eye. "Apparently, that's what sucking on Nick Bruin's cock does to me."

Even though I just came—possibly harder than I have in my life—my dick twitches back to life. "Fuck, why didn't you say something?" I say, palming myself as I watch her rock into Remy's hardness. "I would have eaten your pussy, or–"

Remy yanks down the cups of her top, and while he buries his face in her tits, his fingers push and pull at the garters. The left one snaps, followed by the right. "I can do it. You need to get off?" he asks, licking a path up to her chin.

Her answer is clear, edged with urgency. "I need your cock in me." She rises, fumbling clumsily with his belt. "Now."

"Jesus," Sy mutters next to me, eyes darting between the street and the rearview mirror. "I can head home if you need—"

"No," she mewls against Remy. "No, I can't wait. Can't we just...?"

"Give her what she needs, Rem," I say, bending between the seats and shoving my hand between her legs. I groan at what I feel, her pussy hot and so slick that it's seeped a wet spot into Remy's designer pants.

Was she like this the whole time she was sucking me off?

Straining over the distance, I yank the crotch aside for him. Remy's struggling frantically out of his pants, eyes dark and intent as he shoves them down his hips, slumping lower on the seat. "You good?" I ask, watching him grab the base of his dick.

"Yeah," he says, cradling the back of her neck as he lines himself up, rubbing the head of his cock through her slick folds.

Lavinia sinks instantly down, gasping against Remy's mouth. "*God*, yes," she cries, letting him fill her up. I squeeze my dick as I watch her adjust, Remy's fingertips digging divots into the pale globes of her ass when she gives a gentle, testing rock.

I slide my hand to the crevice of her ass, pushing the lacy thong aside. I don't ask, I just find her puckered hole. Using her own wetness to ease the way, I push a slow finger in, reveling in the way she clenches. "How's that?" I ask, dragging in and out.

"More," she nods, leaning into Remy as I work a second finger inside. Her shoulders shudder with a moan. "I'm not going to last much longer."

"Don't hold back," I tell her, pumping my fingers in and out. I hear the rustle of fabric next to me as Sy drags his hand over his cock. "You held out long enough, baby. Look at him," I say of Remy, whose thighs are flexing in time with her, jaw clenched taut. "He's about to bust, too. Come on Remy's dick."

She's panting like she wants to make it last, but the breaths are short and quick, punctuated with these sharp grinds of her hips. Remy stares up at her, muttering, "Super-fucking-nova, Vinny. Give it to me. Gonna make you so full..."

She claws at the back of the seat when she comes, her ass clamping tight around my fingers. Falling against him, she lets the orgasm roll through her as Remy punches upward, fucking into her hard and fast. He comes with a growl, and through the barrier between him and my fingers, I can feel his cock surging, pumping her full of his cum.

I'm so fascinated by it that when the car lurches to an abrupt stop, I slam into the dash, my fingers slipping free.

"What the fuck!"

But Sy is spitting a low curse, hopping out and slamming the door behind him. I look out the window and see that we're off the main road, headlights shining into a grove of trees. My brother stumbles behind a bush, and it might be dark, but I can see enough to realize he's dropped his pants, hand stripping his cock.

The car is hot, filled with erratic breathing.

I shoot Remy a look. "Guess he couldn't last either."

THE BACON IS SO good that even Sy orders a plate.

"So," Remy says, gesturing between us with his milkshake. "You two have made up, I take it."

Lavinia is tucked into my side, head tipped back onto my shoulder as I lick the taste of milkshake from her lips. Sy and Remy are on the opposite side of the booth, watching us with calculating eyes.

"Because for a second there, up on that stage," Remy goes on, "I thought Nick had really lost his shit."

Lavinia grins, plucking a fry from her plate. "We make a pretty convincing captor-prisoner team, huh?"

"We did have a lot of practice," I point out. In a surlier tone, I add, "Although, at least *I* didn't electrocute you while eating tacos."

Sy and Remy share a look, but my brother is the one to clear his throat, asking, "Electrocute?"

"Tacos?" Remy repeats.

"Eh," Lavinia flicks her hand, "you kind of had to be there."

"You're both psychos," Sy mutters, wadding up his napkin and tossing it on his plate. "And that's my official diagnosis."

Fuck we really have been through a lot. It'll make a good story to tell our kids one day.

Shit.

Kids.

I place my hand over her belly, imagining such an absurdity. A little Nick. A little Sy? A little *Remy.* Jesus, maybe even a little Lavinia.

"I've been thinking," Remy says, his somber tone interrupting my thoughts of blond kids and their dark-skinned siblings. "Maybe you should ask them." When I look up, he's staring at Lavinia, mouth pressed into a grim line. "The thing about Tate?"

Her eyes shutter. "You said it wasn't true."

"What?" Sy asks, looking between them.

Lowering his eyes, Remy rakes the tines of his fork over what's left of his pancakes. "Something Mama B told Vinny about Tate. That she was working for Saul."

Sy and I scoff in unison, the sound punctuated by the sound of my plate as I push it away. "No chance," I insist. "You know how much Tate hated the gun trade."

"Well... yeah," Remy agrees, flicking his eyes up. I sense the reluctance more than I see it—the way Remy fidgets, like he's coming to a decision. Finally, he says, "But maybe it was something else. Saul's got more than one hustle."

My brows pull inward. "What, like gambling? Fighting?"

"Or athletics?" Lavinia offers, glancing between us. "Something to do with Forsyth?"

Sy leans forward, fixing me with a significant look. "She did get that apartment."

Remy snaps his fingers, eyes flashing. "In *East End.* That can't be cheap, right?" He's never been the best at gauging stuff like that, growing up like a spoiled little rich kid. But he has a point. It'd made me curious at the time, but everything went to hell before the curiosity could evolve into something actionable.

Bothered by the timing, I wonder, "Why would Mama B bring this up now?"

Lavinia shrugs, looking up at me. "I don't know, but she was definitely acting weird. Tense. She told me to ask you about it." Teeth worrying at her lip, she looks at Sy and Remy, adding, "I feel like maybe she was hoping it'd be useful?"

Sy runs a palm down his face, looking as frayed and tired as the rest of us. "Mama B has always had a soft spot for me. I'll talk to her tomorrow." He pauses, peering out the window. "Which is in about three hours." He lifts his hips to take out his wallet, pulling out three bills. "You guys ready to head home?"

My brain is moving restlessly around the possibilities of Tate working for Saul, but just the mention of home makes me aware of the weariness in my bones. Lavinia, too, seems to be fading. We pay the bill and pile in the car. Lavinia curls into Remy and falls asleep on the ride home.

All in all, it's a good night.

Until we reach the tower.

22

R ^{emy}

LATER, I'll berate myself for it, wondering if orgasms have really made us so lax and soft that we're off our game. She tells me–the clock tower. She gives me a sign, the odd silence in her voids and vacancies a clear, hushed warning, but I don't even feel the orange until we're pushing through the door.

Nicky has his gun out before the rest of us even realize something is off.

"What the fuck are you doing here?" he asks, gun leveled at Saul's face, despite the fact there are three goons in the room, positioned at the loft, the doorway to Nicky's room, and the entrance to the kitchen.

The tower's air shivers with alarm, though.

There might be more.

Saul's a fucking bastard, but Kings don't survive by playing fast and loose. He's sitting in the leather armchair, still in his suit from the poker game. Unlike the three of us, he still looks immaculate, fingers curled around the neck of a beer bottle–*our* beer. A tinge of goldish orange rolls off his skin like toxic waste. It's worse when he smiles, eyes sharp and menacing. "You must think you're so clever."

Nick doesn't lower the gun. "Only because I am."

"That's the problem with you Bruins," his eyes hold Nick's as he takes a swig. "You're all so incredibly full of yourselves, as if not becoming a stain on your mother's bedsheets makes you special."

My eyes track the room, darting into every dark corner. Saul is most likely aware that Sy and I were both disarmed at the poker game by his men. That means all we came into this fight with is our fists and Nicky's pistol.

Before Nick can reply to Saul's insult, Lavinia pushes between us, eyes flaring in hot irritation. "We jumped through your hoops. We hosted the party, and we put on your fucking show. What more do you want?"

He raises the beer to her. "You certainly did, and congratulations are in order. It seems the esteemed VIPs of West End are ready and willing to see you as a Duchess." His fingers tap against the glass of the bottle, his bulky ring clinking loudly in the stillness. "So I suppose it's time to make you one."

"Time for what?" Sy asks. The tendon in his neck pulls taut.

Saul radiates gold. "To complete her initiation."

Nick throws the keys on the coffee table, wagging the gun. "Your ears must still be ringing from the cheers I was getting, old man. Lavinia's already our Duchess. There are no further initiations."

"It's not really official," Saul disagrees, bending forward to place the beer on the table. "Not until she bears the scar of our house." Without breaking Nick's gaze, Saul turns his head–just an inch–and raises his voice to call out, "Bring the branding tools."

"What?" Vinny says, her eyes wide and confused. "What the fuck does that mean?"

Ewing steps from just inside the kitchen, the straps of a black bag in one hand, his gun in the other.

Fuck me, but I have had enough of this shitstain.

Jolting forward, I angrily grab my jacket from Vinny's shoulders, wrenching her around. "She already has a fucking mark!" I snap, revealing the tattoo on her shoulder. "I put it there myself, on *your* orders, that night at the Hideaway."

Saul hums quietly, touching his lips as his eyes roam her body. "Yes, we've all seen the tattoo by now. It's nice work, Remington. But that was *your* initiation, not hers. At the time, Lucia being a Duchess wasn't on the table. That mark was a warning to the Lords that I'm not to be trifled with."

"Yeah," Nick says, mouth tipping into a vicious grin. "We all know Killian's Lady got the best of you, and you're still sore about it. But that has fuck all to do with *our* woman."

Saul gives Nick a mockingly patient look. "A Duchess bears the brand, Nicholas. That's tradition. Don't pretend like you haven't seen your mother's." His lips curve upward, eyes gleaming hatefully. "I can still smell the scent of her burning flesh as your father held her down."

The shot slams through the room, sending a shrill scream in my ears. In a flash, Ewing has Nick on the ground, hand tight around his wrist. When I regain my bearings, I see that Sy's body is curled around Lavinia, muscles coiled tight as he tucks her into his chest. Looking to Saul, I fully expect to see a bullet hole square in his forehead, his brains spattered over the armchair.

But his hand is on his ear, blood dripping down his fingers, and he doesn't look dead.

He just looks annoyed.

"You missed." He seems as surprised as I feel, turning to seek out a bullethole. The tower has gathered plenty over the years, the lead swallowed whole by the stone.

"No, I didn't." Nick says, the gun has already been wrangled from his hand, his snarling face pressed against the floor. "That was the only fucking warning you'll get, Saul. The next shot I take, you'll be dead before you feel it."

Saul stands, pulling a handkerchief out of his pocket, and

presses it against his ear, face hard. "And here I was going to let you do the branding yourself–as per tradition. I'm not feeling so generous anymore, boys." He lifts his hand, flicking two fingers. "Bring him in."

One of the goons stabs the elevator button, and Sy shoots me a pointed look. If they're planning to cram our girl into that goddamn elevator…

Well, Saul doesn't know it, but she'll be just fucking fine. We've been working with her on being in that steel trap for the last week, and it's not pretty, but my Vinny can handle it, and when she turns, pressing her cheek against Sy's shoulder, I see her readying herself, gathering up all her white and blue.

Unfortunately, when the doors slide open, an enraged, blood-stained Bruce steps out of it.

Hot rage shoots up my spine, my vision filling with crimson and fire. "You've got some fucking nerve showing up here."

"No, it's good," Sy curls his arms around Vinny, voice low and harsh. "It means we won't have to chase his ass across West End to give his 'fuck around' a little 'find out.'"

"I had a feeling you'd refuse." Saul waves Bruce over, frowning at the bloodstain on his handkerchief. "So I brought someone who appreciates the sanctity of DKS's legacy." He looks at Bruce with arrogant eyes, resting a hand on his shoulder. Quietly, as if sharing some valuable wisdom, he says, "It's all in how long you press it, you know. The longer the iron is on the skin, the more the symbols will spread. Restraint is important. Some Duchesses' marks are barely identifiable. The screams *are* fun, though."

When Bruce turns to us, his smirk tugs at the butterfly stitches holding his cheek together. "Oh, I'm gonna enjoy giving this slippery snake a little pain." He lifts his chin, eyes piercing right through her. "And making you assholes watch."

I step between them, catching his gaze. "You're not touching her." Whatever happens here tonight, that much is fact. It's as vital to me as breathing. The thought of someone putting a mark into her skin–*my* skin, *my* canvas–just isn't bearable. Even the mention of it makes my blood throb with the utter wrongness of it. I gesture to Nick. "He'll kill you instantly. Sy will pummel you to death." I tilt my head, holding Bruce's glare. "But you can't even imagine the things I'd do to you. The last time I sawed into someone's body, I could have stayed there playing with his guts for *hours*." Taken by the notion, I idly muse, "I wonder how long I could keep you alive..."

Bruce's face screws up. "You're all a bunch of fucking whack jobs!"

"Clearly." I shrug, shooting Sy a look. "Point still stands."

A gun rises to Sy's back, the goon nodding to Saul, who says, "I don't think you understand. This isn't a request." He ducks his head to meet Vinny's gaze. "Or should I give Killian Payne a call? It's pretty late. I venture he won't be in the most forgiving of moods at three am."

"Vinny," I start, already seeing that spark of panic in her eye.

But she's already twisting free of Sy, snapping, "Fine! Just fucking do it already!" All of the red in her aura becomes tinged with green when Saul takes the bag from Neon, unzipping it to produce a large butane torch.

"Absolutely fucking not!" Nick sneers, bucking against Ewing.

Saul gives her a flat look, taking the iron from the bag. "Get on your knees."

Gripping my hair in two thick fistfuls, I hiss, "Goddamnit."

Sy's eyes swing to mine, the alarm in them meant only for me. He's afraid I'll do something stupid–something rash.

He's right.

"Stop," I say, my shoulders caving in defeat. My stomach roils at the thought of what I'm about to do, but we're outmanned here. If anyone has the right to this, it's me. Despite that, I can't even look at her as I begin rolling up my sleeves, glare fixed to Saul's shiny shoes. "Tradition says a Duke has to do it," I argue, extending a palm. It's only then that I allow myself a glance in her direction. "Give it to me."

Her eyes are wide, shining with unshed tears. "Remy..."

Forcing a smile, I lie through my teeth. "It's okay, baby." From the way Nick is peering up at me, eyebrows crushed together in restraint, he understands.

Unlike Bruce, I won't make it hurt any more than it has to.

Saul looks between me and Bruce, the conflict clear. This man is obsessed with tradition as much as inflicting pain, but showing his power through both?

He can't resist it.

Saul sizes me up, like he's trying to decide which is worse. Ultimately, he decides, "It's your right, Maddox." He tips his chin toward Ewing, who's still holding Nick down. "But if he makes one false move, we *will* kill him."

Saul places the rod of the iron into my hand.

It's heavy and rough, and I test the weight of it, trying to remember back to the summer when I saw this coming. Back then, Verity was in line to become Duchess, and I spent a solid week before initiation trying to imagine it–burning a mark into her flesh. It never sat well with me. Not because it's barbaric and unhinged– although both are true–but because I couldn't fathom pressing a mark into a girl's skin for the purpose of making her mine.

Not until Vinny.

An explosion of red and yellow makes me flinch, Saul sparking up the torch and setting the canister on the table. The flame glows with a hypnotizing gradient of blue and white, and if it weren't for the hiss of butane, I could almost drown everything out and get lost in it.

"Remington," Saul says, voice full of warning. "I do have all night, but I'd rather not waste it on this."

Looking up at him, I step forward, inspecting the tip of the brand. The greek letters of our house, Delta Kappa Sigma, stand out in relief, and I lower it to the flame, feeling the radiating warmth graze the tip of my fingers.

I speak mechanically, turning the iron to heat it evenly. "It has to reach five-hundred degrees to burn through the epidermis,

dermis, and subcutaneous skin." Looking up, I meet Saul's impatient gaze, my own narrowing. "Don't suppose you brought a thermometer."

He smirks. "No."

There's a tension in the air as we wait, my fingers spinning the iron against the torch's flame. "Sy," I say, glancing up at my friend. "Take off your belt."

Dread fills his eyes as he begins unbuckling it, tugging it through his pant loops with a tight, jerky reluctance. "I used to respect you," he says to Saul, folding the belt over on itself–once, twice. "Back before I knew who the real snake around here was. Open." He says the last part to Vinny, gently placing the belt between her teeth. More quietly, he says, "Bite down, baby."

Here's the thing about Vinny, though.

She's not scared.

She meets Saul's eye and clenches her teeth around the leather like she wishes it were him.

"Where?" Sy asks, threading his fingers through her hair, cupping her face. "Where are you going to...?"

I shift my gaze to the flame. Trying to hold myself together long enough to do right by my girl, I answer tonelessly. "Her back."

"Fuck that," Bruce spits, running a finger down his mangled cheek. "Brand the bitch on her face!"

I grip the iron hard, knuckles straining. "The tradition is that her Dukes choose. But I can always shove it up your ass."

Saul flicks a hand. "Put it wherever you want. But you'd better hold it to her skin for ten seconds, just like any other Duchess. No less."

Shifting my gaze to Sy, I work my posture into something believably unyielding, giving him a nod. Without a word, he begins gathering up her hair, shifting it over a shoulder. "Hold on to me," he whispers, Vinny's arms threading saround his neck. He brushes a kiss to her temple, taking a hard, bracing inhale. "Make it quick, Rem."

The first tattoo I ever inked into her skin stares back at me from over her corset. I accept it as a part of her now, but I don't think much of it. It's my work, but not my soul.

This will be neither.

"Keep her still," I tell Sy, watching Lavinia's back go rigid as I lift the iron. Nick raises his head just enough to turn the other direction, looking away, muscles clenching up.

I take a series of short, fortifying breaths, tightening my grip on the iron with each one.

And then I press it to her shoulder blade.

The tendons in her neck go taut, her biceps swelling as she squeezes Sy's neck. But she doesn't make a sound. I count down the seconds in my head, ticking away. *One, two, three...*

"Don't," Saul warns when my arm twitches, "fucking move."

It's not until the fifth second that she finally screams.

It's a horrific sound, gnarled and muffled against the belt. I watch helplessly as her back contracts with the force of it, her lungs emptying themselves of the cry that claws from her throat.

"Stay," Saul commands, his voice barking into my ear. "Hold it!"

My shoulders tremble with the impulse to pull it away, to throw it at Saul's face, to feed it to Bruce through his fucking teeth. Baring my teeth, I count through gritted teeth, "...seven, eight, nine, ten."

The iron falls to the floor with a resounding clatter.

I'd like to be the kind of guy who stays. The kind of guy who gathers Vinny up in my arms and soothes her through the hurt, the sting, the agony, the tears. I want nothing more than to be the one who presses a kiss against her brow and whispers to her about how strong she was. How fierce.

Instead, I bolt to the bathroom, barely reaching the toilet in time for the first retch to hit me. The bile burns–not hot enough–as everything I just ate comes back up. I grip the basin with trembling hands, taking in gulps of air that just get forced back out on the next back-aching heave.

I don't know how long it takes to expel all the green and the orange, my body exorcising it like a demon. By the time the heaves grow dry, my abs twinge from the pressure, hand trembling as I lift it to flush everything away.

Collapsing on the floor, I spend a long moment catching my breath, too cowardly to go out there and face her.

In the end, Sy finds me there, head in my hands.

I don't hear him come in, too distracted with the colors of her hurt to notice him until he's kneeling beside me. I flinch at the feel of his palm on my back, but he doesn't pull away.

He speaks in a detached tone that grips at me, drawing my gaze up. "They're gone. They left."

Nodding, I drag my wrist over my mouth. "Is she…?"

"She's okay," he says, but his eyes are hard and dark, full of a coldness I'm not used to seeing on him. I take his hand when he extends it, lifting me up off the floor. "She needs you," is all he says, tipping his head toward the door.

That's the only reason I leave, catching a glance of my ashen face in the mirror as I pass. I want nothing more than to lose myself in a bottle of booze–or shit, a bottle of pills–but I take one look at her and know I won't.

She's on her knees, back curled as she rests against Nick, panting. One tear-filled, gray eye peeks out at me through limp strands of her blue hair.

I fall to my knees beside them, voice wrecked. "I'm sorry."

Her expression collapses as she pivots away from Nick, clutching for me. "Don't," she cries, winding her arms around my neck. "Remy, it's not your fault."

She smells like panic and pain, green and yellow, ozone and smoke.

Burnt flesh and salt.

I cradle her head, too scared to touch any part of her below the neck. When I look at Nick, he's staring at the mark I left on her back, his body clenched so tightly in anger that he's shaking.

From above us comes Sy's even voice. "Looks like it's time we have that talk, Nicky."

Nick glances up, locking eyes with his brother. "Which talk would that be?"

"The one where we kill Saul Cartwright," Sy says, "and make you King."

23

L avinia

I WAKE up on my side, with Archie curled into the warm curve of my neck.

From the light pouring in through the tall window, it must be past noon already. My throat is dry, my eyes are sticky, and strangely enough, the first hint of pain I feel is on the edge of my jaw where Brice Oakfield's palm struck me.

It only takes one deep breath to remember the wound on my back, though.

The flare of hurt is instant and nagging, throbbing in time to my pulse, making me hiss. Archie responds with a twitched ear, shifting only enough to give my chin an investigative sniff.

His nose is cold and wet.

"Ugh," I grunt, even though I instantly reach up to pet him. His rough tongue curls out to lick my finger, then my wrist, the cursive letters penned there smeared and fading.

The last time I saw the guys, they were stripping me out of my clothes, wiping the sweat and dried cum from my skin. Taking stock, I remember that I'm mostly naked, wearing nothing but the pair of panties Sy tossed to Nick last night before putting me here, into Sy's bed. I remember staring into Nick's eyes as he pulled me down beside him, fingers stroking my hair until I nodded off.

I touch the empty pillow beside me, but it's cold, the vacancy settling heavily in my gut. Out in the main room, I hear voices. I know it's Nick and Sy, but I can't make out the words. I can hear the tone they're speaking with though, quiet and focused. There's a rattle and a squeak, the sound of the main door opening and closing, and then for a second, nothing else.

Luckily, I'm not alone for long. In fact, I doubt even two minutes go by before footsteps sound outside the door, slowing as they approach.

Remy appears, eyes cautious as they fall on mine. He's wearing a jacket and his boots, so I suppose he was the one who came through the door a couple minutes ago. He looks a mess, the hair framing his face straining against an earlier effort to tuck it behind his ears. From the dark circles beneath his eyes, he hasn't gotten any sleep yet, and despite staring right into my eyes, he still lifts a tattooed fist to knock on the frame.

"You awake?"

Nodding, I try to sit up, Archie going stiff when I do. I wince at the way the skin on my back smarts. Remy watches this with an agonized expression, jamming his fists into his jacket pockets.

"Need some help?"

I eye the way he's hovering just outside, like he's afraid to enter. It's the only reason I say, "Please?"

He darts over the threshold and finally approaches me, tucking one hand behind my neck while the other grasps my wrist, levering me up into a sitting position. "How bad is it?" he asks, green eyes full of worry.

I make an attempt at a smile. "It's not so bad." I've had worse, but it's definitely not something I'd choose to do again.

He deflates, eyes dropping. "Vinny, I'm–"

"Stop." I give him a stern look. "No more sorries, okay?" Remy did what he could, and I don't blame him. If Bruce had gotten a hold of that branding tool... I swallow, not wanting to think about it.

The nod he gives me is heavy, and I fully expect to see something painted black today. For the moment, however, he reaches into his pocket and pulls out a plastic bag. "I asked around at some of my usual haunts–managed to scare up some goods."

The bag has pills in it.

My heart sinks.

"Remy," I start, my voice a mixture of disappointment and alarm.

He holds up a hand. "I know what you're thinking, but I cleared it with Nicky and Sy, alright? I didn't involve anyone from North Side. I only asked around the gym, and–hey, look." He eagerly points to the bag. "I scored you two Percocet from Pauly, one hydrocodone from Laura, and," he presses his hand to his chest, expression solemn, "you'll be touched to know that Ballsack generously donated not one, not two, but *three* prescription acid reflux pills."

Despite the topic and the context, I find a laugh burbling from my throat. "Well, it'll help one kind of burn, I guess."

Remy shrugs. "He just wanted to feel useful. I didn't have the heart to turn him away. He's kind of precious in that annoying 'puppy I want to punch' sort of way."

I quickly sober, watching him carefully. "You're supposed to be getting clean."

He frowns. "I'm not getting clean. I *am* clean. Plus, pain pills don't tempt me at all. I mean..." He scratches the back of his neck, uncharacteristically bashful. "If you needed stimulants, we might have a problem. But I'm not about to stiff my girl on pain management just to get a quick high, Vinny."

I feel bad for making him test his restraint, but worse for doubting him. "Thank you," I say, gently opening the bag. He instantly reaches over to the nightstand, producing a bottle of water Sy must have left for me earlier.

After watching me take the pill, Remy inhales deep, shucking off his jacket. "Okay, now lay flat. Let's see the damage."

My face falls. "You don't have to–" But the words bite off, because I see the look on his face, expectant and determined, and realize what this is.

Remy needs to make it better.

Desperately.

Sighing, I turn, scooting Archie aside to lay on my front, baring my back to Remy. I don't know how bad it looks yet, but from the beat of total silence that greets me, I'm guessing it doesn't look good.

Remy shakes it off, however, pulling a pair of black latex gloves from the box next to the water bottle. "I'm gonna try to be gentle," he says, sitting next to me on the bed. "But this cream is top grade. I use it all the time."

"I can take it, Rem."

He bends to press a warm kiss to my forehead, a soft warning to the wet cloth he drags over my blistering skin. I hiss, twisting my face into the pillow. The scream I release is less about the pain and more about the smoldering rage in the center of my chest.

What happened last night was a new kind of violation.

That night at the Hideaway, I negotiated with a masked Nick Bruin as a way to leverage my own power at the mercy of the Kings. They thought I was a virgin. I wasn't, but no one believed me, and by letting the men who broke into my room take me, I made that a certainty.

I had some choice in the matter, though.

At least that's what I try to tell myself.

In some ways, I think that my very first assertion of control is probably what got us to this place. Saul Cartwright can handle a lot of things, but a woman with Royal blood not understanding her place? I don't think that's one of them.

Despite his gentle touch and the way he starts and stops, giving me time to breathe through the sting, the rest of the cleaning process hurts like a fucker, my fingers twisting into the sheets as he works. As much as it hurts me physically, I can practically feel it hurting him mentally–emotionally–when he pauses every now and then to press his palm to the small of my back.

I watch blearily as he rips open a square of sterile gauze, saying, "I'll keep it loose, but this should make wearing clothes easier." He ducks down to catch my eye, arching an eyebrow. "Not that I want to encourage it or anything. Your tits are heaven, Vinny."

I bury a tense smile into the pillow. "Where are the guys?"

He presses the tape to my back carefully, jerking his head toward the living room. "Talking strategy."

When he's finished, I turn and face him, knowing my face must be red. "Well, we better go join them." I grip his arm and pull myself to a sitting position.

Frowning, he insists, "Vin, you don't have to—"

I narrow my eyes. "Yeah, I do."

Giving in, he fishes me a low-cut tank top from my drawer in Sy's dresser, threading my arms through it. As I stand there in nothing else but a pair of panties, I get a flash of memory–me helping Remy into his shirt that night up in the clock room, his shoulder still healing from the dislocation. I was so mad at him back then, but so annoyingly enticed at the same time.

This time, I give in to the impulse buzzing over my skin, straining up on my toes to press my mouth to his.

Remy makes a soft, surprised sound, his movements slowing to a crawl as he eases the shirt down, fingers stalling at the hem. He touches the star on my hip at the same moment he licks out to taste me.

"You're stoned," he accuses, mouth tipping up into a grin.

"Am not." So as to prove this assertion, I take a step toward the doorway, nearly tripping over someone's–Nick's–shoe. Remy catches me gently around the waist, wincing.

"Maybe we should have cut that pill in half."

We find them in the living room.

Sy and Nick sit across from one another–Sy on the couch, Nick in the chair Saul occupied last night. No one's cleaned up the splatter of blood on it yet. There's an open leather binder on the coffee table, the typography inside looking old and antique, pages worn. The heading at the top is in bold ink. *DKS Charter and Bylaws.*

"The frat has to vote," Nick is saying, hands pushed into his hair. He hasn't slept, that much is obvious.

Sy says, "You'll get their vote," with an air of exasperation that signals he's repeating himself.

Nick gestures to the binder. "You can't be sure. It'd be easier if I just took him out. Fuck, I should have just taken him out last night." He looks over, noticing me at the edge of the room. "It would've been justifiable."

Sy leans back, looking just as tired as Nick. "As much as I wish you had, there's a process for a reason. Bruce would call foul, and it's possible he has more supporters in the group than I'd like to admit."

"Then fuck it, I can kill him too." Nick says this as if it's the most simple solution in the world–and I suppose to him, it is. Fuck with what belongs to Nick Bruin, and you'll pay. Meeting my gaze, he holds out an arm. "Come here, LB. Let me see."

I cross the room to him, my legs still bare, and he catches me around the hips, turning me toward his brother. It doesn't hurt when he lifts the tape, and I get a moment of clarity that maybe Remy was right. The pain meds have already kicked in.

Nick utters a low curse at what he sees. "The plan where I kill everyone is looking pretty good right about now." He replaces the tape, then pulls me into his lap.

"No, Sy's right," I say, turning sideways to curl my bare legs over his thighs. "A massacre will do us for a spell, but if we do it the right way, through the proper channels?" I look from Sy to Remy. "That's real, lasting change."

Nick scowls. "Well, we can't just fucking let him keep walking all over us."

"I know," I say, touching his cheek, rough with a couple days of stubble. "But your brother is also right about the fact they'll vote for you."

"We'll see." Not looking terribly convinced, he rests his head back against the bloodstain, muttering, "Tonight."

"Tonight," Sy agrees. In a way, I suspect is more for my benefit than theirs, he adds, "I've already put out the notice. Everyone will be there."

"What about the video?" I reluctantly point out, not wanting to rain on anyone's parade. "Saul said if anything happens to him, it'll be distributed." Fucking Kings and their failsafes.

Nick shakes his head. "I've been working on it. I've got an inside guy who can intercept."

Dread builds in my gut. "An inside guy?"

"A guy like Saul always miscalculates how many enemies he's collected," he explains, palm warm against my knee.

It makes me uneasy. Inside guys are always unpredictable. But I stand by what I told Nick last night. I trust him. "Are you ready?" I wonder, watching him carefully.

"To kill Saul?" He snorts, eyes gleaming in delight. "Absolutely."

I shake my head. "To take over West End?" I know better than anyone what this means. How that title changes a man. Changes their family and the woman that supports him.

And from the way Nick's eyes go dark, he understands this, too.

Remy's voice fills in the resulting silence. "Kingdoms have done worse." Then he yawns, triggering the rest of us. It's the signal we should all get as much sleep as we can before the big vote. It's hard to trudge to Sy's bed with the three of them, knowing that when we wake up everything will be different.

We'll be different.

ONLY IN A FRAT would a meeting be called after dark. But true to Sy's word, the guys roll in the gym, everyone looking alert and eager to find out what's going on. There's no doubt word has spread about the poker game, as there's little hope Bruce kept his mouth shut about what happened during and after. And with the silent looks that I keep getting, I feel like they can see the ugly DKS brand on my shoulder, despite being covered in a bandage and two layers of clothing.

I stand with Sy near the back, nervously watching them all filter in. My blood is energized in a way I'm not used to, rushing thick and fast, as if something monumental is about to happen.

Sy draws my attention with a touch, his fingers lifting my chin so he can assess my jaw for damage. It's the millionth time tonight one of them has made me hold still so they can look at the blossoming bruise from Brice's palm.

His jaw goes taut. "You hear from your girl? Kathleen, right?"

I hold up my phone. "I got a text." It's nothing but a string of emojis. Thumbs up, kissy face, green-sick face, and a cookie.

Sy frowns. "What the fuck does that mean?"

Rolling my eyes, I tuck my phone away. "That means everything's good. She and Greta are entertaining him. You can get started."

Ballsack, who has been manning the door, walks up with a worried expression. "We're at thirty-nine. Should we wait?"

A nervous laugh bubbles in my chest, and I cover it with a cough. He might be expecting forty DKS members, but the Dukes and I aren't. Bruce's interception by Kathleen and the confirmation text means he should be high on enough Viper Scratch to make him forget his own name.

I put that ball into motion the second the three of them fell asleep.

"You know the rules." Sy's arms cross over his chest, striking an appropriately authoritative stance. "A member must arrive at the meeting by the clearly communicated time to gain entry and vote." He jerks his chin to the front. "Lock the door."

Ballsack grins. "Got it."

I still feel a twitch of worry that he'll figure it out and show up, and from the way Sy tracks Ballsack's path to the front, I'm not alone. It's not like things have been going our way lately. I exhale when I see the door shut and Ballsack engages the lock. After last night, I figured Bruce would be in the mood to let off some steam. The goodwill I'd earned from giving the girls some autonomy has paid a lot of dividends.

From beside me comes Sy's quiet rumble. "Good work, Lavinia."

When I turn to him, he's staring out over the faces of the frat, and even though the hard lines of his expression may seem inscrutable to anyone else, I see the tic in his jaw. The burgeoning wrinkle between his brows. The compulsive way he's tapping his forefinger and thumb.

I'm not the only one worried.

I press up against him, fisting my hands in his leather jacket. "You and Nick–you're doing the right thing."

Where Nick is rash and reactive, Sy is deliberate and thoughtful. They're opposites of the same coin, and I know making this decision weighs on him. He's the one who put the words out there, setting this whole thing into motion. Killing a King isn't something anyone does lightly.

"All you're doing is offering it up for vote," I continue, searching his blue eyes. "If it's not what the frat wants to do, then they won't agree to it."

"And we lose," he says, looking down at me. "Until the last few months, Saul has had my loyalty and respect. You've seen him with some of these guys, Lav. As far as they're concerned, they may still trust him."

I give his jacket a tug, as if I could shake the doubt right out of him. "I think Nick has more support than you realize."

"Well," he swallows, eyes shifting over my head, "if we don't, then it's essentially a vote of no confidence–a failed mutiny. We'll have to pack our bags and go."

I shrug, unbothered by the thought. "Hey, moving from shitty place to shittier place is kind of my expertise." I wind my arms around his neck, drawing his gaze to mine. "But at least we'll go together."

He exhales, the line on his forehead smoothing slightly as he tips down to meet me with a kiss.

Secretly, a part of me wonders what my place would be in that scenario. If I'm not a Lucia and I'm not a Duchess, then what am I? If I don't have the tightly constrained boundaries of the Royalty hemming me in, then what do I become?

Maybe I'll just be theirs.

It'd be enough.

"Everyone's here." Remy slides up against my back, interrupting our kiss to press his mouth to my neck. "Ready to make history?"

Nick appears behind him, giving his brother a single, assured nod. "Do or die."

Nick climbs into the ring first, followed by Remy, who reaches down to take my hand and haul me up. Sy lifts me by the hips and then follows after me, ducking between the ropes. The square is occupied only by the lone judge's table they dragged up here on arrival.

Nick walks over to the bell and yanks the cord, drawing the attention of everyone in the room. The boys are clustered around the tables we usually reserve for Family Dinner and they begin turning to us, expectant and eager.

"Let's get started," Nick says, addressing the room. Sy and Remy take their seats on each edge of the table, Nick in the middle. I sit between the two brothers, resolved to remain silent and as unobtrusive as possible. For a win to stick, it needs to be clear that Nick is working independently of any outside influence. There's an official process for all this, and we did our best to absorb all of the information in the charter and bylaws. Saul was right. Tradition means everything here–especially when it involves the sitting King's downfall.

"Here's the deal." Nick's aloof composure comes in handy here, his blue eyes assessing the crowd. "You guys stuck by me when I stepped up to frat leadership, and I've worked my ass off to make that matter. But the truth is, Saul Cartwright feels threatened by having a Bruin in the belfry."

Some of the guys murmur in obvious agreement, Saul's moves the past few weeks not exactly having been subtle.

Nick goes on. "He's exerting his power with a heavier hand than we deserve. Not just the Dukes, but DKS, too. How many wins did Saul cost us with his probation last month?" A sour rumble comes over the crowd and Nick leans back, tapping idly on the table. "It's only going to get worse from here. He's willing to come after not just us, but the people we care about, and that's not something a *real* Duke would tolerate."

Nick cuts his eyes to Sy first, then Remy, but they let him be the one to say the words.

It has to be him.

His blue eyes fall to the ring on his finger, jaw tightening. "That's why I'm presenting a motion to issue a death warrant on our King." The room falls into a sudden hush, all eyes on Nick.

And then it erupts into a roaring, surprised rumble.

"Hey!" Sy stands, knocking his fist on the table to get their attention. His eyes harden as he meets their gazes, one by one. "I know how this probably looks, but you need to understand. We tried working with Saul. We bent over fucking backwards. This was the last motion we wanted to bring in front of you guys." He shakes his head, glancing at his brothers. "You know I don't take this lightly. I'm not just angry at Saul for turning on his Dukes. To be honest, I feel betrayed. Like all of you, I followed Saul for four goddamn years. And what did it get me? A noose around my neck, all because my brother and Duchess happen to have two last names that Saul feels threatened by."

Remy speaks up then, raising his chin. "Saul may be our King, but Nick's a Bruin, born and bred. He has the blood right–"

Porterfield raises a fist in the air, shouting, "Seconded!"

A flutter of something terrifyingly like optimism grips my chest as I watch a couple other guys agree, on the spot. Even Nick looks surprised, his eyes darting to mine, and for a second, Sy is speechless.

He eventually finds his voice, clearing his throat. "It's been a long time since we've had one of these in West End. As most of you know, twenty-five years ago, Davis Bruin was voted out and Saul Cartwright was voted in. I want to reassure everyone that this isn't revenge for some ancient family beef. It's righting a two-decade-long error that has done nothing but put us in a position of risk." There's a short, pointed pause as Sy's shoulders tense for a reaction, but it's unnecessary.

No one argues.

Nick raises his voice to add, "When it comes to this, DKS is a democracy. You all brought your fraternity pins?"

There's a flurry of movement among the guys, pulling the bronze metal from pockets and wallets, plucking them from lapels and baseball caps and gym bags. It'd taken Remy three hours to hunt his own pin down, all of us rifling through his drawers and art supplies only to find it attached to a denim jacket he probably hasn't worn since Freshman year.

Sy shoots Remy a disappointed look, gesturing to the crowd.

Remy casually extends a middle finger.

"If you want Saul to remain your King," Sy continues, "keep them. No hard feelings. But if you want Nicky to do what it takes to gain leadership," he nods to the spot in front of him on the table, "walk up here and give it to him. But understand," he adds, jabbing his finger into the table, "that a vote for Nick Bruin is a vote for removing Saul Cartwright by any means necessary. Any questions?" When none arise, he takes a breath, dropping back into his seat. "Then let the voting begin."

I reach out and rest my hand on Nick's thigh, just so he remembers that whatever happens here, we're going to be okay. But even though I'm not expecting a reaction, he gives me one, dropping his hand to rest it over mine, solid and sure, and I realize that I can't see an ounce of nervousness in him. Just the determination that this is the right thing to do.

Slowly, the frat lines up at the edge of the mat, but for a confusing beat, no one takes the lead. There's a hesitation, a quiet so thick my stomach twists anxiously, and some of the guys are shuffling their feet, looking antsy.

Finally Kaczinski pushes past the first two guys and climbs up into the ring, approaching the table. He stops in front of Nick, rolling his pin between his fingers.

He takes a deep breath and meets Nick's gaze. "It's nothing personal, man. I never bought that stuff about you playing us for North Side or any lack of loyalty. Truth be told, I'd be happy to call you my King."

But he closes his fist around the pin, dropping his eyes.

On either side of me, I see Nick and Sy deflate, even though both remain perfectly composed.

"It's just that he's been here with us from the start," Kaczinski continues. "I know he isn't blood, but he knows how West End works–what we need to function. He's good at this." Gestures to the gym, and the guys behind him. "He makes us better."

Nick gives him a nod, and despite having a million reasons to argue, he doesn't. Jaw tight, he says, "It's all good, Kaz."

It's a bad sign. Sy, I know, has been tight with Kaczinski for a while. He's spent hours training him for his Fury, even when he was a mess after his girl broke up with him. If Kaz isn't in, then there's a good chance none of them are in.

Sy watches as Kaz continues down the mat on his way out of the ring. He stops abruptly in front of Sy, but even though I can see the displeasure in his eyes, Sy still assures him. "It's okay, Kaz. It's a big ask–"

Kaz extends his hand, saying, "To the victor, brother," and places the pin in front of him.

Remy's chair creaks as he peers around Nick. Our eyes meet for a quick moment before we both look back at Sy. His back is suddenly ramrod straight, his blue-eyed glower fixed to the bronze Bruin in front of him. "Wait, that's not–I'm not a Bruin." His words are spoken to Kaz's back, since he's already headed down the stairs and off the mat.

His vote has been cast.

Before I can process it, Grant passes Nick with a nod before stopping in front of Sy, setting his pin next to the first one.

"To the victor."

After him comes Louie, his pin hitting the table with a tinny sound that reverberates. "To the victor."

Sy pales, wide eyes flying to his brother. "Nicky, I didn't–I don't–I never even *implied*–"

But Nick is trying to hide how caught off guard he is, the shutters slamming over his expression as he watches another DKS drop a pin in front of his brother. One by one, they come. Some of them stop to say something to Nick, like Ballsack.

"I'm... uh... assuming you're a bit of a package deal," he asks, looking torn as he pivots toward Sy.

Nick's lips part, but when no sound emerges, he clears his throat, voice gruff. "Of course we are."

Ballsack looks satisfied, dropping his pin in front of Sy. "Then to the motherfucking victor."

It goes a lot faster once they all realize they're getting the three of them, in some capacity or another. The next ten minutes pass with all thirty-nine pins being placed in front of Simon Perilini.

When I catch Remy's eye, he's hiding a grin, even though his peek at Nick is lined with concern. As happy as I am to see the stunned disbelief on Sy's face, with each guy that passes him, my chest aches in sympathy for Nick. He's worked so hard to prepare for this–to make himself an attractive leader to this group of misfits.

Sy never had to work very hard at it.

Maybe that was a sign, and I missed it, so caught up in last names and Royal formalities that I roped him into feeling a responsibility he never even wanted.

Stomach roiling with guilt, I thread our fingers together on his knee, knowing exactly how it feels to have an older sibling chosen over oneself. But Nick just gives me a gentle squeeze back, not meeting my eyes.

When the last member crosses the mat, Remy pushes his chair back and walks around the table, pausing in front of Nick. He holds his fist out to him, and Nick doesn't miss a beat, reaching out to bump their tattooed knuckles together.

Facing Sy, Remy tosses his pin on the pile and says, "To the victor."

And there it is, a stack of bronze pins sitting before Sy in an untidy pile. Only three are missing: Sy's, Nick's, and Bruce's. There's a tense silence that follows, as if the whole room is holding their breath. Sy stares at the pins, his dread unmistakable when he shifts his eyes to Nick.

"Nicky?"

Taking a breath, Nick stands, giving my hand another squeeze before letting go. I watch him round the table with an aching chest, stopping in front of Sy. Nick looks at the pins, a crevice appearing in his forehead.

His words are rough and toneless. "I've followed two Kings already. First Daniel Payne, then Saul Cartwright. I was really fucking good at it, too. Some might say I was too good at it." He stops, mouth tilting unhappily as he regards the ring on his finger. "I told myself when we started making plans that I was never going to be some tyrant's fucking lapdog again." He finally meets his brother's gaze, twisting the Bruin ring from his finger. "I never wanted to be King, Sy. All I ever wanted was one worth following." Holding his stare, Nick sets the ring down right in the middle of the pile. "Now, I've got it."

Sy drags a palm down his mouth, eyes fixed to the ring. "I'm not a Bruin."

Nick snorts, lips twitching upward in a way that makes my chest ease. "I once told our Duchess that a last name is just a series of letters." He shrugs, giving perhaps the most Nick'ish wisdom applicable here. "Who gives a fuck? Your father is a Bruin, just as much as mine is a Perilini. Family isn't blood or the right series of letters, Sy. It has to be something a hell of a lot stronger than that."

He glances at me and I see the truth there just as much as I feel it in my bones.

It has to be love.

Unconditional. Unyielding. Unbreakable.

Without waiting for a response, Nick reaches behind his back and pulls out a pistol. Not just any pistol, but *the* pistol–the one with the Bruin 'B' carved into the barrel. Nick grabs Sy's hand, flips his palm over, and presses the gun into it. "To the victor, big brother."

Sy swallows, testing the weight of it in his hand, and we all watch him, waiting. Sy's never expressed any interest in taking the crown. Where Nick's been preparing to lead, Sy's been preparing to follow. But when he finally looks up, a stony determination settles in his eyes, and suddenly, I know this is what Sy is meant to do.

He raises his chin. "I'll need your help, little brother."

"Didn't you hear me before?" Nick asks, nodding toward Ball-sack. "We're a package deal. All of us."

Sy takes a breath, glancing at me and Remy. I wonder if he sees us for what we are: two wayward Royal heirs, looking for a place to call home. The fact is, we were always all in on these men. These violent, incredible, fierce fighters. Bruin or Perilini, they're all the same to us.

Family.

Sy pushes to his feet, tucking the gun into his belt. "To the victors."

24

S^y

I SPEND the wait turning the ring over in my palm, not daring to slip
it onto my finger just yet.

Every Kingdom only has two rings–that much I know. One is
for the King, the other is for his heir. I wonder which one my father
wore, but that much is obvious. It's on Saul's finger. He didn't take
West End for the purpose of a fresh start. He took it because he
wanted to conquer it.

I'm taking a sip of Saul's scotch when the door to his top-floor
office opens.

"We're two weeks out from the playoffs. Make sure the media
has our new rankings and—" The words abruptly stop, his alert
gaze falling on me. "I'll call you back." Lowering his phone, Saul's
eyes dart suspiciously around the room. "I wasn't expecting guests."

Hearing this, Neon pushes past him and lunges at me. Since my
mama raised me right, I make sure the glass of scotch is firmly on

the table before he arrives, yanking me to my feet. Although, let's face it. I rise on my own more than he lifts me, holding my arms out for what I know is coming.

Neon's narrow eyes hold my stare as he frisks me, hands patting my armpits, sides, back. Pausing, he quickly removes the black pistol tucked against the small of my back, throwing Saul a look as he removes the magazine, emptying the chamber.

Saul commands, "All the way, Neon."

Neon continues patting me down, stilling when he reaches my crotch. I see the look in his eye, like he's trying to decide if the rumors are true. Is that bulge in my pants my cock or a gun? I arch an eyebrow. "Keep your hand there any longer and you're going to need to buy me a drink."

At the last second, he pulls back, tossing Saul a nod. "He's clean."

"Simon," Saul says, not looking any more at ease. "This is a surprise."

"Well," I retrieve my glass of scotch, "I know how much you love an ambush meeting, so I figured I'd play by your rules."

He gestures to the seat I'd been occupying. "Sit down and tell me what's on your mind." More harshly, he adds, "And for once, it'd better not be your Duchess' pussy."

"I can't promise that," I admit, taking a sip of the amber liquid. "I'm here for two reasons, and one is to ask you to back off Lavinia. She's done everything you've asked. If you're just using her to get back at Nick, then maybe what I'm about to say can lead us to a suitable agreement."

Saul leans against his obnoxiously rugged desk, arms crossed. "Shoot your shot, kid."

I twist the glass in my hand, voice measured. "If you leave her alone, I'll handle Nick."

"Is that so?" His chuckle is full of mocking spite. "I doubt our ideas on how to handle Nicholas align."

My jaw tightens as I look up, meeting his gaze. "You made your point yesterday, Saul. You won. *You're* the victor."

There's not a DKS alive that doesn't feel a rush when those words are said, not even Saul Cartwright. I can see the spark of satisfaction in his eyes now, and I can even imagine what he's thinking.

Two Bruins down.

"And what about the Oakfields?" he says, chest expanding arrogantly. "They're an important family–integral to our ammunition supply. Bruce is feeling... underappreciated."

I'm not good at this part of it. The pretense. The acting. Luckily, I don't have to pretend when my teeth clench. "What are you saying?"

Saul pushes off the desk, his stride to the window lackadaisical. "I think it'd be best if you asked your brother to step down and give Bruce his rightful spot."

My eyes track him carefully. "Step down. As in, leave DKS."

Linking his hands behind him, Saul gazes out at the field below. "Yes."

"He's the heir," I point out. "No one has the right to ask him to do that."

He twists to meet my gaze. "Yet, I suspect he would. For her. For *you*."

I pretend to think about it, staring thoughtfully into my glass. Saul lets me mull it over, his goon watching with shrewd eyes. I hedge, "So if I make this happen..."

"I'll let Nicholas live," he assures, tugging a cigar from his jacket pocket. "Just not in West End."

"And if I don't, you'll kill him." The thought is so laughable that I struggle to keep a straight face. In no universe could Saul beat my brother.

Saul shrugs, saying, "It's quite simple, really. A Bruin and a Cartwright can't coexist here." He sets his sights on the couch opposite me, strolling toward it. "Do you know why I didn't kill Davis twenty-five-years ago?"

I watch as Saul takes a seat, puffing his cigar to a bright ember. "Because he left of his own accord. You didn't need to spill blood unnecessarily." The next words taste like acid on my tongue. "I've always held a strong respect for that."

Glancing at Neon, Saul barks a laugh. "How precious is this kid?" He gives me a patronizing smile, like I'm far dimmer than he expected. "Just because I hate something doesn't mean I'm stupid enough to ignore it. Fact is, the Bruin name means something here." Face darkening, he inspects the end of his cigar. "I can kill every man it belongs to–eradicate his whole fucking bloodline–but I can never kill that. The name. The legacy. The reputation. All I can do is give them time to kill it themselves." Bringing the cigar to his mouth, he chuckles. "They almost did, too. Nick going to South Side was damn near perfect. Sullied the name in a single year, and I didn't even have to lift a finger." Pausing, he adds, "Well, not much of one."

Confused, I wonder, "So why bother letting him in the belfry again? Why give him a chance to earn their loyalty?"

"Because I knew he wouldn't," Saul snaps, eyes sparking dangerously. "When your enemy's a fuck-up like Nick Bruin, the best place to put him is front-and-center. Let everyone see that the Bruin name is just as useless as the man it's attached to." He leans back, some of the tight fury smoothing from his features. "But don't think I haven't appreciated the strain that's put on you, Simon. Your brother's return has done nothing but ignite chaos in the tower. First the girl, then Perez, now the embarrassment at the poker game." He looks me up and down, contemplative. "You're a much more capable leader."

Funny. Saul really is DKS. He'd come to the same decision as the rest of the frat. He just didn't realize to what end. Not yet.

I throw the last of my drink back, slamming the empty glass on the table. "Then I accept your terms."

He raises an eyebrow. Someone 'precious' might think he's surprised that selling my brother out was that easy, but I see the understanding in his eyes. To him, power is the strongest allure of all, and that little comment was a message.

Remove Nick, and he'll make me the figurehead of the Dukes.

I add, "With one request," and he tips his head back, assessing me closely.

"I'm guessing I'll need a drink for this," he says, gesturing to Neon, who immediately approaches the little bar by the desk. "Let's hear it, Perilini. Name your stipulations."

I wait until he's holding his drink, looking perfectly at ease, to say, "I want to know the truth about Tate."

There it is.

It's subtle, I'll give him that. The glass doesn't pause on the way to his lips so much as his movement stutters. He plays it off well enough, brows pulling together. "Who?"

Shaking my head, I say, "Don't insult me, Saul. We already know she was doing some work for you."

"Ah, you mean that rowdy girl you used to run around with?" He waves his hand. "Sure, she did some work for me, nothing consequential."

"Then you can tell me about it. What kind of work?" It takes him a childishly long stretch of time to swallow his mouthful of scotch. It's almost amusing–a man as powerful as Saul using toddler-tier tactics. Sighing, I lean forward, elbows propped on my knees as I pretend to level with him. "Look, Saul, I'm here to make things smoother for us, not worse. The time for revenge has already come and gone. Remy and I..." I look down at my hands, fingers lacing together. "We just want to move on, and we can't do that until we understand what went wrong."

I've chosen these words intentionally. Went wrong. There's a lack of blame in the implication something could have been accidental or incidental.

And from the way Saul looks at me, sucking the scotch from his teeth, he takes the bait. "In truth, it was a clusterfuck. All she had to do was get the Lucia girl in position."

Every cell in my body becomes alert. "Lavinia?" But no. That's not right. "Leticia," I realize. Nick and Lavinia had it right. Tate was never the target.

Saul shrugs, flicking the ash from the end of his cigar. "Leticia wasn't the Lucia we got, but she was the one we wanted." His eyes flash lustfully, but I'm too focused on that word–*we*–to process the grossness of it. "Lionel Lucia's precious, pure little viper."

"Pure?" I don't hold back my sneer. "I didn't actually know her, but from what I hear, 'pure' isn't exactly the word I'd use to describe Leticia Lucia."

He leans forward, licking his lips. "Oh, but she was, you see. Leticia played for our team," he taps his temple, "which is something you find out when you run Forsyth's best whorehouse."

My pulse quickens at the implication of who else is included in that 'we'. "Daniel Payne wanted her, too."

Saul nods, eyebrows rising. From the look on his face, someone might think he was sharing a particularly juicy piece of gossip with an old friend. "Well, when his own daughter cut and ran, we were left with a bit of a vacancy." He shrugs, as if he's shaking off an unpleasant notion. "Leticia was better than Killian's slut, anyway. Royal blood. That golden hair. Real haughty, too–just the kind of spoiled little whore you'd love to see put in her place." Shaking his head, he adds, "It was a shame when we got Lavinia. Next to her sister, she just seemed so... disappointing."

My fist curls so hard that, for a second, I don't even want to hide it. I want to fly over the distance between us and slam it into his face until I see blood and bone.

Instead, I ask, "What does any of that have to do with Tate?"

As if such a thing should be obvious, he extends a palm. "A girl with Tate's attributes can cross boundaries, move around in places that were out of reach for someone like me." Sniffing pompously, he finally cuts to the chase. "I paid her to get close to the Lucia girl."

"To seduce her," I realize, stomach dropping. "To help you and Daniel take her."

Goddamn it.

God-fucking-damn it.

There have been a lot of times over the years that I've wished for Tate back, but this is the first time it's been because I wanted to shake her. Ask her what the fuck she was thinking. Tell her that it wasn't worth it. Beg her to explain to me *why*.

Saul continues in a pensive voice. "I actually liked Tatum quite a bit. I knew when I found her running around with you three that she'd have a lot of potential." His mouth presses into a tight line. "Unfortunately, your friend got a little closer than intended. Not that I couldn't understand the physical appeal, but honestly. All that nonsense about being in love." Saul pulls a face, like such a thing is downright baffling.

"She fell for her." A dismal smile springs to my lips, my heart aching. *Of course.* Tate might have been tempted by the money, but she only would have gotten in this deep for something real.

"Enough to double cross her King," Saul says, voice growing serious. "Simon, you need to understand that I wanted things to go smoother that night. I was going to give her a chance to make it right–to give Leticia up then and there." He leans back, mouth pinching unhappily. "But then Remington showed up, so determined to be a hero." The ember of the cigar waves through the air as Saul gestures in frustration. "He pulled a gun on me, you know! Shot out the back window of my favorite truck."

"It was Nick's gun." The words are mechanical, my mind caught up in envisioning them there on that cliff, Remy trying to save our friend. Even knowing at that point what Tate was hiding–Leticia Lucia–he still stood by her. "What happened next?" I ask, trying to resurface from the fog.

But Saul has gone eerily still, his beady eyes observing me. "It wouldn't do you any good to hear the gory details, would it?"

Realizing my posture has sunk, I square my shoulders. "I can take it."

Saul looks skeptical. I don't really understand at first why he glances at Neon. Not until Saul finally answers, his tone cold and business-like. "I disarmed him and then shot her in the head." There's a pause where he waits, like he's expecting me to react badly to the bluntness of it.

I don't. "I see."

Saul gives this slimy little laugh, tucking the cigar between his teeth. "Crazy little fucker, isn't he? Before I could even turn the gun on him, he and the Lucia girl were already diving right off the edge of the cliff."

I blink down at my knuckles. "Yeah, he does that."

"He really doesn't remember?" Saul asks, forehead wrinkling. "To be honest, every time I was face to face with that kid, I'd wonder if he was pretending."

Shaking my head, I shift to the side. "Remy doesn't pretend." My father's pistol is tucked securely between the chair cushion, and I raise it between us, barrel pointing at Saul's head. "But I do."

Even though a split second of alarm sparks in his eyes, Saul vibrates with a low, sinister laugh. "What, you think you came in here to play me or something? You really are precious, aren't you?" He looks at his goon, tipping his head in my direction. "You could do a better job of impersonating security next time, Neon."

Neon looks him right in the eye, not moving a muscle. "Actually, I think I did a pretty good job of impersonating security this time." Neon shifts his gaze to me. "What do you think?"

I give a chilly grin. "I bought it. Although, the grope was a bit excessive."

"Sorry, boss." Neon's lips twitch. "I'll buy you that drink later." Not for the first time, I feel grateful that Nick had been able to suss out Saul's least loyal man. Apparently, working for an egomaniac who doesn't even pay well fosters a bit of resentment.

Saul looks between us, angrily stubbing out his cigar. "What the hell is this?"

"By democratic order of Delta Kappa Sigma, your reign is terminated on death." I rise to my feet, cocking the hammer on the pistol. "The votes have been cast. West End has spoken."

Saul shoots to his feet, face twisted in outrage. "You're lying!" But his eyes zero in on the pistol and suddenly he's whipping his head around. "Come out, you shit! Where is he? If anything happens to me, that video is going straight to Payne and–"

"The video's gone," I say, tilting my head toward Neon, who

helped a competent junior DKS gain entry to the system. The Princes aren't the only ones collecting Forsyth's best and brightest. "And Nick's not here."

His face is turning red as he shoots another glare at Neon, who's casually plugging his ears. Saul whirls back to me to snarl, "He has to kill me himself to take my Kingdom!"

"He would," I concede, "if he'd been the one they voted for."

I thought the moment it settled in would be satisfying. Poetic. It's not that it isn't, Saul's face going an abrupt, pasty-white as he realizes I'm the new King of West End.

It's just that it pisses me off more than anything.

He raises his palms. "Simon, just hear me–"

The shot cracks through the room like lightning, Saul's head snapping back. Before he crumples to the floor like a sack of meat, I see the hole in the middle of his forehead; the life draining from his eyes, the slackness of his jaw as he goes down.

Across the room, Neon unplugs his ears, looking perfectly composed as he plucks up the bin next to Saul's desk and extracts the trash bag from within. Like me, he steps forward and kneels, only whereas I'm yanking the ring from Saul's finger, Neon is quickly slipping the bag around his bleeding head.

"Thanks," I say to Neon as I rise, wondering how many times my brother has gone through these motions.

He looks up, offering me his fist. "To the victor."

I bump my knuckles into his before sweeping out of the office, sliding the ring onto my finger.

The rest of the spoils will have to wait.

As much as I want to go home and curl up in bed with my woman, my night isn't over.

Instead, I find myself being patted down for the second time that night. It's not Neon, but instead a two hundred and fifty-pound former Forsyth linebacker manning the Hideaway's entrance.

The only time I've been to the brothel is through the base-ment window–the night we completed our initiation. One look at the half-naked women situated around the living room, the pulsing music coming from the back patio, and the fully stocked bar, explains a lot about why my brother spent so much time here. This is a place where a man–*fuck*, or a woman–could get lost.

But I don't have the time or interest in getting lost in the sins of this place.

Augustine, wiping down the bar, watches me as I approach. She makes no effort to hide the look of curiosity on her face as she sets a shot glass in front of me. "The Perilini men don't usually come down here. That's more your brother's thing, and even then, it's usually..." Comprehension dances in her eyes. "...work."

I point to the bottle of whiskey behind her. Not quite the caliber of Saul's stash, but it'll do. "Yeah, well, tonight I'm the one with some business. Is Payne here?"

"I can find out." She grabs the bottle and fills my glass halfway.

"To the top." I watch the level rise. "Thank you."

I swallow it in one gulp while Auggie heads through the door behind the bar. She's not gone two minutes when she returns, Killian Payne towering behind her.

He looks confused. "I haven't seen your brother, if that's why you're here."

Sliding the glass away, I say, "This isn't about Nick. We need to talk." Killian weighs it, like he'd rather be doing anything else. Fair. I feel the same. "I've got something you're going to want to hear, and I'd like it to be from me."

He stares at me for a long beat, eyes locked in on mine. There's an intensity that almost makes me run, but I made a promise when those guys gave me their pins, and I'm not about to fail them now. He flattens his palm on the door and pushes it back open, jerking his chin for me to follow.

I stand, reaching into my back pocket and pulling out my wallet. Fishing out a fifty-dollar bill, I push it toward Auggie. "Oh," I say, snapping my fingers. "Remy gives his thanks for teaching Lavinia to dance."

Her eyebrows hike upward. "No shit. She gave him a show?"

I pause. "Of sorts."

That fucking pole dance saved all of our lives. I'm about to find out if that just delayed the inevitable.

I step in the back hall just in time to see Killian disappear through a doorway. When I get there, he's already seated at his desk, gesturing to the chair on the other side. I take it, watching him reach beneath the desk and pull out a nicer brand of liquor and one glass. Filling it to the top, he pushes it toward me, face stony.

"What's that for?" I stare down at it.

"The look in your eye," he explains, watching me a little too closely. "I've seen it before."

Can he really tell? Is there blood on my shirt? My neck? Are my hands still shaking? Suspiciously, I ask, "Yeah, and what look is that?"

He leans back in his seat. "Why don't you tell me?"

Exhaling, I give the words the weight they deserve, holding Killer's stare. "Saul Cartwight is dead."

Killian blinks. "Nick killed him."

"*I* killed him." I reach for that glass, the ring drawing Killian's puzzled gaze when I raise it to my mouth. The burn of the liquor cuts through the numbness in my chest. "We went through our channels. Voted. I did what I was called to do."

His face goes slack as it finally sinks in. "Son of a–" The rest is a silent swear. "I didn't see this coming."

I set the glass down slowly. "Saul dying? I figured you've been wanting that for a long time."

He waves a hand. "No, that Bruin would give up his spot–and that you'd take it." He reaches for a second glass and fills it, this time swallowing it down himself. "Fuck. Fucking fuck."

It's wrong to let my guard down here in another King's domain, but I find my muscles easing. "I know it's not what you really wanted. Saul was a prick, but he was right about some things. The Bruin name means something here." Shifting restlessly, I insist, "But I'm committed. The guys are committed. We're in this. For life."

Killian nods, taking a silent moment to process everything. "How?"

I frown. "How what?"

"How did you kill him?"

Oh. "A shot to the head. He didn't deserve anything else."

"Fucking asshole." He shakes his head. "I wish I could have been there. What he did to our Lady..." Killian looks instantly murderous, and briefly, I start to reassess my need to be here.

But I'm stronger than that. "I know. He came for the Duchess, too."

Killian gives an abrupt laugh. "That's what it was about? Saul's downfall was his dick?" He pauses. "Actually, I can believe that."

I scratch my neck. "That was the final straw maybe, but to be honest, it's been a long time coming. He pushed us to this point." I look down at the ring on my finger, feeling the responsibility that comes with. "I wanted you to know first. Before it's public knowledge."

Killian looks unsurprised. "So I have your back with the Kings."

Rubbing my forehead, I admit, "I won't deny I'm going to need help–the same way you needed Nick's help when you took over your father's Kingdom."

His eyes narrow at the following silence. "Why do I feel like there's something else?"

"Because there is. And to be clear, there's no existing evidence to prove what I'm about to tell you. That's been handled." I waver for a moment, asking, "Got any more of that booze?" Killian's face is lined with the bad kind of anticipation, but he slides me the bottle, looking wary when I use it to fill his glass, not my own.

Finally, there's no more stalling.

"Nicky, Remy, and I..." I look him in the eye, steeling myself.

"We were the Dukes who broke into the basement and assaulted Lavinia."

Slowly, Killian lowers his glass, eyes hardening. "Excuse me?"

"It was our Duke initiation," I explain, the confession settling hot in my gut. "Saul's orders."

I've never needed to question how he got his nickname, Killer Payne, but right now, the murderous look in his eyes amplifies it. "So when your brother came in here afterward, pretending like he was doing my bidding, Nick was actually playing me."

"Honestly?" Sighing, I give him a nod. "Yeah, he was. I'm not going to sugarcoat it."

"He betrayed me," Killian says, voice low and full of uncomfortable intensity. "He betrayed us."

I lean forward, tired but determined. "It was just for her, Killian. He wanted to get her out. It was never about pulling one over on the Lords. You need to–"

He snaps, "Do you know half of my girls wouldn't sleep here after that night?" Tendons straining, he bares his teeth. "Do you know what it did to Story, thinking she was responsible for some other girl getting raped?" He slams his fist down on the table. "She was fucking hysterical!"

With a heavy nod, I point out, "They're friends now. Lavinia and Story–the girls who love us. *Good* friends." Maybe it's a little manipulative, but it's true. It's hard for girls like them to find friends, let alone friends across the boundaries of territories.

And I can see in Killian's eyes that it means something to her.

Therefore, it means something to him.

"Jesus fucking Christ." He tips back in his seat, dragging a palm over his face. "When this gets out, South Side will expect me to–"

"It won't get out," I promise. "Saul was using the proof to blackmail us. That's why I had to kill him and destroy it, for good."

He throws his hands in the air. "Then why tell me at all?"

Fervently, I insist, "Because I don't want to start my reign like that, Killian. Dozens of Kings before us have played that game, and to be honest, I'm not interested. Your house–your brothers, your

Lady–you've been good to us. Maybe that's all political. Maybe you really did just want to put a Bruin in the belfry because it was a threat to Saul. Maybe Nick's been your puppet just as much as you were his." Raising my eyebrows, I add, "Or maybe we can break the fucking chain here. We're a new Generation, Killer. It doesn't need to be like it was in our fathers' days."

Inhaling deep, he pushes his fingers into his eyes, hissing, "Shit."

"If you choose to retaliate there's nothing I can do but assure you that we'll fight back." It'll be a bloodbath, and it's likely neither frat will come away unscathed. "But I wouldn't like it, and neither would Nick or Remy. I just need you to know that."

He watches me for a long beat, the anger in his eyes replaced with something annoyed. "Your house has been a real pain in my dick, you know that?"

I grimace. "We're trying."

It takes a while for that stormy look in Killian's eyes to grow somewhat quieter–pensive. Finally, he grumbles, "Maybe there's an alternative."

My answer is immediate. "Name your price."

"We could use some guns," he says, which is bullshit. The Lords are the second most armed house in Forsyth.

But I'm not in a position to argue. "Sure. We'll do you up right."

"And your DKS boys are good fighters," he says, tapping a rhythm onto the desk. "We could use some more security around here overnight. Make the girls feel... *safer.*" I don't miss the way he's glaring at me, the implication that it's due to my own actions.

Still, I clarify, "You want my fighters to protect your whorehouse?"

He warns, "I'd pay them fairly, if not handsomely."

"Dude, are you kidding me?" I think of Kaz and Porterfield, Ballsack and Grant. "They'd do that for free."

Killian deflates, grabbing for the bottle of liquor. "Then I think we can consider this a new, mutually beneficial slate."

He holds up his glass and raises it, saying, "May you keep what's yours."

Our glasses clink, and an emotion unfurls in my chest. Getting the guys' vote was one thing, killing Saul another, but the approval of my peer locks this all in place. For the first time in months, I realize that what I feel is hope.

THEY'VE WAITED up for me.

I know it the second I see the glowing clock face visible in the skyscape to the west, but I feel it like a hum when I take the elevator up to the top, wrung out and buzzing.

When the doors slide open, the first thing I hone in on are her wide, worried eyes. The second thing is Remy's arm, hooked around her chest, chin resting on the top of her head. Last, but never least, is my brother, who's yanking the gate open with a grunt.

"Well?" Nick asks, giving me that patented devil-may-care stare down.

I step toward them—my brothers, my girl, my family. "It's done."

Lavinia springs into my arms with a relieved gasp, her lips pressing into my neck. "Are you okay? Did he–"

"I'm fine." Cupping her cheeks in my palms, I pull her back, unable to restrain my smile. "Everything went as planned. Nick's not the only one here with good aim, you know."

Remy jumps on me next, pulling me into a full-bodied hug. Partway through it, he catches the insult, burying a fist into my shoulder. "Hey, I have fucking fantastic aim."

Lavinia and I share a look. "Might want to say that to the only person in this place who hasn't cleaned the toilet."

Nick, who's standing off to the side, raises a hand. "That'd be me."

My stomach sinks at the distance between us, dimming the pride in my chest. I only just got my brother back. The thought of losing him again is unbearable. "Are you pissed?" I asked, wishing he'd just hit me and get it over with.

He pins me with a scowl. "Goddamn right, I'm pissed. I spent months trying to be all reasonable and responsible for nothing." When I just stand there, trying to find the right words to say, he rolls his eyes, stomping forward to pull me into a tight, aggressive hug. He speaks gruffly into my ear. "I was trying to avoid saying this in front of Lavinia, shithead, but fine. The second those pins started dropping in front of you, I was trying so hard not to laugh, I think I pulled a muscle. It's such a fucking relief." Pulling back, he glances at Lav. "I would have done it for you, Little Bird." He looks at Remy, then at me. "For all of you. Maybe I even would have been good at it eventually, but if you want the truth? I would have been fucking miserable."

Lavinia's face falls, hands digging into her back pockets. "I'm sorry."

Nick gives my arm a slap, snorting. "Yeah, how dare you think so highly of me that you'd suggest I be ambitious." He pushes his tattooed knuckles beneath her chin, forcing her gaze up. "You thinking I should be King was worth more to me than actually being King."

I grip my brother affectionately on the neck, understanding that completely.

Remy brings his hands together. "So? How are we going to celebrate?"

"We'll celebrate," I promise, taking the gun from my waistband. This was always going to be the hard part, and I find the excitement and thrill leaving me in a staggering wave. "But first I need to tell you something. All of you."

Apprehension shutters in their eyes, and I wonder how long it'll be like this, jumping from one crisis to another, always anticipating the next shoe drop.

I know it won't stop yet.

Not until they know the truth.

"Before I killed him, Saul told me what happened that night." Meeting their gazes, I set the gun down. "I know how Tate and Leticia died."

25

L avinia

"GIVE US A MINUTE?" I hear Sy ask from the outer room. He's not talking to me, but his brother and Remy. His voice sounds as tired as I feel.

I'd walked away at some point, mid-detail. Now I'm staring out the small window in Sy's room that overlooks the city, wondering how I could have been so close, yet so far. Saul was *right there*. I looked him in the eye. I agreed to his terms. I've been in his town, under his command, stripping my clothes off on *his* stage, beneath his stare.

The thought makes me fucking sick.

Worse than that is how obvious it should have been. All this time, Story and Sarah were warning me about Saul. About what he wanted. About what he'd do to get it.

But what makes my stomach tight with unshed tears is the

injustice. Saul died so Sy could become King. Nothing more. Maybe Sy looked him in the eye when he pulled that trigger and thought about his friend, but no part of his death was in vengeance for Leticia.

I hear the door shut, feeling the warmth of his presence behind me before he makes contact.

"I'm sorry." Sy's hand is heavy and warm on my shoulder. I press my wet cheek into it.

I'm not crying for my sister's death. We buried her. Whatever morsels of grief I allowed myself to feel for her, I've let them go. These tears are for the way this city makes me feel. Empty and hopeless. A couple of dead girls is just another day in Forsyth.

"They deserved more," I say, thinking about how they must have thought they'd found happiness. An escape. Am I fooling myself, too? Am I stupid to think that what we have in this belfry is enough to survive?

"That's what we're trying to do here," he says, arms wrapping around my waist. "Tonight was just the start."

I know it's not fair–Sy has been King for only a few scant hours–but I can't help the notion that it isn't enough. He wouldn't understand. He's never been a woman in Forsyth. I turn and face him, jolting in surprise at the sight that greets me.

Sy is in nothing but a pair of boxers, his broad, russet chest on full display. His eyes cast down bashfully. "Nick took my clothes, because... uh, well, you know."

"Evidence. Right." I wrap my arms around his torso, trying to absorb his warmth. His heartbeat sounds strong and loud beneath my ear when I press it to his sternum, breathing in his scent. "Are you okay?" I ask, eyes fluttering at the sensation of his fingers stroking my hair. "What you had to do..."

Saul deserved to die. Honestly, he probably deserved something worse. But Sy doesn't deserve to be haunted by it.

He pauses for only a brief moment, winding his arms around my shoulders, careful of my brand. "I thought it'd be strange to kill someone," he says, voice low and soft, like he's sharing something unbearably intimate. "Maybe it's because it was Saul, or maybe it's because I didn't really have a choice. But it was... easy. I didn't feel anything." I feel his lips brush the top of my head, and then a hesitant question against my scalp. "Do you think that makes me like the rest of them?"

"No." I don't let him finish, tilting my head up to meet his blue eyes. "You protected your family. You protected your community—the people who count on you. The only thing that makes you is brave."

He exhales, tipping his forehead to rest against mine. "It feels like a joke. Like I'm six again, tromping around in my dad's shoes."

Reaching up, I touch his cheek. "My father, Ashby, Remy's dad? They're the jokes, Sy. You're the real deal."

"But—"

I press my finger to his mouth, attempting to look stern. "Don't badmouth my boyfriend. He's a King, you know? He'll totally beat you up."

From the way his eyes bore into mine, I realize he needs this—a place where he can whisper these awful, untrue things. An ear that doesn't belong to the men he has to lead and be strong for. "I have to meet with the other Kings," he says, mouth lined with anxious tension. "What if I fuck it up?"

My answer is instant. "Then we'll unfuck it. All of us."

The kiss I push into his lips isn't just about distracting him. It's to show him that I can be that—a soft place for him to land. The pad of my thumb rasps over the stubble covering his jaw, and he reacts slowly, licking into my mouth as his hands find my hips, pulling our bodies flush.

I'm not exactly sure when Sy became such a good kisser. There at the beginning, when we were in the motel, he mostly treated it as an afterthought. These days, however...

He tilts his head, deepening the kiss with slick, sensuous licks of his tongue. He kisses with his body just as much as his mouth, curling around me as his palms slide over my hips, down to my ass. When I reach down between us, cupping his hardening cock in my palm, the sound he makes is soft and pained, as if he's holding something back.

He shudders when I drag the boxers down his hips.

Breaking away, I eye him indulgently. The man. The fighter. The King. For the first time, he lets me–*really* lets me–knitting his fingers behind his head as he watches me back. He has less scars than Remy and Nick, his dark skin so enticing that I have to run a fingertip down the ladder of his abs.

They flex the lower I get, dipping into the dark thatch of hair, and then lower, skating over the hot shaft of his cock.

He stops breathing when I reach the swollen head, his dick giving a sudden twitch. "Can I call them in?" he asks, voice rough. When I look up, his eyes are hooded, so dark that they're almost black.

I bite my lip, knowing perfectly well what he's asking for.

We don't fuck without Nick and Remy here.

Wrapping my fingers around his length, I give a flippant, "No."

"Oh." He lowers his arms. "Okay."

I strain up to kiss the disappointed frown from his mouth, backing us slowly towards the bed. "I trust you."

His steps falter, and he breaks away, searching my eyes. "You mean...?"

I answer by lifting my shirt over my head, careful not to irritate my wound. Next, I step out of my shorts and panties, fighting a grin at the way his eyes descend, indulging in me just as much as I indulged in him.

"Fuck," he breathes, stepping forward to touch me, his rough knuckles brushing gently over the curve of my breast. "Fuck, you're beautiful."

I've spent all day sore and nervous, pulling at my hair, gnawing at my fingernails, crying and grieving, and I haven't *felt* beautiful for a single second of it.

Not until right now.

He kisses me, and this time when his hands cup my ass, he uses a hard grip to lift me up, dropping to the mattress and taking me with him. He settles me astride his hips, grunting when my pussy makes contact, grinding down.

Lips skating over my jaw, he asks, "You're sure you want to do this? Just us?"

"Yes," I answer, and then his hand rises up to cup my breast in a large, warm palm. "God, yes."

Every press of his lips against my neck feels like a spark, one that travels straight to the cavern in my chest—the one that makes me feel lost and alone. The truth is, I'm not. Neither is he.

I'm struck by the urge to feel him in me, to feel him bury himself inside, so intense, so desperate. Holding his stare, I roll off his body, scooting back until I settle in the middle of the bed, resting on my palms. "Like this," I say, parting my thighs. Even though my toes curl sheepishly, I make myself say the words aloud. "I want you like this. On top of me."

He tears his heavy eyes away from my center. "Lav, your back." Even though he touches my leg, hand gliding up to my knee, a worried crevice forms between his brows. "It'll hurt you."

"Good." Breathing hard, I catch his hand when he goes to pull it away, displeasure flashing in his eyes. Quietly, I explain, "I'm going to look at that scar one day and remember that it hurt. If I'm going to remember the pain, then I'd rather remember it hurting because of something good," I tug him closer, making space for him between my legs.

He relents, ducking down to press a kiss in the middle of my belly. "Sometimes at night, I wake up to check on you," he whispers, his fingers dipping into the slick heat of my folds. "Just in case you're lost in there. Sometimes Nick or Remy catch me–give me shit about it. But it only seems fair." He slides two thick fingers inside, his blue eyes rising to meet mine. "You know that's what you did for me, don't you?" I gasp when he curls his fingers, my hips bucking up off the bed. "I was asleep, Lav. Walking around paralyzed and lost. Just getting from one day to the next. And then you showed up…"

Before I can even think of a response to that, he's dipping down to lick me open, his tongue gliding around his fingers. I clench my fists into his hair and savor the ride, knowing exactly what comes next.

Still, when the third finger sneaks in alongside the other two, I hiss, tugging him up to taste myself on his lips. "Please," I beg, watching the heavy sweep of his eyelashes when he blinks.

"You can always call out to them," he says, thrusting his fingers in and out, stretching me. His blue eyes pierce right through mine as he searches my gaze. "I won't hold it against you."

Groaning, I wind my legs around his hips. "Stop."

Immediately, his fingers are gone, body rearing back.

"No, don't *stop*." I clutch for him desperately, drawing him back in. "I mean… stop assuming a crash position, Sy. I need you inside of me. Now."

His jaw is taut as he hovers over me, grasping the base of his dick. "Yeah?" he asks, running the tip through my folds. His eyes spark, and I think I could get used to the cockiness there. "I haven't even made you come yet."

I chase his cock with my hips, bucking into it when it lines up. "I'm ready. I promise, I'm–"

Sy's whole body flexes when he thrusts, sinking the head of his cock into me. It's not like it used to be. I'm prepared for the stretch, forcing my muscles to relax as I gaze up at him. His eyes are clenched tight, mouth pressed into a tense line. It doesn't even look like he's breathing.

"Sy?" I stroke my thumb over his lip. "Come back to me."

"Sorry, it's just–" His eyes blink open to meet mine, nostrils flaring with a long inhale. "You're so fucking wet." He punctuates this by rocking his hips, easing another thick inch inside. My jaw drops at the feel of it and he reacts by tipping down to lick into the crease of my lips, carefully pushing harder.

An agonized sound punches from my chest as I grip his back, pulling him closer. "More."

He gives a tight shake of his head, and at first I worry he's going to say no. That we've gone far enough. That his control is frayed after a long, tumultuous day. But then he pushes his fist into the mattress beside me and bears down, fucking his dick in deeper, and I realize what it is.

He's trying not to come.

When I spread my thighs wider, making room for him, his growl vibrates against my lips. "Fuck."

I pluck a gentle kiss from his mouth as I rock up against him. Even though he's only half-seated, I still feel overwhelmed by the sheer size of him, throwing my head back to gasp when he pulls back to thrust.

Sy fucks me in a slow, torturous rhythm, damp sweat building between our bodies. Making love to Nick is always all-consuming, and when Remy's inside of me, sex is basically a wild, emotional tornado.

With Sy, I find, it's the edge of a knife. A loaded hand grenade. Two bodies struggling to only take what the other is willing to give. I see the restraint in the tremble of his arms, the guttural grunt that's just below his throat with every thrust. But mostly, I see the way he's watching me—so closely that it's almost as intense as the feeling of fullness between my legs.

"Lav," he breathes, rocking me harder into the bed. There's a tenderness in his eyes that I've grown used to seeing in early mornings, soft and drowsy and so quiet. "Say you'll be my Queen."

I grip his hair, releasing the cry that's been building in my chest. "Yes."

"Say it." He punches in faster, the muscles in his neck going tight. "Say it, baby. Tell me."

Locking my ankles around him, I strain up to meet his lips. "I'll be your Queen, Sy."

His breath escapes in a hard gust that I meet with my own,

because suddenly he's working a hand between us, pressing two fingers into my aching clit. "It doesn't hurt?" he asks, searching my eyes.

So fixed on chasing the sparks of his touch, it takes me a long time to understand the question–the gleam of concern in his eyes. My back hurts, of course, the bandage rubbing between the burn and the bed, but not enough to dull the knot of pleasure in my belly.

But then I look between us, down the length of our bodies.

Our pelvises are almost flush.

"Oh," I breathe, hypnotized as I watch his dick appear, only to glide back inside. "Oh, my god, I'm–" That's how I finally erupt, my body seizing at the realization I'm taking so *much* of him. It escapes me in a strangled cry, my heels slamming hard against his flexing ass as I shudder hard.

A feral sound rips from Sy's chest, forehead pinning mine. His thrusts grow short and more pointed, his cock thickening inside my clenching walls, and then not only do I feel it, but I *see* it, my eyes still fixed on where we meet.

He comes with a harsh groan, his abs tensing as he spills inside me with a wave of sudden warmth. It spreads through me, filling me with hard jerks of his cock.

Abruptly, he lurches back, sliding out of me with a grunt. Before I can do much more than tense, his palm is pressed to my center, wide eyes holding mine.

"Are you okay?" he pants out, ducking down to inspect me with frantic eyes. "Fuck, I got so into it that I just–"

My legs fall limp, a chuckle bouncing from my belly. "Sy, I'm good." I reach out, tugging him to lay beside me. "I'm fucking perfect. Promise."

The tension falls out of him like a boulder, and he falls back, chest heaving. "Christ. Come here."

We're quiet for a moment, just skin and sweat and the feel of what he left between my legs. Next to me he shifts, propping up on his elbow. I look into his face and see the intensity lurking in his eyes. "What?"

"I was serious before," he brushes hair off my sticky neck. "I can't do this without you. I need you to be my Queen."

"There's no need to ask me. Duchess, girlfriend, Queen... it's all the same." I press a kiss on his shoulder. "I'm yours, Simon Perilini. Any name, any time, any place."

~

THE BUZZ DOESN'T WAKE me.

Not for a while.

Somewhere deep in the back of my mind, I hear the sound and just feel an odd sense of serenity, like I know I'm safe with the sound. Looked after. Cherished. I swim in it for a long while, feeling warm and sated, the flutter through my hair not even enough to rouse me out of the goodness.

Eventually, however, the ache in my bladder pushes me to the surface.

When I blink my eyes open, the first thing I see is Nick's chest.

I'm still in Sy's bed, tucked into Nick's side, cheek pressed into his shoulder. His arm is beneath my neck and every five heartbeats, his fingers begin a new stroke through my hair. He's texting someone–Killian, from the looks of it.

Special K: Ashby requested an audience.

So did BK

And the mayor

Find a place that can fit this many egos

Lifting my eyes, I realize the buzzing sound is coming not from the phone, but from across the room, where Remy sits in Sy's desk chair. It takes a few blinks to make out another chair–obviously brought in from the kitchen–and that Sy is the one sitting in it.

He's wearing a loose pair of sweats but is still shirtless, legs spread casually as Remy brings the tattoo gun back to his upper arm.

"Morning, Little Bird," Nick says, suddenly turning off the phone. "We've really got to make some kind of scale between good and bad screaming. You should have seen me and Rem last night. We didn't know whether to bust the door down or give Sy a standing ovation."

Sy's eyes rise to mine, his lips twitching upward at the look on my face. "They really did the standing ovation. Obnoxious shits."

I bury my hot face into Nick's chest, stretching my legs. "Please tell me you're not getting my vagina tattooed on your arm."

Sy scoffs. "Who am I, Nick?"

"Oh no." Groaning, I peek up at Nick's face. "No, Nick. You're not getting my vag tattooed on you."

He rolls his eyes, casually flipping the sheets down to expose my breasts. "You're not the boss of me. Sy is."

Lazily, Sy commands, "You're not getting our Queen's pussy tattooed on you."

In response, Nick lifts his middle finger.

"Can we not talk about my vagina?" I ask, struggling not to feel caught off guard by the title. *Queen.* It's not like I wasn't already preparing to be Nick's, but now that it's real, butterflies erupt in my gut. "What are you tattooing?" I ask, yanking the sheets back from Nick.

Remy's the one to say, "Victory ink."

Rubbing my eyes, I squint over the distance, seeing a smudged outline of a large, intricate bear. "Oh."

Sy winces. "Sorry if it woke you up."

"He wouldn't leave," Nick explains, fingertips dancing down my spine. "Boy gets him some unsupervised pussy and now he's hooked. You thought I was bad? You're about to find out which gene pool that comes from."

After last night, the idea of Sy hounding me doesn't seem so bad.

Nick slouches lower on the bed, nestling his nose into the crook of my neck as he works the sheets back into his grip. "Let me see," he rumbles.

Eyes rolling, I relent, letting him pull the sheet back to expose my naked and well-fucked body. Figuring he just wants to play with my tits, I jolt in surprise when he throws the sheet off, wedging a hand between my legs. "Nick," I say, trying to make my voice stern.

Even though my thighs part for him.

The tattoo on his temple pulls inward when he narrows his eyes. "Just checking." His fingers are rough but gentle as they explore my center, his blue eyes holding mine as he explores. "Sore?" he asks, feeling at my entrance.

I hiss when he slides a finger in, but answer, "Only a little."

His eyelids get progressively heavier, pupils blowing wider as he feels the slickness his brother left in me.

Then, his phone chimes with a text.

Nick freezes, jaw tightening, before pulling away with a frustrated growl. "Great, now I'm a King's goddamn secretary," he complains, jerking his phone up. I use his distraction to roll aside, fishing my panties and top from the floor. "Killian says we need a place to hold a meeting with the Kings. Your choice," Nick says, holding up the phone. I'm already impressed at how easily Nick has taken to Sy's leadership, but maybe I shouldn't be. It's the natural order of things, in more ways than one. Nick is used to working for Kings, and Sy, as the older sibling, has always been the one to hold these guys together. Now it's just official. Watching me get dressed with a surly expression, he asks Sy, "Any thoughts?"

"They're going to expect to come here," Sy says, nose twitching as Remy goes over one spot several times to make the shade a little darker. "But as much as I love the tower, the room downstairs is a party pad, and up here..."

Remy stops his work. "It's private space. Ours."

Nick wraps a lock of my hair around his forefinger, eyes darkening. "The tower is a no-go, regardless. There are only two ways out: the conspicuously blockable stairway, or a very exciting fall from the belfry." When I shiver at the thought, he gathers me close, tucking me back into his side. "There's a reason no one's allowed up here. This place is perfect for an ambush."

"Good point." Sy looks down at the ink, inspecting Remy's work. From what I can tell, it'll take a few more hours to fill it in completely, but the bear is already gorgeous. Majestic. Regal. Painfully sexy. Sy looks thoughtfully at his brother. "Hey, how about the gym? The Kings have all been there at some point."

Nick nods, rubbing his hand over my thigh. "Sure, it's defensible DKS turf, and you're the champion of the house."

"Total BDE," Remy adds, while Sy rolls his eyes.

"BDE?" I ask.

"Big Dick Energy." Remy ruffles Sy's hair, chuckling at his responding glare. "What? I mean, it's not even a metaphor. You can whip that sucker out and prove it if they ask."

"Remy." Sy's tone is exasperated, and his cheeks are red, but I see the smile playing on his lips. All that angst and anger about his oversized cock has vanished.

"No, you're right," I cut in. "The gym is perfect."

Nick's fingers are already flying over the touchscreen. "I told Payne. It's all set."

"I need you to lean forward like this," Remy says, refocused on the tattoo.

"Hold up." Sy grabs his wrist and looks at me. "Will you do it?"

I freeze. "You want me to tattoo you?" But Remy is already waving me over.

Sy shrugs. "It seems... fitting."

Nick snorts. "I knew it bugged you that she inked me and Rem, and not you. Just admit it."

"I'm *not* jealous," Sy declares.

"He's definitely jealous," Nick tells me, helping me sit up. "But you should do it, because you look hot as hell when you're holding that gun."

"Devastatingly hot," Remy agrees, making room for me between his legs. "I'm hard just thinking about it."

It's my turn to roll my eyes. "You're always hard."

That much is confirmed when I take my seat, the solid press of his cock obvious against my backside. Sy's right, though. As Remy preps me to take over, Sy's hand landing warm on my knee, this does seem fitting. The sharp scent of the sterile gloves. The prick of the needle. The speckles of blood as the bear comes to life beneath our hands.

If my first act as Queen is marking my King, then I'll count myself lucky.

WE SPEND the next few days in a tense sort of limbo, as if someone's going to leap out at us and take revenge for killing Saul. It's the reason for the vote, I'm guessing. A house like DKS could turn in on itself so easily with this many hot-headed cubs. Luckily, Bruce doesn't show his face, and if any of the other guys are displeased with Sy's leadership so far, they don't make it known.

The whole house, including the Dukes and their Duchess, makes a convincingly somber appearance at his funeral. In a way, it's the kind of poetry I'd wanted from his death.

Saul Cartwright, Forsyth University athletic director, dead from an apparent suicide.

Just like Tate.

I spend the whole service rigid, anticipating an appearance from the other Kings—my father among them—but they never arrive. In a perfect world, I'd never even have to see him again.

But Forsyth has never been perfect.

"You said the mayor's coming?" Sy asks, watching the doors to the gym. His eyes are sharp and placid, and when he reaches up to adjust the bolt on the punching bag, the ring on his finger gleams in the overhead lights.

From his spot on the weight bench, shoulders forming a casual curve, Nick bounces his chin, loading a round into the rifle between his knees. "Treasurer, too."

It's been five days since Sy became King—two days since Saul's joke of a funeral.

Remy paces back and forth and I track him with my eyes,

wishing he'd sit down. "This is a lot of orange," he's saying, shaking his head disapprovingly. "Killer might clear, but the others are a problem. Three doesn't make white."

Sy releases a sigh, stripping the tape from his fist. "I know, Rem. I'll be careful." Despite the fact he's meeting with the other Kings—and prominent members of Forsyth government–in approximately forty minutes, Sy's still wearing a long pair of athletic shorts and his usual sleeveless workout shirt. He refuses to change for them, to give them the respect of treating them like Royalty, and it makes my stomach churn nervously. They'll take it as a slight, and however much I hate my father and the Baron King, this posturing is done for a reason.

Wringing my hands, I try again. "Are you sure you don't want to maybe put on–"

"I'm sure." He approaches me with an exasperated look, tucking a lock of hair behind my ear. "Baby, I can't let them lead. This is my house." His eyes flick around the gym. "They're going to have to take me as I am."

The rifle clicks as Nick slams the bolt forward. "Young, dumb, and full of cum."

Sy whirls on him, thrusting a finger. "Hey! At least two of those are patently false."

My face heats at the mention of what we did this morning, Sy shooting off into my mouth. "I just think it'd be good if–"

The abrupt whine of the large double doors makes Nick jolt, the barrel of the rifle swinging toward the sound.

"Pops," Sy says, Nick immediately lowering the gun. "Dad. What are you doing here?" He turns a suspicious glare on Nick, who just gives a curt shake of his head. Last I heard, the brothers had been dodging phone calls until they could figure out how to best break the news to their parents.

Manny speaks first. "We got a call—"

"I did it," Remy says, rapping the end of his marker against his palm. "I told them everything."

Sy goes rigid, before hurling a curse at his friend. "What the fuck, Rem?" His voice echoes off the ceiling, making Remy's eyes roll. "This isn't how I wanted it to happen!"

"I know, and I decided that's bullshit." He glances between Nick and Sy, jaw going taut. "Look, it's a big day for you. You've got two really cool dads, and it's fucking stupid to keep them out of the loop just because you're being little bitches."

Sy rubs his face, his perfectly collected facade crumbling. "This is a fucking nightmare."

Davis snorts. "You really think we didn't notice Saul Cartwright's obituary plastered in the media for the past five days? Give us some credit, son." He gestures to Remy. "He just colored in the lines for us."

Looking flustered, Sy meets their gazes. "I know this isn't what you wanted—that it's actually *exactly* what you didn't want."

"Remy said you got the votes," Davis says, eyes zeroed in on the ring his son is wearing.

"Fuck yeah, he did," Nick says, clapping his brother on the shoulder. "Unanimously, as far as anyone who matters is concerned."

"This wasn't about revenge," Sy says, palms raised defensively. "It was about setting things right. Getting DKS and West End back on track." Without even looking at me, his hand reaches for mine, lacing our fingers together. "Protecting the people we love."

"Son," Manny says, leveling Sy with a look, "we just wanted you to find your place—the *right* place—not some role you've been forced into because of tradition and bloodlines." He looks at Nick, his dark hair falling around his shoulders like we're in some kind of shampoo commercial. "You've both taken your own journey to get here, and now that you are, we couldn't be more proud."

Sy's forehead creases, eyes skeptical. "You're serious."

Davis steps forward, giving his son a tense look. "Simon, I wouldn't be your Pops if I didn't tell you how dangerous this is." His eyes pass over all four of us. "The target you've put your back–on all of your backs–is a threat that will always be there. It'll be there when you wake up. When you go to work. When you come home at night. When you sleep." His eyes soften as he assesses Sy. "But since you've done what it takes to become King, then you already know all of that. So all I really want to say is *this*." Reaching out, he grabs Sy by the neck and hauls him into a hard, backslapping embrace. "To the victor, kid."

I step back, letting the Perilini-Bruin men have their moment. After a moment, Remy joins me, slipping his arm around my waist. "That was a bold move, Maddox."

He laughs darkly, curling his fingers around my hip. "Neither of them knows what it's like to have psychopaths for fathers like we do. I didn't want them to fuck this up." Uncapping his marker, he glances at Manny, who's visibly appreciating Nick's rifle. "They needed to know the truth."

At the mention of my father, the flutters of anxiety rise in my belly again. "Are you nervous?" I ask, tilting my head when he grabs my chin, directing it to the side. "About seeing him again?" It's second nature now when he has a pen or marker to just go where he poses me, and the felt tip tickles at the pulse point on my neck.

"Not in the way you're thinking," he answers, distracted as the marker loops and curls against my skin. "I'm nervous about what he'll say to Sy. How he'll treat him. All the ways he'll try to sneak orange into his head." His lips press into a tense line, the fingertips on my jaw holding me steady. "Davis was right. Sy's a target now. That means my father will see him as something worse than his equal." He pulls back, capping the marker to blow a shivering breath across the wet ink. "He'll see him as competition."

"I'm twenty-fucking-two!" Sy suddenly belts, drawing our attention to the standoff happening in the middle of the gym. In a stark contrast to the declaration, he's pouting. Arms are crossed tight, mouth pulled down into a hard frown, Sy looks as immovable as Archie often does.

Looking just as stubborn, Davis replies, "You're not meeting the most powerful men in Forsyth while wearing a sweat-stained shirt with a beer logo on it. "

"You're the one who wanted to be King. That means putting

West End over your own petty values." Manny's holding up the bag they'd walked in with, thrusting a finger toward the locker room. "Go."

Sy relents with a frustrated sound, snatching the bag from Manny's hand. "You," he barks at Nick, "get into position. And Remy?"

Remy jabs the marker behind his ear, pulling his gun from his waistband. "Yeah, yeah, I'm on it."

"Ten minutes!" Sy insists, marching angrily toward the locker rooms.

"Oh, thank god," I groan, trudging to the dads. "I've been trying to get him into something presentable for *hours*."

Manny's eyes flick to whatever Remy's drawn on my neck. "You've adopted a real pair of brick walls here, Lavinia. I hope you're a patient woman."

Shaking my head, I admit, "Not even a little. I usually resort to bribery or threats of violence. I'm just off my game today. You know," I rub my neck, "considering."

Davis gives me a measured stare. "Your dad coming to this thing?"

I shrug. "He didn't exactly RSVP, but that's never been his style." The truth is, my father hasn't shown his face around Forsyth for quite a while, and this would be the perfect opportunity.

"I suppose not." Davis looks at Manny. "We should probably head out. Being here during the meeting would probably cause more problems than help."

"I'll walk you out," I offer, falling into stride beside them. "There's something I need to get from the car."

We step outside into the bright, late fall sunlight. Remy's leaning against the wall, foot propped behind him, knee bent, as he keeps an eye on the street, and I linger beside him.

"See you around, Dads," Remy says, giving them a little wave.

"Thanks for calling us," Manny says. "You'll be at Thanksgiving?"

Remy rubs his belly. "I wouldn't miss Sarah's dressing if my life depended on it."

I grab Manny by the arm, stopping him before he walks away. "Will you tell her thank you for me?"

He looks so much like his son when his forehead creases that it nearly takes me aback. "For what?"

"She'll know," I say, thinking about how that hairpin may not have saved my life, but it sure as hell bought me some time. A little more buoyantly, I add, "And tell her I'll bring a pie for dinner."

"Will do." They both give me a kiss on the cheek, and a moment later, they're gone.

"You need to get back inside, babe," Remy says, thumbing the drawing he put on my neck. "I can't keep up with you and my security duties."

Ducking away, I hold up a finger. "I'll just be a minute." I cross over to the SUV and climb in the front seat, looking for the package I put in the glove compartment. Once I have it, I pause, pulling down the mirror to catch a glimpse of Remy's artwork.

It's a crown.

Car doors slam, and I whip around to realize the Kings have arrived, a long row of black vehicles idling at the curb. I stay in place, watching the men all march toward the gym entrance. Ashby goes first, then Killian, and both of them, for the record, are dressed in nice suits. Thank god for the dads. Obviously, one of my duties as Queen will be making sure Sy understands these nuances. I look down at the wrapped package in my hand. It's a book on the psychology of leadership.

Remy checks them for weapons and then allows them entrance into the gym. Once they disappear through the doors, I fully plan on escaping the car and doing the same, but then the next car arrives. It's a black Mercedes. The windows are tinted, but the man who exits is immediately recognizable as one of the Williams.

He opens the back door and the Baron King emerges, face covered with his mask. It's chilling to know that Timothy Maddox is hiding under there just as much as the knowledge that we're the only ones aware. I wait, anxiety inching up my spine as he and Remy come face to face. Luckily, whatever exchange they have is quick, all business, and I feel my lungs release a slow, relieved breath. After he walks into the gym, Remy's eyes meet mine from across the street, a hard blankness on his features.

I hop out of the SUV, slamming the door behind me. My eyes are on Remy, which is why, as I cross the street, I don't see the car barreling down the road. It stops with a screech, the tires burning against the asphalt. My heart becomes lodged somewhere in my throat, and it sticks there when Lars steps out of the driver's seat.

He gives me a sharp, nasty grin. "Watch your step, Duchess."

Remy's by my side in a flash, that hollow look gone from his face. Instead, it's filled with rage, his palm curling around my shoulder. "Are you okay?"

"Yes," I assure him, eyes firmly on the car. "I'm fine. It's my fault."

Remy argues, "He tried to fucking run you over, Vinny. That wasn't a mistake."

"I'm fine, Remy." I press my hand to his chest, knowing my father is inside that car. "Just watch the door. I'll be okay."

He's clearly not convinced, but he yanks his gun out and slowly makes his way back to his position. Lars ignores Remy's death glare and opens the back door of the car. A familiar, prickly sensation runs up my spine when he finally appears.

My father.

He's dressed in a heavy gray coat, a tone that almost matches his skin color. His face seems thinner. Whatever is going on in North Side is draining him. Too many deaths. Too many failures. Remy said he heard his dog, Amos, is living at the Kappa house. Which for my father is big. He loved that dog more than he loved any of us. It's clear he's losing control.

He barely regards me as he starts across the road, but the urge to speak drives me to follow him.

"I told you I didn't kill her," I burst, my voice small in the empty alley. "Saul Cartwright killed Leticia. He admitted it before Simon put a bullet in his head."

I see the small hesitation, the tiniest curiosity. Of course, for Leticia, he'll stop.

He clears his throat and says, "Wait for me inside, Lars."

Lars looks between both me and Remy, eyes hardening. "But, sir–"

My father flicks his hand. "There's no threat out here."

Lars shoots me a look, then another long one at Remy, before walking inside like a good little lapdog. Remy keeps his distance, giving me space. He understands the need to confront a shitty father–a King.

Looking down, Lionel slowly removes his black leather gloves, finger by finger.

With the book clutched to my chest, I keep talking, my voice steady and sharp. "I thought you might want to know that he was planning to make her into his perfect little Royal slave. He sent a spy into North Side, and you didn't even realize it. Probably because everyone was too doped up to notice."

For the first time, he settles those dark eyes on me, sneering. "Look at you, all puffed up like I care what you have to say. If there's pertinent information regarding my daughter–my real daughter–I'll let your King tell me."

I don't stop. I can't. I'm owed this. "Daniel's virgin step-daughter didn't work out, so he and Saul moved onto the next Royal in line. Someone more pure. Who better than a Lucia, right?"

His eyes narrow as he drinks this in, the glare so familiar that it evokes the scent of old wood and my own sweat. "Except he didn't want you, did he? No one did. You were never anything but a spare. An attempt to create a male heir that went wrong." The words slip from him like the hiss of a snake, evil but mesmerizing. "Your birth devastated your mother so much that she'd rather have died than continued on with the humiliating pretense of raising you."

"That's not true," I snap. My fingers curl around the edge of the book as I remember the way Sarah spoke of her. "Face it. You poisoned her so much that she withered away. Just like Sutton. Just like all your Counts. Just like *Leticia*."

His eyes flash with something unhinged. "Why do you think she needed the drugs, girl? To take away the pain of failure." He steps forward, tall and unwieldy as he bears down on me. "Your little act of defiance in West End has proven that you're exactly what I always thought you were. A weak, pathetic, disloyal bottom-feeder. The fact that you've so easily succumbed to Stockholm syndrome during your time in this dump tells me that I should have locked you in that chest longer—made you stronger than some whore who spreads her legs to the first men that show you an ounce of kindness."

"I am strong," I hiss back, raising my chin. "And I'm *not* a whore, despite your best efforts to make me one."

His eyes drop to my neck, to the drawing. "Ah, right, you're the Queen." A mocking smile tugs at his thin lips.

I square my shoulders. "You're right. I am."

He laughs and shakes his head, like I'm too stupid to understand. "Haven't you figured it out yet? This little game of Royal sluts only exists to keep the young bucks in line. To keep them busy and focused, *believing* they have something to fight for." He looks around, eyes sliding past Remy. "Do you see any other Queens that have survived past producing spawn? Of course not." He eyes me with palpable disgust. "You're nothing but a liability. A poisoned womb. You may as well all be a Princess, for Christ's sake."

Shaking my head, I firm my jaw, insisting, "You're just trying to absolve yourself of the guilt of killing my mother."

He barks a cruel, icy laugh. "What guilt?"

My stomach falls as I comprehend the implication. I've heard it whispered around North Side, in the brothels. Lionel Lucia had a Queen once, but he didn't like it. *Too messy.*

My throat suddenly feels like sandpaper. "You didn't just kill her figuratively, did you?"

Instead of answering, he steps closer, venom dripping from his words. "Best case, Lavinia, is that these men tire and dispose of you.

Worse is that you get them killed before they even have the chance."

I want to tell him he's wrong. To fuck off and stop spewing lies, but there's truth in his words. I was never built to be Queen. I feel it in my bones. "My King loves me," I say, hating that I feel the need to prove it. "The men in the West End know true loyalty–real honor–unlike your Counts." I gesture behind me, toward North Side. "Your entire enterprise is crumbling. Your Count and Countess are both dead. The entire frat is doped up on Viper Scratch. We don't need to destroy you. You're doing it to yourself."

His eyes flare dangerously. "Careful, girl. You're talking to a King."

I laugh, raising my arms. "Look around you. The guard is changing. Old men are getting picked off one by one, replaced by younger, stronger, savvier men and the women who support them."

"Is that so?" He doesn't look the least bit threatened. "You think I got to this place, this position, by being scared of a bunch of children? You forget, I can destroy this entire city, every quadrant of this godforsaken town, with the press of a button." He bears down on me, lips pulling back to bare his teeth. "If you or any of your thugs come after me, you all go up in flames. The clock is ticking, Duchess." His eyes brighten for the first time since he arrived. "Tick-Tock."

Click.

Eyes shifting to the side, I see Remy standing a couple feet away, the barrel of his pistol pointed at my father. "Couldn't help but notice that you're getting a little too close to our Queen."

Lionel exhales, rolling his eyes at what I assume he thinks are Remy's dramatics. He won't show fear. Not to him. Not to me. I don't breathe until he's sweeping away to disappear inside, behind the metal gym door.

Remy's green eyes follow him the whole way, mouth twisted unhappily. "It'd be unwise to interfere with Sy's first Royal meeting." He doesn't lower the gun until my father's gone, tossing his arm over my shoulder. He tucks me close, adding, "But just say the word, and I'll put a bullet into his head when he walks back out."

"No," I say, thinking of the threat my father just leveled–a reminder that this entire city is wired with bombs. His failsafe. *Tick-Tock*. I look up at Remy. "If anyone is going to kill Lionel Lucia, it's going to be me."

26

Nick

"Do you want to know?" Sy asks, sliding his gaze to mine when we get out of the car.

Knowing he's talking about what happened in that office with the other Kings, I arch an eyebrow. "Do I need to know?"

He doesn't think about it very long. "A bit, yeah."

Nodding, I look around and answer, "Upstairs."

West End is quiet.

It took me a long time to re-adjust to that after South Side. The lack of screams, gunfire, and traffic felt eerie at first, as if the streets here were holding their breath, waiting for the crash. I realize now the serenity isn't a trick. Instead of making my shoulders tense, West End has become the thing that unwinds them. The sense of home.

The girl by my side as we approach the tower is just as silent, and I feel it now–the tension. The discomfort. The alert.

I toss Sy a look and he shrugs, casting her the same curious glance. But it's been a long week. We all deserve some quiet to wrap our heads around the fuckery.

Sy holds the door for us and we filter through, but when we reach the bottom of the stairs, Lavinia says, "Wait." She stops and Remy pauses just ahead of her, turning to look back down. "I need to do something. I'll meet you upstairs."

The three of us watch as she turns, approaching the elevator.

"Whoa, hey," I say, following her. "What's going on?"

The line of her shoulders goes rigid. "I just... I need to do this. For myself."

It's been a few days since we've worked with her on it, so busy and preoccupied with Royal business. Eyeing her carefully, I stab the button. "I'll go with you."

She gives me a tight smile. "Thank you, but I need to... go alone." The door opens, and it takes her a second, but she finally crosses the threshold. Turning, I see that her eyes are tight and shiny, but there aren't any tears. "See you upstairs."

The door shuts and I stand there for a long moment after it's gone, just listening for her screams. "Remy," I say, twisting to meet his gaze. "*Run.*"

He's the fastest, and I don't even have a chance to see the acknowledgement spark in his eyes before he's darting up the steps, disappearing around the bend.

Sy waits for me at the bottom of the staircase, staring at the elevator uneasily. "What the fuck is that?"

"I don't know," I answer, beginning the climb, "but I plan on finding out."

The door is open by the time we reach the top, Lavinia and Remy sitting on the couch, her face buried into his shoulder. He strokes her hair, and from a panic standpoint, she seems to be doing okay, but putting herself in that situation? Something drove her there.

The way Remy is looking at her makes me think he knows more than he's saying.

"Someone explain what's going on," I demand, dissatisfied when Remy just looks from me to her. "Now."

Lavinia turns her head, peering up at me through swimming eyes. "I ran into my father outside the gym."

"You what?" Sy's shoulders square. "You talked to him?"

Well, that was messy. The plan had been to minimize contact between Lavinia, Remy, and their fathers. Now they're both on the couch looking small and tense, shifty and miserable. Fucking assholes.

Palming her own forehead, she takes a shuddering breath. "I know it's dumb to let him get to me–"

"That's not dumb," Remy says, ducking down to watch his thumb rub a tear off her cheek. "That fucked up muscle memory? He built it himself, Vinny. He had all the best tools–they always do. And people like you and me are trying to tear it down with nothing but a pair of spoons. It takes time." Huffing, he stresses, "It takes for-fucking-ever."

Sy's fists clench. "What did he say?"

When she shakes her head, I figure she won't say anything at all. Miraculously she does, eyes fixed on her fingernails as she picks the cuticle. "He said a lot of stuff. About you. About Leticia and my mother. About the fact I'm going to drag you down. And the thing is, he's probably right." She looks up, eyes swimming with panic. "Sy, my father raised a Queen, but it wasn't me."

"LB," I say, sitting on the coffee table, eyeing the way Remy has both their pants undone, star and moon tattoos exposed. "I need you to listen to me. Your father is a narcissistic, toxic piece of shit."

Frustration flares in her eyes. "I know." She does know, but Remy's right. He's fucked with her head for so long, all it takes is one interaction with her and she loses all ground. She looks at Sy. "You called it, okay? I'm a Royal cliché with daddy issues."

My brother shakes his head, some of the stoniness falling from his expression. "Yeah, and like you said, that's not your fucking fault. That's on him. Not you."

She shrugs, idly reaching out to touch the moon on Remy's hip.

"It doesn't change anything. The second I see him, I'm that scared little girl again, one wrong move from being locked in the box." She presses her cheek to Remy's shoulder, looking wrung out. "He said I'm weak-willed–that I've been Stockholm Syndrome'd."

"So you went in the elevator to prove you could do it." His arms are crossed over his chest and there's the slightest tilt of his head—like he's assessing—fuck. He's analyzing the situation.

"Sy—" I start, knowing none of us like to be under Dr. Freud's microscope. But he waves me off.

"I was wrong. You don't have Daddy issues," he says, sitting next to her. "You don't want his approval. You don't want *any* man's approval—"

"That's for sure," I blurt. Sy glares at me and I shut up.

Taking her hand in his, he lifts it to his mouth, kissing her knuckles. "Lavinia, you fought us every step of the way, setting up boundaries, forcing us to work on your terms, making us adapt to you." He forces her to look at him. "Each one of us has hurt you, but you're still here–not because we changed you. Because *you* changed *us*."

"That's not weak-willed," Remy agrees, brushing her hair back. "You're a star, Vinny, just like the sun. You pulled us into your orbit."

Darkly, Sy adds, "And let's make one thing perfectly fucking clear. No one gets to tell you if you're fit to be our Queen but *me*. And you're it, baby." He tips her face upward, brushing his lips over hers. "And you're not just mine, you're theirs, too. And that makes you even more special."

Remy shoots me a look, eyebrows raised. He's thinking what I'm thinking—that my brother, who spent his life pent up and angry, has got some serious game.

Lavinia melts in his hands like butter, head tipped back against Remy's shoulder. Her eyes slip closed. "Will one of you–" Teeth digging into her lip, her words bite off.

"What?" Sy asks, cupping her cheek. "Tell us what you need, Lav."

Slowly, her eyes flutter open. "Will one of you make love to me?"

Sy's eyes meet mine and Remy's, a silent understanding passing between us. "Just one of us?" I ask, raising an eyebrow.

I once told Lavinia I don't want one-third of her–I want it all. Even though it was an unreasonable request, she's kept her promise. Anything they get, I get, too. But whereas Lavinia gives each of us everything, she accepts us in pieces–one by one.

It doesn't *have* to be that way.

Her breath stalls at the implication, lips parting in surprise, and I take that as my answer.

"I think," sliding off the table and down on my knees, I run my hands up her thighs, "our Duchess needs to be reminded that she's a Queen. By all of us." I grab the waist of her pants and tug them down. "Lift up for me, LB."

Her breath quickens as she jolts with the force of my tug. "Nick, what if I can't take—"

Remy cups her face, turning her to meet his kiss. It's a filthy thing, his tongue visible as it licks into her mouth, tangling with her own. The moan she makes is quiet and pleased, and almost like an afterthought, her hips rise off the couch, allowing me to peel the pants from her legs.

Sy watches this with darkening eyes, ducking in to whisper into her ear. "You can take it, Lav. You can take anything."

Remy's hand lands on her thigh, dipping between her legs to spread her. Without missing a beat, Sy palms the other thigh, pulling her legs open for me. Remy releases her from his slow, wet kiss just in time for her to watch me lean in, licking a hot path up her inner thigh.

"Oh," she breathes, mouth slick and red. "Oh, god, Nick..."

Her pussy tastes like heaven, wet and warm. As I kiss the hot fire of her clit, I hear the hitched breath she tries to take, see Sy's hand duck beneath her shirt, easing it up her body, feel Remy restless beside her, vibrating with anticipation.

Sy must get her shirt off, because the next moment I glance up, his dark-skinned palm is gently massaging her tit, his mouth sucking a mark into her shoulder.

"I want to touch you too," she says, the words a breathy pant. Her hands flail, looking for something to hold on to, and at the same time she finds it, her thighs give a tremble.

"Shit," Sy curses and I look over, seeing her hand cinched around his cock.

"Let me touch you," she says again.

Immediately, he and Remy begin fumbling with their pants, pushing them clumsily down their hips and legs, kicking them off with an aggression that borders on comical. There's nothing funny about the way she reaches for them though, her hands just as greedy as the kiss Sy gives her, pushing his tongue through her parted lips.

It's easy to feel left out as I watch her slender fingers wrap around each of their dicks, Sy and Remy bucking into her fists with varying degrees of eagerness. Where Sy slams his hips up into her grip, Remy rocks into it, coaxing her mouth back to his with a finger on her chin.

But they don't get to do *this*.

I spear my tongue into her entrance, feeling the way her muscles melt at the sensation. It's what allows me to work my hands beneath her thighs, pushing them higher and higher. Glancing up, I catch Sy's eye, pushing her knee toward him. Somehow, he gets the hint, hooking his hand beneath her knee and raising it for me. It spreads her so deliciously that I'm able to lick lower.

Her whole body goes rigid, eyes dazed but widening. "What are you—"

My tongue meets the puckered flesh of her asshole, a chuckle rumbling against it as she gasps. "Relax, LB," I command, palming each side of her ass open for me.

Remy's the one to whisper, "Feels good, doesn't it?" and I flick my eyes up just in time to see him descend on her tit, tongue looping wetly around the peaked nipple.

"T-that's..." she stutters, arching into Remy's mouth. "That's... *new*."

It's necessary, is what it is. Not just because I need her ass stretched and wet for us, but also because there's no square inch of Lavinia's body I don't want to know. I acquaint myself with this one hungrily, jabbing my tongue into her tight hole, teasing it with the tip of my finger until I feel it fluttering eagerly for me.

It's only when I shove her hips up, easing back to aim my spit right into the dip of her asshole, that it hits her. "Oh my god, you're really going to—" Her words fade off into a strained fricative when I glide two fingers inside, pushing the spit into her.

Remy reaches between her legs to stroke her clit. "You'll do it, won't you? You'll let us fill you up?"

I thrust my fingers in and out, cock so hard that it aches. "We'll get you nice and ready for us, baby."

Lavinia begins shuddering, her breaths coming in sharp, pointed gasps. The tendons in her thighs tremble and flex as she tries to chase the feeling, but suddenly Sy's fingers are there joining us, two sliding right into her slick pussy.

We work her like a symphony, Sy and I fingering her holes as Remy teases her clit. Her cries grow louder and more desperate as she breaks away from Remy's mouth to look down at what we're doing to her. Our hands are all jammed up together, relentless as they rub and stroke and thrust. Remy might call it art. Sy might call it a fight.

I call it perfection.

She comes with a strangled yelp, hands grasping frantically at our wrists as she goes rigid and seizes. I don't know about the other two, but I can feel it around the third finger I sneak into her ass–the way her whole body clamps down on us, like it wants us to stay.

Her pussy is so soaked that it's dripping down to my fingers, slicking the way as she goes abruptly lax. I watch Sy's thick, glistening knuckles as he eases them free, bending down to press a kiss to her flushed cheek.

"So fucking beautiful," he says, bringing his fingers to her gaping lips. He paints her slickness on like lipstick before licking out to clear it away.

"That," she pants, chest heaving, "was insane."

Fingers still buried in her, I climb to my feet, thumbing the button of my jeans with my free hand. "Oh, Little Bird. That was just to loosen you up for Remy." Evenly, I explain, "I'd do it myself, but a deal's a deal. It might hurt the first time, though." I'd told Remy months ago that he could have first shot at fucking her ass, and I try really hard right now not to feel sour about it.

Remy meets my gaze, giving me a loose, sex-glazed smirk. "Ah, it's not her first time, Nicky."

I freeze three knuckles deep in her asshole. "You already tapped this?" I ask, brows crashing together. "You never said anything."

He gathers her tit in a palm, holding my stare as he kisses the swell of it. "Because I knew you'd get all jealous and annoy the shit out of her about getting yours."

I thrust my fingers in and out, scowling at him. "When was this? Where?"

Shrugging, he says, "A couple weeks ago, maybe? We were upstairs."

My brain fogs up for a solid minute at what this means.

Her thick voice cuts through. "Nick?"

Blinking, I absorb this naked woman, slick and primed. Bending over her, I take her mouth in a deep, frantic kiss, working off my pants in the process. "I apologize in advance," I say against her mouth, pressing a palm against Sy's shoulder to get him to move.

"Apologize for wh—"

I pick her up, flip her around, and drop her on Remy's lap. He shifts sideways, catching her with a surprised sound that morphs into a grunt when she lands on his cock. His hands instantly move to palm her tits. "Fuck, you're dripping all over me," he groans, kissing her jaw.

My focus is on one thing.

Pounding her sweet, tight, ass.

27

R emy

I KNOW Nick Bruin well enough to see what he has in mind. He wants to feel us both in her at once, stretched out and full, cum spilling out of her.

Fuck, I want it too.

"You turn the prettiest shade of lilac after you come," I say into her neck, the deadhead moth that I inked into her just below. I bask in her halo of purple, the way she's rocking her pussy into my cock, making me slick. "I'm gonna fuck your pussy, Vinny. You'd like that, wouldn't you?" She makes a soft, agreeable sound and I pluck a kiss from her lips. "And then Nicky's gonna fill your ass and make it feel so good."

She shudders against me, eyes shifting over to Sy, who was pushed aside by Nick's little jealous tantrum. Sy takes it in stride, eyes focused on Lavinia as he moves around the couch. She watches him closely. "And Sy?"

I thumb her mouth open, feeling the heat of her tongue swipe over the pad. "He's going to fuck this sweet little mouth and feed you his cum."

She flattens her hands across my chest, indulgently squeezing my muscles. "What if I can't take that much?"

I frame her face, making her look at me. "You'll try for me, won't you, Vinny?" I've been thinking about it for so long–being inside of her with one of the others. Feeling the way she stretches for us, making room, taking every drop of each Duke.

My cock jerks in excitement.

"You don't have to," Sy says, leaning over the back of the couch and kissing her neck. "But I like seeing you like this, baby. Fucking your Dukes. Watching my brothers fill you up." I see it ripple through his neck like a shockwave, and I bet his cock is jerking eagerly, too.

"I want to taste you," she says, licking her lips. "Please?"

Sy leans over my shoulder, his massive cock swinging overhead. A lesser man would be intimidated, but that shit doesn't bother us. Whatever it takes to satisfy our girl. And from the way she immediately surges forward to mouth at the swollen head, this is it. I don't see Sy's face, but I see his hands, slamming down hard into the back of the couch and digging in hard, knuckles turning white as her tongue curls out to catch his precum.

He curses low and harsh, "Fuck, Lav." She hums, kissing the tip of his cock like a lover–slow and sweet and slick. From the spread of wet heat coating my cock, what she needs now is to take my dick. I meet Nick's gaze over her shoulder, raising my chin. "Me first?"

His jaw tightens like I'm asking him to do some gravely Herculean task. "Fine," he grinds out, grabbing her hips and tilting them upward for me. I reach between us to grab my cock, sliding it through her folds so she knows what's coming. She responds by moaning around Sy's cock, wriggling her hips to chase me.

I slide into her with a long, torturous exhale, Nick bringing her down slowly to my lap. It feels like velvet lava, so wet and warm.

Our tattoos are lined up, her star meeting my moon for a kiss when she sinks all the way down, our hips touching.

Since she's already come, she's lost that frenzied desperation I love so much, but it's replaced with a languid sigh, her hips rolling into my thrust. Sy's fingers tangle in her hair as her red mouth engulfs the tip of his cock, cheeks caving with a soft suck.

He lets out a strained groan. "Remy, come on. Give her something." If he wants me to start fucking her hard and fast, then he's going to be disappointed. I want this moment–her Royal coronation–to last.

So I respond by rocking up into her, reveling in the soft mewl that vibrates through her chest. Easing us into a slow pace, she tips her face upward for Sy, watching him as she licks and sucks his cock. This means her tits, so soft and perfect, are right in front of my eyes, undulating with another roll of her hips. There are worse things I could be staring down. The swell of them is flushed a vivid fuschia, or maybe that's just the color she's become with the three of us on her like this.

I grab them with both hands, soft and supple, pushing them together to caress them with my tongue. Her nipples are hard between my teeth, and when I give one a gentle nibble, her whole body kicks forward.

Her head falls back, releasing Sy's cock, and she gives a short, wet gasp. She's right. She can't take us all at once, but only because we're so damn good at driving her wild. Behind her, Nick is watching with a glazed, drunk expression.

"You know why I never tattooed your tits?" I ask, rolling my hips upward.

She shakes her head, hair cascading over her shoulders. I see Sy fist his cock, stroking himself patiently until Vinny's ready for him again. "W-why?"

"Because," I take one nipple in my mouth and lazily tongue the peak. When it's stiff and hard, I do the other. Her hips lurch forward and she hums overhead.

She leans into me, her silky veil of hair shielding us from my brothers. "Why, Remy?"

"They're already perfect," I explain, holding her glazed stare. "So many good colors. Pink and umber. Ivory and porcelain. Sensitive, too. Absolutely fuckable." She grinds down, heat engulfing me. "Shit, Vin." I hold onto her hips, lifting my foot to the coffee table for leverage.

"Oh, god," she gasps, hips rocking faster. Her hands land on my chest and she looks down at me, eyes blazing.

The words tumble from my lips. "I love you, Vinny. I love your wet pussy and your perfect tits. I love how you turn amethyst when you look at me like that." I touch her bottom lip, slick and wet from Sy fucking her mouth. "I love the way you look sucking Sy's cock. And taking Nick's bullshit."

"He's doing this on purpose, you know?" Nick says. He's naked and slowly rising from his sex-fueled stupor, shoulder shifting with the slow stroke of his palm gliding down his cock. "Dragging this out so that when I finally get in you, it's gonna last all of two seconds."

"I'm an artist," I argue, "even when I'm making love. Shut the fuck up." I roll my eyes, but I can feel that she's eager for more, so I palm each of her ass cheeks. "You ready for him, beautiful?"

She glances at Nicky over her shoulder, teeth raking over her swollen bottom lip. "Nick," she says, the name emerging with an edge of desperation that has him springing forward. He curls over her for a barely coordinated kiss, their tongues meeting in the space between their clumsy lips. I'm so hypnotized by it–Nick kisses like he wants to fucking devour her–that I don't see him dropping a hand between their bodies. I feel it though, his fingers brushing my cock as he gathers her slickness onto his fingertips. From the way his shoulder begins shifting, I'm guessing he's using it to coat his cock.

His jaw tightens when he pulls away, voice a thick rumble. "Open her for me, Remy. I'm gonna need some space."

I gather her up close, the feeling of her tits pressing against my chest making my balls tighten. With both hands, I pull her ass apart for him, watching the look on Nick's face as I expose her hole. His eyebrows crouch low, something frantic crossing his features as he fists his cock.

If I'd thought my having first dibs on her ass might have taken the thrill out of it for him, then I was wrong. Right now, he looks like a man on the edge of getting everything he wants.

He doesn't need to get it first.

He just needs to have it.

She stiffens at the sudden exposure, but I run my fingers down to her puckered ridge and tease the muscle, whispering, "It's gonna feel so good with us both in there, baby. Nicky and I are gonna take care of you. You know that, don't you?"

She melts at my words, opening for us like the petals of a flower. "I know you will."

Nick's knee presses on the couch just against my inner thigh, his large frame hovering over us. Sy is still behind me and we're being pinned by two of the biggest, horniest fuckers in Forsyth. I feel it the instant Nick makes contact, her walls tightening up, a small, surprised sound escaping her throat.

"You need to let me in, LB," he says, jaw tight. She can't see him, but he's straining to control himself, blue eyes fixed to her ass with a laser-like intensity.

I run my hands over her ass, gently massaging. "Relax. Just like we did before."

"It's so much pressure." She exhales, but it doesn't loosen her muscles. When she reaches out to clutch at Sy's hand, still strangling the back of the couch, he crouches to meet her eyes, lips brushing over her knuckles.

"Bad pressure?" he asks, shooting Nicky a warning glance.

But she shakes her head, gulping in a hard breath. "No, it's just... so much."

Stroking my fingers through her hair, I turn my head to meet his gaze. "Give her your dick, Sy. It'll help distract her."

When he springs back up, his cock hard and heavy over the back of the couch, I tip her face toward it. "Take his dick, baby."

She licks her bottom lip, and he gives her the tip. "Just suck on it," he says, reaching out to stroke her hair. These two have some kind of mind-meld when it comes to Sy's cock. All those nights of training him in self control, and now he's the one coaching her.

I watch her mouth hungrily at the tip, lips stretched gorgeously when she takes him in. "That good?" I ask her.

Her eyes flutter closed. "Mmhmm."

I feel her relax incrementally, all of her focus narrowed in on licking and suckling on Sy's cock. He grips the base for her, but he's good. He doesn't fuck into her–not yet.

We gotta get Nicky inside first.

And he looks like he's about to explode.

The tendons in his neck strain as he bows his head over her shoulders, panting. "I'm gonna try to–" I nod at him and he pushes in a little more, threading her slowly on his cock. She's loosened, distracted by the taste of Sy. When she doesn't resist, my boy looks me right in the eye, curls his fingers over the cut of her shoulder, and pushes in.

Now it's my turn to seize up. I can feel every fucking inch of his dick as it fills her, crowding me up inside her pussy. "Holy shit," I hiss, pushing the words through my clenched teeth. I see the same emotion I'm feeling cross Nick's face, as if we're the ones over-whelmed by the force of this. His jaw hardens the deeper he goes, the stony line of his brow collapsing in bliss.

For a blink of eternity, I think about the sky. I think of how when Vinny and I fuck, we *fly*. It's always been that way with her, thrilling to the most extreme heights, and cataclysmic when we finally fall. But with Nicky and Sy, it's different.

We're not just a star and a moon, we're a whole goddamn constellation.

28

S^y

I LIFT a prayer in thanks for all those frustrating, humiliating, relentless hours Lavinia and I spent wrangling my cock into submission, because otherwise, I would have shot my load the second I felt her tongue. It's one thing when she's sucking me off, taking me in deep, but what she's doing now...

There's this thing she does with my swollen tip, licking just under the ridge and swirling the point of her tongue against it.

Sweet. *Jesus.*

I didn't even know that was a thing.

But that's Lavinia Lucia, the bearer of surprises.

It's my turn to distract her as Nick and Remy fill her up, working their way inside her at the same time. It's hard to decide where to look. Her lips are stretched wide around my cock, but her body is making these small, testing hitches of movement against them. It's the way she looks, eyebrows knitting together as she tries so hard to take them inside, that makes my fingers claw divots into the upholstery.

"Nick?" I ask, voice thin and worn. "You in there?" I can tell he is, not just from the rush of air that leaves him, but the way she clamps down on my head and gives a sharp, tugging suck.

My balls may explode before this whole thing is over.

Nick answers with a rough, "Yeah," and glides a palm down her spine, nudging his hips into her ass. "Remy?"

He gives Nick a tight nod, thighs flexing as he plants his feet, rocking up at the same time Nick's back curves, shoving into her.

She cries out around my cock, and I take her hand in mine, lacing our fingers together. "Fuck, look at you. You're such a good girl for us." She surges up at the praise, lips sliding wetly up my cock, before falling back into Remy's lap.

Remy grunts, digging his fingers into her hips. "That's right. Show us how you want it, baby."

There's something about this moment. Watching my two brothers take our girl like this. I don't know when it happened, but at some point, we all stopped fighting each other, and now this just feels right. The familiarity, the cohesion that was missing for so long, is present in every movement. Remy thrusting up on Nick's backstroke, Nick driving forward when Remy eases down, the press of Remy's lips against Lavinia's throat as she sucks me.

If we can do *this,* share this woman, this Queen, I truly believe we can do anything.

Even change Forsyth for the better.

I grip her neck, running my hand up and down the column of it, keeping her eyes focused on me as Nick punches into her with an agonized sound. He's nothing but power, taut muscle and hard lines. I remember thinking once that Nick would be happiest holding the leash attached to her collar. But the way he looks at her now, the soft desperation in his eyes, I realize it's not like that for him. Not really.

He loves her.

Pretty Nick Bruin isn't just obsessed. He's not just coveting. *He's loving.* It's the same love that I feel in every pump of blood. Every time I see her. Feel her.

My cock twitches and I hold back a groan.

Why is love so fucking hot?

"Fuck," Remy whispers, his green eyes rising to Nick. "You feel me, too?"

"Yeah," Nick says, his voice strained as he thrusts in opposition to Remy, who turns to run the tip of his nose along the shell of her ear.

"I thought you were tight before, Vinny." His tongue peeks out to curl against her earlobe and I feel her responding shudder. "Your pussy is goddamn magical."

"Can you take more, baby?" Nick asks, ignoring Remy. He presses deeper, hips snapping tight, and she pants out against my cock. Eyes flicking up to mine, she gives me a slow, heavy blink.

"She said yes." I reach out to touch her cheek, feeling the swell of my cock on the other side. "You'll tell me if it's too much. Don't let them hurt you. Understand?"

She gives the barest nod.

Nick pulls back slowly, eyes dropping to watch his cock emerge from her hole, then, jaw going taut, he snaps his hips forward, both him and Remy releasing low grunts. Lavinia reacts with a long keen against my dick, fingers squeezing mine.

"She's good," I say when Nick's dark eyes flick up to mine. "Just take it easy."

He gains a slow but intense rhythm, pulling back lazily only to punch forward. Every time he does, Remy bucks up with him and a small cry lurches from Lavinia's throat, muffled around my shaft. I see Nick and Remy watch each other, coordinating, planning these little huffs of air that gust over my cock with every lurch of her body. They look indescribable as they take her, their inked skin and flexing muscles against her soft, delicate skin, and it strikes me that she's not panicking.

Even though she's boxed in.

I watch her face as they fuck her, her body loosening with every thrust. The suction of her mouth grows hungrier, greedier, and my hips chase the friction, pushing deeper. *Fuck.* When her hand reaches for me, wrapping around the iron rod of my cock, I grunt. The added sensation drives me to thrust shallowly against her tongue.

I press a hand on her shoulder and ease off.

Her heavy eyes blink at me, lips looking red and abused. "You're holding back," she rasps.

I run a finger down her cheek. "This is enough."

Her expression crumbles with another of Nick and Remy's pointed thrusts. "I want all of it. Please, Big Bear? Let me show you I can take it." There's a spark in her eyes–that challenging defiance that makes her such a perfect Duchess, but I don't have the chance to really appreciate it.

Nick catches my eye over her writhing body, tightly mouthing, "Big Bear? What the fuck?"

I don't give a shit that my brother knows my girl's nickname for me, because Lavinia is actively guiding my cock into her mouth. And when Nick thrusts into her the next time, the wet, hot heat closes in on all sides, and I'm powerless to disobey her wishes.

I cradle the back of her head and fuck into her mouth.

She practically goes limp between them, head tipped up in supplication as I thrust into the wet heat. It used to be hard not to just slam myself into the back of her throat. It's not exactly easy now, but it isn't lingering on the edge of my nerves like a threat. I only hold back what I know she couldn't physically take, fucking into the press of her lips.

I feel sorry for the guys because they don't know what it's like to be this big, to feel how tight she is all the fucking time. Everything is a stretch for me–her pussy, her mouth. She blinks up at me with watery eyes before dropping her hand to squeeze my balls.

"Holy fuck."

Somehow, I'm not the first to blow.

That'd be Remy.

He curls an arm around her back, the tendons in his forearm

tightening as he hooks his hand around the back of her tattooed shoulder, pushing her down. He bucks up wildly, tense and just as flushed as Lavinia as his lips pull back, baring his teeth.

I know he's coming when he goes rigid, slamming upward so hard that Nick has to chase her. Not far, though. Remy clamps down on her hard, holding her flush as he empties into her with a strangled grunt. Nick takes the opportunity to quicken his strokes into these tight, pounding bursts, his muscles bulging as he flings out a hand, clamping it over the back of the couch, just over Remy's shoulder. He fucks her hard–animalistic–before crashing his hips into hers.

The snarl rips out of him, and what results is a shockwave of Remy's groan, Lavinia's garbled cry, and my low, strangled curse.

As much as the way I'm fucking into her mouth has me on the razor's edge, I think that's what finally does it. Seeing my brothers fill her up like this, knowing that I'm the only missing piece, is what pulls me over the edge.

I try to be careful–I swear to fucking god, I do–cradling each side of her jaw as it begins cresting through me. But then she looks up at me with those eyes, so goddamn trusting and tender, and I'm powerless to do anything but yank her closer, the head of my dick grazing the back of her throat as I come.

I watch with a hard growl as my cock surges between her stretched lips, pumping wave after wave of my cum into her hot, bulging mouth. Her back swells with the effort of keeping it all in, but instead of backing off, she just nudges closer, unblinking as she methodically swallows it down.

When the texture of her tongue is enough to send my nerves flaring, I finally tear myself away, fighting to catch my breath as Nick does the same. She's left in Remy's lap, boneless and panting, letting out these little hitches of overwhelmed whimpers that have Remy laying her out on the couch beside him.

"You okay, Vinny?" he asks, but even though she nods, he throws Nick and I a meaningful look. We don't spring into action so much as limp, me going for a warm, wet washcloth as Nick lifts her from the couch, carrying her toward my room.

When I arrive at the threshold, they're already in my bed. He's got her tucked into his side, her cheek resting on his chest as Remy spoons in behind her, brushing his lips over the curve of her shoulder. I climb up from the foot of the bed—which is feeling less like 'mine' and more like 'ours'—and give her calf a nudge.

"Open up for me, baby."

She shivers, but it's Nick who reaches down to hook a hand behind her knee, hitching it high over his hips to bare her center to me. Their cum is leaking out lazily and as much as I know they'd both want me to push it back inside, I clean it away. As I check her holes carefully, Remy and Nick bring her down with kisses and caresses.

"Will you let me make you something to eat?" I ask when I'm done, leaning down to brush a kiss over her round ass cheek.

Her tired eyes lift to meet mine, and she nods. "Thank you."

"For feeding you something that isn't my spunk?" I snort, watching as Remy traces the smudged ink on her neck.

If possible, her cheeks get even redder, but the smile she sends me is small and sad. "No. For making me stronger."

Uncaring of how it wedges me between the three of them, I force myself over her to press a kiss to her damp forehead, hovering there for a beat. "You made *us* stronger, Lavinia. We just showed you how strong you already were."

29

L avinia

Tick-tock

   Tick-tock

   Tick-tock

The sound is faint, like it's on the other side of a wall. I push my hand out and feel the hard surface. My feet meet a similar block. My back seizes, achy and bent, and in the inky darkness, I know I'm trapped. It's too far away to grasp, but Nick told me something once about a box being a frame of mind. Right now, my limbs are frozen, my brain running haywire.

"I have a secret."

Blinking, I suddenly see Leticia. Her shiny blonde hair. Her mean, coy smile. I realize the dark isn't the chest, but instead the oppressive darkness of an overcast night. We're on that cliff again, but even though I'm not in a box, I still can't move—can't scream.

My sister's not alone. Her hand is intertwined with another, as the girl I recognize as Tate is beside her. She grins back with her black hair and almond-shaped eyes, but says nothing. The side of her head is shiny with blood and clumped matter. Slowly, I remember that I don't even know what her voice sounded like.

And every day that passes, I'm starting to forget Leticia's.

"I don't have time for your games," I try to tell her, my own voice seeming slow and garbled. "I have to kill him."

Him. Lionel. Did she ever love him, I wonder? All the attention and favoritism… did it ever endear her to him? Or did she spend our childhood trapped in a different sort of box, always pretending, surviving?

My eyes zero in on her lips, forming around the words she speaks. "I gave you what you need. Are you really going to waste it?"

I try to reach for her, but I just can't break through the barrier. "What? What do I need?"

"Leverage," she says, her face transforming. Before my eyes, her skin melts away, leaving nothing but teeth and bones. "You better hurry," she whispers, her fingers blowing away into dust. "Tick, tick, tick—"

My eyes pop open, prepared for the pitch black of the chest. Instead, light comes through the tall window nestled in the tower wall. I'd exhale but my lungs are paralyzed like the rest of my body.

The clock is ticking, Duchess, tick-tock.

Tick, tick, tick…

"Hey. Vinny." Remy's face comes into view, his hand stroking a warm caress down my arm. I realize I'm curled into his chest, Nick's arm slung around my waist from behind. "Come back to me, baby." Remy catches my lifeless hand, pressing my fingers to the crescent tattooed on his hip.

The touch–the memory–draws me from the cobwebby dream, warming my frozen veins. I blink and then swallow, my voice rusty. "I-I'm okay."

"I felt the goldenrod," he rumbles, and from the slouch of his eyelids, he hasn't been awake very long, either. "What did you see?"

I instantly shake my head. "Nothing." I doubt he wants to hear about his friend appearing in my dream, her brains all exploded from her temple. "Go back to sleep."

Climbing over Nick, I sling my legs over the edge of the bed, stretching my toes, trying to regain feeling. Rousing a little more, Remy's green eyes track me as I look back at Sy's bed. We ended up here after showering and late-night grilled cheese, and I feel warmth bloom in my chest at the sight of them. Sy and Nick are sprawled out, both asleep, still naked. I stretch my hands over my head as I observe them, letting my spine loosen.

Remy makes an unhappy noise when I step into a pair of panties, grabbing a hoodie off the back of Sy's desk, but he rolls over and closes his eyes. It's the first time I've dreamed of Leticia since Sy and I buried her skull, putting her to rest. She doesn't feel restful now, rustling around in my head like gossamer.

The living room is chilly when I step out, but the air cooling my skin is a welcome sensation. It's not long before Archie finds me, winding around my ankles.

"Hey, buddy," I whisper, bending to scoop him up. He's getting so much bigger now, his legs lankier, ears pointier. He hasn't lost any of his softness though, and I press my face into his fur, letting the low vibration of his purr soothe me. He indulges the snuggle only briefly before squirming out of my arms and bolting off.

The tower feels stuffy, or maybe my lungs are still frozen from my dream. I climb the spiral stairs to my loft, and it's cast in a blueish glow, the early morning light filtered through the clock face. Those maddening hands are, as always, eternally frozen.

7:32.

Tick-tock.

I climb higher, going straight to the staircase that leads to the belfry. Stopping in the area that holds the mechanics, I look around me. On the floor, the remaining pieces of the dismantled inner workings are laid out just like I left them. I haven't touched it in weeks—not since Sy and I got the two levers to work. I've been too frustrated with it, and anyway, my Dukes are keeping me busy both in and out of the bed.

The clock is ticking, Duchess, tick-tock.

My father's voice rings in the half of my brain that's still caught in the web of my dream, and I keep moving, climbing the ladder to the belfry. As soon as I emerge from the hatch, my breath comes a little easier. The sun is rising from the east when I look out the archway, casting the Princes' territory in a pinkish glow.

For so long, I hated this town. All I wanted was to run as far away as possible. Leticia tried to run, and look what it got her. I was trapped, held captive, turned into a prize, and look where *that* got me. I touch my neck, knowing the permanent marker is still there.

It made me Queen.

I no longer hate Forsyth–I just hate the people in control of it. I have a home here. People I love. Even people like the cutsluts and Story, who I actually like. I see the value in the women working at the Hideaway, too—Auggie and Mrs. Crane and all the rest- who are just trying to keep afloat. They aren't bad people.

Except my eyes fall to the North, and my blood thins.

I'd threatened my father with extermination, but he's right. In the end, he's untouchable. He has the city in his grip, and we're one lunatic's trigger finger away from being dust if pushed too far. There's no Perez to oust him. No heir waiting in the wings. No hope of waiting him out. There's just him and his drugs and dysfunction.

And those goddamn explosives.

I gave you what you need.

The hatch suddenly rises, Remy's head appearing. His eyes search for me in the dim light, eventually catching my gaze. "Hey," he says, climbing up. He's still shirtless, and if I'm not mistaken, wearing Nick's jeans, the denim looser on his thighs as he crams his fists into the pockets. "I feel kind of like you might want to be alone, but—"

"I do." I stop him with a pointed look. "But Remy?"

His forehead knits. "Yeah?"

"That doesn't apply to you," I explain, extending a hand. I can't think of anyone better to get lost in my head with, and when he stalks forward to wrap me up in his arms, I breathe him in deep.

He smells like *us*.

All of us.

He holds me there for a long while, letting me rest my temple against his chest as I stare out over the city. From up here, it's so easy to believe we're untouchable, floating through the clouds, a bird and her bear.

The sun's rays have only just begun to reach us when he finally speaks. "I've been working on something," he says, releasing me only to pull a sheet of paper out of his pocket. One of the edges is frayed, as if he's yanked it out of one of his sketch pads.

Taking it in my hands, I unfold it, eyes drinking in the dark ink. "Are these the clock parts?" I recognize them from my hours of trying to make this puzzle fit back together. I study the drawings, which are precise and very unlike his normal style, and glance up in surprise. "Wow." It's almost like an instruction manual. "These are so good, Remy."

"I took a mechanical drawing class last year." He shrugs, green eyes flitting over the skyline. "I was trying to, like... work backwards and see what was missing. Those ancient manuals you had weren't complete even before they got all old and torn and stained to shit." He tips his head toward the hatch. "So I studied the actual components up here. One of the principles of the class was that we needed to be able to break things down into individual pieces so that whoever's looking at the parts can figure out how to get them together."

I drop my gaze to the paper again, not allowing myself to be distracted with the way his fingers reach out to catch a fluttering lock of my hair. The thing about the clock is that it's unnecessarily intricate. Probably places with mechanisms as ancient as this one have already gutted the heart of their clocks and implanted something more reliable and modern.

The thought makes my brain scream with an immediate, visceral *no*.

"Wait," I say, squinting at the ink. I point to a specific spot, not recognizing the component. "What's this? It wasn't in the original diagrams–or what you could see of them." I'd memorized every visible, usable inch of that old musty paper, and this was one of the few parts of the strike chain that was legible.

He steps up beside me, ducking down to look. "Yeah, I looked at that for a while, but didn't understand what it was. This little cover here," he guides his finger over the section, "doesn't even look like it belongs. It should look like this–" He points to a different drawing, a screw with threads, not rounded. "I'm not a mechanic or anything, but if I had to guess, it's fucking the whole thing up."

My brain spins, much like the pieces of the clock, one gear after the other, clicking into place. I push past him, heading for the hatch door. Once I'm down the ladder, I grab the flashlight off the floor, bending into an awkward position to beam it into the spot Remy had drawn.

Everything in this room is dark, making the parts sometimes virtually indistinguishable from one another, but getting at anything from this angle was always off-limits to me. The space is too cramped, barely enough room beneath it for someone to maneuver. But even at a distance, the more attention I pay to it, the more I suspect Remy might be right.

Something is jamming up the gears.

Something that doesn't belong.

Excitement pumps through my veins as I get down on my belly, taking a series of slow, calming breaths. If I could make it through the elevator alone, then this should be a cinch.

Without giving myself the time to panic over it, I begin belly-crawling beneath the machine, pulse thrumming with a confusing mixture of emotions. There's the thrill of finding the problem, but also the quick, nervy thing that always arises when I'm in cramped spaces.

Behind me, I hear Remy approach, the wood beams hard and rough against my knees as I push myself closer.

"Hand me that screwdriver," I ask, straining to extend a hand toward my feet. "Flat head. The big one."

The sound of Remy picking through the tools is faint under the pounding of my heart.

Tick-tock.

"Here," Remy says, crawling in right next to me. It's both better and worse, his presence making the space impossibly more tight, but also soothing me in a strange, intrinsic way. Wordlessly, he trades the screwdriver for the flashlight and holds it up to the spot in question. I wedge the edge of the screwdriver under the edge of the cap, prying.

But it doesn't budge.

After watching me try this a few times, grunting at the effort, Remy reaches over me, hand closing over mine, and together we apply the leverage to force it loose.

Leverage.

The word rattles around my brain as I stare into the revealed spot.

"Are those..." he asks, holding the flashlight steady.

They're wires. Three of them. Red, green and black. They coil around the screw and vanish under a piece of conduit, down into the wall.

Clocks—especially this one, which I know inside and out—are made of metal and wood. Brass and steel. Not the plastic and copper I see peeking out of the workings like the head of a snake.

"Remy," I say, my voice quiet against the stone. "The clock doesn't work because it's been rigged." Looking over, I meet his green eyes, my breath quickening. "With explosives."

There's only one person deranged enough to put them there.

Tick-tock.

"Vinny," he says, chasing me into the living room. "Slow down."

"You don't understand," I snap, not stopping. "We need to get out of here. My father threatened me yesterday. 'The clock is ticking,' he said." I palm my forehead, heart pumping wildly. "Jesus Christ. I thought he was being dramatic, but he was laying it all out there. We're literally living in a bomb!"

"Hey," he catches my arm and brings me to a lurching halt. "You've been a little–" he grimaces, and I get the sense that he's choosing his words carefully, "–*off* since you got up. Take a deep breath and let's figure this out. Start at the beginning. What fucked you up when you got out of bed?"

I don't want to slow down. I want to get my men to safety and drive to my father's fucking mansion that he built on lies and death, and end him. For good.

But when I look into Remy's eyes, I realize he's right. He and I do this, get caught somewhere between real and not. My nightmares and sleep paralysis. His episodes and mania.

I need to be sure.

Taking a deep breath, I let his grip on my shoulders ground me. "I had a dream," I confess, hurriedly amending, "I *have* dreams. It's not the first time. I wake up stiff. Frozen, you know? Back in the box." He gives me an understanding nod. "But Leticia is there, Remy. She... talks to me. Tells me things about the secrets she knows."

Now that I say it aloud, it sounds ridiculous.

Remy takes it in stride, though. "So your sister is a bitch even in your dreams." His hands settle on my hips, warm and steady.

Fuck, it's true. She'd probably be proud of it. "I guess so, except..."

He holds my eyes. "Except what?"

"Except she's always like... making me feel dumb, like she's telling me stuff. Things I should know." None of this is coming out right and I shake my head, trying to find something coherent.

"Ah," he nods in understanding. "She's not Leticia. She's you– your subconscious."

I make a face. "Don't get all 'Sy' on me."

He doesn't look insulted at the comparison. "I mean, I'm no Dr.

Freud like your Big Bear in there," he shoots me a smirk, "but I've had my share of brain probing. Your sister–your brain–is trying to tell you something you already know. You just have to be open to whatever it is." His thumb rubs a circle in my hip. "Can you do that?"

I exhale, pulling in air. I close my eyes and pull at the cobby webs of the dream. "She said something about having already given me what I need."

Frowning, he says, "Okay. Any idea what that means?"

"Leticia never gave me anything but an inferiority complex and bruises," I snap, not liking the feeling of being manipulated–neither by dream Leticia, or as Remy says, my bullshit subconscious. "It's all just mind games. Like father, like daughter."

Although, I realize, Leticia did give me something. The box hidden under the floorboards, the receipt, the phone number, the detonator Nick and I discovered she'd programmed to give her–

My eyes fly to Remy's, widening in realization. "Leverage."

"Huh?"

"Leverage," I repeat, grabbing Remy's upper arms. She had to have left it for me. She must have known if anything happened to her, I'd find that box. "That's it. Remy, she gave me her leverage."

SY RUBS HIS FACE–PARTIALLY to wake up, the rest out of frustration. "Is there a reason you didn't tell us about all this when you found out?" The question is directed at me and Nick. Remy is on the other side of the clock room, video chatting with a sleepy and irritated Tristan Mercer.

"Yes," Nick says. He's alert, but his face is still puffy from sleep, a long line from the pillow pressed into his cheek. He looks at me because we both know the answer to Sy's question. We'd come home from talking to Tristian that night fully planning to tell Remy and Sy. Instead, we found a party at the tower, and the night ended with Sy hurting me and leaving. Nick sighs. "But that ship has sailed, and is sort of irrelevant to the fact our house has been wired to blow."

"Yep." Tristian's voice echoes against the walls. "That's a bomb, alright."

"Jesus," Sy mutters, coming more awake by the moment.

Tristian continues, "It's like we talked about last time–remote detonation. I mean, we've all heard the rumors that Lucia has this place wired up. We all figured he planted them underground, but it's kind of genius. Guy's got us crawling through the sewers when we should be checking our roofs."

Nick moves toward Remy, grabbing the phone, face set into a hard expression. "Remote detonation? Like the kind someone could set off with a phone?"

Groggily, Tristian says, "Yeah, possibly."

I gave you what you need.

My mouth goes dry, face growing clammy, and from the laser intensity of Nick's meaningful stare, he's coming to the same conclusion.

He asks Tristian, "You remember that phone Leticia Lucia asked you to rig up for her? Could it have been used for something like this?"

Tristian sighs, aware that his fuckup from all those years ago is still wreaking havoc. "I don't see why not." When he shifts, the phone moves, revealing what looks like Dimitri Rathbone's bare ass behind him. "Keep us posted on this. If you need help, you've got it."

"Not sure how much you can do, but thanks," Nick says, hanging up. He tosses the phone back to Remy and runs his hands through his hair. Sy paces the room, while I try to process everything.

"So you have the passcode to this phone," Sy says, putting the pieces together. "And from what Mercer told you, he programmed it so that she could detonate specific locations as needed."

"Yep," Nick says. "Leticia Lucia was hardcore."

"No wonder Tate fell for her," Remy says, eyes fixed to the phone's dark screen.

"But to what end?" Sy asks, always trying to pull on all the threads. The motive. The reason. The *why.*

"For leverage," I say, forcing the words through the lump in my throat. "This isn't Leticia's bomb, you guys. It's my father's. To get away from him–to live her life freely with Tate–she had to find a way to use his own weapon against him."

Because she understood this game better than I did. To gain her freedom, true freedom, she'd have to be willing to take our dad's life. Or at the very least, make him think she would.

It's the exact thing he's done to me.

"Smart," Remy says, drawing me from my thoughts. "Fucking psycho dads, Forsyth's biggest export." He looks at the guys. "Promise me we won't be like that."

Nick glances at me, eyes on my belly, then up to my face. "If we knew what Leticia did with that phone detonator, I'd feel a lot better." He approaches me, blue eyes boring into mine as he cups my cheeks in his big, warm palms. "Think, LB. You sure you don't know where she might have stashed it? That floorboard beneath her bed... it didn't have anything else in there?"

Shaking my head, I wrack my brain. "There wasn't anything else down there, and let's be real, Nick. She would have kept something that important–that dangerous–as close as possible. If she had it on her when she fell from the cliff, then it probably–" My lungs snatch the words back into my throat, eyes snapping up.

The Barons would have gotten it.

Nick's eyes meet mine, but I'm already springing into action, zipping across the room.

"What–" Sy asks, but I don't stop.

"This whole fucking time," I mutter. Nick's hand reaches over my head, shoving open the door. Just as urgently as I'm moving, he dashes past me, jumping down the five steps of the loft in one leap.

He waits for me at the bottom with outstretched arms, grabbing my hips and lifting me down.

"Son of a bitch," Sy yells, Archie darting out between his feet. "Please don't tell me you have more secrets you didn't share."

Nick and I do have secrets. The things that happened between us in the motel, the cage, a dicey game of Russian roulette, the visit to Ashby's security guy–but this isn't one of them. This is us being too blind to see what was right in front of our eyes the whole time.

"I just saw it," I tell Nick, racing to Remy's messy desk. "When we were looking for Remy's bruin pin, the day of the vote, it was–" I flip through a pile of markers, sweeping them aside.

Upending Remy's desk drawers, Nick grumbles, "I should have known. I should have *fucking* known."

"What the hell?" Remy walks in, aghast at the sight before him. Nick and I are tearing through his things frantically, sending tubes of paint skittering to the floor.

In unison, Nick and I whirl on him, barking, "Where's the phone?"

"What phone?" He's confused and I don't have time for it.

"The one you stole from your dad," I urge. "The red phone!"

Recognition lights up his eyes, and he pushes Nick aside, walking to the nightstand beside his bed and wrenching open the bottom drawer. We hurry to flank him as Remy pulls out the old red phone, yanking a cord off the end.

"I've been keeping it charged ever since we found out who my dad was." He looks between us and Sy, explaining, "Just in case someone called for him–another King. Intel, right?"

Nick shakes his head at Remy, but I hold out my hand. He presses the smooth metal into my palm and I spend a long moment staring at it, testing the weight of it. How odd to think Leticia held this in her grip for days–weeks, maybe.

When I press the power button, it boots up with a glow, a security screen prompting me for a passcode to access it.

"I need the–"

Nick recites the numbers in a tight rush, having them memorized. "Four, zero, zero, nine."

I punch in the number and the home screen flicks to life.

Sy and Remy hover quietly nearby, and through the paralysis of shock that we were right–this was my sister's weapon–I recall what Tristian told us that night.

"...if this is the one I'm remembering, she needed help with a remote detonator... I left a group of contacts on it. All she had to do was call the contact of her choice, and the fuse would blow."

I thumb open the contacts, and there it is.

Dad's House.

Below it are contacts for *Dad's Office, Stash House,* and *Kappa Frat House.*

Nick laces his fingers behind his head. "He knew," he says, pacing away only to pace right back. "Remy's dad knew that phone had something important, but he couldn't get into it. *Fuck.*" Despite the context of it all, Nick's eyes are alight with the excitement of this missing piece of the puzzle.

"We're not here," I tell them, looking at the four contacts. I don't why, but there's a knot inside me that unwinds at the realization. Looking up, I meet Sy's gaze. "The tower, the brothels, the Prince's palace, the Baron's crypt... none of them are in here. It's just North Side."

Leticia never planned to use Forsyth as a pawn.

Remy holds up a hand, saying. "Wait. Why would your father plant bombs in his own territory?"

"He wouldn't," I answer, holding his green eyes as it dawns on him.

"Your sister planted them," he says, looking impressed. "She really was hardcore."

Hungry for more, I begin searching through the rest of the phone, but it's all blank, practically in factory condition. No apps. No browsing history. No texts.

Except the call history.

The one, lone entry is dated three days before Tate and Leticia's deaths–a call that lasted seven minutes and was made to a number that I somehow recognize immediately.

My father.

"So what you're saying," Sy begins, looking over my shoulder, "is that all you have to do is press a button, and North Side..." He doesn't speak the words aloud, but we all hear them anyway. With this phone, I hold Lionel Lucia in the palm of my hand.

There's a long stretch of silence as the truth of it washes over us. I don't know what the others are thinking, but my thoughts are as solid as steel. I wonder how it felt for my sister. Did she hesitate? She could have ended him days before her own death, but she didn't. Was she hoping she wouldn't have to? Was it all a very convincing bluff?

When I look up, I become pinned with the intensity of Nick's knowing stare. A frisson of understanding passes between us. All those long nights at the Crane Motel, in the basement of the Hideaway, here in the tower...

They taught me how to read Nick Bruin.

And they taught Nick Bruin how to read me.

He nods slowly, pulling his own phone from his pocket. "I'll call South Side," he says, already aware of my next move–maybe even before I am.

Remy sighs, having already caught the significance of the moment. "I'll reach out to my dad." At my alarmed look, he offers a tight grin. "Don't worry, Vinny. He might not understand family, but he understands business." I watch, an eerie stillness settling over me as he and Nick leave the room, phones pressed to their ears.

Sy stands in the doorway, arms crossed against his bare chest. "Lavinia," he says, gazing at me with a similar eerie stillness. "Are you sure?"

"He threatened us," I say, willing him to understand. "Leticia left me a gift. Maybe she didn't plan to die, but she left me the pieces, just in case she did, and that's..." Head shaking, I try to remember her as she was. Elegant and strong, but also ruthless and cold. "It's the only nice thing she's ever done for me." These little hints of Leticia–these secret, kind, compassionate things–should mean something.

He searches my eyes, and I wait. The truth is, if Sy ordered me to stop, I'd do it. I wouldn't like it. It'd eat at me, corrosive and ruinous until there was nothing left inside but an empty pit of resentment, but I'd follow his orders like a good Queen should.

All he has to do is say it.

His arms unfold, hands reaching for me. When he pulls me against his bare chest, the kiss he brushes against my forehead is slow and soft, unbearably warm. He speaks the words against my brow. "I'll call Ashby."

I should feel apprehensive or scared when I look back into the phone, Sy wandering away into his own room, but all I really feel is sure. So sure, that when I open the call history, it's easy to punch in the last call, bringing the phone to my ear.

I walk sightlessly into the main room as it rings, hearing the distant voices of my Dukes arranging the formalities. I'm already up the staircase and entering my loft when the other end picks up.

There's a long, static-laced pause, and then, "Tisha?" Hearing my father say her name like that–quiet and surprised, so full of cautious hope–makes my fist clench around the phone. "Tisha," he repeats, "where are you?"

I've already reached the clock room by the time I answer, voice casual. "She's in the ground–locked away in a box."

His sucking breath pierces right through my ear. "How did you get this phone?"

"Do you know what it is?" I wonder, carefully climbing the ladder to the open hatch. "How far did she even get into her plan before Saul messed it all up?"

Frustration rings in his voice when he snaps, "What the hell are you talking about?"

So he didn't know.

He didn't know *anything*.

The thought is both amusing and infuriating. "What did you

talk about?" I ask, the idle curiosity piercing to the surface. "When she called you on this number–which you obviously saved as belonging to her–what did you talk about?"

His answer is spoken with a viciousness that twists around my vocal cords. "We talked about you, Lavinia. How intolerable you were, up there in your bedroom, banging away in that chest. How long I was going to keep you in there." I can practically hear the satisfied sneer in his voice. "Indefinitely, if I recall."

The confirmation pushes a hard breath from my gut, but I continue. "We found your explosives," I say, rising out into the cool morning air of the belfry. "Planting them inside the clock? Clever. Of course, now that I think about it, it's obvious. You always did have a thing for symbology. I guess I'll never know if you actually have the guts to kill me, seeing as how Tristian Mercer helped us disable it."

There's a stretch of silence, and then a low, unpleasant chuckle. "You really think I'd only plant one?"

I answer without missing a beat. "Yes. You're too arrogant to have a failsafe for your failsafe. That's why, with Leticia and Perez gone, your whole territory is falling apart."

"What do you want?" he snipes, the barb making its target.

"I called to say you were wrong," I say, staring out over Forsyth. "I actually believed you–for a while. But then I woke up this morning, and I had this... epiphany." I shift my eyes to the horizon in the distance, spotting Widow's Rock–the cliff. "Leticia loved me."

He snorts. "You're delusional."

I shake my head. "Even after you poisoned her against me. Even after all the years of competition and fighting. Even after you tried so hard to make her into you. You couldn't strip the soul out of her." It's exhilarating, this new awareness bringing a prickle to my eyes. Laughing thickly, I say, "I think I might have suspected it. It's why I grieved for her so hard, even though she hurt me so much. It had me twisted up there for a while, but I was right." Nodding, I confirm it to myself more than to him. "I was right to mourn her."

His reply comes, sharp and impatient. "Leticia didn't love you."

A bittersweet smile touches my lips. "She did. I know she did, because she was smart. Wasn't she so smart?" I don't give him a chance to answer. "She knew how to play this game, and that means she knew she'd have to kill you. But she didn't." I tilt my head back, imagining all the stars just out of sight, hidden beneath the veil of sunshine. "She didn't use this phone because it would have killed me, too."

In a twisted, complicated sort of way, my father was right all along. I did have something to do with my sister's death. If she'd killed our father and secured her place as Queen of North Side, she would have been bulletproof. Saul and Daniel wouldn't have been able to touch her. But she hesitated. For *me*.

My father argues, "If Leticia ever had the chance to kill you, she wouldn't have hesitated!"

But it doesn't penetrate.

Not anymore.

My sister loved me. My mother loved me. The only Lucia who never did isn't worth mourning.

And I won't.

"You're home alone, aren't you?" Hearing a shuffle behind me, I look over my shoulder, seeing all three of my Dukes standing feet away. I blink, wondering how long they've been there, listening. Emotionlessly, I tell my father, "You would be. There's no one left to show you real loyalty. Just cockroaches running at the first sign of disorder."

Nick dips his head in a nod, while Remy smirks.

Sy's eyes are fixed to the distance–to North Side–waiting.

Nastily, he asks, "Why do you care? Thinking of sending your little guard dogs over?" From the sound of my father's voice, he'd love nothing more than to see that happen.

But I shake my head, turning back to watch the sky. "No. I think I just like the idea of it. You all alone in that big, empty box. You don't even have *your* guard dog anymore."

"I don't need one!" he explodes. "I don't need a Queen, and I certainly don't need a daughter. My house is empty because none of you have what it takes!"

I nod, back straightening. "That's all I needed to know."

The call ends with a sharp vibration and I turn to them–my Dukes and our King. They're all wearing the same sort of expression–a fighter's scowl–ready for the punch to be thrown. Their faces harden even more as they watch me pull up the contacts.

"Do you remember the day you taught me how to throw a punch?" I ask Sy, recalling my own surprise at how much it hurt. "You said to never strike out in anger–that if I let anger drive, I'd crash."

Sy nods. "I remember."

I hold his stare, because if there's one thing I need them to know, it's this. "This isn't anger, even though I have the right to it. And it's not revenge, either." My gaze stops on Nick, whose blue eyes gleam proudly back at me. "This is freedom."

In the end, Sy was right.

When it comes to men like Saul and my father, it's easy. My thumb touches the screen, and the truth is, I don't feel anything. Not excited. Not guilty. There's no fear or regret, no instinctual, last second wish that I can take it back.

There's just me and my Dukes, turning our gazes to North Side.

There's a moment of absolute stillness where my exhale remains caught in my throat. Remy's hand tangles with mine, and I'm thinking of the cedar chest–the one at the end of my old bed–when the flash comes. It's a sudden glow in the distance, as if Forsyth herself is discharging a weapon, there and gone. Nick's fingers lace with my other hand, and above our heads, birds startle from their perch in the top of the belfry, rushing into the wind. They feel it first, before the quake, and our eyes are all fixed to the fiery ball to the north, dust clouding the flames.

I can feel Sy behind me when the sound arrives a second later, his warm palms curling over my shoulders. The *crack* rebounds off the empty streets and their derelict buildings. It's odd. I think it should be bigger–louder. Instead, it flashes and immediately wanes, the people beneath us going about their day as if nothing's happened at all.

I lean back against Sy, the man who made me a Queen, and feel it rushing through me like a breath of fresh air. In the distance, a box is burning, and all I feel is relief.

The Lucia name won't live on.

But Perilini, Maddox, and Bruin will.

30

N ick

"GOD ALMIGHTY."

I fall over Lavinia's back, cock twitching inside of her warm pussy. Her elbows are on the top of my old dresser, giving me a fantastic view of her tits in the mirror. All in all, perfection.

Breathlessly, she asks, "Satisfied?" Her eyes lock with mine through the reflection, her cheeks the most delicious shade of pink.

'Just been fucked'-pink.

Remy may be onto something with this color thing.

I bend to suck a kiss into her neck. "Partially. That was only fantasy number one for fucking my girl in my childhood bedroom. There are like," I run it over in my head... six different ways in bed, against the bedroom door, titty fuck, blow jobs, obviously... "ten other positions on the list."

She sighs, but it's laced with contentment. Should be, too. I dragged her up here after Thanksgiving dinner to give her the dessert she really needed. "Well, you're going to have to pace yourself, because I already feel weird enough knowing that your parents are fully aware of what we're doing up here."

Snorting, I say, "My mother, the *sex therapist*, raised two teenage boys. This house was nothing but dirty sheets and long showers for a good eight years. She'll just be happy I didn't mess up the bed." I open the top drawer of the dresser and remove an old t-shirt. Pulling out slowly, I catch my dick in the cloth with one hand and reach between Lavinia's legs with the other, dragging the leaking cum back up to her slick, well-fucked pussy.

She hums as I push it back inside, spreading her legs wider for me. The movement is automatic, an afterthought to the wistful look I see on her face as she laces her fingers with the hand I'm bracing against the dresser. "I can't wait to get home. Do you think Remy was serious before?"

"Yes," I answer instantly, balling up the cum cloth to clean her inner thighs. "Remy is *never* not serious about making promises."

All three of us keep searching for traces of regret, or even grief, from Lavinia after killing her father, but we never find it. All I find is *this*–the soft, assured look she gets when she inspects my fingers. If anything, she seems happier. Settled. Even Remy says that all he sees is clean, pure white. It's why he asked her to get her next tattoo with him.

It's why Sy and I demanded the same.

"It's not exactly something we can take back." There's a soft sort of skepticism in her eyes. "Are you sure Sy–"

"Yes," I insist, tipping down to brush a gentle kiss over the scar on her shoulder blade. "Sy and Remy are just realizing what I already knew two years ago. There's no one else for us, Lavinia." Still, I make sure she knows, "You can say no. If you're not ready, or–"

"Nick." She meets my gaze, giving me a small, satisfied smile. "I'm ready."

Nodding, I glance around, trying to find a spot to toss the dirty shirt. Coming up empty, I reopen the drawer and stuff it inside.

Lavinia jolts up, jaw dropping. "Oh my god!"

"*Anyway,*" I ease her skirt over her hips and spin her around, "if you didn't want me to fuck you today, you would've worn underwear and pants. Instead, you're all commando beneath a skirt."

She pulls at the hem, smoothing out any wrinkles. "Pretty Nick Bruin, always the romantic." If this girl wasn't being a smartass, she wouldn't be true, but I see the glint in her eye.

My Little Bird loves me.

I grab her cardigan off the bed and hand it to her. As she covers up, her eyes shift toward the door, and she asks, "Do you think they're finished talking down there?"

'They' is no doubt a reference to my brother and our mom. Remy and the dads took off for the basement as soon as the kitchen was clean, and I dragged Lavinia up here. But my brother is most likely sitting at the table, regretting that third piece of pie, and getting the lecture of a lifetime about his new title.

Buckling my belt, I answer, "I doubt it, but I suppose my job as a brother, and second-in-command, means I should go save his ass."

She rolls her eyes but kisses my cheek. "Go ahead. I'll be in the bathroom for a moment, cleaning up all the cum you barely pretended to wipe away."

Winking at her, I watch her ass as she struts out. I hear the hallway bathroom door shut as I jog down the stairs. Pausing at the kitchen door, I hear my brother's perturbed voice. "Mom, I know. I promise—"

"Don't make promises you can't keep, Simon." Her tone is laced with something she usually keeps under wraps. "Taking out Saul is one thing. I don't like it, and I hope you're talking to a therapist about the emotional toll of taking another human's life, but going after Lionel Lucia?"

Hotly, he argues, "I had nothing to do with Lionel's death. He's the one who wired this city with explosives. It was only a matter of time before that backfired—literally."

This is the official line. That the explosion at Lionel's house was an accident. That he was taken down by his own hubris. That the explosion was the consequence of neglect and carelessness. It's believable enough that no one is asking questions.

Unless, apparently, you're our mother.

"Simon—" mom starts, the warning tone the signal it's time for me to be a good soldier.

"What time does the game start?" I ask, strolling into the room. Forsyth's annual rivalry game is a big matchup. DKS usually shows it on the big screen down at the gym.

"Seven." Sy makes a show of looking at the time. "So we should probably get going."

"We're not through," mom says, as much to him as to me.

"Of course not," he says, standing and giving her a kiss on the cheek.

Remy walks into the room, having linked up with Lavinia at some point. The two of them have been wound around each other a little intensely these past few days, and right now is no different, their fingers tangled together loosely between them as they filter in.

Remy looks hopefully at the dishes. "Any leftovers?"

Mom smiles up at him. "Already packed up."

He touches his chest with a solemn expression. "You never fail me, Sarah."

With our mom distracted, Sy gives me a hard, annoyed look. "Thanks for taking your time saving me," he quietly hisses.

Sniffing dismissively, I say, "I was busy."

"Yes," he rolls his eyes, "we all heard."

If he wants me to be embarrassed that people could hear my fuck-rhythm when the dresser hit the wall, he's out of luck. I pat his shoulder. "Jealousy is a bad shade on you, big brother."

He shakes his head. "You're a fuckwit."

"A well-fucked fuckwit."

Piled with leftovers and two additional pies, the drive back to West End is spent in a quiet sort of anticipation. At the main intersection, Sy flips on the signal to the left—toward the gym.

Lavinia leans between the seats, looking between us. "Hey, guys? I know the game is a tradition, but..."

She doesn't need to finish the sentence.

We've spent the week following the explosion living out of a hotel–a nice one next to the university, paid for out of the King's coffers, while the tower was methodically swept for additional signs of explosives. Turns out, being a King in Forsyth comes with a heavy stipend, and since Saul didn't have an heir, he'd left everything to his successor. His accounts and real estate, including his penthouse, all belong to Simon Perilini now.

But none of us have an interest in moving into Saul's property. At least not yet. We just want the tower and its staircase, the belfry and its open sky, the floors and walls that Remy swears are living, breathing things.

Our eyes all meet in the rearview mirror and Sy flips the blinker again, turning toward the towering structure in the distance. The clock's hands are still frozen in time, but the building is safe. "Let's go home," he agrees.

~

MOST OF THE TIME, I know just who I am and exactly what I want. Pops used to tell me I'm a manifester– and then Dad said if I ever want to get a conventional job, I should use the term 'motivated self-starter'. Really, it's not often I surprise myself.

But sometimes I do.

I'm sitting on Remy's bed, bringing a beer to my mouth as I watch the way he curls over Lavinia's hand. She's on his weird table-chair-bed thing, but only perched on the edge. Her palm is flat against the table and Remy has this look on his face, all focused and soft. I've seen him give dozens, maybe even hundreds of tattoos by now–a lot of them on me directly–and he's always methodical and precise.

But I've never seen him work like he does with Lavinia. He keeps tucking his hair behind his ear, but it's not quite long enough to hold, so it springs back, and he does it again, and again, not even looking frustrated. He's too distracted for all that. His green eyes hone in on her skin like it's something religious–something worth worshiping.

The surprise is that I like it. The way they look together. How Remy treats her so reverently. The adoration in Lavinia's eyes when she takes over the task of holding his hair back, the fingers of her free hand curling it behind his ear.

Something clinks against the neck of my bottle and I look over, my brother pulling his own beer back. "Yeah," he says, eyes moving back to Remy and Lavinia. "I feel that."

The Archduke, having been returned to us by Verity an hour ago, is currently nestled in Sy's lap, aggressively cleaning his tail. Despite being the one to put his foot down about a hotel room not being a fit place for a cat, he's monopolizing Archie's affection like he's missed him.

"You look ridiculous," I say, taking another pull from my bottle.

Sy's eyebrows snap into a glare as he assesses himself. A hulk of a man, a skilled fighter, a killer, the reigning King of West End.

And his fluffy white kitten.

Sy shrugs, raising his beer to his lips. "He's the Archduke," he replies, as if this is a perfectly valid explanation.

I suppose it is.

The buzz of the tattoo gun suddenly stops, drawing our gazes to the table. Remy purses his lips as he inspects his work, wiping down her finger before tilting the hand from side to side. She watches with him, but I already know she's pleased with it when she looks up to catch my eye.

In a tone that's clearly meant to convey her thoughts on my earlier whining, she says, "It wasn't so bad."

I scoff. "Fingers hurt like a bitch. You're all fronting."

Sy fidgets with the gauze around his own finger. "Pretty easy, as far as victory tats go."

Remy looks Lavinia straight in the eye as he raises her hand to his mouth, pressing a kiss to her knuckles. She flushes under the intensity, because it's not *just* a victory tattoo. The sad fact of the matter is that three men can't marry the same woman. It doesn't really mean much in a place like Forsyth, where relationships like ours aren't exactly a rarity.

The rings tattooed on each of our fingers aren't legally binding in any way.

But they're still a promise.

He pulls Lavinia from the table with his hands on her hips, giving her ass a little slap. "Nicky will do the ointment."

She climbs into the bed, moving to sit between me and Sy. Archie gives a little squawk when he sees her, and she reaches out, running her finger over his nose.

"Give me your hand," I tell her, and she rests it on my knee. I look down at the delicate design–four narrow lines–creating one band. "You sure that didn't hurt?"

"I know pain, Nick," she touches my chin, "and this isn't it."

There's no accusation in her tone, just facts. Lavinia proved one thing in her time as Duchess, she doesn't do anything she doesn't want. And this tattoo–this ring—proves one thing for certain.

She wants us.

THE NEXT MORNING, she hauls us all out of bed and up the stairs to the clock room, eyes alight as she directs us back down with the supplies and components. At some point over the last few decades, a group of Dukes clearly decided this godforsaken clock was never going to work again, and took down the mechanisms that connected it to all the guts upstairs.

"You're not lifting it high enough," she says as she stares up at me, hands on her hips. She's wearing this teeny little tank top that isn't exactly helping me stay focused, especially given that I'm looking right down the neck of it, but I try.

Good *god*, I try.

The last time I climbed up into these rafters, it was to spy on her. This time, it's because she bullied my brother and I up here to be the muscle to lift the pinion, or shaft, or whatever-the-fuck it's called. It's more like an enormous metal rod that weighs a metric shit-ton. We have it rigged with ropes so all we have to do is pull, and about twenty feet down the rafter, my brother fixes me with the most insincere look of concern he can manage.

"You need to do more bench presses, Nicky." He wraps the rope around his fists, looking cool as a cucumber. "It's not really that heavy."

My eye twitches, jaw clenching. "On three."

I'll show this asshole who needs to do bench presses.

Remy, who's on a ladder in front of the clock, is holding the end of the pinion, attempting to guide it into the threads in the center of the clock face. Apparently, this monstrosity will be responsible for turning the hands on the clock.

Who knows if it actually will.

"One, two, three." Grunting, I pull. Sy is careful to keep pace, making sure the shaft doesn't just slide right out of the rope cradle and crash into the living room.

"Almost there," she calls out, tipping her head back to watch Remy. He directs it a little to the right, arms straining, and then–

"There!" I can feel it locking into place, Remy rushing to slide the threaded bolt to it, tightening it hastily. Lavinia brings her hands together in a victorious clap. "Now we need to attach the–"

"I'm on it," Sy says, tying the rope off on the beam he's straddling. It holds the shaft steady as Remy hauls the ladder back down to where the coffee table used to be, climbing until he's teetering at the very top.

Lavinia watches this all while grasping the ladder from the ground, gasping every time the ladder shifts. Fortunately, Remy's never been sketchy about heights–even when he really fucking should be–and he easily catches the rod that emerges through the ceiling, affixing the transmission joint to the monstrosity that's currently making my arms ache.

He gives it a testing shake, Lavinia on the edge of having a stroke as she watches the ladder wobble, but he had all the parts right.

It's solid as fuck.

I let the rope go slowly, more for her sake than mine, watching as her face goes from panicked, to cautious, to bright enough to light up the room.

"You did it!" she yells, catching Remy in a celebratory embrace the second his feet touch the floor. To us, she orders, "Text me if it moves!" and drags him by the hand up the staircase to the loft, disappearing through the door that leads to the clock room.

Sy watches them go, leaning back to wait with his phone in his hand.

I never really understood Lavinia's obsession with the clock. I doubt she ever has, either. Now that we know what was lurking inside of it, it's a bit eerie, as if somehow she could feel her father had something to do with it. It was broken long before he came along, but there was never a hope of fixing it when it was all jammed up with his device.

Now, there's a chance, and Lavinia has been working 'round-the-clock–*pun intended*–to get it into working shape again. I'm sweaty and sore and tired, and I'm also pretty sure when we go to crank that thing, nothing is going to happen.

Still, I turn to watch the clock face.

Apparently, there's some mechanism up there that allows them to set the time.

I ask Sy, "You don't really think–"

Only then, the transmission jolts to life, turning.

Turning the hands of the *clock*.

Dusty rust rains down to the loft as the hands spring to life, inching toward the top of the face. I'm frozen, a part of me feeling it deep down, like a wound. This clock has been sitting at 7:32 for as long as I've been alive. It's a snapshot in time. It's such a big part of West End's identity that I have it tattooed on my temple, for fuck's sake.

But a bigger part of me knows that some paralyzed, broken thing shouldn't be our identity at all. I watch with a silent, complicated sort of respect as it moves forward, the hands pausing on 3:53.

When I look back to Sy, he appears just as stunned, even though he hides it better, tapping his phone screen.

The squeal from upstairs is audible, even through the stone and distance.

So we slink down the ladder and then trudge up the steps, finding our girl waiting impatiently by the crank lever. The clock room looks completely different now, all the pieces put back where they belong, clean and greased.

Lavinia presents this to us like a game show hostess, making sweeping gestures to the machine. "We've already cranked the striking mechanism and set the counterweights. It just needs to be wound now." She looks at my brother, giving him a firm nod. "It should be you."

Remy's in the chair by the table he usually files serials at, hands laced lazily behind his head. "Fuck it up, Sy."

My brother sends him a thumbs up, giving his palms a good rub before stepping up to the lever. I'm the one to tug Lavinia into the curve of my body, lifting her chin to lock eyes with me.

"Look, I know we got the hands connected, but keep in mind, this might not work," I warn, already dreading her disappointment. "This clock has a million moving parts. The chances of them all coming together and working after a few tries... realistically, it's slim."

I should know better than that, though. She holds my eye and I don't see someone who's ready to be disappointed.

I see a woman who's willing to fight until she wins.

The corner of her mouth tips up. "Wind her up, Sy."

Glancing at her, my brother grasps the crank, smirking. "That's usually my goal." His muscles flex as he gives it a push, grunting. The lever gives, whirling around with each push and pull, and the cable above begins moving, winding around the barrel. Lavinia grasps my hand, watching anxiously, as her eyes keep flicking to the back of the room, where the counterweight is located, then up toward the belfry, then back down to the strike train, continuing the circuit.

It takes a while, Sy's sweat-dampened hair flopping into his eyes as he turns and turns, tendons shifting beneath his dark skin.

Finally, it's wound.

He pulls away, huffing with the exertion, and asks, "What now?" I can see it in his eyes, the seed of his own excitement, and it grows when she nods to the little dial beside him.

"Push that pin and it'll engage the gears."

Sy points to it, and at her encouraging nod, turns to regard it with a dubious stare. Never one for a suspenseful pause, Sy just reaches out and pushes it.

Tick.

Tick.

Tick.

Our eyes dart around to meet one another's, breaths caught in our chest.

And then Lavinia tips her head back, letting out an ear-splitting victory cry. Both of her fists thrust into the air, and I'm speechless as I watch the joy transform her face. That, plus the shock of watching all the gears turn and tick, is why I almost don't catch her when she launches herself into my arms, barking out a jubilant laugh.

"We did it!" Grabbing my face, she plants a hard, aggressive kiss to my lips, springing back with a beaming smile. Sy and Remy look just as floored, and maybe it's a testament to the complete fuckery of our tenure as Dukes that it takes a moment for us to begin celebrating too.

"Holy shit," Sy says, taking in the moving clock parts. He palms his forehead as he watches. "It is working, isn't it?"

Lavinia excitedly suggests, "Let's go downstairs to–"

From one breath to the next, the air around us suddenly explodes.

We all drop to the floor, Sy diving to cover Lavinia as we clap our hands over our ears. All I can think about are hidden bombs and failsafes. I see the same panic cross Remy's eyes as he crawls toward us.

But the longer we brace for it, the more we realize this isn't an explosion.

It's the goddamn *bells*.

Sy's hands drag slowly from Lavinia's head. "Oh," he mouths, looking upward with a bloodless face. "Oh, hell no. *Fuck* no!"

Remy belts out a relieved laugh, but I've got to agree with my brother. Yelling over the *bong* of the chime, I ask, "We're supposed to sleep beneath that thing?"

Lavinia is absolutely awestruck, though. She climbs slowly to her feet, gaping up toward the noise. I know where she's going before her feet even move, and I groan as I follow her, Remy and Sy not too far behind.

If I thought the bells were loud in the clock room, then they're even worse when we climb out onto the belfry, a gust of air whipping her blue hair around her face. Sy sticks his fingers into his ears and sends the bells above us a sharp glare, but Remy and Lavinia look absolutely fucking captivated.

"Holy shit," I hear Remy yell over the noise. "Vinny, you fucking did it!"

She turns to say something to him, eyes alight with wonder, but I'll never know what it is. Her gaze drops to the streets below, and I don't understand at first what the slack, shocked look on her face is meant for.

And then I turn to look, too.

Below us, the streets are growing speckled with people.

They spill out from warehouses and buildings, arms raised as they point upward, to where the four of us are standing. We can't hear them—we can hardly even make out their expressions, they're so far down—but I can imagine well enough what they're thinking, because I'm thinking it, too.

One day, at 7:32, West End stopped breathing. For decades it's been here, quiet and solemn and so fucking angry about it that we grew into a group of desperate fists.

Today, we have a heartbeat again.

I sling my arm around Lavinia's shoulders as she stares out over them. The lost people. The broken people. The fighters. People like us. Pressing a kiss to her temple, I tell her, "I love you so fucking much, Little Bird."

There's no way she can hear me over the bell chimes, but she still turns to give me a proud, fierce smile. "I love you, too."

Those words will never get old. I couldn't have predicted it two years ago, when a hurt, terrified girl slammed the sole of her boot into my jaw and made an imprint on my soul. I couldn't have known during all those long nights in the old Crane Motor Inn. I didn't even realize it when I placed the dominoes that would fall to make her my Duchess.

Little birds, striking vipers, and angry bears...

These are all wild, resilient things.

And a cage could never hold her heart.

EPILOGUE

L avinia

"WELL, THIS IS…" A snowball whizzes past Sy's ear, smashing into the wall behind him.

Nick reaches for his gun.

"Seriously?" Sy's look is a characteristic mixture of deadly and exasperated. He holds out his hand. "I specifically said no firearms."

"It could have been an assassination attempt." Nick sighs, but puts the gun into Sy's palm. Like we don't all know there's a knife in his boot.

"Sorry, dude." The thrower, a guy wearing a stocking cap with the Greek letters LDZ across the front, shrugs, before bending over to grab another handful of snow. "My bad."

"This is *a lot*," Sy finishes, glaring at the kid who almost hit him across the Lords' backyard. It's been transformed into some kind of magical winter wonderland.

"Tucker!" Dimitri Rathbone appears out of the crowd. "Stop being a fuckhead."

Tucker drops the snow, which scatters at his feet. "Yes, sir."

"Go get our guests a drink."

"On it." Tucker runs off without a glance backward, rushing to the bar across the yard. Ducking into my scarf, I notice a lot of LDZs are much like Tucker. Drunk, happy, and playful.

"This is fucking elaborate." Remy's eyes are a vivid green, taking in everything. He loves seeing something new and different, and a snowy, glowing patch of South Side is definitely different. "Can you really sled down that?" he asks, jerking his chin toward the hill in the distance.

Rath follows his gaze. "Yeah, it's fun as hell, especially if you're going down it with your girl. It's engineered to make you feel like you're falling right off a cliff."

Remy and I share a look. "*Ugh*, maybe later."

"Lav!" Story's happy, inebriated voice rings out. A moment later, she has me in a tight, crushing hug. "I'm so glad you and your guys could make it!"

I embrace her back with a laugh, her enthusiasm infectious. "Me, too."

It's not completely unheard of for the frats to invite the leadership to each other's events. We all go to the Baron's equinox celebration, and all the house girls compete in Screw Year's Eve. I suppose, if things stay peaceful, we'll get an invite to the Prince's Valentine's party. But when it comes to the Counts…

How wrong is it to make a barbecue joke right now?

Killian and Tristian walk up behind her and the two Kings share a nod.

"This might sound really inappropriate," Tristian starts.

"Then don't say it," Killian says, eyes narrowed.

He does, anyway. "That explosion was better than a wet dream." Killian shakes his head while Rath actually slams his fist into his shoulder. Tristan grasps his arm, glowering. "Jesus! What? I'm just congratulating the Dukes for a job well done."

"Yeah," Killian says, eyeing Tucker and another LDZ who return carrying a drink for each of us. "You're lucky things went well–since you're the asshole that programmed the phone in the first place."

"You know how it is," Tristian winks. "Things have a way of working out for me."

Story grabs one of the drinks, a mug of something warm and chocolatey with whipped cream on top, and hands it to me. She then links her arm with mine, and says, "Why don't you guys go try out some of the activities? Lav and I need quality girl time. No boys allowed."

Nick studies the two of us, his arms crossing over his chest. "I don't know."

Is he worried about the two of us getting close? Probably, considering the way we ganged up on him a few months back. I can admit it's weird, but I can also accept that I need a friend. The cutsluts are great, but I really need someone who understands this life. "Nick, it's fine. Go."

He doesn't relent without staring Story down for a good second. "Okay, but Screw Year's Eve is in less than a week and she's the reigning champion. This better not be some kind of sabotage."

I look at Sy for help and he rolls his eyes, clapping his hand on Nick's shoulder. "Come on, little brother. Is that curling over there? You'll love it. It takes almost no upper body strength to push a rock."

Nick turns to him, and–

Oh no.

I know that spark of intensity in his eyes. "Bet I'd be better than you."

Sy might be the leader, but he's still a Duke, and the hunger for competition–the chance to win–still breaks through. "You're on."

Leaning over, Nick plants a warm kiss on my cold cheek before walking off with the others.

Story watches them go, head shaking. "They're going to be menaces with those brooms, aren't they?"

I give her a weary look. "You have no idea. Last night, I had to referee a confusingly violent round of competitive gift wrapping."

Her head tilts curiously. "Who won?"

This is an easy answer. "I did."

She barks a laugh, and a few minutes later, we're next to a roaring fire pit, bundled in blankets and sipping spiked hot chocolate. I have a thought that this isn't too bad for a Christmas, and it reminds me of the last two, both spent under Nick Bruin's intense, watching gaze, and somehow even those were better than the Christmases back home in North Side.

Loud voices erupt from across the yard and I cringe. "Do you think it's really okay for them to be left alone together?"

"We'll find out." She raises her mug, her eyes sparkling in the firelight. "We should make a toast."

Perking up, I wonder, "To what?"

"Girls who are fucking three guys? Being Queens?" Some of the mirth fades from her eyes. "Being a member of the shitty parent club?"

I hold up my mug and clink it to hers. "To all of that." The drink burns going down, less from the heat and more from the liquor.

"How are you doing?" she asks, pinning me with a reluctant look. "Really."

Shrugging, I don't really need to think about it. "Better."

Something reluctant pops up in her eyes. "When Daniel died, Killian felt... complicated. I gave him some really profound wisdom that I'm way too buzzed to remember, but I think it went something like this." She holds my stare, face growing serious. "It's okay to grieve for people who don't deserve it–to grieve the people they could have been."

I feel my face soften. She's too good for this town. "I'm okay, Story. The truth is, I grieved my idea of who my father could've been a long time ago. He was already dead to me."

She searches my face, but finding no thread of insincerity, she raises her glass. "Then we'll toast to new beginnings."

I touch my cup to hers, grinning. "To new beginnings."

"Oh, my god," she suddenly says, back straightening. "Speaking of, did you hear about the Princess?"

"No." We've been firmly cocooned in our bubble since moving back in the tower. "Everything okay with the baby?"

"As far as I know, the baby is healthy," she says, "but there *is* a problem."

I frown. "What kind of problem?"

Story leans in with a conspiratorial smirk. "It's not any of the Princes'."

My jaw drops. "What? Holy shit."

"Right?" She looks as shocked as I feel.

"How do they even know?" I wonder, since the Princess is barely showing.

Waving her hand, Story explains, "Auggie told me that it's standard protocol that once the Princess reaches nine weeks, they perform a DNA test on the baby." She leans forward, letting her fingers warm up. "Turns out, Piper had a boyfriend before she became Princess. Non-frat. They kept hooking up this whole time, which—as I'm sure you know—is a clear violation of the Psi Nu covenants."

"Oh," I reply, blinking. "That's, like... a contract?"

"Well, yeah," Story leans back, taking another sip. She notices my baffled expression. "Wait, you didn't sign a contract to be the Dukes' house girl?"

"No," I say, wondering if that's strange. The Counts don't do it—that much I know. But even if the Dukes did, I came to them as a prize. A captive. There's no contract for that. "But I guess everyone's arrangement is different," I offer. She nods, leaving it at that. "The Princes must be furious."

She shakes her head. "Oh, not this time. From what Killian hears, they knew she was cheating and were okay with it, because they'd been fucking around, too."

This can only mean one thing. "So Ashby is going to assign new Princes." It's the rule of their house. If they don't produce an heir by the three-month mark, they get the boot. It's why they fuck so doggedly, desperate to get a baby into her before the deadline comes and reduces them back to mediocrity.

"And a new Princess, too," she adds, eyeing me over her mug. "I guess that's one less Royal to worry about for Screw Year's Eve."

I snort. "Please. I don't think any Princess has ever gotten into the ring. They're always pregnant by the time New Year's rolls around."

"Vinny!" My name is shouted across the yard. "You've got to come see this."

"I'm being summoned." I stand, gathering the blanket around my shoulders. "Let's make sure everyone is playing nice."

I'm not surprised when I see a group of guys surrounding the flat sheet of ice. Competition is contagious, and now it's not just the Dukes battling it out for whatever the hell curling is... rock sliding? Ice scrubbing? Winter bowling?

"How is this an Olympic sport?" Story asks, easing against Rath's side as his arm comes around her.

Killian Payne is beside Nick, who's propped against his broom handle. "You hear about this shit with the Princes?" he asks.

Nick dips his chin in a nod. "Never a shortage of drama in the purple palace."

"There are rumors," Killian says, ducking closer to keep his voice low, "that Ashby's going to put his sons in the palace."

Nick's eyebrows knit together. "He can't do that. Lex is graduating this year, and Pace just got out of prison for that stuff over spring break."

Shrugging, Killian notes, "It's what I've been hearing, and Ashby might just be nervous enough to buck tradition. My father's dead. Saul's dead. Lionel's dead." Killian glances up, catching my frozen eye for a split second. "Three out of five, Nick. The old generation is pissing their pants."

Sy strolls up, having obviously heard some of this. "I say let them. Better off with Ashby's spoiled little misfits than someone who poses a real threat. None of them are even real Royalty, anyway." Pausing with a beer halfway to his mouth, Sy glances at

Rath. "No offense. I obviously don't buy into the bloodline bullshit."

Nick says, "Ashby does, though." I don't like the look in his eyes, as if he's struggling to come to a decision. The seed of something dark grows, turning his gaze on Killian. "Did your dad ever tell you Wicker's real last name?"

Killian frowns, watching as an LDZ stokes the fire across the yard. "No. I didn't even think he knew anything."

"It's Kayes," Nick says, keeping his voice low. "Wicker Kayes."

I jolt forward, eyes wide. "You mean like Clive Kayes?" I look at Remy, who's currently crouched down on the ice, sliding a rock.

Story tips her head to the side. "Who's Clive Kayes?"

I clutch my mug close, swallowing. "He's the Baron legacy." It's not a lie. It's just not the whole truth, either.

Rath asks the question we're all thinking. "What the fuck is a relation to the Baron King doing in East End?"

But that's the thing. Clive Kayes isn't the King of the Barons.

And we're the only ones who know it.

Nick locks eyes with me, a silent understanding passing between us. "And what's he doing with Ashby's last name?"

The question hangs in the air, enticing but full of worry. If Wicker is a Kayes, and Ashby is a collector, then who are the other two, *really*?

Over the heaviness of my thoughts, I hear Tristian Mercer and Remy approaching. It's an odd tableau, the eight of us. North and West. Lord and Duke.

"So," Tristan says, cleaving through the tense silence. "Have you ever heard of a game called Candy Cocks?"

"Is this really necessary?"

Remy's pupils are blown wide as they fix on my nipples. "Babe, you have to be slippery as fuck out there. Can't let her get a hand on you."

Remy's been massaging oil onto my tits for a solid three minutes under the guise of covering me in what he claims is 'absolutely necessary' baby oil. The tenting in his jeans reveals an unmistakable erection.

"That's gonna leave a mark!" Nick's voice echoes into the lounge as he calls the match before mine.

"Rem," I say, growing both exasperated and completely horny, "please finish up so I can get dressed."

He sighs and squeezes them one last time before stepping back and assessing me. "God, the crowd is going to lose it over your nipples."

"Are you trying to make Nick lose his shit and fly into a jealous rage?"

He grins. "I mean, it would definitely add an extra dose of excitement to the night." His fingers grab for my hips but don't make purchase, sliding right off. His smile falters as he realizes that *he* also can't get a hand on me. "Just kick her ass, okay? This is the first time we've had two Queens battling it out, and there's a lot on the table."

I level him with an unimpressed look. "You mean bets."

"Bragging rights, money, who gets to fuck you first tonight..." He hooks a finger in my bikini bottom and drags me close, capturing my mouth in a tongue-thrusting kiss. I slide my hands into his hair, and it isn't long before I begin wondering how much time we have to maybe, possibly–

Knock knock.

He groans against my mouth. "I'll get rid of them."

"*No*," I say, grabbing my bikini top. "See who it is and give me time to get dressed."

He cracks the door open, greeting, "Hey, Verity."

"Oh, thank god," I say. "Come in, please." His eyes dart down to my tits, barely covered by the arm I have pressed over them, the bikini top hanging from my fingertips. I give him a stern look. "Let her in."

He swings the door open to reveal Verity, her red hair pulled up into a high ponytail. She assesses me with a wince. "Sorry! I can come back later. I know you're busy, I just–"

"Please," I say, shooing Remy out the door. Verity enters and I reach behind her to flip the lock. "This bikini that Remy's friend made for me has some intricate strap system that I can't manage by myself, and the person who's supposed to be helping me is as distractible as a two-year-old."

She eyes the tangle of straps and sets her purse on a chair, chuckling. "Sure, happy to help."

We move in front of the dressing mirror and I manage to get my tits into the cups–sort of. Verity's job will be to navigate the criss-cross mess in the back. "So you needed to talk to me?" I ask, noticing how quiet she is.

Her eyes jump to mine in the mirror. "It's not important. We can talk about it when you're not about to jump into a pit filled with Jell-O. I'm sure you need to focus."

"Verity." I catch her eye in the mirror. "I need a distraction from the horror that has become my life. Do I really look like the kind of girl who wants to wrestle my friend in front of two-hundred horny frat boys?"

She pauses before saying, "Not really," but there's a small smile on her lips as she untangles the straps and begins criss-crossing them over my back. "But you did kick Haley's ass. I feel like you have a pretty good shot at winning."

It wouldn't be a lie to say I'm flattered. "Thanks. Now, what's going on?" I've spent enough time around her to know when that usually sweet bubbly demeanor is being weighed down with some-thing serious.

Scrunching her lips, she ties the strings in a knot, tugging on it to make sure it's secure. "Well, there is... something." Turning, she bends to unzip her purse, extracting an envelope. She thrusts it out to me while averting her gaze.

Frowning, I step closer to read it, seeing her name written on the front in a fancy script. *Verity Sinclaire.* "What's this?" I ask, noting the thickness of the paper. Lush. Wealthy. "A wedding invitation?"

A nervous laugh escapes her lips. "Not exactly." She removes a thick piece of cardstock and holds it out for me to see. I don't touch it, not with all this oil on my fingers, but I can see it definitely is an invitation. There's a crown embossed at the top, and it's embellished with shiny gold and silver foil. The text is broken up into lines of simple script and elegant cursive.

It reads:

Verity Sinclaire has been cordially invited to attend the Princes' seventy-eighth Masquerade ball, which will be celebrated at the purple palace on January 6th.

As an esteemed guest of honor, you'll have the opportunity to become Forsyth's next Princess, a position of the highest prestige.

Your attire and accommodations will be provided.

Respond by January 3rd.

"I don't know why I would get an invitation like this." She looks down at the paper like she's trying to find a missing clue. "Usually, they pick girls from the higher tier sororities or daughters of former non-heir Princes. Cutsluts wouldn't even rank."

I try to find the missing clue myself. "That is weird." I squirm around as I adjust my top. "Do you think it's a joke? A way to get back at us for some reason?" I wouldn't put it past those guys to bring in some unsuspecting girls just to cut them down and humiliate them for kicks. Invite the low West Ender to their fancy Princess coronation as if she has a chance, and then completely dump on her.

"Seems pretty elaborate."

Unhappy by this possibility, I ask, "Have you shown your mom?"

Verity's eyes widen, snatching the paper back. "God, no. She'll either be completely furious or super excited. I don't think I'll like either option."

I think about my first Friday Night Fury as Duchess, when Verity asked me what I wanted to wear. It had been the first time anyone had ever asked me for my opinion. I'd been so over-whelmed and confused. She has that look on her face now. "Well," I say, "what do you want to do?"

She worries her lip between her teeth, staring around the lounge. "I don't know, Lavinia. I've been so... *aimless* these last six months. All those years of prepping to be the Duchess, and it isn't even an option anymore."

My heart sinks. "I'm sorry."

She looks up, a smile touching her lips. "Don't be sorry. You're an amazing Queen, and I'm so glad it was you. I just..." She looks at the invitation again. "I don't know what's next for me, but being humiliated by a group of Princes doesn't make the list." But then her eyes rise, locking with mine, and I see it. A flicker of temptation. "Right?"

There's a bang on the door. "Vinny—you're up."

"Listen," I say, taking out my earrings, "don't do anything yet. Don't tell your mom or RSVP. We can meet tomorrow, and I'll help you work it out, okay?" It's the least I can do. Verity has helped me through enough crises these last few months that I owe her.

"Okay." Still looking a little overwhelmed, she tucks the invitation back in the envelope and looks me up and down. "Now, go kick some Lady ass."

Our palms meet in a high-five as I exit the lounge.

"Ow," I groan as I reach for the salt shaker, my breast aching. It's been twelve hours, and it still hurts like a bitch. I give it a surly rub as I narrow my eyes at Story. "I can't believe you slapped my tit. *Twice.*"

Frowning into her pancakes, she shifts uncomfortably. "Shove it, Lucia. You kneed me in my vag."

We're at the diner, which is on the boundary lines between North Side, West End, and East End. Not the best locale for Story, who's far enough from South Side that her Lords would probably shit bricks.

"And anyway," she adds, eyes hardening, "you won."

Damn right, I did. "It doesn't feel like it." We're both bruised and sore today. In truth, the match was so close that it had to be called by adding up our points. My knee to the vag put me over the top. However, "To the victor go the spoils." I smirk, holding up my milkshake.

Smirking back, she touches her mug of coffee to my glass. "To the loser go the amazing consolation sex. I'm not mad."

Just then the bell above the door chimes, drawing our eyes to the redhead who enters, and my belly flutters uncertainly.

"I don't know if this is such a good idea," I whisper, smiling tightly when Verity catches my eye.

Story, however, disagrees. "We make our pitch, and she makes the move. Give her a choice, Lav. It's more than you got."

I toss Story an unamused look. "You're such a dirty bitch." She blows me a kiss just as Verity approaches, dropping onto the bench next to me.

"Sorry, I'm late," she says, looking harried. "It was noon, and the bells..."

I slap a hand over my face. "Shit!" I'd completely forgotten.

Sy and I worked for two weeks tweaking the strike chain to make it only chime at noon and midnight. The West Enders weren't happy about it. The bells ringing out over our corner of the city had everyone excited and enthralled. But it just wasn't tenable. A week into the bells going off at the top of every hour had the four of us exhausted and frayed, not to mention poor Archie who spent every second on edge, awaiting the next assault.

Now that they only chime twice a day, people come out to appreciate them fully, clogging up the streets.

Verity pats my hand. "It's okay. I actually really like the bells, and the novelty will wear off soon." She shifts her attention to Story, thrusting out a hand. "Hey, I'm–"

"Verity Sinclaire!" Story gives her hand an eager shake. "Lavinia has told me so much about you. It's really great, you know? When I became Lady, every girl in South Side hated me. I couldn't find a friend anywhere." She gives a small, self-deprecating laugh, but Verity's eyes sadden.

"That's terrible."

Story nods, cutting into her pancakes. "It's okay, though. I found Lavinia, and she's... well, nice isn't quite the word." She wriggles, shooting me a glare.

"Oh, please," I demand, poking at my milkshake. "Stop pretending your vag hurts because of my knee and not all that fantastic loser sex you got at the end of the night."

Her jaw drops in outrage. "How dare you. My Lords are gentle creatures with nothing but tenderness for my Lady parts." But even she can't keep a straight face, cracking up at the look I give her.

"Wow." Verity looks between us, flushing. "I can't believe I'm having lunch with two Queens. And you're not plotting to kill each other."

All of the mirth falls out of me like a boulder. It's strange that it should be like that. Queens against Queens. It's the reason I find the strength to turn to Verity and say, "I think you should tell Story what you told me yesterday."

Verity's eyes widen, the side glance she gives Story a confirmation that she doesn't trust her the way I do. At least not yet. "Are you sure that's a good idea?"

I wipe my chin and rest the napkin next to my plate. "Do you know what one of the last things my father said to me was?"

She looks between me and Story. "I have no idea."

Gesturing out the window, to the boundaries, I explain, "He told me to look around. That there are no Queens around for very long. That we're given to the Royal men to keep them in line until they don't need us anymore." I exhale, shoulders sinking. "The sad thing is, he wasn't wrong. My mother. Sy's mother. Killian's mother. Hell, probably even *your* mother. They were toys."

Story clears her throat. "But Lavinia and I aren't willing to be expendable. Not anymore."

Placing my hand over Verity's, I duck in close to tell her, "Story helped me when no one else could. She stuck her neck out for me and Sy when Saul sent his goons to jump us. She didn't have to do that, and I've learned to trust her." I lower my voice. "I think you should trust her, too."

Verity doesn't react right away. She looks down at her wringing hands and thinks about it, which is something I like about her. This isn't a girl who was next in line for Duchess because of her blood. She has a cool head for conflict.

When her mind is made up, she unzips her purse and takes out the invitation, showing it to Story. She knows what it says already. I told her. We needed to come up with a plan, but there's no lack of surprise when she reads the invitation for herself.

Story gapes at the card inside. "Wow, so they've asked you to, what? Audition? For Princess?"

Verity shrugs. "We all know Ashby picks the Princess this time around. If it is an audition, then he's the one they'd all be bowing and scraping for." Her face screws up at the thought. "No, thanks."

Story and I share a look. That'd explain the conflict. Princess is the most coveted Royal position in Forsyth for a woman. It's not all just being their baby factory. The Princess is known to be pampered and spoiled, set up for life. Less known are the women like Autumn, who get spit back out.

Story wonders, "And he wants you to be a part of it. Why?"

"That's the question, right?" Verity pushes a lock of hair behind her ear. Her nails are perfectly manicured.

"He saw you that night at the gym," I say, remembering her being cornered by Wicker. "Maybe he got a good look at you and liked what he saw."

The words alone are enough to make my skin crawl, but it makes sense. Verity just has that look about her. She wears makeup that's subtle but striking. Her clothes cover enough to be presentable but show just enough skin to make a guy wonder what she's hiding underneath. She's been raised for this role–house girl. Ashby's not stupid enough not to see it himself.

And, like every other King, he wants what he can't have.

Taking a breath, Story says, "We think you should do it," and Verity's head snaps back in surprise.

"What?" Her eyes flit wildly between us. "*Why*?"

I glower at Story for a moment—the plan had really been to break it to her a little more tactfully. "My point before was that things are changing in Forsyth, Verity."

Story nods along. "And this may be our only chance to get in the double doors of the purple palace."

"*Our* chance?" She looks between us, comprehension dawning on her features. "You want a spy."

She's not wrong. The idea came to me last night, up on the belfry. For all the trouble the bells have caused, I love being up there to hear them, the evidence of what I've built here ringing out like a physical force over the landscape.

I push my plate away. "Not just for me and Story, but for our Kings—Killian and Sy. Nick didn't just spend two years in South Side causing trouble." Snorting, Story and I lock eyes. "Well, not *only* causing trouble. He stuck around, waited until the right time to make a move, and claimed his title. Then he leveraged that trust with Killian to get me out of there." I reach across the table and touch Story's cuff, running my finger over the gold skull. "Every move we make is methodical. Tactical. And it's about more than just surviving, Verity." I look over, holding her stare. "It's about changing this place and how it works against us."

Story raises her chin. "It's about seeing two Queens having lunch and not wondering why they're friendly. It's about—"

"Sisterhood," I cut in, grinning.

Verity takes this in with a hard inhale, and we give her a moment. "But what if I don't make the cut?"

Story leans forward. "They invited you for a reason, Verity. Like Lav said, every move is methodical. Ashby sent you that invitation for a reason, and we need to know why."

Verity gives an uncomfortable laugh. "You have a lot of faith in a rejected South Side Duchess."

"You're not a reject," I stress, grabbing her hand. "You're a trained assassin. Sexy. Smart. A virgin–"

Story snorts. "Oh yeah, girl, you've already got the job."

I shake my head. "You've said it yourself. Mama B spent her life raising you to be a house girl. Maybe she just didn't realize which house that'd be."

Squirming, she asks, "And what if they do want me? Then what? I let them..." Her words trail off, because yeah, we all know what the Princes do. They make heirs.

Story and I share a look because we both know she's going to have to fuck them. Probably a lot. And I know in my gut it's going to hurt. For all the Princess is a coveted position, girls like me and Story know the pampered facade is almost certainly just that.

A facade.

I take a breath, stomach churning uneasily. "I won't pretend that what we're asking doesn't come with sacrifices. Story and I... we carry the evidence of our own on our bodies–our souls." The brand on my back says it all. The puckered scars on Story's chest. Girls like Autumn and Regina, who never found love in those dark, angry places, probably carry it somewhere even deeper. And then there's Sutton. "You can say no." After a beat, I add, "You probably should say no."

Verity looks up. "I'll do it."

The decisive tone startles me, drawing my eyes to Story. "Well, you should think about–"

"I don't need to think," Verity says, sliding my milkshake in front of her. "If this is going to help you and Sy–if it'll help change Forsyth into a place where women like my mother and the cutsluts can become something other than Royal waste–then I'll give it a shot."

Story looks just as worried as I feel, leaning over the table to ask, "You know what it means, right?"

Verity sighs, taking a sip of my milkshake. "I always wanted a big family. I always wanted kids. Did I ever want the Princes' kids?" She grimaces but lifts a shoulder in a shrug. "My mom raised me all by herself, and she did just fine, but a little security would be nice. There are perks that come with the job right?"

It's not until I get it that I realize it isn't the answer I wanted to hear. Verity is sweet and kind, and far too good to be chewed up by this wretched machine. But then she looks me in the eye and I remember Verity is something else.

She's West End.

She's a fighter.

"It's okay," she says, voice softening. "I know what this means, and to be honest, it's a good idea." She looks at Story, nodding. "A sisterhood, right? One that doesn't need Royal blood or special last names. A sisterhood for everyone."

"For everyone," Story says. It's an agreement as much as a promise. What happens over this table today shouldn't be a deal made between warring houses or competing territories. It should be something new.

In fact, I decide, "We won't call ourselves Royals." Looking at the two women who have been a big part of making this place a home, I think of the moth on my chest and how I got it. The day I asked Remy to give me wings, he made me promise not to fly away. But wings aren't just for running away.

Sometimes they're for soaring.

"We'll call ourselves the Monarchs."

AFTERWORD

You've met the Lords. Survived the Dukes. But are you ready for the Princes?
Three new Royals are called to deliver the fraternity's greatest duty; creating an heir.
First, they'll have to find the perfect Princess who can handle the demands of the position.

The next installment of the *Royals of Forsyth: Princes of Chaos*, will be available in 2023.
Preorder Available @amazon

ACKNOWLEDGMENTS

Wow, our TENTH book. That's double digits. As someone who rarely finds it in myself to finish creative things, this is a huge accomplishment for me, and probably owed to Angel more than myself. So my first thanks goes out to her. Thanks for keeping me in the car instead of letting me go to Buc-ees. Whatever that is.

Lisa, as always, you are our heart. Nikki, you're definitely an artery or three. Vicki, we haven't even met yet, but I need you to understand that I'd protect you with my life.

Most of all, I have to thank our readers. This journey with Lavinia and the Dukes has been so intense, and I sincerely mean it when I say that we wouldn't have been able to push through it without your support. The reviewers, the group members, the kickstarter supporters... you're the reason I open the document and let myself overthink things. You're the reason I don't just settle for the easy thing, and instead put in the work, however difficult, to hopefully give you something as beautiful to you as you are to us.

Lastly, a big thanks to Crowley, who labored ceaselessly as my assistant over the course of writing this book. Every single day, when I went to write, there he was, so disciplined and motivated, always keeping me on track. His little snores lifted my spirits, even during the darkest of moments.

(Yes, Crowley is my cat.)

Much love and skulls and kittens,

Sam

~

I'm going to let Sam do the heavy lifting on the thanks! I agree with everything and all the people, although my cats are unhelpful and keep bringing dead things into my house and pretend to have forgotten litter box etiquette, so, no-thanks to them.

I do want to say a major thank you for the understanding when we had to push the book back. That kickstarter-yo. It was crazy! We jumped in with no idea what was going to happen and you showed us that the men of Forsyth own all of us a little more than we realized.

Lav is one of those characters readers sometimes just don't get —you know, like most women in the world. Therefore we insist on writing people like her because we can see this bigger world and can't help ourselves. I can't wait to dive into Princes because whoa. I don't think even I'm prepared.

To The Victor!

Angel

ALSO BY ANGEL & SAM

Have you met the Wilcox Brothers?

The Royals of Forsyth aren't the only books written by Angel & Sam. Their first series, The Boys of Preston Prep is a four-part, standalone, dark prep school m/f romance. In these books you're introduce to the Wilcox Brothers, Sebastian and Heston, both of who love and fight hard (including one another.) We included a few Easter eggs of these boys in Dukes! If you want a little more here's a bonus sneak peek of Touched by the Devil.

Sebastian

There's something ironic about how the uber-wealthy go to tiny, back wood, hick towns for vacation. God forbid we go to one of the five-star resorts that line pristine beaches, or the comforts of a modernized summer home in the mountains. Nope, every year the Wilcox family makes the trek to the little town of Briar Cliffs to stay in our hundred-year-old, musty cabin, overlooking the river that my father has been coming to since he was born, and *his* father came to since he was born. Apparently, it's family tradition to bore the hell out of the Wilcox men, which is just a dangerous fucking move.

It makes us restless, and if history has proven anything, it's that there's nothing worse than a restless Wilcox.

Makes no damn sense. Even my dad hates it; he holes up in the makeshift office, drowning himself in work. When Mom actually decides to get sober enough to leave the house, it's only to spend time with the other summer wives, who she doesn't even like. Gossiping and trying to show each other up isn't her scene. Being locked in the cabin with my absent father isn't her scene, either. I pace around like a lion in a cage, trying to find something to do with my hands, going crazy with the ripple of unspent energy sparking beneath my skin. And Heston. Well, Heston is the worst of all. Putting him in any contained area with me and our mom is a recipe for disaster. This has never been a quality family bonding experience, is what I'm saying.

It's my sense of restless, energy-rippling boredom that ejects me from the cabin one summer night on the hunt for weed, pussy, and maybe a fight. Three things a determined seventeen-year-old can find pretty easily, even here.

"Yo, Wilcox."

I look up and see my friends Reid and Mitchell walking down the cracked sidewalk. I jerk a nod in greeting. "Thing One, Thing Two. What's going on?"

"In the Briar Cliffs?" Reid asks, bumping his fist with mine. "Jack and shit."

"Except," Mitchell says quickly, "we heard there's a party down at the dock. Wanna come?"

"Let me check my schedule," I joke, pulling out my phone, which predictably has no service. I've had shit-all to do for weeks now but work on my tan and try to charm the pants off a few girls. "Yep, looks like I'm free."

We head off, passing the antique shops and pharmacy, taking the turn to the dirt road that heads down to the water. I know this place like the back of my hand, every nook and cranny. The steep cliffs overlooking the river. The seedy liquor stores. The mom and pop shops. The suburbs ten minutes north of here. Parents feel secure in letting their kids roam free around the Briar Cliffs from a young age—the wisdom being that there's not much trouble to get into, and whatever trouble we do find, they'd done it all before.

Reid reaches inside his jacket and pulls out a silver flask. It's pretentious and a little douchey, but when offered, I take a swig. The liquid burns like fire down the back of my throat, then warms my belly. I hand the flask back over and ask, "Is this a townie party or summer people?"

There's a distinct difference between the two. Summer people, like myself, have the kind of parties you write home about. Great booze, big boats, and freaky bitches dying to be the center of some rich boy's attention. Townie parties, though. Those are thrown hastily together on a wish and a prayer. The booze is cheap swill, the boats aren't safe for occupancy, and the girls...

The girls are dicey as fuck.

Not always a bug, sometimes a feature.

"Probably a mix," Mitchell says, taking a drink and then wiping his mouth with the back of his hand. "I got a text from Karen telling me to come."

Karen is a local girl who works down at the marina. She's a sexy ginger that Mitchell had the pleasure of hooking up with last weekend on one of the docked boats. I spent last weekend bare-knuckling it with some douche from Rockport and won two-hundred bucks, a loose molar, and a bag of weed. For the Briar Cliffs, that's a pretty great night.

We reach the top of a rise, and down below is the public dock. During the day, little kids jump and dive off the end, and families picnic on the beach. At night, it's an infestation of older kids and a few college students. This is the place to be if you're looking for some trouble. I head down the hill toward the crowd that's already gathering.

"Hey, Bass," a girl calls out. I look over and see Madison, a girl who's spent summers here almost as long as I have. Mostly I see her tits pressed tight against the fabric of her tube top.

"Hey, Mads, how are you?"

She walks over, gait a little wobbly. She's already drunk. "Fine, fine, fuckin' peachy."

I slide my arm around her waist, peering down her top. "You sure look fine."

"So do you." Her hand presses against my abs, feeling the muscle. Madison has never been shy, but we've only hooked up once. "I've been wondering something..."

"Yeah?" I lick my lips, thinking I might be ready to raise that number to two. "What's that?"

"Where has your brother been this summer?"

And scene.

I drop my arm but try to keep the easy expression on my face. "Heston didn't come down with the family," I say, trying not to grit my teeth over his name. "Busy getting ready for college."

"Oh," she pouts, "too bad."

"Yeah." I reach out to Reid and swipe the flask from his hands, taking another too-long swig. "Too, fucking, bad."

It should make it better, not having him here. Not having to listen to the way he talks to our mom. Not needing to jump in and push back against the way he spits at and ridicules her. Not spending weeks on end, tense and mindlessly pissed off, wishing him away.

Instead, I just keep feeling all the spaces he *should* be. I keep coiling for fights that never come, bracing for snide remarks and hateful glares, always ready but never spent. It's like the fighter's equivalent of blue balls.

"Hey!" he complains, rightfully.

I swallow it down and shove it back at him. "Sorry." I reach into my back pocket and pull out a small bag of weed, tossing it to him. "Take it."

He nods appreciatively. "Come on, let's light up."

But I've already started skimming the crowd, looking for something, someone, a *reason* to blow off a little steam. It doesn't take long when I spot a few kids that I'd beefed with a week ago over a parking spot following my last fight. They'd parked too close to my car—my sweet Jasmine—and these motherfuckers showed her no respect. Downright rude, really.

The biggest guy leans against the boat house, cat-calling a group of clearly uninterested girls nearby. They all shift uncomfortably when he says, "Come on, sweet thing! Don't be like that."

My hackles rise in a familiar way, shoulders going tight, face smoothing out.

"Meet you in a few," I say to Reid, and start toward the dock. I sweep past the huddle of girls—townies, I gather, from the accents and clothes. Back home, I'm used to conservative uniforms at school and trendy outfits at parties. But these girls have an edgy grittiness that Preston Prep girls can't buy. Frayed cut-off shorts. Worn boots. Stony expressions. I make eye contact with a pair of hard, hazel eyes and dart my gaze down to her lips. They're pressed in a tight line. Whatever she sees in me, she's not impressed.

Well, sweetheart, I think, *justwait until I'm done with these fuckwits.*

"Sugar," the big guy pushes off the wall, leering at her, "you know, you'd be a lot prettier if you smiled every once in a while."

Hazel eyes scowls and cuts her eyes at him, jaw setting. She's wearing a loose flannel shirt, which should be universal code for unsexy. Unfortunately, it just makes us really wonder what's hiding underneath. Which is exactly what's got this dumbass up her grill.

She bites back, "You'd be a lot prettier if you fucked off and died, Derek," and the other guys all laugh.

Derek presses a hand to his chest, feigning hurt. "Come on, Sug, I bet I could make you smile for once." He moves closer and the group of girls parts like the Red Sea, giving him berth. The only one still holding her ground is the girl he's harassing. She's tiny, yet her stature implies she's tough as nails. Long black hair hangs over her shoulder, the tips dyed blue. "We've fought this thing between us for too long. Stop playing frigid princess and let me warm you up."

"Sure, I can probably find some lighter fluid," she says, all faux-casually, looking around. "Setting you on fire could get me downright toasty."

I snort, but he takes a step forward, and something wavers in her eye. A flicker of fear. A hard swallow bobbing her throat. I dart between them and look up at the stupid oaf.

"Looks like this girl isn't interested in what you're selling, *Derek*," I say, looking behind me to shoot her a grin. I get nothing back but hard glare. *Okay, then.* "Why don't you move along."

The oaf laughs. He's got a couple of inches on me, and he's big, but it's not the lean mass that I have. I'm fast. Quick. And I already feel the building hum of anticipation in my knuckles, ready to slam into something hard and meaty. Beating his ass would be a pleasure. "Why don't *you* move along, pretty boy. This isn't about you."

I grin. "First, thanks for the compliment. I really am pretty. Second, I've seen how you treat other people's things, and it's not great, Derek, it's not great." He tilts his head, assessing me for a minute, like he's trying to place me. "Third—and not to sound egotistical or anything—but *everything* is about me."

Derek narrows his eyes at me and a twisted grin tugs at the corners of his mouth. A moment later he lifts his two meaty paws and shoves them at my chest, pushing me back. The girl I'm defending skirts out of my way, but I keep my eyes on this asshole. He hardly moved me, but he's just given me the opening I need to justify ruining him.

"Thanks," I say, grinning. "This was getting boring." I jerk my elbow back and slam my fist right into his jaw. I barely feel the pain in my knuckles, just the momentum of my arm propelling them forward. I follow through on the punch and then slam a second fist right into his gut. He growls like a beast and swings, but I jump back fast enough that he misses. He tries to barrel into me next, hoping to take me down to the ground, but it's easy to step out of his path and bury a fist into his kidney.

"Oh, so close!" I taunt, seeing some of his boys gathering in my periphery. Fucking classic. Can't take someone one-on-one, just keep adding dudes to the pile. Fine by me. "Everyone can get a turn," I assure them, swiping one of Derek's flying fists.

"Stop!" a girl cries from the growing crowd. "Stop fighting!"

I play for a second like I'm deeply considering it. "Nah. Not until this piece of shit learns a little respect." But Derek's had time to recover. He doesn't lunge at me, taking in my stance—fists up, legs loose and quick. Instead, he shakes out his shoulders and braces himself, mirroring me. The sight of it pulls a laugh from me, high-pitched and crazed. "Now we're talkin'."

No more of this clumsy rage-driven shit. It's too easy.

His fist flies forward, but I duck it. I'm not counting on his left fist following it, but it's a messy, badly-coordinated punch. This guy is no south paw. His knuckles barely graze my cheek. Even though he's not here, I can hear my brother's voice in my head, vicious and taunting.

You're such a little bitch, Bass. Look at you, gonna get your ass beat by this loser? Typical. Can't even handle a drunk townie. Fuck, you're embarrassing. This is the only thing you're good at, and you can't even win.

It makes my focus narrow tightly in on him, filling my head with a violent red and something so chaotic that I can't pin it down long enough to understand it. I just know it makes me want to pound this fucker's face in.

I reach back and slam my fist forward, getting in a solid hook that rocks Derek backward. I don't stop. I plan to keep burying my fist into his face until it's bloody and limp. A flash of movement comes from the side, and I know one of his boys is coming to help him. I react on pure instinct, jerking back and slamming a tight fist into the face coming at me.

The sound is almost sickening—the sharp crack, the loud gasp, the soft sound of a small body hitting the ground.

It takes me so long to realize that it's *not* one of Derek's boys that

I'm already turned back to the oaf, fist raised. But I freeze, doing a bewildered double-take.

Because that was not a hard jaw.

That was not a man.

The body on the ground has long dark hair, with blue tips. A girl, the girl I've been *defending*.

My fist drops to my side.

"Fuck," I say, and the crowd shifts, her friends shuffling forward with palms covering their mouths, watching her lifeless body.

I had to have killed her or something. She's not moving, and I don't punch like a little bitch. I follow through. That had been a hard hit—a devastating hit—to someone smaller than me. To someone who's not used to it. To someone with soft skin and a delicate neck. I move forward in horror, looking down at her limp body, but notice instantly that her eyes are open. Unfocused. Squinting, like she's confused.

"Hey," I try, bending down to touch her arm. "I'm sorr—"

Her hazel eyes finally go into focus, landing on mine. She opens her mouth, dragging in a big inhale, and releases it in a bone-chilling scream.

I jerk back first, and then everyone else does. The scream—it doesn't stop. It keeps building and climbing, but it doesn't die. Even when she drags in another breath, it's just to feed that blood-curdling shriek pouring from the pit of her chest.

I look around nervously, but the crowd is frantically dispersing. This is too loud, too much attention. The cops will come. People will ask questions. We'll all be fucked.

Thick with terror and a pain that goes far beyond the punch I'd landed. I stare at her for another for a moment, and then I do the only thing a Wilcox can in a situation like this.

I run.